Sarah Lefebve is a former jour
sticking to the facts for making st

By some minor miracle she fits writing romantic fiction in around a full time job in event management, being mum to two children, running as many miles every week as her love of red wine, cheese and chocolate dictates, and sharing the odd night out with her husband.

She values and treasures the friendships in her life and firmly believes that "friends are the family we choose".

Her best friend loves and trusts her enough to look after her children if there were ever to come a day when she can't.

A Mother's Second Chance is her second novel.

Also by Sarah Lefebve

A MOTHER'S SECOND CHANCE

SARAH LEFEBVE

One More Chapter
a division of HarperCollins*Publishers* Ltd
1 London Bridge Street
London SE1 9GF
www.harpercollins.co.uk
HarperCollins*Publishers*
Macken House, 39/40 Mayor Street Upper,
Dublin 1, D01 C9W8, Ireland

This paperback edition 2025
1
First published in Great Britain in ebook format
by HarperCollins*Publishers* 2025
Copyright © Sarah Lefebve 2025
Sarah Lefebve asserts the moral right to be identified
as the author of this work

A catalogue record of this book is available from the British Library

ISBN: 978-0-00-878926-8

Printed and bound in the UK using 100% Renewable Electricity
by CPI Group (UK) Ltd

For my friends

"a friend is one of the best things you can be and the greatest things you can have" — SARAH VALDEZ

Prologue

There are times in life when you *just know*. That you have met the love of your life. That you just have to have that dress you saw in the window of your favourite store. That peanut butter and jam are the perfect combination.

That's how it was with Louise Dalewood.

The moment she stepped onto the bus on my first day at Crakeleigh High School – her skirt a good bit shorter than it should have been, her tie just a little bit looser than was considered smart – I just knew she was someone I wanted to be friends with.

I assumed she was a second-year student at the very least – someone with at least a year under her belt at this place. When she appeared beside me in our form room after the bell had gone, though, looking for a spare seat to park herself, it was clear she was as new to this game as I was. But she was definitely more prepared.

I quickly learned she was a rebel. She wore make-up when the rules said we shouldn't, earrings when we were told they were strictly forbidden, and her long blonde hair loose around her shoulders when she was repeatedly asked to tie it back.

She was a risk taker. She was ballsy. She said what she thought, did what she wanted. But she also worked hard. She handed her homework in on time. She got straight As. She aced every exam she took. She had just very quickly determined that the length of her school skirt had absolutely no bearing on her ability to learn algebra, or all the elements of the periodic table, or how to ask for directions to the nearest station in French.

She was also very funny, fiercely loyal to anyone she called a friend, and incredibly thoughtful. She never missed a birthday – even my first as her friend which fell just a few short weeks after we met, when she bought me the scarf I'd spotted on a shopping trip together.

———

When we were turning fifteen Louise – or Lou, as I knew her by then – came to school wearing a pair of earrings in the shape of little jesters. Sterling silver. Delicate. Pretty. I loved those earrings. I wanted a pair so badly, but the shop where she had bought them had sold out. When my birthday came around, Louise presented me with the nearest alternative that she'd been able to find. And they were lovely – in a Pinocchio-meets-The-Tin-Man kind of way. But they just weren't the same.

So Lou made a promise that she'd leave me those jester earrings in her will. And we laughed. We were fifteen. We knew nothing about wills. We just knew they sounded grown-up. Which was exactly how we liked to think of ourselves in the year we took our GCSEs – a far cry from the young girls we were when we met on the bus on our first day of secondary school.

Today I find myself staring at those very same earrings. Sitting, a little lost, in the bottom of a gift box decorated in multicoloured

2

giraffes, as pretty and as delicate as I remember, if a little less shiny than they once were.

It seems my friend of more than thirty years has kept her promise.

But she had to die to do it.

Chapter One

The offices of Massey & Stewart are impressive. From the marble floors in the entrance, to the oversized coffee machine with all the frills in the reception area – there solely for the purpose of caffeinating the visitors to this London-based law firm – no expense has been spared. It's hardly surprising that Lou didn't object to doing the two-hour commute three times a week.

My best friend had hoped to make named partner one day. *Massey, Stewart & Smithson.* It was a while off, but there was no doubt she had the ambition to make it happen. She had always worked so hard. Maybe even *Smithson, Massey & Stewart* hadn't been beyond the realms of possibility.

Patrick Massey takes a sip of water from a crystal glass. The sunlight beaming through the floor-to-ceiling window bounces off the glass and projects coloured patterns on the papers in front of him. I stare at them, numb.

"Do you have any questions, Mrs Henry?"

I've been divorced a year now. Even though I've had this name for almost twenty years, and have chosen to keep it, it now feels ever so slightly odd when I hear it. Like an old well-worn pair of jeans that are just a little tighter than you are used to, or your favourite cup of coffee that has a splash more milk than you would normally have.

I put the lid gently back on the giraffe-covered box and place it on top of the papers in front of me.

"Mrs Henry...?"

"Please, call me Zoe."

"Zoe..."

"When did she change the will?" I ask him.

We have not read through every detail of Lou and Rich's joint will – that is just the stuff of movies – but I do know that they made one significant amendment in the months leading up to their deaths.

He looks at me blankly.

"My husband – my *ex*-husband – and I – we were both guardians," I tell him. "When did she change that? When did it become just me?"

It makes sense, of course. That they would change it. Mike and I are divorced. The children will live with me. They just made that official. Unequivocal. I will be their new family.

And it is just words on a piece of paper. I know – or at least I hope – Mike will help. A little. Or a lot, maybe. They are his godchildren too.

"I am not sure when it was changed," Patrick says. "Let me look."

"Don't worry," I tell him, waving my hand in the air with an indifference I am not really feeling.

The answer *is* irrelevant though.

It doesn't matter when Lou changed her will.

It only matters that she changed it. And that she didn't tell me.

"Are you sure?" he asks, and I nod.

"Thank you, Patrick," I say. "I think everything is clear."

"I'm so very sorry we haven't met under better

circumstances," he tells me. "Louise meant a great deal to us all here. And I know you and she go back a long way."

He's right. We do. It's safe to say I wouldn't be sitting here right now if that were not the case.

———

Lou and I were just eleven years old when we met, on that first day at Crakeleigh High.

"Is this seat free?" she had asked me.

"Yes," I had replied, moving my backpack off the seat and casually dropping it under the desk, whilst making a mental note to hitch my skirt up a little higher the following day. And there – in that uncomplicated five-word conversation – was the start of a friendship that had lasted the next three decades and more.

Until just two weeks ago.

"She certainly left everything in very good order for you," Patrick Massey continues.

I have no doubt of that. Louise Smithson – as she has been for the last thirteen years – gave new meaning to the word *organised*.

"Financially you will not need to worry at all," he adds. Like this is supposed to make up for the fact that I have lost my best friend. I'm being unfair, of course. Patrick Massey is just doing his job. But that's how it all feels right now – so bloody unfair.

He shuffles the papers in front of him, signalling that – if I do in fact have no questions – then we are done here.

It made perfect sense for Lou to have her will registered with her own law firm. She will have wanted to ensure her wishes were in the best possible hands. Heading up the Wills & Probate department, Patrick Massey has those hands. Ready for retirement in five years or so, he has known nothing but the law, setting up his own firm at the age of twenty-six. He joined forces with James Stewart ten years later and the two of them quickly became a household name in London. When Lou graduated from Cambridge it was the only company she wanted to work for. Patrick Massey got a gem in my best friend. She was one of the firm's best criminal defence lawyers. And now he is repaying her hard work, by seeing that her wishes are honoured.

"Read through everything in your own time, and – please – give me a call with any questions you have – no matter how big or small.

"And let us know, when you are ready, what you decide about the house. I understand it is all very raw right now, and we have of course updated the purchaser's solicitors, but if you are able to give it some thought that would be very helpful."

He hands me his card. I take it. It's the third one he has given me. I drop it in my handbag with the others. And then I shake his outstretched hand. Which makes it feel a little like I have just been for a job interview, and not for the reading of my best friend's last will and testament.

———

My journey home includes two underground trains, one mainline train, and a taxi, all lasting a total of just under two and a half hours, door-to-door – including a pit-stop at Waterloo Station where I cry discreetly into a cold cup of coffee and an uneaten blueberry muffin.

But I still don't feel ready for this. To face the next step in the toughest thing I have been through in my life so far.

I tell the taxi driver I need a minute and to keep the meter running.

He looks at me in the rear-view mirror, quietly switches off the meter and waits patiently for me to gather my thoughts.

Whatever happened to the two girls with the matching Forever Friends keyrings on their schoolbags? And the signed photographs of Take That on their bedroom walls? When did we get so grown-up that we had husbands, and houses, and children? And wills to make sure they were taken care of if anything ever happened to us.

I miss my friend.

Thoughts gathered and taxi fare paid, I slowly put my key in the door – buying myself just a few more seconds before I have to face the world.

And then it is time.

The latch on the door clicks as I push it shut.

Stanley, our four-year-old springer spaniel, rushes out from the kitchen, always the first to greet me, his tail wagging frantically.

"Auntie Zoe, you're home!" my goddaughter Phoebe shouts excitedly, joining the welcoming committee in the hallway.

"Phoebs!" I shout, as brightly as I can. "I missed you!"

"You weren't gone that long, silly," she says giggling.

"What have you been up to?" I ask, scooping her up for a cuddle.

"We've been playing in the den," she says.

The den.

It used to be a playroom. Until about three years ago, when my youngest nonchalantly tossed a board game onto the shelf for the last time, and – what felt like overnight – became more interested in painting her nails and FaceTiming with her friends.

The toys and games were all boxed up, the times table charts and solar system posters were taken off the walls and the room was turned into a den. A place to go for anyone looking for a bit of peace and quiet – something that's often in short supply in a family with three children and an overexcited spaniel.

It will need to be turned back into a playroom…

"Uncle Mike got the colouring books out and then Isla found Monopoly Junior in a box in the garage," Phoebe tells me excitedly. "I was the cat. And she had to give me all of her money.

So I won. And Uncle Mike gave us Maltesers. The big bags, not the mini ones," she adds with a little giggle.

"Oh, he did, did he?" I say, pretending to look cross.

"Yes. On the sofa," she adds cheekily, sure that this will get him in even more trouble than the Malteser provision alone.

Evidently done with telling me about her day, Phoebe skips away happily, instructing a reluctant but obedient Stanley to follow her.

I walk through to the kitchen and drop my bag on the worktop.

Isla walks in, clutching her phone in her hand.

"You okay, love?" I ask.

I wrap my arms around my youngest daughter. Just fourteen, but so grown-up in so many ways.

"I've played Guess Who seven times, and Monopoly Junior three times," she says, confident this answers my question.

"Thank you, darling. I'll make it up to you, I promise. Where's your dad?"

"Upstairs, changing Zack's nappy." She screws her face up. A messy one, then. "Can Dad stay for tea?" she asks.

"Well – if you like. Maybe," I say, my heart sinking.

There was a time when I would have wanted Mike here more than anyone else – the person who knew me best of all and could cheer me on through any crisis. But things are different now. I tell Isla I'll ask him but that he will probably have plans. No doubt he will need to get back to his laptop – or to Charlotte. The unfairness of it hits me again. Mike has replaced me, but I will never be able to replace Lou.

Chapter Two

I got the call on the Saturday night. At 10.17pm.

I had been looking after Phoebe and Zack for the weekend while Lou and Rich were at the wedding of an old school friend, Heidi. Lou had stayed in touch with her but I hadn't.

I was listed as ICE2. That's "In Case of Emergency" for those who are not as organised as my friend is. Was. The number "2" because she took being organised to a whole new level. Dialling ICE1 took the emergency services through to the man in the back of the taxi with Lou – the man whose fate had tragically been the same as hers. Then they tried number 2 and reached me.

From what they could establish without too much effort, a deer had run out into the road. The taxi driver had swerved to avoid it, skidded on some diesel on the road and gone straight into a tree. It's unlikely any of them – including the deer – would have known anything beyond the impact.

That has been left to the rest of us.

We will be dealing with everything beyond that impact for the rest of our lives.

I have lost my best friend.

And her beautiful children have lost not just one but both of their parents.

Chapter Three

L ou and I were virtually inseparable from that first day at school.

But we were very different.

Lou liked to push the boundaries, while I liked to stay well within them. Lou liked to stand out in a crowd, while I liked to blend in. And right from those early days Lou liked to point out which boys in our class were cute, while I was firmly of the opinion that absolutely none of them were. That came later for me – around the age of fourteen when Jamie Cooper passed me the pencil I had dropped under his desk and I blushed, conscious that for the first time I was aware that a boy might be in the slightest bit worth bothering with.

I was a goody two shoes. I hitched my skirt up – but quickly pulled it back down when I realised I was about to pass the headteacher in the corridor.

Lou didn't care, though. About breaking the rules.

She would bunk off school because she didn't fancy learning about electromagnetic waves.

She would tell the teacher that they didn't know what they were talking about.

And she would smoke weed because she wanted to know what it was like – but she wouldn't do it discreetly to avoid getting caught.

But she was smart. And she was popular.

She aced every test. And she was liked by everyone.

When the school was handing out the Head Girl and Head Boy roles in our last year I think it was only Lou's eagerness to break the rules that stood between her and that coveted title and ensured she lost out to Caroline Jenkins.

I think the teachers thought that if a girl like Louise Dalewood was made Head Girl then her disregard for authority would spread through the student body. Like playing hooky or smoking weed was a contagious disease or something.

My parents thought Lou was a bad influence when we were growing up.

"She does stupid things that get her into trouble," my dad would say.

"Why can't she just follow the rules?" my mum would ask.

I loved Lou, though, and nothing was going to stop me being friends with her.

But I was smart enough to know that bad choices usually come back to bite you.

Chapter Four

I am pouring myself a glass of wine when Mike walks into the kitchen.

"I would offer you one, but you're driving," I say.

It still feels odd that he no longer lives here. The last house we bought together. The one that was supposed to be our forever home.

He is only a few miles away – in a flat we bought as a buy-to-let just before our marriage started to fall apart. But it sometimes feels like the other side of the world.

Both properties – the flat and our family home – will be sold when our children have all left home – the proceeds split down the middle – a business transaction finally marking the end of a life together that we could once never imagine not lasting.

He flicks the kettle on and takes the milk out of the fridge.

"I've put Zack down for a nap," he tells me. "I thought you might need a little time."

I'm waiting for him to ask how it went. But he doesn't. He knows how it went. He knows I am now the legal guardian of two small children. He knows their parents will have crossed every *t* and dotted every *i* to make sure everything was in place. He knows today was just a formality – the day that will simply become a date in history when the arrangement was formally acknowledged.

And he knows I'll be doing it alone. Because we are divorced now. Because we couldn't make our marriage work.

I put the bottle down and take a deep breath. A solitary tear travels down my cheek. I hastily brush it away, afraid it will attract others if I leave it there for a second too long.

My phone rings.

Simon.

I click it to silent and leave it ringing. I can't do this right now.

"Isla wants you to stay for dinner," I say to Mike, opening the fridge to see what I can cobble together to feed us.

I notice him glance down at my phone, but he says nothing about the unanswered call.

"I'll order us a takeaway," he says, and the simple kindness of it almost tips me over the edge, threatening to release the emotion that I have been fighting hard to hold back.

Mike holds out a hand to me as I gulp back my tears.

I want to take it. It is what I have always done. But I can't. Not today. Not anymore. So instead I turn away. I put the wine back in the fridge. I pull my hair into a ponytail. I run a cloth over a worktop that is already clean.

When Lou and Rich asked me and Mike to be Phoebe's legal guardians should they do something as daft as both die, of course we said yes. But when you agree to something like that you never expect it to actually happen, do you? You don't expect you'll ever have to live up to that promise. The chances of one parent dying are slim, right? But both parents…

By the time Zack was born, Mike and I were divorced. Just. So maybe it was when Lou and Rich added their newborn son to their will, that they changed the guardian details to just me.

Lucky me.

And I mean that. Genuinely. I really do. I love those children as much as I love my own. I held Phoebe when she was just two hours old. A six-pound bundle of joy that ended five years of sadness and hopelessness for my best friend. And five years of guilt for me. Guilt that my three children had come along so easily. Guilt that my eldest was the very happy product of a moment of carelessness, and my two younger children both the result of very little effort. When Zack was born – a surprise addition just nine months ago – Lou and Rich had already agreed to feel blessed that they were a family of three. You couldn't help but love that little boy who scared us all senseless when he threatened to make his debut appearance eight weeks early. He hung on an extra four, thank God, and we were all so relieved when he arrived safe and healthy, just a little smaller than expected.

So yes, lucky me. Lucky me that I am the one that gets to tell Phoebe and Zack – when they are old enough to understand – what amazing people their parents were. Lucky me that I am the one that can try and make the world feel a better place than they are entitled to think it is. Lucky me that I get to watch them grow up into the kind of people their parents would be so incredibly proud of.

They will forever be the love that links me with the best friend I ever had.

———

But let's be honest. This isn't going to be easy.

This is my second time around at all this. My children are all long past the age where they really need me for anything. Other than money, of course. Oliver is almost twenty – and in his second year at Bristol University studying Medicine. Sophie is seventeen and doing her A Levels this year. She recently started dating Josh, so of course we barely see her. And then there's fourteen-year-old Isla, my youngest. She has no significant objections to my company just yet, but it is only a matter of time…

I have already done all this once.

I have changed a thousand nappies – more, I'm sure.

I have pureed apples, and pears, and carrots, and potatoes, and tried to persuade three dubious babies that the green mush in front of them really is delicious.

I have read a million bedtime stories – sometimes the same one over and over again for a month or more.

I have sung alphabet songs, nursery rhymes and times table poems.

I have said a tearful goodbye on the first day of nursery – three times, and again on the first day of school – three times.

I have taught three children how to ride their bikes, how to tell the time, how to tie their shoelaces, how to tie a tie on their first day of senior school.

I've done all of that. And now I'm teaching them how to go for what they want in life, how to pick themselves up when things don't go right, how to keep smiling when that person they think they love doesn't love them back.

I was only twenty-two when I fell pregnant for the first time. For the almost four years Mike and I had been together we had always been so careful. The one and only time we ever took a risk it gave us Oliver.

After we had had him, it made sense to add to our family while he was still young, so Sophie followed two years later, and Isla another two after that.

But Lou and Rich took a different path to parenthood. For a long time their careers came first. And then, when they decided they were ready for children, children it seemed were not ready for them. After three years of trying, four failed attempts at IVF followed. Phoebe was their fifth and final go. Not because they had run out of money, but because they had run out of tears. And then Zack was their little miracle. The child they say can come along when you have stopped trying. Lou and Rich had stopped trying.

So, while my own children are all but grown-up, my godchildren are both still so young.

Lou and Rich were still in the early years of parenting – still perfecting the art of peeling a crying child from around their legs in the school playground, still negotiating vegetable consumption in exchange for the promise of chocolate buttons and an extra five minutes of TV before bed, and still stair-gating the shit out of their home.

And now it's my turn to do it all over again. Only this time I'll be doing it alone. Will I be enough for them? Will I remember what to do? Will I know what Lou and Rich would have done? The values they would have instilled in their children? The traditions they would have created? The decisions they would have made for their futures?

Chapter Five

It took Jamie Cooper another two and a half years after handing me back my dropped pencil to ask me out. By which time I was more than ready to say yes.

Dating is not easy when you rely on your parents to take you everywhere, so a lot of the time we spent together was at school – a quick snog in the cloakrooms, a lunch date in the canteen, a knowing glance across the desks in double Maths – but we were quickly besotted, convinced this was the real thing.

Every minute I spent with Jamie was a minute I didn't spend with Lou. This was new ground for both of us.

I think we were both surprised that I was the first of us to have a boyfriend. It should have been Lou. She was the one who was always interested in the boys – always pointing out the good-looking ones, always engineering opportunities to sit next to them in class. I wasn't bothered. Not until Jamie passed me my pencil that day.

I think Lou missed me.

I was careful never to cancel plans with her to see Jamie, but there was a definite shift. Lou was so used to monopolising my time – and me hers, of course – but now there was someone else who was taking their fair share.

Things were easier when Andrew Robson came along – transferring to Crakeleigh from a school up north just after we'd started our first year of A Levels.

Lou was smitten.

And so was Andrew.

And then it was the four of us who were inseparable.

Chapter Six

By the time Zack wakes from his nap we have played three more games of Monopoly Junior and I have poured my third glass of wine.

It's late. He'll never sleep tonight.

If I have learned anything from being a mum three times over, then it's to never leave a baby to sleep for too long in the day. No matter how tempting it may seem while you are enjoying that cup of tea, or when you've got your nose buried in a good book, or in my case when you are getting annihilated by a small child in a game of Monopoly Junior.

He is standing up in his cot, holding onto the bars and smiling when I go into the guest room to fetch him. When I pick him up, he cuddles into me, and I hold him close.

He is so young. Not even a year old. Robbed of having even one birthday with his parents. Will he even remember them at all as he grows up?

I change his nappy, put him in a fresh babygrow and straighten the blankets in his cot. A travel cot left here two weeks ago for the weekend I was looking after them.

I need to go to their house, but I can't bring myself to do it. Not yet.

Mike has collected the essentials but that won't keep us going for long. They need their toys. And more clothes. And books. And all the other million and one things that two small children need. All the things I had for so many years but no longer have.

———

When I walk into the kitchen Phoebe is helping Isla set the table with napkins and glasses.

"The pizzas will be here in ten minutes," Mike announces, handing Isla the plates.

Zack holds his arms out to him.

"Hey big man," he says, taking him from me and throwing him up in the air. Zack giggles.

I remember how he used to do that with Oliver. Always Fun Dad.

"Careful with him," I'd say – an anxious first-time mum.

"He's okay, he loves it," Mike would argue. And he was right.

———

The pizzas arrive at the same time as Sophie, back from Josh's house.

She brings the boxes through and drops them on the table.

"Hi, Dad," she says, wrapping her arms around Mike. Grown-up in all the ways she chooses to be, but never too old to give her dad a hug.

"Hi, honey. How's Josh?"

"Fine," she says, her tone firmly indicating the end of that conversation.

A classmate with good grades and hardworking parents,

Sophie's new boyfriend has had Mike's seal of approval. But attempts to get any information beyond that have so far proved futile.

Mike recently went so far as to offer to take them both out for dinner one evening so he could meet Josh properly. But "Oooh cringe, you're so lame, Dad, as if!" was how that went.

Sophie opens the lid of one of the pizza boxes and pulls out a slice.

The doorbell goes.

"Oh yeah," she says casually, mid-bite, "The Domino's guy is waiting for his money."

———

As usual, Mike has ordered far too much food.

"There are only six of us," I point out, looking at all the leftover pizza on the table, "and one of those is a baby."

"So you can all have pizza for breakfast," he suggests.

Sophie rolls her eyes. Isla pulls a face. Phoebe's eyes widen in excitement.

"Yummy," she shouts. "I love pizza!"

And then, "Auntie Zoe, when will Mummy and Daddy be back?"

The table goes deafeningly quiet, except for Zack who is gently bashing a plastic spoon on the table, sporadically poking it into a slice of apple.

Isla looks at Sophie. Sophie looks at her dad. Her dad looks at me.

How do I tell her that her mummy and daddy are *not* coming back? That we are her family now.

When it happened, we told her that Mummy and Daddy had decided to stay on for a few days, that we were lucky because we got to have a bit more fun together.

I needed time. I needed to work out how I was going to deliver the worst news a child will ever have to hear, to a child whose heart I just can't bear to break.

How do you tell a five-year-old that she will never see her parents again? That they left her here for a weekend but won't ever be coming back?

As a forty-three-year-old adult I am struggling to understand it, so how can I expect her to?

I brush my hand across her cheek and take a bite of pizza – a move meant only to buy myself some time, and though the smallest of bites, it is the toughest mouthful I've ever had to swallow.

"Maybe it will be tomorrow," she says with a happy smile.

"Not tomorrow, Phoebs," I answer softly.

And then, just like that, she saves me in the way that children often do without even realising.

Out on a dog walk, a four-year-old Sophie once asked me how Isla got into my tummy. I was two sentences into a hastily but well-thought-out age-appropriate explanation of the facts of life, when she lost all interest and asked me instead why Bella, our black Labrador, didn't do her poos in a toilet like she did.

I am not sure how I will ever explain the unexplainable to Phoebe, but for now – in the same way that Sophie once saved me from explaining the birds and the bees – Phoebe saves me from breaking her heart, for another day at least.

"What's your favourite pizza, Uncle Mike?" she asks.

"My absolute favourite pizza is a Hawaiian," Mike tells her, gently squeezing her hand.

It isn't. It's a Meat Feast. Always has been. He has said Hawaiian for me. Because it's Phoebe's favourite. And that will keep this conversation going, while I swallow back the enormous lump in my throat.

"Mine too," she says, grinning.

"No way! Well, what I want to know, Phoebs, is this… Would you rather have no more pizza for the rest of your life, or have pizza for breakfast, lunch and dinner, every single day, forever?"

Wide-eyed at the very thought of it, this gorgeous girl giggles infectiously, while she tries to imagine a world where she eats pizza three times a day.

And for now at least, that is far better than her imagining a world that doesn't include her mummy and daddy.

Chapter Seven

Mike and I went out for pizza on our first date.

We met at Bristol University. Mike was a second-year Maths student when I started my degree in Veterinary Medicine. Jamie and I had just split up and I wasn't ready to meet someone new. Or so I thought. I met Mike on day six – during Freshers' Week – where he was manning the rowing club stand and was trying to entice new members with free pens and Murray Mints. I wasn't in the least bit interested in joining the rowing club. But I was definitely interested in Mike. He was gorgeous – tall, fit, with tanned skin (from all the rowing, I assumed), a thick mop of dark hair and a cheeky smile. He's still gorgeous, still has the same tanned skin, the same dark hair (with a few bits of grey here and there that he blames on me and the kids) and the same cheeky smile.

He regaled me with the benefits of joining the rowing club.

"It will help get you fit. Well, even fitter," he said with the first flash of that cheeky smile.

I enjoyed the banter, and the free Murray Mint.

But I had no intention of joining the rowing club. I was a

runner, not a rower. I just stayed long enough to remember his face when I saw him again – and to make it acceptable to take a second mint.

He called me the next day and asked me out.

We went to Pizza Express and I ordered a pepperoni pizza with mushrooms and sweetcorn.

"Mushrooms *or* sweetcorn?" Mike asked me, before taking a sip of his beer.

For a moment I thought he was being tight – that this was some cost-saving exercise, that I was required to make a choice after which the waiter would reduce the bill accordingly.

But instead he wanted to know what I couldn't live without.

So I weighed up the benefits of both, concluding that whilst I loved sweetcorn, I wasn't prepared for a world without mushrooms – my ultimate favourite vegetable. And we both laughed at the serious consideration I had given this make-believe dilemma.

And right there – in Pizza Express Bristol – began a tradition that would eventually help us make many a decision throughout our lives together.

If push came to shove, what would we choose? What would we rather have? What could we give up?

The south-facing garden or the double garage?

The platinum wedding ring or the new dining-room furniture?

The career I had worked so hard for, or the baby that came along long before we would have planned?

In my fifth and final year at university, Mike and I moved in together, renting a small one-bedroom flat. It was our first non-student accommodation, with nice carpets and furniture that wasn't falling apart, and crockery that actually matched.

By then Mike had earned himself a first-class degree and started a financial analyst internship at one of London's most reputable investment banks.

He was away a lot, and I was in my last year of my degree – working through my clinical rotations. So we barely saw each other. But when we did we certainly made up for it.

And then I fell pregnant with Oliver.

We had been to visit my parents for the weekend, and I had left my pill there.

Back at home after sharing a bottle of wine with dinner, we were just a little too drunk to be as sensible as we might otherwise have been, when Mike snuck his hand down my shirt while we watched some inane rubbish on the telly. Long story short, we thought we could get away with it.

And we couldn't.

When I saw two blue lines on the first pregnancy test I had ever had to stick between my legs, I cried.

I wasn't ready to be a mum. I was ready to be a vet.

Being a vet was all I had ever wanted to do from the age of ten when my dog Toby was hit by a car. Tom Linton – who had been our family vet for years – saw Toby's lifeless body and told us to prepare for the worst. But somehow he saved him. I decided there and then that that was what I wanted to do with my life. When we arrived to pick Toby up and I shared that decision with Tom, he promised me that if I contacted him when I was qualified, he would give me a job.

And in the final year of a gruelling five-year degree, I was so close.

How could I give it all up now?

Mike and I had so many sleepless nights agonising over our decision.

We both knew we'd found our someone. And we both knew that one day we would want children. But would we have chosen to have them now? Still studying? Not married? No real money to speak of? Of course not.

We went round in circles – lots of them – trying to come to a decision.

We would go to bed confident we'd made up our minds, only to wake the next morning more confused than ever.

In the end it came down to a simple choice.

Mike came home from a run one day, sat me down, and said: "Zo, would you rather give up having a career, or give up having a family?"

We knew it wasn't real. We knew – or at least hoped – that I didn't really have to choose between the two, that I could have both – eventually.

But hearing that question, looking at the man I loved more than anything, my hands on my tummy – on the life growing inside me – I knew. This baby was wanted.

It wasn't easy, of course.

I knew our decision would mean putting my career on hold, and I had come to terms with that prospect, but I was determined to ensure I did as well as I possibly could. One day I'd be going back to it. Of that I was sure. One day I would be the vet I had dreamed of being ever since that day we almost lost our beloved Toby.

The baby may have shifted the timescales a little, but I resolved that that was all he – or she – would do.

I finished my degree.

And three weeks later Oliver was born.

Mike completed his internship and on the back of his exemplary performance, was given a full-time job. He was now a legitimate financial analyst. Truth be told, twenty years later I still don't really understand what it is he does – I just know he crunches numbers every day. Which, if you ask me, sounds really – really – boring, though I guess it would be a very boring world if we all got our kicks from picking maggots off a rabbit's bottom. But it earned him a lot of money. Which meant we could have the life we had dreamed of.

Knowing we'd never have stopped at one child if we'd sorted our timing out a little better, we decided to carry on what we had started. So almost two years to the day after Oliver was born, Sophie came along.

And because we just weren't sure our family was complete, we tried for a third, Isla arriving with the same precision timing as Sophie.

By the time Isla started primary school Mike had started his own company. Contracting his services more than doubled his salary overnight.

Every penny he earned came at a cost, though. Mike was spending more and more time making money *for* us – and less and less time *with* us.

Monday to Friday, I might as well have been a single parent. He was out the door before 7am and rarely home before 7pm. Gone before the kids were even awake, and home after they'd drifted off to sleep, trying desperately – but failing – to keep their eyes open for a glimpse of their dad, knowing that he'd be gone again by the time they reopened them in the morning.

But his salary did mean that we could afford help with after-school care, which meant I could finally get my veterinary career off the ground.

We were living back in West Sussex by then. By the sea – in the village of Hartingley, just a few miles from Crakeleigh where I had grown up, and where Lou and Rich had lived since they were married. I applied to thirteen different practices – some local, others less so. My first-class degree helped me get interviews, but my eight years of post-graduation with no experience stopped me getting the jobs.

In the end it was Tom Linton's practice – run by then by his nephew Nathan – that kept a twenty-year-old promise and offered me my first job. It was on the condition, though, that I completed a whole load of refresher courses. Which meant I was juggling three children with a full-time job *and* night school – and the hours and hours of study that that involved. Which left little time for Mike and me to be just that – Mike and me. Not parents, not people with careers they cared about, just him and me, a boy and a girl who once fell madly in love.

That was when the first cracks started to show.

With so many other priorities, there was just no time to prioritise each other.

We spent less and less time together, until there came a point when I realised I barely knew him anymore, and though he would never admit it, he barely knew me either.

And so eventually the cracks got deeper, until they were impossible to ignore.

Chapter Eight

S ophie is putting Zack to bed for me while I read Phoebe a bedtime story. One of Isla's favourites.

So many of my children's childhood toys and books have been donated to charity shops over the years. But I have always kept their favourites. Oliver's first ever Woody toy, that he played with day in, day out for eighteen months at least, faded and a little battered at the edges but still bearing the last of the Sharpie pen ink used to write Oliver's name on the bottom of his boot – just like the "real" Woody. Sophie's Disney chest full of princess dolls, complete with an array of costumes that put my own wardrobe to shame. And Isla's Sylvanian Family animals that, sold on eBay, could go a long way towards paying off the mortgage!

They have all always loved books, so those I have no shortage of.

Tonight Phoebe has chosen *The Giant Jam Sandwich*. I open the book and that lump catches in my throat again. Inside the front cover is a message from her own parents:

To our lovely Isla. Love you always.
Auntie L & Uncle R xxx

Phoebe starts to read it.

"That's Mummy and Daddy," I tell her, and she giggles.

"My mummy and daddy?" she asks.

"Yes. They bought this book for Isla."

She cuddles in, ready to listen.

"One Hot Summer in Itching Down," I begin, wiping the corner of my eye and taking a deep breath, "four million wasps flew into town."

"I'm not sure I can do this," I tell Mike after I have tucked Phoebe in and kissed her goodnight.

He is getting ready to leave, his keys in his hand.

Putting his keys on the side, he puts his hands on my shoulders, the way he has always done when reassuring me.

He did it when I waddled into university, six days before my due date, to sit my final exam. He did it the day Nathan Linton offered me a job and I suddenly wondered what the hell I was doing, thinking I could be a vet after all this time.

And he did it when my eyes filled with tears as I prepared to say goodbye to my firstborn – to send him out into the big wide world to become the wonderful doctor I know he will be.

But that was then and this is now, so I gently pull away from his grip.

"Yes, you can, Zo," he tells me, pushing his now empty hands into his pockets. "I know things are different now, but you know I'll always be here for you. I'll help you. As much as I can."

I know that he wants to. I *believe* that he wants to. But with our own children he was hardly ever there. Why would he be any different now?

"But it's me that's responsible for them," I say, my mind once again picturing the document put in front of me in Patrick Massey's office. The one declaring me sole guardian of Miss Phoebe Elizabeth Smithson and Master Zack David Smithson.

"It's me that has to make all the decisions. Me that has to try and make up for what they've lost."

"I know," he says. "And this won't make you feel any better right now, because you've lost your best friend. And those gorgeous kiddies up there have lost everything. But you've got all the things you need to do this, Zo. The experience. The money. The space. Look at what we had when Oliver was born. We had no money. And no idea what we were doing, really. And we lived in that pokey little flat…"

He's right, we did. Our flat in Bristol was definitely pokey. But it was ours. We bought it when I was six months pregnant with Oliver. Mike's parents had lent us the deposit, and his small salary from the internship was enough to cover the payments. Just.

"I loved that pokey little flat," I tell him, suddenly no longer able to hold back the tears.

Mike wraps his arms around me while I cry. And I let him. Maybe I shouldn't. Maybe it's wrong to let him be the one to comfort me, but I can't stop myself. I cry for everything. For the pokey little flat where we brought our son into the world, for the days when we were happy and everything was great, and for the friend I thought I would have forever.

"I know you did," he says eventually, when I have wiped the last of the salty tears from my face. "And so did I. Because it was where we started our life together. But look at what we've got now.

"What *you've* got," he says, quickly correcting himself. "Six bedrooms, four bathrooms, a back garden big enough to actually lose the kids in, the study, the den, the kitchen-diner... It's everything we ever dreamed of."

"Yes, but at what price?" I ask.

It's not the million-pound price tag I'm talking about, and he knows that.

"I'm sorry," he says.

"I'm sorry too."

I remember the day we moved into this house like it was yesterday. It was our third house move as a family.

It felt like we had barely finished unpacking all the boxes from the last move when Mike came home and announced he thought we should move again.

Newman Gardens was a brand-new development on the edge of Hartingley. Just a short walk from the beach. Twelve plots, each with six bedrooms and a quarter of an acre of land. Mike was so excited. But I didn't want to move. I was happy where we were. I loved the home we had built for our family. It took him four and a half months to break me. For four and a half months he went on and on – and on – about how amazing it would be. The kids could all have their own bathrooms, a playroom – "somewhere to shut away all their shit" I believe Mike called it, a back garden where they could make as much noise as they liked without us fearing a knock at the door from the neighbours... We'd have the big kitchen-diner I had always wanted, a laundry room, an office, a gym (to store all the fitness equipment Mike had bought but never had time to use)...

And the real reason for my hesitation? (Because, let's face it, who in their right mind wouldn't want all of that?) The simple fact that I had so far managed every house move single-handedly.

Mike would generously add his signature to all of the

necessary paperwork before leaving me to organise every bit of every move – from packing everything up at one end to unpacking it all at the other. He was so busy earning the money to pay for the houses we were buying, he had no time to contribute anything to the actual move. On the day we moved from Bristol back to Sussex he actually buggered off to London for a meeting. I was making the third round of teas for the removal men, feeding one child a bottle and buttering slices of toast for the other two before throwing the toaster into a packing box, when he sauntered into the kitchen, grabbed a triangle of toast, and planted a kiss on my cheek.

"I'll see you tonight," he said casually, like it was the most normal thing in the world to be disappearing to London on the day you were moving house.

"Come again??" I said in response, utterly confused.

"I've got a meeting," he explained helpfully. "Didn't I mention it? You can handle everything here, right?"

And that was the story of our life, really. He worked, I picked up the pieces at home.

Until I went back to my career. And then I picked up the pieces at home – *and* did a full-time job.

So when Mike fell in love with the idea of Newman Gardens, scarred by the memories of our previous two moves, I did eventually agree – on the strict understanding that this would be our very last move.

It *was* our last move. But, of course, it wasn't Mike's.

"If anyone can make this work, you can," Mike says eventually, pulling us both back from our own personal thoughts of regret, of loss, of fear about what the future holds.

"Do you really think so?"

"Yes," he says, putting his hands back on my shoulders. This time I don't pull away.

"It may not feel like it right now, but those children are lucky to have you, Zo. You love them, and right now that is all they really need."

Despite the tears threatening to fill my eyes again, I manage a smile.

"Thank you," I say – to the man who, a year ago, would have been doing all this with me.

"What for?" he asks.

"Just being here," I tell him.

He goes to hug me and his phone pings in his pocket.

He pulls it out and glances at it before pushing it back in his pocket.

"Charlotte?" I ask.

He nods.

"I bet she's thrilled that you're spending all this time at your ex-wife's house," I tell him.

"She understands," he says. "And Simon?"

"What about him?"

"Is he okay with me being here?"

"He understands too," I say, bringing a quick end to this line of conversation. It just feels too weird.

The truth is, I don't know how Simon feels about any of this.

Mike looks at his watch.

"I should probably get going," he says.

"Sure."

"I said I'd go over," he adds. Hesitantly. Needlessly. He owes me no explanation.

"It's fine," I tell him. "Honestly. We're fine."

"Are you sure?"

My turn to nod, afraid if I try to speak, I might cry.

Chapter Nine

Mike says goodnight to the girls and leaves, his phone ringing as he gets in the car. I hear him answer as he pulls away. He is just leaving, he says. He'll be there in ten.

Charlotte.

I'm not sure how serious it is. It has only been six months or so. Honestly, I think it's Mike's way of accepting what has happened between us. But I may be wrong. It was me that pushed for the divorce. I just couldn't do it any longer. I couldn't live with the man who had once been my everything but had become more like a close friend I happened to share a house with – and three children, of course.

He met her at a colleague's wedding – or so the girls informed me. Nothing like me, apparently. Blonde, shorter, quieter, no children of her own. They have met her a handful of times. She cooked for them all at the flat the first time they met. Paella and home-made apple pie. Isla told me she didn't like either. But I think she could have served them Domino's and chocolate brownies and they'd have said the same thing. Kids don't ever really want to see their parents with anyone else, right?

I asked them to give her a chance. For their dad. Because I want him to be happy. But I am not going to lie. It all does feel pretty strange.

I give him a quick wave and shut the door before checking my own phone, which has just beeped.

Simon.

How are you? I'm thinking of you. X

I have been seeing Simon for a few months now. He has twins in the year below Isla at the girls' school, and I made a great first impression during parents' evening in the summer when, whilst making small talk in the queue to see Mr Harris the Chemistry teacher, I asked him his wife's name. Gesturing towards the teacher who was waiting for me to take a seat, he politely informed me that he was a widower.

I waited for the ground to swallow me up, and when it didn't, I mumbled my profuse apologies and quickly took my place in the seat opposite Mr Harris.

We met again at the school gates as I was leaving, where he told me not to feel bad, he had been widowed for nearly ten years now. At which point I felt compelled to tell him that I was newly divorced in a kind of "look at us – single parents ruling the world" conspiratorial fashion. He smiled, nodded, and probably completely understood why it was I was now single. And then we said our goodbyes.

A month or so later he brought his dog into the surgery.

He'd never been to the surgery before, and after I told her the story of the clanger I dropped at parents' evening, Robyn, my friend and colleague, was convinced it was just a ruse to get a date.

I'm sure I am not the worst catch in the world, but equally I am under no illusion that a grown man would fabricate his dog vomiting all over another dog walker's shoe, just to get a date with me.

But you never know.

Yogi, his German shepherd, seemed happy enough after the embarrassing episode, but I gave him the once over anyway.

I was handing Simon back his credit card (an administrative task I wouldn't normally get involved in, Robyn had observed) when he asked if I would like to join him for a drink some time.

"She'd love to, wouldn't you, Zo?" Robyn quickly answered for me, putting her arm around me – I was still dressed in my attractive mint-green scrubs.

I was mortified.

I wasn't looking for someone else. I was happy being on my own.

But in that moment I found myself thinking why the hell not, and so I said yes. Because I could. For the first time in twenty-five years I was being asked out on a date. By a not-unattractive man. And though I had absolutely no idea what to do on a first date, my last one being when I was a mere teenager, I was ready to take the plunge.

I later asked Robyn why she'd accepted the date on my behalf when she'd spent months trying to stop Mike and me from splitting up. To which she answered: "You're right, I didn't want you to get divorced. But now you are, it's time you both got laid." Which kind of sums up my lovely friend. Direct and to the point.

We met for a drink, where I spilt my wine, and talked about Mike and the kids the whole evening. Old habits die hard, I guess. But by some stroke of luck it didn't put him off and he came back for a second date. This time dinner at a Mexican restaurant, where I successfully conversed on subjects other than my ex-husband and the three children we share, found out a few facts about Simon that ensured it wasn't our last date, and even shared a brief kiss at the end of the evening.

Before long we were seeing each other regularly.

I didn't know what to do about the kids. When to introduce them to Simon. This was uncharted territory. He didn't push, though. He was happy to go at my pace. In the end the girls met him by accident – in the supermarket, of all places. We'd popped in on our way to my parents to pick up some apple sauce, as it's a standing joke that my mum always forgets to buy it when she is cooking roast pork.

I introduced him as a friend, of course, but as soon as we got back in the car the girls knew.

"Is he your boyfriend?" Isla asked quietly.

"Of course he is," Sophie snapped, in a rare confrontational moment with the younger sister she has always got on so well with.

I didn't need to answer the question. Sophie had already done that for me.

And I could see that they were both crushed.

The jury is still out four months later.

They like Simon. But they love their dad. They miss him. And they are fiercely protective of him.

―――――――

Simon was with me the night of the accident.

I'd put Phoebe and Zack to bed and we were waiting for a takeaway to arrive when I got the call.

When I fell to my knees he was there to pick up those first fragile pieces of grief.

He has seen me at my worst.

Seeing her mum absolutely floored, Sophie called her dad and when he arrived at the house less than an hour later, Simon reluctantly stepped aside to leave him to support his family.

I didn't have the strength to question whether this was the right thing to do.

Should I have asked Simon to stay? Told Mike to leave?

All I knew was that my children needed their dad. And in a way so did I, I guess. Lou and Rich were *our* friends, not just mine. And the children sleeping soundly upstairs were *our* godchildren, not just mine.

I haven't seen Simon since.

This is the third message he has sent me.

And it's the third time I am completely at a loss as to how to reply.

How am I?

Devastated.

Heartbroken.

Daunted.

Overwhelmed.

Not exactly your average response to a text from a new-ish boyfriend.

I call him. And when all I can do is cry, he simply tells me he'll be straight over.

He arrives twenty minutes later and for the next hour he says nothing. He knows there is nothing he can say that can make this better, that can make this go away.

Simon is an attractive man. Slightly shorter than Mike, but still tall – and certainly taller than me. Athletic, like Mike. With light brown floppy hair and a soft covering of facial hair.

He's really funny without trying too hard, which I find incredibly sexy.

And he is the kindest man I have ever met.

There is nothing he wouldn't do for his girls, and – it seems – for me.

Which makes me feel terrible for shutting him out over the last two weeks.

"I'm sorry," I tell him.

"What for?" he asks, running his hand through my hair as I lie with my head in his lap on the sofa.

"For not answering your messages. For shutting you out. For making you feel like you had to leave. That night, I mean. When Mike arrived."

He runs his hand through his own hair, contemplating the apology.

I needed to say it but I also know he gets it, that he understands, that it's an incomprehensible situation. For all of us.

"I get it," he says, and I smile.

"What?" he asks.

"I knew you'd say that."

I clasp my hand in his and he takes it as his cue, kissing me gently on the lips.

I sit up and find my spot in the nook of his arm, which he wraps tightly around me, pulling me close.

"I'm scared," I whisper.

"I know," he whispers back. And he really does.

He has been where I am now.

I have lost my best friend, and I am now raising her children on my own.

He lost his wife and has had to raise *their* children on his own.

The twins were just three years old when Simon's wife died. She had breast cancer. By the time they realised, it was too late to save her.

His girls don't even remember their mum.

That will surely be the case for Zack. Will it be the same for Phoebe?

"You will find ways to keep their memories alive," Simon tells me. "Talk about them. Don't be afraid to mention their names. Tell stories about them. Tell Phoebe and Zack all the things you loved about them. They will want to know it all. And though it might sometimes feel painful, they will bank all of those stories and they will help them remember their mum and dad.

"Trust me. When Mia was four I told her how her mum once dressed up as Where's Wally for a fancy dress party. It really made her giggle, picturing her mum – who she really had no mental image of other than the photos I'd shown her – as Wally from her favourite book.

"From that moment on, whenever we'd look at that book together she'd say to me 'Daddy, do you remember when Mummy dressed up as Where's Wally?' It was as if it was her own memory. Of course it wasn't – she wasn't even born when we went to that party. But that didn't matter – that story helped keep her mummy firmly in her mind. We still talk about it now. In fact I think Mia still has a picture of Helen in her costume on her bedroom wall somewhere."

"Does it hurt to talk about her?" I ask him.

"Not really. Not anymore. I'll always love her, but I had to move on. For my own sake and for the girls'."

I learned on our second date that Simon was on his own for six years before he finally allowed himself to let another woman into his and his girls' lives.

The first woman he dated wanted children and Simon made it clear he didn't want any more. After six months she realised she wasn't going to change his mind and walked away. The second lasted for two years, until Simon broke her heart when he told her he couldn't see a future together.

I am the third.

"You'd have liked Helen," he says. "She was very like you."

"How?"

"She was smart. Funny. She was a good person."

I tuck myself into his nook just a little tighter at this and he lifts my head up to kiss me again. And then there's no more talking for a while.

"So what did you go as?" I ask him eventually, as he's putting his shoes on to go home. He understands, without me saying anything, that it would be too much for Phoebe to see him here in the morning.

"To the fancy dress party?"

I nod and he chuckles.

"Well … the theme was book characters, right? So I went as the Gingerbread Man."

I laugh and realise that for even just a brief moment, I have forgotten my grief. And that Simon has made me do that.

Chapter Ten

I wake on Saturday morning to the sound of Zack playing happily in his cot, his babbling coming through the monitor on my bedside table. It is 6.30am. I won't be needing an alarm clock again for a while. I take some degree of comfort from the fact that I know all too well it could be worse. Far worse. Isla was a terrible sleeper. From the moment she started sleeping through – if you can even call it that – she woke relentlessly at 5am. It didn't matter what I tried – cutting down her daytime nap, putting her to bed later, attempting to soothe her back to sleep – her mornings started at 5am. On the dot. No arguments.

I remember Lou's reaction when I told her my youngest was not following in her sleep-loving siblings' footsteps.

"That's insane," she had said. "That's not even morning, by my calculations, it's the middle of the night."

And I couldn't agree more. So, I'll take 6.30am. and be grateful.

I put my dressing gown on and pull my hair back into a scruffy ponytail before heading to the spare room where I am greeted by the sunniest of smiles that simply melts my heart.

As I lift him out of his cot and take him over to a makeshift changing area on the spare bed, he spots a toy fire truck on the floor. Holding my hand on his tummy so he doesn't fall – an instinct you never lose once you have had a child – I bend down to pick it up and hand it to him. It goes straight to his mouth.

It's Oliver's first fire truck – saved for when my career-driven friend eventually decided she wanted to start a family, and then for another five years while we all waited for it to happen. And then another five when Phoebe showed zero interest in playing with fire trucks and cars and chose dolls and princesses instead.

He is not even a year old. He literally has his whole life ahead of him. Without his parents.

But he is such a happy boy. Always smiling. Always ready for a cuddle.

I zip up his babygrow – when did the makers of baby clothes realise this was easier than the million and one buttons that I had to navigate with my own children? – and grab the elephant from his cot before heading downstairs to the gentle hum of three girls aged five to seventeen chatting and eating breakfast.

"I don't remember the last time you were up this early on a Saturday," I tell my eldest with a smile.

"Me neither," she says, yawning.

"I woke her up," Phoebe announces proudly, leaning affectionately into Sophie and popping her thumb into her mouth.

The girls have been amazing. I literally couldn't have asked any more of them.

They are both devastated. They have known Lou and Rich their whole lives.

But they have both put Phoebe and Zack first, and their own grief second. And I am so proud of them for that.

Sophie pours Rice Krispies into a bowl for Phoebe, taking a

bite of her toast and Marmite at the same time. She's already sussed out the multitasking involved in parenting.

"Do you think Mummy will be picking us up today, Sophie?" Phoebe asks.

Sophie looks at me.

"I don't think so, Phoebs," she says.

"Auntie Zoe?" she says, looking at me, looking for a different answer.

"No, Phoebs, she won't be picking you up today," I tell her gently.

"Why not?" she asks, as Sophie pours milk onto her cereal. "When are they coming back?"

I hand Zack to Sophie and sit down next to this confused little girl, who will face so many things in her future without the most important people by her side.

I hold her hand in mine and take a breath.

I have researched this. Read books. Consulted friends. Googled relentlessly.

The one thing they all said was to tell the truth. And to keep things simple.

And I have rehearsed the conversation a million times, trying out different words, different ways to explain it. But nothing has felt quite right. But then, how *can* a conversation in which you are telling a child her parents have both died ever sound anything even remotely resembling right?

"Phoebe," I say. "Mummy and Daddy won't be coming back."

"What, not ever?" she says, looking confused. And I can understand that. What a ridiculous thing to say. Of course they're coming back. They're her mummy and daddy.

"No. Not ever," I tell her gently.

She drops her spoon in the bowl and her eyes fill with tears.

"Why?" she asks, wiping the first of the tears from her cheek with the back of her little hand.

Out of the corner of my eye I see Isla doing the same thing. Her sister holds her hand, while I fight to control my own emotions.

"Don't they love us anymore?"

"Oh, Phoebe," I say. "Your mummy and daddy loved you and Zack more than absolutely anything in the world."

"Then why don't they want us anymore?" she asks.

It's only natural, of course. But it breaks my heart to hear her doubt their love.

"Phoebe," I say. "Do you know what it means when someone dies?"

She nods.

"Mummy said my grandma died. And she went to heaven to be with my grandad."

"That's right," I say. "Well, Mummy and Daddy have died."

For a minute she says nothing. She just looks at me, confused, as if she is waiting for me tell her that it's not true. That of course Mummy and Daddy are coming back for her. Why on earth wouldn't they be?

When I don't, her eyes fill with fresh tears.

"They've gone to heaven like Grandma and Grandad?" she asks eventually.

"Yes, Phoebe, they have," I tell her.

She looks at me, confusion still etched all over her little face.

"Why have they gone to heaven?" she asks. "Why have they died?"

Instinctively I pull her onto my lap.

I want to know that too. I want to know why my best friend has been taken from me so soon. Why she has been taken from her children when they needed her most. Who decided we didn't need her anymore? Because I want to tell them they were wrong. We do still need her. These children need their mother and I need my friend.

I squeeze Phoebe's hand, trying to find the words that will make her understand. I'm not sure there are any. How can I make her understand something I don't understand myself?

Sophie quietly slips Zack into his highchair, hands him a banana and sits back down in the empty chair opposite Phoebe and me.

She lifts her leg up and rests her foot on her chair, clasps her hands around her knee then leans back.

I've seen this pose a million times. It's what she does when she is thinking hard about something. Simultaneous equations, the hidden meaning behind a Shakespearean sonnet, what she'd really like for tea…

"You know, Phoebs," she says quietly, "I don't think there were enough angels in heaven. I just think God needed some more. And he picked your mummy and daddy."

Phoebe looks at Sophie, and I struggle to fight back my own tears.

She is thinking about this carefully. I can see it in her eyes.

"How did they get there?" she asks eventually. "How did they die?"

My instinct is to hide the "how" from her, to protect her from even greater sadness, but I know I have to tell her, so I keep it as brief as possible.

"You know Mummy and Daddy were going to a wedding?" I say. "And that's why you and Zack were staying with me and the girls?"

She nods.

"Well, on their way home they had an accident in their car. And that's how they died."

"Will they be able to come back?" she asks, with the heartbreaking innocence of a five-year-old that, sadly, we all lose eventually.

"No, Phoebe, they can't come back," I tell her. "When you die your body stops working. And that's when you go to heaven."

"Oh," she says. Just that. "Oh."

And in that one word lies an incomprehensible heartache that no child should ever experience.

She lets go of my hand and rubs her eyes.

The three of us – Sophie, Isla and I – all watch her and wait. Wait for her to take it all in. Wait for her to tell us she doesn't understand. Wait for someone to say something – anything – to mark the start of our next chapter as a family.

Eventually it is Zack who breaks the silence.

Blowing an enormous raspberry, he proceeds to try and eat a piece of banana that is literally as big as his hand. And his timing is quite literally perfect.

Phoebe looks at him and giggles, her tears already drying. For now.

"Oh, Zacky," she says, rolling her eyes in the way she has seen all of us do.

Happy to have an audience, Zack responds by blowing an even bigger raspberry.

In spite of ourselves, in spite of the overwhelming sadness of the news we have just delivered, we all laugh.

Slipping off my lap and holding her baby brother's hand protectively in her own, Phoebe takes another mouthful of Rice Krispies. Chews it. Swallows it. Wipes a dribble of milk from her chin with the back of her hand.

And then…

"Sophie," she says. "Would you rather live in a box of Rice Krispies or in a jar of Marmite?"

I am not foolish enough to think that that's it. That she is now more interested in talking about cereals and toast toppings and which would make the more comfortable home. That the job is now done, and we can all move on. She is just five years old. She will take time to fully understand the meaning of what we have just told her.

But for now, it is a step in the right direction.

"Definitely a box of Rice Krispies," Sophie tells her, nodding.

"Me too," she says. "It would be very dark in a jar of Marmite, wouldn't it?"

"Very," Sophie says. "And quite smelly too!"

And they both giggle.

Listening to their laughter as they explore the pros of cons of Marmite jars and cereal packets as places to live, I take myself into the pantry – seeking solace amongst the tins of spaghetti rings and bags of Hula Hoops that now fill the shelves. It used to be the place I'd hide to take a sneaky bite of a bar of Dairy Milk after singing the praises of raisins and banana chips to my children. And of course it will be that place again. But right now it is where I come to shed a tear for my friend. Because I have lost her too.

"Are you okay, Mum?" Sophie says, joining me – no longer the gullible child who doesn't question why I emerge from the pantry empty-handed after saying I was just getting something for tea.

"I'm worried about you."

"I'm okay," I lie. Because I may not be right now, but I will be. Because I have to be.

In the days that follow, inevitably, so do the questions. Lots of them. And I answer each one as honestly as I can.

Did I see them die?

Will she die too?

What about us?

Some conversations are brief. She asks a question, listens to the answer, and then skips off happily to play with one of her toys.

Others are longer.

Like when she tells me she doesn't think Mummy and Daddy will like it in heaven. When she tells me she thinks they will miss her and Zack too much. That they will probably want to come home.

I tell her she is right. I tell her Mummy and Daddy will miss them very much. And I remind her that they can't come home. But that she and Zack have us now. That we will look after them.

Where will they live, she asks. Will they ever go back to their house?

Who will teach her how to ride her bike now?

Who will do her reading with her?

Who will make her birthday cake?

I will do all of these things, I tell her.

I tell her that we are her family now. Me, Sophie, Isla and Oliver. And Zack.

"And Uncle Mike?" she asks.

"And Uncle Mike," I say.

"But he doesn't live here anymore?"

"No. Uncle Mike doesn't live here anymore. But he still loves you. Very much."

"And Stanley?" she checks.

"And Stanley," I confirm. For a little girl who has been desperate for a puppy since she knew what one was, this is a big deal, and her face lights up. It's not much but it's all I have for now.

Chapter Eleven

W hen you agree to be listed as a guardian, it's a quick conversation. Will you do it? Of course. You don't want to think about the nuts and bolts of the arrangement. The how. The 'what do we do in this situation?' The practicalities. You just agree to it and move on – you get back to the glass of wine you were enjoying together, the shopping trip, the dinner party. But where does that leave you when it actually happens? You haven't discussed what you should do in every situation you will ever face in taking on that role. From the monumental to the absolutely mundane. Do they want their children to stay in their own home? Would they be happy if you moved them to a different school? If they wake at night do they want you to comfort them until they fall back to sleep? Do they want you to encourage them to love music? Sport? The outdoors? Are there toys they have avoided buying? Foods they would rather they didn't eat? Television programmes they think might corrupt their little minds?

You don't cover any of this stuff. So I am having to make it up as I go along.

On Friday night – exactly three weeks after arriving at my

house for the weekend – Phoebe screams out in the night. A nightmare. The first of many, I am almost certain.

With the quick reaction that never leaves you once you are a parent, I throw back my covers and rush to her side.

She is sat up in bed – her eyes are wide, her forehead clammy.

I sit down next to her.

"Did you have a bad dream, sweetheart?" I ask her.

She doesn't answer, but crawls into my arms and holds onto me.

I stroke her hair, aware of a dampness underneath me. The bed is wet.

"I was trying to hold Mummy's hand, and someone was pulling her away from me," she tells me eventually.

"Auntie Zoe's here," I say. "You're safe."

I strip her bed of the wet sheets and put her in some fresh pyjamas and then I put her into my bed.

Is that what Lou would have done?

I climb in next to her and stroke her cheek. She opens her eyes and smiles up at me, holding on tightly to the fluffy pink rabbit that she brought with her three weeks ago.

"I sleep with Mummy sometimes too," she whispers, giving me the answer I didn't really need. "When I wake up in the night. And sometimes I go into Daddy's bed too," she adds.

"Daddy's bed?" I ask. Because she must be confused.

"Yes, in his new bedroom."

I immediately want to ask her why. Why her daddy had a new bedroom. Why he wasn't sharing a room with her mummy. But I don't.

Instead I wrap my arms around her.

"Maybe Daddy's snoring was keeping Mummy awake," I say quietly, and Phoebe giggles.

But soothing her back to sleep, I find myself wondering if that was the real reason why my best friend was not sharing a bedroom with her husband in the time leading up to their deaths.

In the morning, at the first sound of Zack stirring, I make his bottle before bringing him in with us. We switch on Saturday morning television and the two of them cuddle into me, transfixed by the cartoons that swim nonsensically across the screen. An hour later Isla joins us – at an age where she desperately wants to be grown-up but at the same time doesn't want to feel like she is missing out. She tickles Zack and he giggles, waiting expectantly for her to do it again each time she stops. Phoebe grumbles that she can't hear the television, so Isla tickles her instead. And she laughs. And then Stanley leaps on the bed, clearly concerned he may be missing out on something here too. When Sophie appears at the door, she rolls her eyes and smiles at the sight of us all – her mum, her sister, her two new siblings and a dog who I'm convinced really does think he is one of us. Deciding she might as well complete the picture, Sophie jumps onto the bed, and everyone giggles together. And in that moment – in the middle of overwhelming sadness – I dare to hope that we might just be making some new memories. All of us together.

"Let's go to Granny's," I say.

I'm not ashamed to admit I need my mum. I need to not have to be the strong one. Even for just half an hour.

Sophie stays behind as she's made plans to see Josh, but after a breakfast of pancakes with maple syrup the rest of us make the half-hour journey to my parents' house.

They are still in the house where my brother Luke and I grew up, our bedrooms long since having been turned into bedrooms for their grandchildren when they are on sleepovers, which I am lucky to be able to say have been frequent over the years.

My mum and dad are as wonderful grandparents as they were parents.

Their grandchildren's photos fill their walls, there are always treats in the cupboards, and they have always made sure there are toys in my old toy chest to keep them entertained – particularly after the long journey we used to have to make from Bristol.

My mum opens the door and I crumble.

While my dad scoops up the children and takes them to the park, my mum makes us both a drink and we sit at the kitchen table.

"I just miss her, Mum," I say. "But I feel like I'm being selfish, because they miss her more."

"You are allowed to miss her," she says gently, reaching across the table and holding my hand. "You don't have to be strong all of the time."

I look around me, conscious that my parents' house is full of memories of Lou and me. The photos of us on the walls, the misshapen jug on the shelf that we made together in Art in our third year at Crakeleigh, the netball hoop still on the wall at the back of the house that we used relentlessly to practise our shooting one summer, both of us desperate to make the team. Even the table where we are sat is full of memories – of us enjoying fish and chips after school on a Friday, revising for exams, baking cakes...

"How will I do it, Mum?" I say, suddenly gripped by the enormous task ahead of me. Not just the practical stuff – feeding them, getting them to school, teaching them all the things a parent teaches their child – but the emotional stuff too – getting them through the heartache when they desperately want their mummy and daddy to make it all better and I can't give them that.

"You just will," my mum tells me, because she knows I have no choice. "You're not alone," she reminds me. "You've got Dad and me. And your brother and Jess. Oh, good news by the way – he can make the funeral after all."

"What?" I say, confused.

"Why wouldn't Luke have been coming to the funeral?"

My brother knew Lou for as long as I did. I never imagined for a second that he would miss her funeral.

"I'm not sure," my mum says. But I don't know if I believe her.

"Mum? What's going on?" I ask. "Why would Luke have missed Lou's funeral? That doesn't make sense. Unless he was going to be on holiday?

"Was he?" I ask, when my mum doesn't answer.

"No. Look, Zoe, you probably need to speak to your brother about this."

"I'm speaking to you about it," I say, a little more harshly than intended. "What's going on, Mum?" I say, a little softer.

"I'm not really sure," she says eventually. "They had not seen each other for such a long time, and I think they did have a bit of a falling out when you were younger, so they weren't particularly close. And I think he just thought maybe he shouldn't be there."

"What falling out?" I ask. "I don't remember them ever falling out."

"Oh, I don't know, Zoe," she says, probably bitterly regretting ever starting this conversation. "It was something and nothing, I'm sure."

"And why wouldn't he want to be there for me, if nothing else?" I ask.

"Well, exactly. That's probably why he *is* now coming, I imagine."

But I'm not convinced.

What was going on with my brother and Lou that would make him not want to be there at her funeral? It doesn't make sense.

"It's okay to miss Lou, but don't confuse that with thinking she was perfect, Zoe," my mum says eventually. "Or that you are not enough for Phoebe and Zack. You have been a great mum to your own children and you will be a great mum to them too."

My mum has never hidden the fact that she wasn't Lou's biggest fan. Right from when we were teenagers, when she made it clear she thought she was a bad influence on me and openly tried to encourage other friendships.

It didn't help when I told my mum about the party Lou had when her parents went away for the weekend. (We'd needed my dad to help fix the patio door which had come off its rails after someone had fallen into it. Drunk, obviously.) Or the time she parked her dad's car in town one night in a car park that he had told her explicitly not to park in, as it was notorious for break-ins – and of course, it was broken into. Or the time she cheated on Andrew when we went on holiday together after our A Levels.

It didn't matter that Lou got straight As or that my friendship with her made me happy. Even as adults my parents have not been able to shake the notion that she was far from perfect. But aren't we all?

I'm relieved when my dad arrives home with the children, saving me from further discussion of my dead friend's flaws. He puts his arm around me, leans down and plants a kiss on top of my head. Like he used to do when I was a child.

My dad is a man of few words. But that kiss is loaded with so many of them.

I love you.

I'm here for you.

I believe in you.

He gets Zack out of his pushchair while Isla takes Phoebe

upstairs to look for a board game to play. Moments later Phoebe runs back downstairs, clearly excited.

"Come and see my bedroom," she tells me.

I look at my mum and she just smiles.

I know immediately what she has done, and it melts my heart.

When Oliver was born, I think my mum was determined to win the new grandparent of the year award. She immediately turned my old bedroom into a second nursery for her new grandson – complete with a cot she'd bought from a colleague, a chest of drawers with a changing mat on top, a lick of blue paint and a huge basket full of cuddly toys. And on the bedroom door my dad had fixed colourful wooden letters that spelt out his name. When Sophie came along her name was added, and then Isla's and eventually – seven years ago – my niece Molly's too. The cot was eventually sold and replaced with two sets of bunk beds for the four of them, and new toys and board games were added to the teddies. But the names on the door were there to stay, and are still there today.

But now there are six names on that door – all in order of age.

"Look," Phoebe tells me, pointing to the door.

"It's me and Zacky."

And then a puzzled look crosses her face.

"Am I living here now?" she asks – her voice suddenly hesitant.

"No," I remind her. "Do you remember how we said you are going to live with me? And Sophie, and Isla. And Oliver sometimes – but he's away at big school right now, isn't he?"

She nods.

"But if you like, Phoebe, you and Zack can come and stay with me and Grandad Bill," my mum tells her. "And we can take you to feed the ducks like we used to with Sophie and Isla."

"And Oliver?" Phoebe asks.

"And Oliver," my mum confirms. "Would you like that, Phoebe?"

Phoebe nods.

"And we can get sweets from the shop again?" she says, hopefully, looking at my dad, who puts his finger to his lips and looks conspiratorially at his little friend.

And in that moment, I think I love my mum and dad more than I have ever loved them.

On the way home Phoebe asks me again if Mummy and Daddy might ever come back. She asks if it is possible to un-die once you have died.

If only it *was* possible.

If only we could un-die as easily as we can undo so many other things in life.

I tell her it's not possible.

But I so wish it was.

Chapter Twelve

Lou and I had it easy at school.

We were sporty, we worked hard enough to get good grades, but not enough to be considered nerdy, and if you asked the boys we were both considered hot.

We were popular. Well, Lou was popular. I was then popular by default.

People wanted to be our friend.

But our popularity was wasted on us.

We didn't need anybody else.

We had each other. To study with, to have lunch with, to sit with on the bus on our way home at the end of every day.

We spent every weekend together.

It was rare to see us apart.

"Where's Lou?" they'd ask me when I was alone.

"What's Zoe up to?" they'd ask my best friend.

As soon as we were both old enough to get away with it, we spent our Friday and Saturday nights at the local pub.

It was round the corner from Lou's house so we'd get ready there and then walk round in our skin-tight jeans and stiletto heels – no coats, of course, even in the dead of winter when there was ice on the ground.

It wasn't the coolest of places, but it was convenient. A starting point for our blossoming social lives.

We forced down alcoholic drinks that we didn't like the taste of – just because they made us feel grown-up, and we played pool, which neither of us was any good at.

By the time we were sixteen we were venturing further afield – to the nightclub in Ferringham – if you could call it that, with its miniscule dance floor and cheap disco lights.

We'd jump the queue and use our fake IDs to get in and then dance the night away.

Ecstasy, as it was inappropriately named back then, was where Lou had her first kiss.

He was older than us. Early twenties, maybe. He bought her drinks all night and then pulled her into the disabled toilet where he kissed her and tried to put his hand up her skirt.

She was drunk enough to go with him, but sober enough to stick her knee between his legs when he tried it on.

She cried all the way home.

She was annoyed that her first kiss had been with a complete jerk.

She said she wanted to find a nice boy like Jamie.

Her second kiss was with Graham – the older brother of a girl in our class.

Their parents were away and he had a house party.

In exchange for not blabbing on him, his sister got to invite a few friends. Lou and I were at the top of that list, of course.

Lou spent the entire night snogging Graham in his parents' bedroom – on their Laura Ashley bedspread, no less – during which he stuck his hand down her jeans and had an enthusiastic fumble.

It was soon after that that she and Andrew got together.

I had just passed my driving test and drove the 2.7 miles to Lou's house in the next village – a journey that remains the most exciting 2.7 miles I have ever driven. The very first miles on my own at the wheel of a car.

I honked the horn outside Lou's house and she ran out shouting "We will" back at her dad as he instructed us to be careful.

She got in the car and handed me a gift bag containing two purple furry dice to hang in my mum's car when I was allowed to drive it.

I immediately hung them from the rear-view mirror as we set off to the shop in her village. We'd have walked it just as quickly but wouldn't have felt nearly so grown-up.

And it was as we sat on the swings, swigging Fanta and crunching Pringles that day, that Lou told me she liked the new boy, Andrew Robson.

We then spent the next thirty minutes working out the probability that they would get together.

Lou and I grew up in the era when girls wrote their names on a piece of paper, together with those of any boys they liked the look of, plus the word LOVES and then worked out – with great accuracy, of course – the percentage chance that it was "true" love.

Lou and I had played that game so many times over the years, but this was the first time I could tell she really liked a boy. It didn't even matter that they only had a "scientifically calculated" 18 per cent chance of true love.

She asked him out the following week, and he said yes.

It wasn't hard to see what Lou saw in Andrew.

He was good-looking. He was sporty. He was funny. And he brought out the best in Lou. She was a better person when she was with him. She worked harder. Laughed louder. Cared more.

They dated for four years. And she quickly forgot that her first kiss was with a complete jerk, and that her second meant she'd never be able to look her friend's parents in the eye again.

Because she'd met the one.

She was in love.

It was young love. But she thought it would last forever.

Like we all do when we are head over heels.

It didn't last, of course. Because it was Rich she married.

And now she is gone.

Chapter Thirteen

The funeral is as you would expect. Painful. Sobering. Two coffins. Two lives taken far too early, from two small children who, as yet, have no real comprehension of the enormity of what they have lost. A church full of tears and complete and unanimous disbelief that this could have even actually happened.

I have not been to many funerals in my life. That makes me lucky, I guess. Not to have lost many people I love.

The last funeral I was at was for Louise's mum. Gone just three years before her own daughter, as it turns out. Audrey had been living with cancer for the last two years of her life. When it finally got the better of her it was a blessing, really. Lou had watched her suffer terribly in the final six months. And I had watched Lou as she watched her mum's decline and felt completely helpless.

She had already lost her dad in her early twenties to the same thing.

Twenty-four hours after her mum's funeral she had asked to see me. With no siblings between her and Rich, cousins they had barely spoken to since childhood and Rich's elderly parents rapidly nearing the day a nursing home would become inevitable, they had looked at their little girl asleep in her cot and wondered what the hell would happen to her if they were both gone.

"You love Phoebe, right, Zo?" she asked me, a cup of tea in her hand, her face free of the make-up I had known her to wear without fail – such was her grief, her hair haphazardly tied back in a messy bun.

"Of course," I said, confused where this conversation was going. She had just lost her mum. She was grieving. Her mind was clearly racing.

"Would you take her?" she said. "You and Mike? If I died? If Rich died?"

Her voice was desperate. She needed to know. She needed to be sure her baby would be okay. Always.

I just nodded and held her in my arms. I let her cry for the mum she had already lost, and for the little girl she hoped she never would.

We never spoke about it again – until Zack was born, when she reminded me of her emotional request the day after her mum's funeral and asked if taking on two children would be too much to ask of me.

I laughed and told her no.

"The more the merrier," I said, pulling her in for a hug.

Here was the child they had given up hope of ever having. And already she was worrying about the day she might not be there for him.

She was less emotional this time, of course. She had not just buried her mother. But I heard the same desperation in her voice.

"You would never split them up, would you, Zo?" she said. "If it got too much, I mean," she added, for some kind of context, I guess.

It seemed like an odd thing to ask, but then what conversation in which you are asking another human being to one day –

maybe – take care of the children you have brought into world, would ever sound normal?

And just like the first time, we never spoke about it again.

It's an easy thing to agree to when your friend is stood in front of you, describing a time when they might not be here anymore, and their children are left with nobody. Of course you say yes. Of course you agree to anything they want. You metaphorically stick your fingers in your ears and tell them you'll do whatever they're asking, if only they'll stop talking about this awful scenario that is never going to happen. Not in a million years.

And then it does.

The vicar is kind. He tells us a little bit about their lives, he tells us that they were wonderful people, wonderful parents, wonderful friends, and that they were taken from us all far too soon.

The funeral is well attended. Lou and Rich were clearly loved. Friends, neighbours, colleagues – they all crowd into the church to say their goodbyes.

Rich's dad died last year but his mum is here. She is in a nursing home now and is here with one of her carers.

She has early-onset Alzheimer's, but today is a good day.

She remembers who we are and why she is here.

It would be better if today she didn't remember, of course, if she didn't have to say goodbye to her own son.

She asks me to take Phoebe to see her and I promise her that I will. Just as soon as things have settled down.

I see Heidi and Stephen, whose wedding Lou and Rich had been travelling back from at the time of the accident. I can only imagine what they have been through since that phone call that probably turned the best day of their lives into the worst. Stephen is holding his new wife's hand, his spare hand tightly gripped around a rolled-up order of service.

I see Jamie too, and my heart catches in my mouth. My first love.

He looks over at me and I can see in his face that he understands the intense pain I am feeling. It's his pain too. Lou is wrapped up in so many of our shared memories. He touches his fingers to his lips, his wife Amy by his side.

I spot Patrick Massey, and another man I assume is James Stewart. They both nod politely in my direction. I see Lou and Rich's nextdoor neighbours and a group of women – mums from Phoebe's school, maybe – sitting at the back, not wanting to impose. I see my own parents, and my brother.

Evidently he decided that whatever it was he and Lou fell out about was not big enough to keep him away.

I want to ask him what my mum meant, but I know now is not the time or the place. That is a conversation for another day.

The mourners are mostly in black. They bring flowers. Some of them bring gifts for Phoebe and Zack. And everyone tells me and Mike how sorry they are.

Simon did offer to come to the funeral. But it didn't feel right. He'd never met Rich and he'd only ever met Lou once. Well, twice.

He met her by accident.

The girls were at Mike's and it was the first time Simon had been to the house when Lou dropped by on her way home from work. To ask if I could have the children overnight in a few weeks' time, as she and Rich both had work things on that they couldn't miss.

I wasn't ready to introduce her to Simon. It was too new.

But I had no choice.

A couple of weeks later he saw her again.

At one of the pubs in Ferringham. With a man. Sat at a table in the corner.

She didn't see him. And he didn't go over.

"You should have done," I told him. "You could have met Rich."

But he picked up a picture of Lou and Rich and Phoebe on my windowsill, and told me that the man in the pub wasn't Rich.

"A colleague, then," I said, nonchalantly, pushing spaghetti into a pan of boiling water.

But the expression on his face was enough to tell me that would not have been his guess.

"They seemed a bit close to be colleagues," he said, raising an eyebrow, before hastily backtracking. "I mean, what do I know, I'd never met the woman before she dropped in here that night," he said, before pulling me away from the hob and kissing me.

It was a good kiss. It was enough to distract me. But I have wondered since who that man was.

I wish I had asked my friend back then. Before it was too late.

Would she have reassured me that of course he was a colleague. Or a client even, that she was prepping for an upcoming court case.

Or would she have told me that she was doing something she shouldn't have been doing? Again.

The girls are with us. And Oliver.

Phoebe and Zack are not.

I spent so long researching what was the right thing to do.

Should we bring Phoebe? Should we not? Would she understand it? Would she remember it? Would she want to say goodbye? Would she resent us later if we didn't give her the chance?

I even turned to Google.

I sometimes wonder if we have all become completely inept at making decisions without the assistance of the worldwide web.

Help, my hair dye has turned my hair green.

How do you solve a Rubik's Cube?

Why doesn't my boyfriend love me anymore?

Should I take my five-year-old goddaughter to her parents' funeral?

Some sources said yes, she should go, she should be given the chance to say goodbye; others said no, she was too young to understand.

And then I asked Simon. I should have asked him first. He has been where I am now. He has had to walk a child through unspeakable grief. He has had to bury a mother of two small children.

"What did you do?" I asked him. "Did you take the girls?"

"I asked them if they wanted to go," he said. "I tried as best I could to explain what a funeral actually is, and then I gave them the choice."

"And?"

"They came. But they were so young. They don't remember it. And nor will Phoebe if you take her. But it's important to involve her in the decision.

"Whatever decision you all make, Zoe, you will have doubts that you are doing the right thing. But there is no rule book on what we do in any of these situations. If there was, I'd be giving you my copy, I promise you."

I hugged him in that moment. Because there he was, making me smile again, in the face of utter devastation. And despite the overwhelming grief I was still feeling, I felt lucky. I *feel* lucky.

So in the end we did give Phoebe the choice, explaining as simply as we could what a funeral was, and what would happen.

And she chose to stay at home with Zack and Auntie Robyn.

After the service we head to Lou and Rich's local pub for a wake, where we eat doorstep sandwiches and chunky chips and share memories of two people taken far too soon.

Everyone comes to find me – to offer their condolences – but no one knows what to say – not really. Other than the obvious.

How am I doing?

How are the children doing?

Do I need any help?

Except for Heidi. Heidi has something different to say.

Heidi was in the same year as Lou and me at school. When it wasn't just Lou and I, Heidi was there. Part of our wider circle of friends. In another life, where Lou didn't find that empty seat next to mine on that first day at Crakeleigh, she might have been Lou's best friend. She was more like her than I ever was. Another rule breaker. Another boundary pusher. Someone else who always said what she thought.

I lost touch with her when we all left for university, but Lou was better at keeping in touch with people than I ever was.

Putting her drink down on the bar, she wraps her arms around me and holds me tight.

It's been more than twenty years.

"I don't even know what to say," she tells me.

"Most people don't," I reassure her.

"I know you two were still very close. I'm sorry you and I lost touch."

"It's hard," I say. "To keep in contact with everyone, I mean. Life gets in the way. But yes, Lou and I were always close."

She is looking at me like she has something to say. Something significant. But she's holding back. I can tell.

"What is it?" I ask her.

She hesitates for a moment, like she's about to start a conversation that maybe she shouldn't.

"Did Lou seem happy to you?" she says eventually.

I want to say yes.

Out of loyalty? Or because that's what I actually believe? I'm not sure.

Did she seem happy?

I didn't see her as much as I would have liked. We both had busy lives, we were both running around after children – albeit at very different stages. But when I did see her, did she seem happy?

Yes. In many ways I think she did.

The family she had wanted for so long was finally complete. She was excelling in her career. Heading in the direction of partnership. And she had a wonderful man by her side, who as far as I know worshipped the ground she walked on.

But why was he sleeping in another room? And who *was* that man in the pub that Simon saw her with? Do I really believe he was just a colleague?

These things are enough to make me doubt that my friend was truly happy, but they are not enough to know for sure she wasn't.

"Did she not seem happy to you?" I ask Heidi, turning it back on her. Maybe I need someone else to answer the question.

"She just seemed distant. And her and Rich…"

She hesitates again.

"What about her and Rich?" I say.

"Well … they just seemed like … well … almost like they were strangers…"

Were Lou and Rich having problems? Was their relationship in trouble?

I want to ask Heidi what she means.

But I can't.

Not here. Not at their funeral.

Or maybe I just don't want to know the answer.

Maybe I don't want to know that my friend was unhappy when she died. Maybe that will just make her death all the harder to bear. Or maybe it will make me question our friendship. Make me wonder if maybe I wasn't there for her when she needed me most. Or that I didn't really know her.

So I say nothing.

And we are both saved from the uncomfortable silence when Jamie appears by my side.

"Jamie," Heidi says, with the nonchalance and familiarity of someone who clearly sees him regularly.

She leans in to kiss him on the cheek and then squeezing my arm affectionately – sympathetically – she slips away, leaving us alone.

Jamie immediately wraps his arms around me, saying nothing.

I can feel myself crumbling once more so I pull away and brush a solitary tear from my cheek.

You never forget your first love. And though I quickly stopped thinking about Jamie once Mike was in my life, there was a time when I never thought I would love anyone like I loved him.

We shared lots of firsts. All the significant ones when you're a teenager. Our first date. Our first kiss. The first time we'd ever slept with anyone. And at the time they all felt unsurpassable. But we were young and inexperienced. What did we know?

At exactly the right moment – when the silence between us has said enough – we are joined by Jamie's wife Amy.

She and Jamie got together six months after Mike and I started dating. I first met her during a weekend visit home from uni, when a bunch of us went to the pub. Lou was there too and seemed to take an instant dislike to Amy.

"Jamie and Amy," she had said, enunciating their rhyming names more than was strictly necessary after being introduced. "That's unfortunate."

It was said with enough of a smile to be seen as being said in fun. But if you knew Lou well you could detect something else.

And I knew her well. What I didn't know was why she was being like that.

Out of some misplaced sense of loyalty to me, maybe? If that's what it was then it wasn't necessary. I was happy. I was with Mike. I was in love with him in a way I'd never really been in love with Jamie.

She told me later that she wasn't sure about her. That she didn't think she was right for Jamie. But she could never tell me why.

"It's just a feeling," she had said dismissively.

I've barely seen Jamie – and Amy – since that night. Lou and Rich's wedding… Lou's mum's funeral… Maybe one other random get-together. I have no idea where all the years have gone. We met when we were kids and now we have our own kids.

While Jamie and I silently scan our many shared memories, Amy does the talking.

"I'm so sorry Zoe," she says softly. "Jamie was absolutely devastated when you called to tell him the news. I can only imagine what you're feeling. What you're all going through."

She has a kind voice. Genuine. You can tell she really does care, that it's not just empty words.

Lou had no reason not to like Amy. She was a good person back then and she is still a good person now. But once my friend had made up her mind about someone, there was no changing it.

I knew instinctively when I met her that she was to Jamie what Mike was to me. The real thing. The one that made everyone else seem insignificant.

"How are the children?" she asks, putting her hand on my arm as she does so. "You will tell me if there is anything I can do to help, won't you? I mean it. Honestly."

And she really does. It is not – like so many others are – an empty offer.

Everyone says it, don't they?

Please let me know if I can do anything, they say.

All you have to do is shout, they clarify.

Anything, they add. Just to be clear.

But there is no follow-up. No phone call to check you haven't suddenly thought of something they can do to help. No WhatsApp reminding you of their kind offer.

Or when you do think of something, they are suddenly busy.

I wish I could, they say.

I'm so sorry but I'm busy that day, they apologise.

With Amy it really is different.

Amy is a child therapist.

So I tell her how I'm worried about Phoebe. How she has been having nightmares, and wetting the bed, and constantly asking whether Mummy and Daddy might actually come back for them one day.

I tell her how I catch Phoebe sometimes, snatching a toy from Zack, telling him that he can't have it, because Mummy gave it to her.

I tell her that I've seen her playing with her dollies, telling them that their mummy has died, but that they mustn't be upset because she will look after them now.

I tell her that she will ask me from time to time whether I might die too one day, and what will happen to her if I do.

And she assures me it's all normal. That it's still early days. But I take her card anyway. Its presence in my pocket is strangely reassuring.

"We missed you at the wedding," Jamie tells me, attempting to have something resembling a mundane conversation.

"Heidi and I lost touch a long time ago," I tell him. "This is the first time I've seen her for years."

"It was a bit of blast from the past," he says. "The wedding, I mean," he adds, painfully aware that the funeral too is not unlike a reunion. Former school friends coming together – wearing dark clothing and a sombre demeanour – to say goodbye to an old classmate.

"Rebecca and Phil were there too. And Andrew and his wife."

"Is Andrew here?" I ask.

Out of everyone, it was Andrew I thought I'd see.

I expected him.

I expected him to want to say goodbye.

Lou's first love.

"He's on holiday," Jamie tells me. "They tried to change their flights, but they couldn't make it work."

Is he really on holiday, I wonder. Or is it just an excuse? For not wanting to come?

Andrew was heartbroken when Lou ended things with him after four years. He loved her, and continued to do so for a long time after they broke up.

Was saying the ultimate goodbye just too painful?

I have dismissed the notion as ridiculous before I have shared it with Jamie.

Lou and Andrew broke up more than twenty years ago.

Remembering the weekend the four of us spent camping in our final year of school, I smile to myself.

"What?" Jamie asks.

"Do you remember when we went to Bournemouth for the weekend, camping, and Andrew forgot to bring the tin opener?"

Jamie laughs.

"It was the only thing he was asked to bring," he says.

This should feel odd. Discussing the past with my first love, his wife standing by my side. But somehow it's okay. Somehow it feels normal. And it allows me to remember a time when I *do* know for sure that my friend was truly happy.

"Lou was furious," I say. For Amy's benefit more than anything. Jamie was there. He knows the story as well as I do.

"She made him drive all the way to the nearest supermarket to buy one because she was too embarrassed to ask the people in the tent next to us. 'What kind of idiot forgets to pack a tin opener when they go camping?' she shouted as he drove off. By the time he got back we were all tucking into baked beans on toast, washed down with bottles of Smirnoff Ice."

Amy looks at us quizzically.

"What about the can opener?" she asks.

"Turns out Lou had bought the expensive cans," I laugh. "The ones with the ring pulls!"

We all chuckle at this.

And I realise in that moment that funerals don't need to be sad. Not completely. They can be a celebration too. A chance to remember the good times.

When Amy slips away to get a drink, I pull Jamie in for another hug. I breathe him in and I am taken back to my youth all over again. To snatching time together in between lessons just to hold hands; to sneaking him out of my bedroom in the early hours of the morning, hoping my parents wouldn't catch us; to lazy days spent on the beach with Andrew and Lou, talking about how we would all travel the world together one day. We thought that was it. We had it all, and we could not have imagined a life without each other.

"Did Lou seem happy to you?" I ask Jamie, releasing my grip on him and slipping my hand in his.

"Yes," he says. A little too quickly. Naively. Optimistically?

"Really?" I ask.

"Yes," he says again. "I mean, I guess everyone has their shit to deal with, and I think Lou and Rich were no exception, but she seemed happy enough."

"Shit to deal with?" I ask him.

"You know," he says. "Same as all of us. Busy lives. Kids. Not enough time to just be."

Yes, I do know. All too well.

I look at him and he knows I need more.

He sighs.

"Were they okay?" I ask. "At the wedding? Lou and Rich?"

"They were clearly having some kind of disagreement," he says, letting go of my hand and running his own through his hair, the way he always used to when he was uncomfortable. Like the time my dad caught him sneaking out of my bedroom and told him he was absolutely fine with whatever was going on in his daughter's bedroom, as long as it didn't result in him becoming a grandfather prematurely. Ironic, really, given that that was exactly what happened a few short years later. Absolutely mortified, Jamie turned a lovely shade of crimson, ran his hand nervously through his hair and quickly mumbled his assurances that he would indeed not get me pregnant – or words to that effect.

"What kind of disagreement?"

"I don't know, Zo. Just a disagreement. I didn't hear it. I just saw them arguing intermittently throughout the day.

"But like I said. We all have our shit to deal with. Life is hard. It's not like it was when we were kids. When all we had to worry about was remembering to bring a can opener on a camping trip, or whose house we were going to get pissed at on a Friday night. Lou and Rich had stressful jobs. Two young kids…"

Realising what he has said, he squeezes my arm.

"Heidi said they're with you?"

I nod my confirmation.

"That's amazing, Zo. *You* are amazing."

"Not really," I tell him. "I am just keeping a promise."

"Listen," he says. "You've got enough on your plate without worrying about some stupid argument that Lou and Rich had before they died. She was happy. They were both happy. Put all your energy into getting those little kiddies through this. That's what's really important."

Wondering what on earth happened to my carefree childhood sweetheart, I promise him I'll do just that. And then I kiss him on the cheek and tell him I'll see him soon. I'm not sure I will, but somehow it is comforting to pretend I will. Because he is part of the past I shared with Lou that I'm just not ready to say goodbye to yet.

Soon after Jamie and Amy leave, everyone else begins to drift off, each coming over to give me a hug, or a sympathetic squeeze of the hand, or a reminder to call them, should I ever need anything.

And then we all head home too.

Mike has taken the girls back to the flat for the night, so after I have dropped Oliver at the station I drive home by myself, wondering whether everything will start to feel better from this moment on.

As I pull up on the drive, Robyn opens the door and Phoebe runs out in her socks.

"Look what I made for you, Auntie Zoe," she tells me excitedly. "It's a necklace made out of pasta!"

"How lovely," I tell her, scooping her up for a cuddle.

As she slips it over my head, I smile at my friend waiting to put her arms around me.

"Thank you," I tell her, once Phoebe has skipped away to terrorise Stanley with another pasta necklace. He's not so keen.

"How was it?" she asks me. "I'm sorry. That always feels like such a crass thing to ask after a funeral," she adds. "But I can't not ask."

"It was heartbreaking," I tell her honestly. "But with some lovely moments of reflection, if that makes sense."

She smiles in confirmation that it does.

I don't know what I would have done without Robyn these past few weeks.

Besides keeping the surgery going in my absence, she has been a great friend, pure and simple.

When I called her to tell her what had happened, she told me to go and be with my family and that she would handle everything else. And she has lived up to her promise.

She spoke to Nathan. She organised for a locum to take my place. She delivered meals, and shopping, and freshly ironed uniforms for the girls. She took Isla to her Maths tutor, and to dance class, and hockey practice, and she walked Stanley for me. She did everything I would normally do, so that I didn't have to. So that I could literally just be with my family.

And so in the middle of soul-shattering grief I feel lucky. Because though I have lost my best friend, I have another truly wonderful friend who will do everything she can to help get me through it.

I met Robyn on Oliver's first day of school. It was her son Charlie's first day too, and as our children's friendship has grown over the years, so has ours.

For the last three years she has worked with me at the surgery as our practice manager, dragging our clunky old patient database into the twenty-first century – a huge administrative undertaking that was well overdue.

Today, though, she is just my friend. And whilst we have been saying goodbye to Lou and Rich, Robyn has been making sure Phoebe has been doing what every five-year-old should be doing – having fun. Making pasta-tube necklaces and covering my kitchen table in every imaginable colour of glitter. She is sweeping up the last of that glitter while I put Phoebe and Zack to bed.

Zack goes down with no trouble at all. A bottle of milk and a quick cuddle and he is a happy boy.

Phoebe is a different matter altogether.

She asks about the funeral. She wants to know what happened. Was it sad? Who was there? Did Uncle Mike and I cry?

And when I have finished telling her – as briefly and as carefully as I can – that it was a sad but incredibly beautiful celebration of her wonderful mummy and daddy, and everything they had accomplished in their short lives – her and Zack being at the very *very* top of that list – I sit with her until she falls asleep, her hand gripped tightly onto my arm, as if she's afraid that if she lets go I will disappear overnight, just like they did.

"Everything okay?" Robyn asks, when I finally slip away, my arm still bearing the imprint of her little fingers pressed against my skin.

I fight back a fresh wave of tears, which tells Robyn everything she needs to know.

"This stuff literally gets everywhere," she laughs, dusting her hands off into the bin.

It's the distraction she knows instinctively that I need right now. More hugs, and more platitudes of sympathy are not what I need.

"I don't know why you do it to yourself," I tell her. "She'd have been just as happy with a piece of paper and a packet of crayons!"

"What can I say, I'm a glutton for punishment."

Sitting down, I pull my phone out of my pocket.

Three new messages.

One from Oliver telling me he got home safely.

One from Mike telling me he'll swing by in the morning so that the girls can change into their school uniforms.

And one from Simon.

Thinking of you x

Vaguely aware of Robyn talking to me, I look up.

"Do you want a cuppa?"

I shake my head and look back at my phone.

"Simon?" she asks me, intuitively.

I nod my confirmation.

"Can you stay?" I ask her.

"I thought you'd never ask. Now get out of here. I'll call you if you are needed."

"Are you sure?"

"Hundred per cent."

———

Twenty minutes later I am knocking on Simon's front door.

"The girls are at my sister's," he says before I'm even in the house.

It's all I need to know.

"How was…?" he starts to ask. But I stop him, covering his mouth with one hand and pulling him towards me with the other.

"I just want to forget," I tell him. "Just for tonight."

So he kisses me. And I do forget. And it feels good.

Just for one night I need to not be grieving for my friend, I need to not be worrying about putting back together the broken pieces of her children's lives.

Just for one night I need to forget it all. I need to feel alive. I need to feel wanted.

And that's exactly how Simon makes me feel.

Without saying anything he takes my hand and leads me upstairs.

In seconds, the black dress I decided was a respectable cut, and a respectable length in which to say goodbye to my best friend, is abandoned on the floor and I am pulling Simon into me.

Being with a man other than Mike still feels strange.

But not tonight.

Tonight I am so lost in the moment, it doesn't feel strange.

It feels vital.

Simon is good at this. Really good. I clamp my hand over my mouth as I am about to scream out and he laughs.

"I told you, the girls are not here," he says, sliding off me, breathless, his body glistening with sweat. "So make all the noise you like," he adds.

I blush and he pulls me into his arms.

"Was that good?" he asks, with a little smile.

"Do you really need to ask?"

"Well, not really, no," he says, and we both laugh. "I'm guessing I helped you forget!"

We fall asleep like that, and early the next morning I slip out of Simon's bed and drive home, ready to face whatever it is that comes next.

Chapter Fourteen

Mike is at the house when I get home – waiting for the girls to change into their uniforms before he drops them off at school.

He watches me as I drop my keys on the kitchen table, pour coffee into a mug, drop a slice of bread into the toaster.

He doesn't ask where I have been.

The fact that I'm still in the same dress in which I held his hand at my best friend's funeral yesterday makes it pretty obvious I've not just been out to the local shop for a pint of milk. Well, that and Robyn's presence at the kitchen table feeding his godchildren dippy eggs and fruit smoothies.

"Do you not think you should have been at home last night?" he says eventually. I look at him and know instantly that he is regretting it.

I say nothing.

The silence is deafening – broken only by the sound of my now cooked slice of bread emerging from the toaster, and the sound of a jam lid dropping onto the kitchen worktop.

"Do you want more smoothie, poppet?" Robyn asks Phoebe. Anything to fill the quiet.

Phoebe nods, happily oblivious to the inaudible argument raging around her.

I walk out of the kitchen calmly and call the girls.

"Are you ready?" I shout. "Your dad's waiting to drop you off."

"Hi, Mum," Sophie says, appearing at the top of the stairs with her toothbrush in her mouth. "You okay?"

"Top of the world," I tell her. "Top of the world."

He tries to talk to me – when the girls are waiting in the car, but I am too angry, so I politely tell him I'll see him at the weekend when he comes to collect his children, and I shut the door.

"Are you okay?" Robyn asks, wiping yoghurt from Zack's face.

Phoebe gets down from the table and follows Stanley into the living room.

"How dare he?" I whisper. "How dare he question the fact that I wanted one night to myself? One night to forget the hell that I'm going through. To forget that I have lost my best friend and that her children have lost everything."

"He shouldn't have said it," Robyn says. "But I think he knew that."

"I mean, it wouldn't hurt for him to come and help out once in a while," I say.

Sensing I have stuff to get off my chest, Robyn stays quiet. She lifts Zack out of his highchair and puts him down on the floor, scooping up a stray piece of banana in the process.

"They are his godchildren too. They were his friends too. Why am I the one left dealing with all of this?"

Of course, I know why I am the one left dealing with all of this. Lou chose me. She picked me to love her children when she would no longer be here to do it herself.

Even if Mike and I hadn't divorced, even if she'd never changed the will, Mike would only ever have been the second parent.

I pick Zack back up off the floor, suddenly needing to hold him. He cuddles into me and my eyes fill with tears.

"Was he right?" I ask. "Should I have been here? Should I have been with Phoebe and Zack? Was I being selfish?"

Robyn pours fresh coffee into my cup and brushes an imaginary piece of fluff from the sleeve of my dress.

She has something to say and she is contemplating how best to say it. I can tell.

"Do you want to know what I think?" she says, sitting down and pulling out a chair for me to do the same.

I sit down, and nod.

Yes, I do want to know.

"I think you needed last night," she says.

I let myself smile and she smiles back knowingly.

"I think you have been amazing these past few weeks. The way you have taken those children in as your own. I am honestly in awe of you.

"But you are only human, Zoe. Everyone has their breaking point, and last night I think you were at yours. So I think you did absolutely the right thing.

"Mike was wrong.

"The kids were fine. They were asleep, they didn't need you. They had me. And I am pretty amazing, after all."

She grins and so do I, signalling my unequivocal agreement.

She *is* amazing.

"Let's be honest," she continues. "Mike was out of order. And I think he knows that. I think he just probably feels incredibly guilty that you are now bringing up two more children on your own. If this had happened a year ago, he'd have been doing it all with you."

"I wish he was," I tell her.

She looks at me curiously.

Robyn was gutted when Mike and I split up. In the same way my parents were. I guess we were the couple everyone just assumed would always be together. And then we weren't. And not only did we have to get used that, but so did they.

"I just mean it would be so much easier if he was still here," I tell her. "If there were two of us. If I had someone to navigate all this with."

"So anyway. How was last night?" Robyn says, evidently deciding that if I'm not suddenly wishing that I had never left my husband, then the least I can do is share some A-rated gossip.

So I take a deep breath and a sip of coffee and do just that.

Chapter Fifteen

M ike phones me on his way into work after dropping off the girls.

"How dare you?" I spit, before he has even said a word.

He says nothing in response. A wise decision.

"One night," I say. "One night. That's all I needed. Just to forget this living nightmare. And you couldn't even let me have that without snide comments about whether or not you deemed my behaviour appropriate.

"Well, I've got news for you, Mike. We are divorced. You don't get to comment on what I'm doing or not doing. And it wouldn't hurt you to offer to help out occasionally. They are your godchildren too, you know. In case you'd forgotten. Then maybe I wouldn't need to rely on Robyn looking after them, just so I can have a break."

"Are you finished?" he asks quietly.

Am I?

Probably not.

I am so pissed off with the world right now, I could rage for hours.

But what good would that do? It won't take the pain away. It won't bring my friend back.

"I'm sorry, Zoe," he says.

"You were out of order," I tell him.

"I was. And I'm sorry."

"Why did you say it then?"

"I don't know. I was being a dick."

"Phoebe is going back to school on Thursday," I tell him, changing the subject. "It's time. And I need to go back to work. Nathan has been beyond understanding. Can you help?" I ask.

"Of course. What do you need?"

"Can you pick her up? A couple of times a week, maybe? At least until she is settled. Her school is a right hack from the surgery, which means I'll have to leave super early just to get there in time."

"What time does she finish? Four?"

"Three," I correct him, immediately feeling frustrated.

Of course he doesn't know the time a typical primary school finishes. Because he never had to worry about it. That was always left to me. He was too busy working. Even when we both worked, it was down to me to pick them up – or arrange for someone else to.

I'm not sure why I have even bothered asking. This is never going to work.

"I'll have a look," he says. "But I usually have meetings all afternoon."

"Uh-huh," I say. Because of course I never have meetings, or appointments, or surgeries in the afternoon. What could he possibly be talking about?

"What about Zack?" he asks. "I could pick him up. He finishes later, right?"

Yes, he does. Which is exactly why I don't need help with Zack. I can manage a 6pm pick-up just fine.

"Zack isn't the problem," I tell him. "It's Phoebe I need help with."

Silence.

"It's just the school is so far," he says. "Have you thought any more about moving her?"

This is not the first time Mike has brought this up. And I know it won't be the last. He thinks I should move Phoebe to a school that is closer to our house. Hartingley Primary, even, where our own children went. And yes, I agree that that would make things a lot easier. But right now I think it is more important to keep her in a place she is familiar with. There has been enough change in her little life without ripping her away from that too.

"I can't," I tell him. "Not now. It's too soon."

"When you move her…" Mike starts hesitantly. "If you move her…"

"Forget it," I tell him, abruptly. "I can ask Simon."

It's childish, I know, but I can't help myself.

It's also absolutely not true. I wouldn't ask Simon to help with my children, any more than Mike would ask Charlotte. Though maybe he would, I don't know…

"I do want to help, Zo," he tells me, wisely ignoring the Simon comment. "Honestly."

The unspoken "but" hanging ominously in the air between us, I say my goodbyes, reasonably certain that there will be no help coming from Mike any time soon.

Chapter Sixteen

It is hard to pinpoint the exact moment Mike and I stopped being husband and wife and started being more like two single parents who just happened to live in the same house. The moment that he stopped being the man I always thought would get my heart racing just by looking at me, and started being the man who was too busy to even look at me.

He supported me in my return to work. He encouraged me to go for it. He said all the right things when I returned home with stories of refresher courses I had completed, of surgeries I had performed for the first time, of animals I had saved. And he paid for the childminder so our children would be looked after when I couldn't be there to do it. But his job was always more important. His job always paid more money. His job always meant I was the one who had to do the school pick-up or arrange for someone else to.

Time for "us" disappeared. Gradually at first. Evenings together were interrupted by meetings that ran over, by urgent phone calls, by report writing that couldn't wait until the next day.

At first these things were still interspersed with a kiss, or a romantic gesture – an "I love you" or a "Fancy a quickie later?" or a "You look nice today" (even though I was wearing yesterday's make-up and clearly had spaghetti sauce down my top). He would climb into bed after working until gone midnight, wrap an arm around me and plant a quick kiss on the back of my head. And I would do the same after staying up late to catch up on the never-ending surgery admin.

But eventually those things disappeared too.

Communications would revolve not around us and our love for each other, but around the children, and the house, and the chores. "Don't forget Isla has the dentist at 4.15pm", "Don't forget to get the chicken out of the freezer", "Don't forget to turn the tumble-dryer off when you leave the house." And the odd but significant quick kiss on the head was suddenly conspicuous in its absence, replaced by a quick shove when one or the other of us was snoring.

At some point life calmed down a little. But by then we were both so out of practice at prioritising each other, we no longer even tried. Instead, in those precious few hours we found ourselves with, we were arranging to see friends, to go for a run, to take a class. We made time for everything except our relationship.

Before I knew it I was reaching for the towel if he walked into the bathroom when I was showering. I was turning my back to put on my bra if he was in the room with me. I was sleeping facing away from him, when I'd always slept the other way.

We went for six months without sex. How does that even happen? It happens when two people are living for their children, and for their work, but not for each other because there are simply not enough hours in the day. It happens when one person crashes out early from exhaustion, while the other carries on working, waiting for exhaustion to get the better of them too. It happens when you wear yourself out racing from one thing to another, with no let-up – work, after-school clubs, dinners for five, drop-offs at friends – and pick-ups a few hours later. It happens when every hour of every day is taken up with something vital – cramming in a couple of extra hours of work or study because there is always something that needs to be done and you're paid well so you can't not do it; tidying the house; emptying the washing machine; going to put the laundry in the tumble-dryer and finding it's already full with yesterday's load, dry but creased beyond recognition; emptying and reloading the dishwasher; wiping down surfaces for the umpteenth time…

Before you know it, life – or married life at least – is passing you by, and you don't know each other anymore. Or you have just stopped seeing each other the way you used to.

One day I looked at Mike and I realised I didn't see him in the way I thought I always would.

He was the man who worked his socks off for his family – the family he loved more than life itself. But he wasn't the man I couldn't keep my hands off anymore. I had spent so long with no real opportunity to get my hands on him, that I had stopped trying all that hard when the opportunity did come along, and eventually it was too much effort to even bother trying at all. I would rather take the run, or the Spanish class or the night out with my girlfriends.

I have never stopped loving him. I just began to resent him too much. And that eventually stopped me from loving him in the right way.

Chapter Seventeen

I need to go to the house. I can't bring myself to think of it as Lou and Rich's house. It makes everything too real. So in my mind it is just a house from which I collect things. Bit by bit. Until we have everything we need.

Lou and Rich moved back to Sussex the year before Mike and I did. Lou had always wanted to come back to her roots. It was where her parents were. It was where a lot of her friends were – the friends that she had kept in touch with but I hadn't. She was well established at Massey & Stewart by then and was prepared to do the long commute.

They moved to Crakeleigh, where Lou and I had grown up – to a new development of houses far bigger than the semi the young Lou had lived in.

It was only a few miles from Hartingley where Mike and I settled, but the school they chose for Phoebe was the other side of Crakeleigh to us.

If I could never go back to this house again, I would. I would buy everything new. Toys, and clothes, a walker for Zack, furniture, duvet covers with dinosaurs and fairies on them, everything that two children could possibly need to start a new life. With their new family. But that would not be fair on them.

They need their things. They need memories, and I can't give them those without going back.

On my first visit to "the house" we started with the essentials – a few toys and books, some teddies. Some clothes. And Zack's bibs. Because there are only so many times you can wash the same bib, and tea towels tucked into his babygrows were just not cutting it.

Phoebe was very specific. She wanted her pink dress with the yellow spots, the Hungry Hippos game that Father Christmas brought her, and her ladybird hair slides.

Who knew a pair of ladybird hair slides could break a grown woman.

When I dropped them in my handbag three days after losing my best friend, I cried like I have never cried before.

And then I got back in my car and drove home. Delivering the requested items to their little owner. Like nothing had happened.

Today I need school uniform. So that Phoebe can go back to school.

I have no idea whether I am doing the right thing. Should she be going back now? Should I have sent her back sooner? Should she be at home with me for longer? I honestly don't know. What I do know, though, is that she needs to start her new normal. And so do I. We all do.

I take Robyn with me for moral support.

I park on the drive and she takes hold of my hand.

It's weird how normal the house looks. That sounds ridiculous, I know. I'm not expecting it to be obvious that the two adults who lived here a month ago are now dead. But it looks like nothing has happened, which doesn't feel right either. The For Sale sign is still up, reminding me that I need to speak to Patrick Massey and give the go-ahead for the house sale to proceed.

But this was Zack and Phoebe's home, so I just can't do it yet.

The house looks no different to how it did just a month ago.

Imposing. A house to be envied. One whose owners worked hard.

A modern house that was far bigger than a family of four really needed, but one that symbolised the success of the people that lived within its walls.

A house where the windows were cleaned every week, where the outside was kept as tidy as the many rooms inside, with olive trees either side of the front porch and a silver door-knocker free of fingerprints.

A bed of daffodils underneath the living-room window is just beginning to bloom. The start of spring. A beautiful but painful reminder that life does not stop. Even when your best friend dies.

Lou loved daffodils. She always joked that she liked designer clothes, and expensive things for her home. But buy her a seventy-five-pence bunch of daffodils and she was more than happy.

The security light still comes on as you approach the house. The stone statue of a rabbit is still standing guard at the front door. The nextdoor neighbours are home. Both their cars are there. They'll probably have just got home from work. They'll be making dinner shortly. Putting their children to bed. Talking about their day. All the while the house next door is sitting completely empty. The owners gone. The children that used to live there starting a new life without them.

"Ready?" Robyn asks me.

I nod, take a deep breath and put the key in the lock.

It is three weeks since I was here last and our first steps into the house are reminiscent of returning home from a holiday – the pile of post on the mat inside the front door, the slight chill in the air where the house has been sitting empty.

I drop my handbag on the floor and scoop up the post – the sight of those words "Mr & Mrs R Smithson" through the envelope windows stings. I hold the pile of letters to my chest – as if having their names close to me will take the edge off the pain.

"Shall I put the heating on for an hour?" Robyn asks. "It feels a little damp."

I nod my agreement, leafing through the pile of letters in my hand.

It doesn't feel right, opening someone else's mail. But I have to. It's the only way of knowing who I need to tell.

Every letter means another phone call. Another company to inform. Another hour of my life, explaining the unusual circumstances, being passed from one department to another, no one quite sure who it is I should be speaking to.

Today's list includes the building society where the children's savings accounts are held, a furniture company that Rich once bought a desk from offering a 20 per cent discount on a matching cabinet, and the dentist.

Phoebe missed her check-up.

The letter politely requests twenty-four hours' notice in future if appointments cannot be kept. Missed appointments are a drain on NHS funding, it explains.

Please accept my sincere apologies. Her parents just died. But – of course – I'll try to give more notice in future.

I stuff the letter back in its envelope and put it in my handbag along with the others.

I am trying to set up a redirection service for their post, but it is proving difficult. Why am I trying to redirect post that is not addressed to me? What authority do I have to redirect said post?

Fortunately most communication these days is via email or phone.

And as legal guardian to their children, Lou and Rich's phones were handed over to me by the police three days after the accident – though I've not been able to bring myself to look at them in detail yet, other than to look up all the contact details I needed.

Brushing a lone tear from the corner of my eye and telling myself not to waste my energy getting upset over a bloody letter from the dentist, I head upstairs to Phoebe's bedroom.

The room is tidy – the fairy curtains open at the window, every toy in its place, every pretty dress hanging neatly in the wardrobe.

Her teddies are all lined up on her bed. Like they are ready to welcome her back with open arms.

Any day now, they are telling each other. *Any day now and she'll be back to cuddle us.*

There is just one lone story book on the carpet. Lou or Rich must have been reading it to her, the night before they dropped her off with me.

It was there the last time I visited, and of course it is still there now. I can't bring myself to move it, to alter this moment in time that was one of their last together.

I open the wardrobe and take out her school uniform. Grey pinafore dresses with butterfly zips, white polo shirts with a slight frill around the collar and navy cardigans.

I pull her little tights out of the top drawer of her dresser, along with some extra underwear and the last of the pyjamas that I've not already collected, and I put it all in the holdall I brought with me.

Closing the door behind me, I put the bag down in the hallway and brace myself to do something I don't really want to do.

I open the door to the spare room.

Daddy's bedroom, as Phoebe called it.

I have allowed myself to believe she was just confused. That he wasn't sleeping in a different bedroom. Or, worst case, that he really was just snoring, booted out of the master bedroom on occasion so that Lou could get a decent night's sleep ahead of a big court case.

She wasn't confused.

The bed looks slept in – the duvet not quite straight, the pillows hanging off the edge.

But it's more than that.

Rich's things are in here.

Everyday things.

Antiperspirant, and aftershave.

A pair of jeans and a lightly creased shirt hanging over the back of the armchair in the corner.

A used pair of socks by the side of the bed – kicked off just before going to sleep, maybe?

Phoebe was right.

This *was* Daddy's bedroom.

Was my friend really unhappy? Was her marriage over? Were they even discussing going their separate ways the night they were killed?

Without thinking, I straighten the sheets quickly, as if I can eliminate the possibility just by making the bed – just by making it look like it hasn't been slept in.

But I know it is not that simple.

It's in my head now.

And if it is true, why didn't I know? Why didn't she tell me? I thought we told each other everything.

———

Lou was the first person I told when I met Mike. I phoned her that night and told her about the boy who had chatted me up with a bit of flattery and a Murray Mint.

She was also the first person I told when I realised I didn't love him anymore. Not in the way I always had.

"People change," she said. "If we can fall out of love with a dress we once thought was the best thing we'd ever own, then why not a man we once thought we'd love forever?"

She was pregnant with Zack at the time. We met at the coffee shop in Crakeleigh. The same coffee shop we'd been meeting at for as long as we could both remember. Once a family-owned business, now just another Starbucks. I remember her holding my hand across the table, her other hand resting gently on her baby bump.

Was that the day she phoned Patrick and changed her will, removing Mike's name and making me the sole guardian to her daughter and her unborn son?

"I will be here for you," she said. "Just like I always have. I'm not going anywhere."

If, less than a year later her own marriage was in trouble, why didn't she tell me?

"I think Lou and Rich were having problems," I tell Robyn on the way home.

It's a relief to say it out loud. But it scares me how likely it sounds.

I tell Robyn what Heidi said at the funeral. About Lou not seeming happy. I tell her what Jamie said about her and Rich arguing at the wedding. And I tell her what Phoebe said about them sleeping in separate rooms.

"She was right," I say. "They were."

"That could be for any number of reasons," she tells me.

"Maybe he was snoring? Maybe Zack was waking a lot and Rich was struggling to sleep? Scott moved out of our bedroom for three months when Charlie was born, just to get a decent night's sleep."

"Rich was better with Zack at night than Lou was," I tell her.

"Okay, well, there could still be any number of innocent explanations. It doesn't have to mean anything sinister. It doesn't have to mean they were having problems."

We travel in silence for the rest of the journey, my mind racing amongst the innocent explanations for two married people sleeping in separate bedrooms, desperately trying to make one of them stick.

Before Robyn gets out of the car she turns to me, and I know she is weighing up how best to say what it is she has to say.

"I know this won't be easy to hear, Zo," she says. "And please know that I'm saying it as your friend, with your best interests at heart."

I nod.

"But?" I say, ready to hear it.

"What difference does it make now? What difference does it make whether Lou and Rich were happy, or whether they were already in the middle of a divorce? An awful one, even."

She is right, I know.

It makes no difference whether my friend was happy or not. Whether her husband had been sleeping in a different bedroom. Whether they were arguing on the night they died.

They are gone now. Knowing the answers will not bring them back. Knowing the answers will not change what happens now.

Chapter Eighteen

"Rich and I are thinking of selling," Lou told me a few months ago, over a glass of wine. Isla was plaiting Phoebe's hair and Zack was sat on Sophie's knee – all of them transfixed by Peppa Pig – the episode where she meets the Queen.

"What? Why?" I asked.

It didn't make sense.

Their home was amazing.

They had always talked about it being their forever home.

"You love your house," I told her. "Why would you move?"

"I just need a change," Lou said. And I didn't push it.

I had no reason not to believe her. They were happy.

"Where will you go?" I asked her. "Not back to London?"

"No," she assured me. "Phoebe is at school now. It wouldn't be fair."

"Please don't move away," I joked, now confident it wasn't even on the table. "What would I do without you?"

A month later the For Sale sign was up outside the house and the search began for the house that would give Lou and Rich the "change" they craved.

"We want something a bit older," Lou told me. "Rich wants to have a go at fixing something up. Because we've got so much time on our hands," she joked. "Maybe we'll find something in Hartingley," she added, with a twinkle in her eye. "We could be neighbours!"

They sold within a month.

We all knew they would.

Who wouldn't want to buy that house?

A respectful three weeks after the accident, the solicitors handling the sale phoned me.

What was I going to do, they wanted to know.

Was I going ahead with the sale, or keeping the house?

In their will Lou and Rich put everything they owned into trust for Phoebe and Zack. But they included a clause that gave me the authority to make financial decisions on their behalf.

Which included whether or not to sell the house.

And the responsibility is suffocating.

Mike thinks I should push forward with the sale.

It's what Lou and Rich wanted, he says.

But if they'd known they were going to die, would they still have wanted to sell it? Would they have wanted to take away the home that held the only memories their children had of the short time they had their parents in their lives?

I don't know.

"What are you going to do with it?" Mike asked, the first time I mentioned not selling it. "Keep it as a shrine to Lou and Rich?"

He immediately apologised, of course.

But it was a valid question.

"Keeping their house isn't going to bring them back," he said.

The buyers have been patient. But patience eventually wears thin. And theirs is getting thinner by the day.

Chapter Nineteen

Today is not a good day.

For any of us.

Zack is teething really badly and won't go to anyone other than me.

Sophie has had an argument with Josh at school and is refusing to speak to him, so our afternoon is being interjected by the gentle vibration of her phone what feels like every five minutes but probably isn't.

Phoebe is upset because I don't know the words to the song that Mummy always used to sing her.

And Isla is annoyed that her dad won't take her to her friend's party tonight.

I'm annoyed too.

He's seeing Charlotte tonight.

But it's making me angry in a way that it never has before.

Irrationally so.

Not because he won't take Isla to her party – he said if he'd known about the party then he'd never have made plans, which is fair enough.

Or even because he is seeing his girlfriend.

But because he is making time for Charlotte in a way he couldn't make time for me.

He's finishing work at a decent hour. He's probably booking a nice restaurant. Maybe scanning his wardrobe for his best shirt.

And I resent that. Today more than ever.

―――――

Maybe it's because my freedom has gone. Overnight. In a puff of smoke. In the dramatic crash of the taxi my best friend and her husband were travelling in.

And today it all just feels unachievable. Like this mountain is just too big to climb.

I mean, for heaven's sake. How am I supposed to know the words to a song that Lou sang with Phoebe?

She never told me.

She never prepared me for any of this.

She just left me to pick up the pieces.

She left me to tell her children she's not coming back.

And she left me without my best friend.

Some days my heart aches for her in a way I didn't think was possible.

When I close my eyes at night I see her. Getting onto the school bus looking like she ruled the world. Dancing with Andrew at the school disco – certain she was going to spend the rest of her life with this boy. Proudly showing off her growing baby bump when she finally fell pregnant. Holding her mum's hand as she slipped away.

―――――

It won't always be like this, Simon tells me, when I phone him – when I ask him to come round. Because I need to feel prioritised. Because I need to feel wanted. Even if just for a few hours.

He drops Isla at the party for me (which isn't "cool", apparently – being dropped off by your mum's new boyfriend – but it beats missing the party) and then he gets us a takeaway.

I tell him about my visit to the house. I leave out the bit where I discovered my best friend and her husband were definitely sleeping in separate bedrooms. That would feel like a betrayal, somehow. Instead I tell him the only thing that really matters.

"I miss her," I say, brushing away a tear.

He doesn't say anything. He just listens.

Sometimes I feel guilty talking to him about all this.

Am I bringing back memories of when he lost his wife? Of when he was left to raise two three-year-olds all by himself?

"I'm sorry," I say, absentmindedly folding a tissue on my lap over and over until it is a neat square of white in the palm of my hand.

"It's okay," he says, putting the tissue on the arm of the sofa, and taking my hand in his. "I promise you. One day you'll wake up and though the pain will still be there, it will be a little duller. A little easier to bear.

"You'll find things to laugh about again.

"You'll have found the words to a new song that you can enjoy together.

"And pretty soon you'll realise you've gone a whole week without any tears or tantrums at all.

"From you or the kids," he adds, with a smile.

And then I kiss him.

For knowing the right things to say.

For making me feel important.

And for staying, despite this crazy, devastating, unexpected turn my life has taken.

Chapter Twenty

I read once that sudden loss is world-stopping.

But it can't be, can it? Not really.

Life has to go on.

The sun will still rise every morning and set at the end of each day.

We have survived the aftershock – the first painful weeks without Lou and Rich – and we have the beginnings of a new routine.

Today I am going back to work. And Phoebe is going back to school.

———

I'm under no illusion that it will be a walk in the park.

Four weeks ago my mornings were easy.

I had nobody to get ready but me.

Long gone were my days of having to wake up sleepy children and make their breakfast, lay out their uniforms or tie their ties, and their ponytails, and their shoelaces…

But today I am back at the beginning. Where my mornings will be consumed with getting other people ready. And where I can probably kiss goodbye to the luxury of brushed hair and a hot cup of coffee.

It's a daunting feeling.

When my alarm goes off at 5.45am the house is strangely quiet. It is the first day since he came to stay for the weekend that I have been awake before Zack.

By 6.15am I am showered, dressed and on my second cup of coffee and the last bite of a still warm slice of toast. I have given Phoebe's school shoes a cursory polish, I have dropped Zack's nursery bag by the front door, and I am looking up the stairs, marvelling at how calm this house of five currently feels.

I am putting my plate in the dishwasher when a sleepy Phoebe appears in the kitchen.

I look at her and chuckle. It seems that she was so excited when I told her she was going back to school today that she snuck into her freshly washed and ironed uniform last night, which now looks like … well … like she has slept in it.

She holds her arms out for a cuddle and I pick her up.

"Are you excited?" I ask her.

Putting her thumb in her mouth, she nods.

And I am relieved.

Her teacher – Mrs Chandry – has been wonderful. She has spoken to each of Phoebe's classmates and their parents. To tell them what has happened. To ask them to be extra kind to Phoebe. To sit with her, to give her cuddles, to play with her.

I, on the other hand, have instructed Robyn to ask the complete opposite of my team. Don't sit with me, don't hug me, don't offer to make me a cup of tea. Well okay, maybe make the cup of tea. But that's it. No "How are you?"s, no "How are the children?"s, no sympathetic glances. Just treat me how they always have. Let me get on with the job. Let me feel normal.

I know it won't be easy. I know it will be excruciatingly hard at times. But we are ready.

We drop Zack off at nursery first.

He doesn't even look back when I leave him with Clare, his key carer. To him it is just a normal day at nursery.

The school playground is a different story. The moment we walk through the gates of West Hill Primary School, everyone immediately turns and looks in our direction. At least that's how it feels.

And then they all look away, just as quickly.

Phoebe holds my hand tightly and I scan the playground for a familiar face.

I know very little about Phoebe's school. I've never needed to, until now.

In size and appearance West Hill is much like Hartingley Primary School where my own children went – a small village school with one class per year group and idyllically surrounded by green fields and country lanes, down which mums in gym gear drive with purpose.

Just as I am starting to lose the feeling in my hand, I see Diana Holland – West Hill's headteacher – walking towards us.

"Good morning, Phoebe," she says, both as gently and as positively as she can. She is clearly a comforting presence for Phoebe, who loosens her grip on my hand.

"Hi, Zoe," she adds, my face now familiar after our meeting last week to discuss the plan for Phoebe's return.

"I thought you might like to go in ahead of everyone else

today and get settled," Diana tells Phoebe. "Lilly says she'd like to come in with you. How does that sound?"

Lilly is Phoebe's best friend.

She nods.

Mrs Holland beckons to Lilly who is waiting patiently by the door, excited to see her friend.

She runs over and the two of them hug.

"I thought it might be helpful to introduce you to Lilly's mum," Diana says as the girls skip across the playground hand in hand.

"Mrs Jones, Mrs Henry," she says.

"Allison," Lilly's mum tells me. I recognise her from the funeral. One of the mums sitting discreetly at the back of the church.

I blow Phoebe a kiss, before turning to Allison.

"Zoe," I say.

Satisfied that her job is done here, Diana gives us both a little smile and heads back into the school building.

"How are you all doing?" Allison asks quietly, the second person in as many minutes to ask this. And no doubt not the last today. "I can't even begin to imagine what you've all been through," she adds, touching my arm. "None of us really knew Louise very well. She wasn't in the playground to chat to very often. Not that that's a bad thing, of course," she says quickly.

"Thank you so much for coming to the funeral," I say.

"I wasn't sure what to do for the best. But in the end I felt … well, I just felt that I should…"

"Thank you. It meant a lot to see so many people there."

"Lilly is keen to have Phoebe over for a play. And some tea. If she'd like to. When she's ready, of course."

"She would love that," I tell her. "We're trying really hard to create some sense of normality for the children, so that would be great. Perhaps in a few weeks?"

"Perfect," she says. "Shall we swap numbers?

"You will let me know if there is anything I can do to help, won't you, Zoe?" she says, once we have saved each other's numbers. "Mrs Holland mentioned that you're a vet over at the surgery in Ferringham. I'm sure this can't be easy for you – for so many reasons, but juggling all of this with a job like that… Well, anyway, if you ever need someone to pick Phoebe up, or if you are stuck on a morning… I'd be more than happy to help."

"Thank you, that's really very kind of you," I tell her. "I may well take you up on that."

"Please do. Will Phoebe be coming back to dance class?"

"Dance class?" I ask. Phoebe hasn't mentioned it.

"Wednesday evenings. After school. At West Hill village hall."

When the look on my face tells her that this may be the straw that breaks the camel's back, Allison tells me not to worry, that she'll text me the details. Then she tells me about a class list she'll add my details to. For reminders about forms that need to be completed. And collections for teacher gifts. And children's party invitations. That kind of thing.

"Sounds great," I tell her, the primary school admin rapidly coming flooding back and already threatening to overwhelm me.

I look at my watch. It's 8.23am.

"I'm really sorry, Allison, but I'm going to have to dash," I say.

It is 8.27am when I get back in the car. My chances of making it to the surgery for the 8.45am meeting are slim to none. It is thirteen miles from West Hill to Ferringham. I know, because I have driven it four times in the last five days, in a bid to shorten the journey somehow. I did inadvertently shave off half a mile when I took a wrong turn on the third attempt, but this added another three minutes due to the number of passing points in which I had to pull over.

By the time I reach the dual carriageway it's already 8.40am. I call Robyn through the car.

"I'm going to be late, Rob," I tell her. "Go ahead without me. You can fill me in when I get there."

"Of course," she says. "Don't worry about it, Zo. How did it go? Was she okay?"

"Yes. Absolutely fine."

"And you?"

"I'm okay."

"Okay. Kettle's on. Drive carefully. I mean, well … see you soon…" And then the beep as she hangs up.

I know my friend. She will have put the phone down and kicked herself for that last comment. But life goes on. And the last thing I want is for everyone to be walking on eggshells around me. Robyn would have told me to drive carefully before the accident, and I want her to feel like she still can.

When I eventually pull into Linton Veterinary Surgery car park I look at the clock.

8.51am.

There is no point in rushing. These meetings run like clockwork and it will be six minutes in already. I know. I set them up that way. Ironically, lateness is my pet peeve. Although, I'd like to think I have a good excuse. My best friend died and left me in charge of her two young children, for instance.

I walk in, mouth a quick "Hi" to our receptionist Jenny, who is talking to a client holding a shoe box (a hamster, a guinea pig, or a tortoise is my guess), and slide round the back of the desk to the office.

As I open the door, I am met with multiple sympathetic stares, and one standard stare – from a work experience student who clearly knows nothing about my recent change in circumstances and just thinks I have rubbish time-keeping skills. I think I prefer it that way. At least that's one person who will just treat me normally.

"Hi, everyone," I say, hastily shoving my handbag in my locker on the back wall. "Sorry I'm late."

"We were just finishing up," Robyn tells me. "We've got quite a packed day."

"Great," I say, as everyone starts to disperse.

"Right, let's go and meet Bruce," Liz, my chief veterinary nurse, tells the work experience girl – a GCSE student called Becky from Sophie and Isla's school.

"Who's Bruce?" she asks.

"He's a guinea pig," Liz tells her. "And I think he may be depressed."

Becky raises her eyebrows, no doubt wondering if Liz is joking.

She's not.

"I know the feeling," I tell Robyn when it is just the two of us left in the room.

"Welcome back," she says, wrapping her arms around me.

"Don't be too nice to me," I say.

"I won't, you bitch," she says with a giggle, and I laugh.

"Seriously, though – you okay, Zo?"

"No. Yes. I have to be, right?"

"No," she says. "You don't have to be. But I get it," she adds. And I know she does.

She hands me a coffee.

"It might be a bit cold now," she says. "I can make you another."

I shake my head, take a quick gulp, and look at my watch.

"I might have to change the 8.45am meeting," I say.

"I don't think you'd get any objections," she says sarcastically.

"So what have we got?" I ask her, abandoning my coffee and casting my eyes swiftly across the ops board.

A quick scan tells me I will not be in for a gentle ride on my first day back.

My phone rings from inside the locker, so I open it and pull it out of my bag.

"Hi," I say.

"Mike," I mouth at Robyn, and she raises her eyebrows. The movement is miniscule, but I know it's there.

Robyn's husband Scott is one of Mike's best friends.

The four of us have always done so much together and we have all noticed the change in the last year.

Evenings that we once all spent together are now splintered – with Mike and Scott meeting independently of Robyn and me.

Just after we split up Robyn did invite us all to Charlie's birthday party. The kids were all there too, so it didn't feel as weird as it might have done. But now we both have other people in our lives, things have to be different.

"So what's my first appointment?" I say, looking back at the board when I have finished updating Mike on how Phoebe was at drop-off. I grab a pair of scrubs and pull my sweatshirt off.

Robyn runs through a list that both exhausts and exhilarates me at the same time – then tells me that things can be moved around if required. That I can finish early to pick Phoebe up from school if I need to.

She is already making allowances for me, which I both love her for and can't stand in equal measure. I don't want to be that person. The one that exceptions need to be made for. I have never been that person. Even when I was heavily pregnant in my final months of veterinary school.

"Thanks, Rob," I say. "It's only for this week. I'm hoping if she settles, then I can book her into an after-school club a couple of times a week."

"It's fine, honestly, Zo, take your time. We are all okay here. Do whatever you need to do."

"Is it wrong that I feel like this is what I need?" I ask my friend. "A bit of normality, I mean. I love Phoebe and Zack. You know I do. But this has all been so overwhelming."

"Of course it has," she says. "You are only human, Zoe. Don't be so hard on yourself."

"Thanks, Rob. What would I do without you?"

"I have absolutely no idea," she says, with a grin, before heading out of the staff room so I can finish getting changed.

When I had young children the first time around, I put my career on hold.

I gave them all my time.

I was there for every nappy change, every mealtime, every first.

I took them on every playdate, to every baby group, to every toddler class.

Every hour of every day was dedicated to caring for them, being their mum, being their everything.

It has crossed my mind – more than once – that I should be doing that again – that I should be putting Phoebe and Zack first in the same way I put my own children first.

But I know Lou, of all people, would not have expected me to do that. She was a career woman. She wanted children, yes. But she wanted a career too. And she accepted that with that choice came sacrifices. She wouldn't always be the one at the school gate at pick-up, or at the other children's houses when her children were invited for playdates. She wouldn't always make the parents' evenings, or the sports days or the nativity plays, and when the PTA sent out the pleas for cake contributions, while other mums would send in beautifully crafted home-made cupcakes, Lou would grab a tray of Waitrose's finest on her way home from work and save herself the grief.

I made the same sacrifices when I became a vet. Though I have to admit, I never was a mum whose edible contributions were made with my own fair hands – I mean, why bother when the supermarkets have already gone to the trouble for us?!

And it took a lot of hard work to get where I am today. I'm not sure I could give it all up again.

Does that make me selfish?

I hope not.

When Nathan Linton took me on almost eleven years ago I had so much still to learn, so much to go back and relearn after such a huge gap. I worked so hard. When I wasn't working, I was studying – snatching precious moments with my children in between. I was up at 5am, and often didn't see my pillow again until midnight. But it paid off. I worked my way back up to where I would have been if I'd never taken the break. And when Nathan decided to take a back seat two years ago, he made me Clinical Director. Second only to the births of my three children, it was the proudest moment of my life.

And they may have become the kids who went home with the childminder at the end of the day, the kids who didn't always see their parents when they scanned the audience on the night of the nativity performance, the kids who turned up with the shop-bought cakes, not the home-made ones, but they were also the kids who very quickly learned that if you work hard, you can achieve anything.

It's a good day.

I work my way through vaccinations and neuterings. I treat cats and dogs, a hamster that has lived longer than he should have and a parrot that won't stop talking.

Then I leave on time, pulling up outside the school with a good six minutes to spare.

And that's how you do it, I think to myself, as I grab my phone – smugly fitting in a phone call to book Phoebe a place back in her dance class.

When she skips out of school as happily as she skipped in, I literally feel on top of the world. It's a great feeling. It's exhilarating. Liberating. Unexpected.

And of course, it's short-lived.

Chapter Twenty-One

Day two does not go well.

I start the day – as we seem to start a lot of days right now – stripping Phoebe's bed, running her a bath and reassuring her that it's fine – that it will pass, even though I sometimes wonder if it will.

When I can finally peel her away from me – with the help of Mrs Chandry – there is significantly less of a spring in her step than yesterday.

I am late to work, obviously.

And then, just as I am about to go into surgery, I get a call from the school, which is not unexpected, given the way our day started.

Phoebe can't find her "hug".

I don't even know what that is.

"Her hug?" I ask the school receptionist on the end of the phone.

"Yes," she says. "It's a little wooden heart, apparently."

"She hasn't mentioned it," I say. "She wasn't bothered about it yesterday…?"

"I know. I get it. Some days these things matter more than others," she explains.

That's true enough.

Sophie once had a full-blown meltdown at school because she'd forgotten to give her dolly a kiss goodbye that morning. The next day she left her face down on the kitchen floor and barely gave her a second's thought. And Oliver once refused to go into school because he realised he had his Wednesday pants on, and it was Tuesday. He went in eventually, of course, when I didn't give him the option not to. The following week he was more than happy to wear his Saturday pants on the Monday and looked at me like I was crazy when I queried whether he might want to change them.

Life was busy, I explained, and I didn't have time to be bringing dollies into school for their missed kisses or taking my children home to change their incorrectly labelled underwear. They just had to suck it up and get on with it.

But do I say the same to Phoebe? When she has just lost her mummy and daddy?

"We have tried distracting her," the receptionist tells me. "But she is very upset. Would you be able to talk to her?"

"Of course," I say, gesturing to Robyn that I am going to need five minutes. She disappears to let the team know.

"Hi, Phoebs," I say when they put her on the phone. "What's up, sweetheart?"

"I can't find my hug," she tells me tearfully.

"Where did you put it?" I ask her.

"It was in my bag," she says. "But it's not there now."

Now, if I had a pound for every time one of my children swore blind that something was somewhere that it turned out never to have been, then I'd – well, let's just say I'd have an awful lot of pounds.

"Did you check in your tray, sweetie?" I ask.

"Yes. Mrs Chandry looked with me. But it's not in there."

"Did you have it with you yesterday? Maybe it's at home?"

Home.

I say the word without thinking.

Does she see it as her home? Or is home still the house where she lived with Mummy and Daddy?

"It's not at home," she says. "I keep it in my school bag. Mummy gave it to me so that I don't miss her when I'm at school."

And in that moment I realise that today Phoebe's heart – real or otherwise – is more important than anything else in the world, and that Mrs Pelton's cat's balls may well live to see another day.

With an hour to spare before my next appointment, I race home to look for the little wooden heart. Despite Phoebe still having minimal things at my house, I fear it will be like looking for a needle in a haystack.

When after fifteen minutes I am no closer to finding it, I conclude that today a real hug will have to do. If necessary, I will buy another one. Once I have found out exactly what it is, that is, and where the hell Lou got it.

I race to the school, the roads feeling very familiar already, park up and throw myself out of the car and through the school gate.

I am out of breath and mildly sweaty by the time I arrive in front of the receptionist, who calmly tells me that they have found the heart.

"It was in a secret pocket in her school bag," she says, cheerfully.

"That's great," I say, through gritted teeth.

"Can I hug her anyway? Since I'm here?"

"Of course," she says with a smile.

Three minutes later Phoebe is brought to reception.

"Hello, Auntie Zoe," she says, looking delighted, but surprised to see me.

I am beginning to think the "suck it up" technique might be the way forward after all, especially when my little charge continues to look at me with complete confusion and I realise she is wondering what the hell I am doing here – the most logical options being that I am either incredibly early for pick-up or I have come in to school to deliver a talk on hamsters and guinea pigs.

***

And it is blatantly obvious at this point that my day is not going to go according to plan.

So after a manic afternoon which includes a routine dental clean on a greyhound that ends up being a two-hour operation to remove eleven rotten teeth, it comes as no surprise when I find myself pulling up outside the school gates no less than seventeen minutes after I am meant to.

And the little girl who five hours ago was wondering why I was so early, is probably now wondering why I couldn't manage to pick her up on time, even just two days in a row.

***

There are two kinds of mums in life, I have come to realise. Those who get their kids to school on time, and who are on time to pick them up. And those who don't, and who are not.

I hate being late. And until I went back to work, I wasn't. Ever. I was proud to be a member of that first group of mums. Always on time. Never late. Always frowning at those who rocked up in their cars on a morning just as you were getting back in yours after delivering your kids into the playground and giving them goodbye kisses. Always sat outside the school a good twenty minutes before the kids were kicked out at the end of the afternoon – just so you could get a decent spot in the miniscule parent parking area and wouldn't have to walk a tiring hundred yards to the school gates. There in plenty of time to see their smiling faces as they prodded the teacher and pointed you out in the crowd, awaiting permission to leave the invisible boundary that stood between you and them.

When Oliver was at Hartingley there was one boy whose mother was always the last to drop him off, and the last to pick him up. Every day, without exception, he could be seen stood by his teacher until after the last child had been collected, still waiting for his mum to pull into the lay-by outside school, at breakneck speed.

Did she work? No. Did she have seventeen other children to pick up from other educational establishments? No. Did she live beyond the boundaries of the limited catchment area? No. Truth was, she was a stay-at-home mum with no other children and lived five minutes down the road. She just had incredibly poor time-management skills. And I just couldn't understand how anyone could be that rubbish at getting somewhere on time.

Is it so difficult to pick your damn child up on time? I'd think to myself, driving away with my own children already halfway through regaling me with stories of their day in the back of the car – or rather, telling me what they'd had for dinner and who'd been in trouble with the teacher, which was pretty much all I ever got out of them.

And then I went back to work. And overnight I became that person I had muttered about under my breath on a daily basis.

Today it is Phoebe who is the lonely child stood with the teacher. And the guilt is as crushing as it was the first time I was late picking up Isla after I went back to work.

More so. Because if it will never again be her mum picking her up at the end of the day, then whoever it is really needs to step up, and be here on time to make up for that.

I jump out of the car before I have even got the key out of the ignition, and belt across the playground shouting profuse apologies at the teaching assistant who is stood by her side.

"She's fine," she assures me. "Aren't you, Phoebe?"

Phoebe nods quietly.

"I'm sorry, Phoebs," I say, because she clearly isn't.

There is no point in explaining what I was in the middle of, or that the traffic was terrible, or that my car wouldn't go any faster… None of that makes any difference to a child who just wants to see someone standing there waiting for them when they walk out of their classroom at the end of the day.

She is still quiet as we get in the car, and not quick to volunteer any information about her day.

I need to make it up to her. So I start by visiting the bakery in the village on our way home. They do the most amazing cupcakes, which have saved me after many a late-for-school-pick-up. She chooses a unicorn rainbow cupcake, and an elephant for Zack, and we grab a couple of triple chocolate chip cookies which are the girls' favourites.

By the time we are back in the car she is almost smiling again and an hour later, when we have collected Zack and arrived home to two big sisters and a dog ready for some fuss, she is back to her happy self.

So I reassure myself that I might just have got away with it. This time.

But what about all the other times that I know I'm going to let her down?

Chapter Twenty-Two

When Mike and I first moved back to Sussex, Lou and I were like those two eleven-year-old girls who had just met for the first time. Just a couple of decades older.

I loved living near my best friend again.

I'd missed her.

It was like old times, except we now talked about our husbands and our careers, not the boys we liked or the teachers we couldn't stand.

We went running together again.

We had drunken nights out where we'd call our dads to pick us up at midnight – for old times' sake, and because our husbands were at home looking after our children or working away.

We had dinner parties where we'd look through old photo albums and bore the men senseless with stories of our teenage escapades.

We'd spent so many years living apart, we were drunk on the memories – each one making us laugh more than the last.

Once again we were intrinsically linked.

"Where's Mummy?" my kids would ask.

"With your Auntie Lou," Mike would tell them with a chuckle and a roll of his eyes.

"Is Lou here?" Rich would ask, dropping in on his way home from work, her car in our driveway rendering the question redundant.

Occasionally we'd meet up with some other friends from school – but more often than not, it was just us. Just like at school.

Lou once suggested we meet up with Andrew and Jamie. For old times' sake.

But I said no.

I hadn't seen Jamie – or Andrew – in years, and I had no desire to.

"It'll be a laugh," Lou had argued.

I said no.

I was the voice of reason. Just like at school.

So instead we reminisced. About the crazy things our boyfriends had got up to when we were young – including the time they ended up at a house party when they were supposed to be out with us. The party was out of control and the boys made the sensible decision to leave before the police got there, but when they went to pick up their bikes they had been dumped in a field down the road from the house, the saddles both removed. Remembering how they arrived at Lou's house, both of them cycling as if their lives depended on it, whilst trying desperately not to put their backsides down on the poles where their saddles should have been, the pair of us were hysterical.

"Those were the days," Lou said to me, the smile on her face as big as it was back then.

I wasn't ready to lose my friend.

We had so many more memories to make.

Years later, watching Lou and Rich struggle to conceive, the laughter was overshadowed by moments of extreme grief, when all I could do was hold my friend, and tell her that everything would be okay.

I didn't know that it would be.

It was, of course.

But until when?

When did it stop being okay?

Years after Phoebe was born, Zack was the baby they believed would never be theirs.

He is not even a year old. Were they having problems before he was even born? Were they trying to make it work out of a sense of duty? Were the separate bedrooms a temporary measure while they worked on their marriage?

We got what we always wanted – so now we have to be happy. How ungrateful would it make us to not be?

Or were they ready to call it a day? The argument at the wedding sealing the deal, maybe? Were the separate bedrooms a temporary measure only until it could be made more permanent?

Chapter Twenty-Three

The first full week of our new normal starts well.

Everyone gets out of the house on time, and everyone has someone waiting for them at the end of the day.

I manage to treat a few animals at work, and to save the lives of a few others.

I even manage to find time for my boyfriend, though I will never get used to using that word as a forty-something-year-old.

And I start to think maybe I can do this after all.

Which is, of course, where things go wrong.

On Wednesday I am late for pick-up again. Thanks to an emergency caesarean required to deliver seven puppies, and a tractor that had broken down a mile away from the school.

Not only this, but I also manage to completely forget to pick Isla up from an after-school hockey match.

I am halfway to nursery for Zack when she phones me.

"Where are you, Mum?" she says when I answer.

And I am halfway through telling her exactly where I am – two and a half miles from Zack's nursery – when it dawns on me this is not the answer she's looking for.

"Oh shit," I say, remembering two seconds too late that I have a small person in the back of the car.

I look in the rear-view mirror and catch Phoebe looking at me.

"Auntie Zoe said a bad word," I tell her, apologetically. She says nothing and looks down at the Peppa Pig magazine on her lap.

"I'm sorry, Isla," I say. "I'll grab Zack and be with you in twenty minutes." Even with a straightforward pick-up, and no hold-ups on the way, that's optimistic at best, completely unattainable at worst. But it seems to appease her for now.

"We could stop at McDonald's on the way home?" I suggest, shamelessly using fast food to ease my guilt.

"Are we going to McDonald's?" Phoebe says excitedly.

"Okay," Isla says, begrudgingly.

"Looks like it," I say – for the benefit of both girls.

"I'll see you shortly, Isla," I say. "I'm sorry, sweetheart. I'll pick you up outside the entrance."

An hour later I arrive home with three tired children and a car that smells of chicken nuggets and French fries.

And I am exhausted too.

So despite my best efforts to establish a routine, we skip bath time and go straight to stories and bed.

I fall asleep on the spare bed, next to Zack's cot, waking a few hours later to the sound of Sophie coming home from Josh's.

She comes in and lies next to me. She says nothing but holds my hand, and I feel my eyes filling with tears at this simple gesture.

A year ago, when Mike and I told her we were splitting up, she did this a lot. She would sit quietly next to me and hold my hand. And I would give her hand a little squeeze – to reassure her that I was going to be okay, that we were all going to be okay.

I do the same now – but I'm not sure who I am trying to reassure – my eldest daughter, wise beyond her years, or myself.

"Are you okay, Mum?" she asks, in the darkness.

"I'm fine darling," I lie. "I'm just tired."

"This is hard, isn't it?" she whispers, holding my hand a little tighter.

"Yes, it is," I tell her honestly. "But we will get through it."

Zack stirs in his cot, so we leave the room, and I pull the door shut gently.

We go downstairs to the kitchen and I make us both hot chocolate.

"Do you think they miss them?" Sophie asks, dipping a stick of KitKat into her drink. "Phoebe and Zack, I mean. Do you think they miss Auntie Lou and Uncle Rich?"

"Yes, I'm sure they do," I tell her, stroking her hair, the way I did when she was Phoebe's age. "But they are both so young. Zack will quickly forget. If he hasn't already. And Phoebe may too. She is only five. How far back do you remember?" I ask my daughter.

She thinks about it for a moment.

"I remember when Isla broke her arm," she says. "When I was at primary school. How old was I then?"

"About seven or eight," I tell her, my own mind suddenly transported back to that day around nine years ago now when I got a frantic call from Isla's friend's mum to say she had fallen whilst on a playdate at their house.

Mike was in London at the time and I had scooped her up, dropped Sophie and Oliver off at Lou's and gone straight to A&E where less than an hour later we learned she had broken both the bones in her forearm and had to have surgery to pin them back together.

And then I smile at the memory from a few days later when, in adapting her school cardigan to accommodate her plaster cast, I had cut the wrong arm off.

"What?" Sophie asks, seeing my smile.

"Do you remember when I cut the wrong arm off her cardigan?" I say.

"Oh yes," she giggles.

She thinks again.

"I remember when I played Mary in the nativity play. Holly Bainbridge's mum was supposed to bring a doll in and forgot, so we had to wrap up the class teddy bear instead."

"Oh yes," I say. "You were so cross. I got an absolutely cracking photo of you scowling at the little boy who played Joseph, as if it was his fault your newborn baby was a bit on the furry side."

Sophie laughs at this.

"How old was I then?"

"Five?" I say. "Six, maybe?"

"I don't have many memories from that age," she says, her voice tinged with sadness. "Phoebe is so little, Mum. I don't think she will remember anything from her life with Auntie Lou."

I say nothing. I just hold her hand in mine.

"That's so sad," she says. "Will she even miss them when she's older, do you think? How can you miss somebody that you don't remember?"

It's a good question.

Can you miss something you have no memory of?

I guess it's down to us to help her.

To fill in the gaps.

To tell her what wonderful people they were. How hard they worked. And how happy having her and Zack made them.

I will tell them how I can barely remember a time when I didn't know their mum. How I have too many memories of her to ever recall them all. I will tell them about how we would be paired together for science experiments in our first year at school together and how Lou would run straight to the front of the class for the equipment, grabbing the test tubes and the Bunsen burner and two pairs of safety goggles. And while I was meticulously planning the experiment, she would return to our desk wearing the goggles and doing a funny dance. And we'd both laugh.

I will tell them how their mum once got sent out of a Maths class for laughing when our teacher Mr Parkson let out a quiet but unmistakable fart at the front of the class whilst trying to explain Pythagoras' theorem. It started out as a quiet giggle, but by the time he had written the equation on the blackboard, Lou had completely lost it, and was digging me in the knee under the desk to check I hadn't missed it. Sending her out of the room, I suspect, was all Mr Parkson could do to cover up his utter mortification. When they are old enough, I know that story will make Phoebe and Zack laugh as much as it made their mum and I laugh at the time.

I will tell them that their mum knew right from wrong but didn't always like to follow the rules. That she once got sent home from school for wearing too much make-up, and when she was asked to attend detention and write "I will not wear too much make-up to school" a hundred times over, she refused on the basis that it wasn't true, because she knew she would very likely do it again.

I will tell them how their mum and I both knew soon after that first day at Crakeleigh that we'd met someone who would be in our lives forever. We just never knew forever would be so short.

Chapter Twenty-Four

"We're going to be late," I tell Phoebe on Monday morning, when she is unpacking and repacking her unicorn backpack for the third time.

I have a meeting at the surgery that I can't miss, so she is going to Lilly's after school and she's very excited.

"All you need is one dress to change into after school," I say, opening her bag and removing a pair of pyjamas, three pairs of socks and the new dressing gown I bought her at the weekend.

"I want to show Lilly my dressing gown," she says, looking forlorn.

I kiss her on the head and push it back in the bag, aware this is a battle I really don't need to win if it means we can leave the house in the next five minutes.

"Okay, sweetheart."

"And I need my dolls, and my finger puppets," she says.

"That's it though, Phoebs? We need to go."

She nods and I usher her down the stairs, pulling the bag behind her so that it bumps against each step along the way.

"Are you sure this is okay?" I say to Lilly's mum Allison as we arrive in the playground with just a few minutes to spare.

Hopeful that she hasn't changed her mind, I hand her Phoebe's bag before giving her a chance to answer.

She nods, looking at the bag curiously.

"Don't ask," I laugh. "Didn't you know that ladybird dressing gowns, dolls that change colour when you get them wet, and Disney Princess finger puppets are the regulation playdate kit these days?" I say. "Well, shame on you."

Allison laughs for a second then stops herself.

I wish people wouldn't do that.

I wish people wouldn't stop themselves from laughing around me.

I don't want people to think they can't laugh when they are with me. That I am too fragile. That it would be inappropriate because my best friend died. And because I'm raising her children.

I want them to be normal.

I want them to be happy.

I want them to laugh out loud. Especially when I say something funny!

"I'll pick her up around six thirty, if that's okay?" I say.

I did ask Mike. But he's working. Of course he is. He couldn't possibly finish early in order to pick up his goddaughter.

He said he could help tomorrow.

To which I pointed out that, given I was needed at the surgery this afternoon, and not tomorrow afternoon, this was of absolutely no use whatsoever. And then I took him up on his offer anyway, as I honestly don't know when there will be another one.

"Six thirty is fine," Allison says. And I tell her she's a life-saver, which I imagine makes her uncomfortable all over again, so I give Phoebe a kiss and beat a hasty retreat.

Just knowing I don't need to worry about being at the school gate at 3.15pm changes my day completely.

I treat patients, and I laugh with colleagues. I take an extravagant lunch break of at least twenty minutes, and I get paperwork done that would normally have to wait several more days. I do the job I have trained so hard to do. And I never once worry about the time.

I'm not worried about disappointing anyone – Phoebe because I'm late, or my team because I'm abandoning them to rush off to the school gates.

I feel in control.

I feel like me again.

But that makes me feel guilty. Because I'm not that me anymore. I'm a new me. And I do have to worry about being at the school gate by 3.15 p.m. Not today. But every other day. And I don't know how I'm going to do it.

For the first time in three weeks it is Zack I pick up first. Second children never get quite the same attention as the first. You take less photos; you do fewer baby classes; you buy fewer toys because you've already got so many. A fifth child is a whole different ballgame. Ever since his parents left him with me seven weeks ago, Zack has just fitted in. He's gone to nursery when I've needed him to. He's been put in and out of his car seat while I've ferried the rest of them around – from school, from clubs, from trips into town with their friends. He's sat in his highchair while we've navigated our way through grief, and funeral planning, and making sure his big sister is given all the support she needs.

But what about him? What does he think about all this?

Does he feel the loss of his parents as acutely as the rest of us, but just can't tell us?

When I walk into his nursery he spots me immediately and crawls over, reaching up to me to be picked up.

For Zack I will be the only mummy he will ever remember. I know that. But for Phoebe I will always be the substitute. No matter what detail she forgets, I think she will always remember a time when she had a different mummy.

When I arrive at Allison's to pick her up, Phoebe's happiness at seeing me on the doorstep is as great as Zack's was – tempered only by the fact that no child is ever ready for a playdate to end.

"Can I stay a bit longer?" she asks me, barely looking up from the doll whose hair she is busy brushing.

"I could put the kettle on, if you've got time?" Allison says.

"Yes, yes," Lilly and Phoebe both shout.

"Just a quick one then," I say.

"Thank you so much for today," I tell Allison later, one hand gripping a cup of coffee, the other wrapped around Zack, who won't leave my knee.

"It's honestly no problem at all," she says. "The girls play so nicely together. It makes my life easier, if anything. When we made the decision to have only one child, I'm not sure we realised how much they crave someone to play with." She laughs gently at this, and then, I know – like me – she is thinking about how I now have five children.

"This must feel quite strange for you, though," I tell her. "It's not your everyday situation. A couple of months ago it would have been Lou you'd be sitting here drinking coffee with. And now it's me."

"To be honest, we rarely did anything like this," Allison tells me, twisting her coffee cup on the table. "We had Phoebe quite a bit," she continues. "But Lou would never really stay when she picked her up. She didn't really socialise with anyone at school, to be honest. I think she was just very busy with work. She was usually on her way home from London when she picked Phoebe up."

Just then the back door opens and a golden retriever comes bounding into the kitchen towards a very excited Zack.

"This is Barney," she says.

I give Barney a stroke before draining my coffee and standing up.

"It's late. We should be going."

As I'm fastening Phoebe's coat she watches Barney playing with Lilly.

"I'm going to have another dog," Phoebe says.

I want to tell her that Stanley is more than enough for us. But I don't. Instead I wait, a sixth sense telling me there is more to this than meets the eye.

"I'm going to have a dog at my daddy's house."

And there it is.

Allison looks at me. I look at Allison. Both of us, I'm sure, are thinking different things.

While Allison has clocked only Phoebe's use of the present tense – her absolute belief that this is possible, that she could actually have a dog at her daddy's house – I have noticed only the fact that she was going to have two different homes.

"Thanks again," I tell Allison, ushering Phoebe out of the door with one hand whilst juggling Zack and a hastily packed unicorn backpack in the other, my mind racing at a million miles an hour.

Chapter Twenty-Five

"She was probably just getting confused," Mike tells me the following evening.

True to his word, he has picked Phoebe up for me, so I could do another long day at the surgery. Or a normal day, at least.

"I don't think she was, Mike," I say. "She seemed very sure. She was going to have a dog. And it was going to be at Daddy's house. If they weren't separating, why wouldn't she just have said she was going to have a dog?"

"She's five years old, Zoe. She doesn't know what she's saying."

"Are you staying to see the girls?" I ask, changing the subject.

"If that's okay?"

"Of course it is."

"Why don't I put the kids to bed?" he says. *While you chill out,* he wants to say, but doesn't. "I could order a takeaway for us?"

"Sure," I tell him.

"Have you thought any more about moving Phoebe to a school closer to here?" Mike asks me later. I've had a glass of wine, so maybe he feels safer bringing it up.

"Why? Because it would make it easier for you to help once in a while?" I say. I can't help myself. "Sorry," I say.

"Don't be. I know I need to help more. I'm trying, Zoe. And yes, it would make it easier for me if she was at Hartingley. But it would make it easier for you too. And she'd soon settle. It's a lovely school. You know that. We wouldn't have put our own children there if it wasn't."

His choice of words hangs heavy in the air.

Our own children.

I can't blame Mike. I do it too.

Without meaning to, we are implying that Phoebe and Zack are not our own children.

But they are now. Well, they are mine, at least.

I agreed to that the day I walked out of Patrick Massey's office.

Mike is right, of course. It would make it much easier for all of us if Phoebe moved to Hartingley. But it just doesn't feel fair. Not right now.

"Not yet," I tell Mike. "It's too soon."

He doesn't say anything. He just reaches across the table and tops up my drink.

"Do you think Lou and Rich were happy?" I say, gently twisting the stem of my wine glass.

"Yes," Mike tells me.

Too quickly.

"Really?" I ask him.

"I don't know, Zoe," he says. He sounds frustrated. "But why are you asking? All you are going to do is drive yourself crazy. It doesn't matter now – whether they were happy or not, whether they were planning to split up, whether they were going to have a dog each, or no dogs, or a thousand dogs. They're gone. And none of this is going to change that."

I know he's right. I know it won't bring them back. But for some reason I just need to know.

It never occurred to me that Lou and Rich were selling the house to go their separate ways. Why would it? She always told me everything. She would have told me if she was leaving Rich. Or if he was leaving her. Wouldn't she?

The next day I phone the solicitor.

The week before the accident Lou said they'd found a house.

"Not a fixer-upper," she declared dramatically, though none of us were remotely surprised. Rich barely knew one end of a hammer from the other.

It was in the next village. Closer to Phoebe's school. A slightly bigger garden. A loft conversion.

"It's Zoe Henry," I tell the Junior Associate on the end of the phone.

By now my name is familiar. The staff perhaps even drawing straws for who gets to avoid speaking with me. The one with all the questions. The one whose best friend has died. The one who has inherited two children.

"I was hoping you might be able to tell me a bit about the house Lou and Rich were planning on buying," I tell him.

My question is met with silence.

"Were they still planning on buying the house in Lentbury?" I ask.

More silence.

And I know what he is thinking.

They're dead, he is thinking. *What difference does it make where they were buying a house?*

"That's right," he says eventually.

"And just that house?" I ask.

There is a brief pause where he is likely weighing up what he can and can't say. Customer confidentiality and all that.

And then, presumably concluding that customer confidentiality ceased to be a requirement the moment they both died, he takes an audible breath.

"I believe the house in Lentbury was for Mrs Smithson and their children," he says.

My heart immediately starts thumping.

"And Rich?" I say. "Mr Smithson?"

"I understand he was in the process of renting a property in the same village."

And now it is my turn to be silent.

"Is everything okay, Mrs Henry?" he eventually asks.

I nod, to convince myself more than anything.

And then, "Yes, thank you."

"Did you want to go ahead…" he asks. But before he can finish I have hung up.

He has only told me what I already suspected when I picked up the phone. But it still hits hard.

And just like that, I wonder whether I actually knew my friend at all.

Chapter Twenty-Six

When Lou and I both went to university, it was the first time we'd really been apart since our friendship began.

In the beginning I barely saw her. She was still with Andrew so would travel from Cambridge to Edinburgh every weekend to see him, while I was at the start of a new relationship and stayed in Bristol to be with Mike.

Whenever I came home she was always too busy.

I'd been with Mike for six months before she finally came home on the same weekend to meet him.

"I've been busy," she said, after giving him her seal of approval. But I never really felt like she was telling me the whole truth.

"Is everything okay with you and Andrew?" I asked her, and she assured me it was. Things felt different, though. I was scared we were growing apart.

We weren't, of course. We were still us. Still the best of friends. We were just growing up. We had our own lives. And we were living them.

It was when Lou moved to London that those lives started going in very different directions.

I was spending my days changing nappies and singing nursery rhymes with other mums and their babies, while Lou was spending hers going to battle in a court room.

Our evenings were even more different – with Lou spending hers drinking in trendy London bars while I spent mine getting as much sleep as I possibly could.

Lou was with Rich by the time Mike and I married, and by the time *they* were married we had two young children.

They had been back in Sussex for several years when they decided they were ready to start their own family. Which meant I could be there for my best friend while she went through four heartbreaking rounds of IVF.

I will never forget the guilt I felt every time she phoned, sobbing, to tell me it had failed. Again.

I will also never forget the day she phoned to tell me it had worked.

———

Why had it been falling apart? Why were they letting the family they fought so hard for break into pieces?

"You have to let it go, Zoe," Mike says when I phone to tell him what the solicitor told me on my way out of the house to pick Isla up from hockey practice.

"They are gone. Sell the house. And then we can all move on."

"Yes, that would be nice and simple, wouldn't it?" I say sarcastically, gripping my phone between my shoulder and my ear while I put Zack's coat on.

"Phoebe!" I shout. "Come and put your shoes on. We have to go and get Isla."

My request is met by tears and a half-hearted stamp of her

foot. She doesn't want to go back out. Nor do I, truth be told, but we all have to do things we don't want to do.

"I don't want to sell," I tell Mike. "It's too soon."

"Then don't sell. But you've got to move on from this obsession about whether or not Lou and Rich were happy. It's nonsense. What difference does it make now?"

"Thanks for the chat," I say. "Super helpful."

And before he can apologise, or protest, or have another go, I hang up.

Chapter Twenty-Seven

Mrs Chandry wants to see me.

Apparently there has been a "bit of an incident" at school – involving Phoebe and a little boy in her class, and some alleged "pinching".

It's not the first phone call I've had like this.

Last week Phoebe called Lilly a liar, because she told her she couldn't have a dog at her daddy's house, because her daddy was dead.

Allison phoned me that evening, apologising on Lilly's behalf. And I in turn apologised for the fact that Phoebe called her a liar. Because, let's face it, the kid was spot on. By the following morning they were the best of friends again, of course.

And now here I am, on my way into school for "a little chat" with Mrs Chandry about Phoebe's behaviour.

―――――

The truth is, this is a lot harder than I ever imagined it would be.

We have some good days, of course we do. But at the moment, on the whole, life feels like an uphill struggle.

I'm trying to be everything to everyone and I am failing miserably.

I am not giving 100 per cent of myself to anything. To my job as a mum. Or to my job as a vet.

Not because I don't want to. But because it's physically impossible. I just don't have 200 per cent to give. Who does?

If I am on time to pick Phoebe up, then it means that I have left work early, that I've abandoned my responsibilities at work.

And if I do my job properly, then I am late to pick Phoebe up. Sometimes only by a couple of minutes. But a couple of minutes can make all the difference to a child who is the last one standing at the gates, a teacher standing sympathetically by their side, their presence like a neon sign declaring "this child's parent doesn't care".

I keep promising I will be there on time, which I know doesn't help.

Under-promise and over-deliver. That's what Mike told me when I went back to work and missed Isla's first nativity. We had an emergency caesarean at the surgery for a bitch who had been hit by a car and though I was in no way ready to assist in any meaningful way, with eight pups to deliver it was literally all hands on deck. I walked into the school hall just as Isla and her class were finishing their rendition of 'Away in A Manger'. She cried all the way home. And so did I.

"The mistake you made was telling her you'd definitely be there," Mike had told me that night, handing me a tissue after tucking Isla in because she'd refused to let me do it.

"I wasn't there either, but I hadn't promised I would be, so I'm not the bad guy," he said, before assuring me she would have forgotten all about it in the morning. She had.

At home things are spiralling. The house is a mess, the laundry is stacking up, and Stanley is lucky if he gets a walk around the block most days, let alone anything more substantial.

I honestly thought I would do a better job.

I'm good at multitasking.

I thought I could do my job, and pick up the pieces for two young children who've lost everything, and keep everything going at home, and meet the needs of two teenagers, and find the occasional evening for a bit of romance…

What on earth was I thinking?

Last week Phoebe asked if she could stay at home with me – maybe under the illusion that not being at school was the only way to ensure she wouldn't be the last one to be picked up at the end of the day.

I told her I had to go to work. I told her there were sick animals who needed my help. She asked if she could come with me, said she could help the sick animals too.

I told her that I knew she'd be brilliant at looking after the animals, but that I thought she'd miss her friends.

And yesterday she asked if she could go back to her old house. The innocence with which she asked made my heart ache. This wasn't just the curiosity that we all feel when we think about the homes in which we once lived. This was as important to Phoebe as the air that she breathes.

I thought about it. I have even thought about us all moving there – in the fleeting belief that it might make it easier for her. The truth is, there is not much I haven't considered in the past few months. It is just so hard to know the right thing to do.

"I feel bad for dragging you in, Zoe," Mrs Chandry tells me when I arrive at Phoebe's school. There are still thirty minutes until pick-up so the children are still in class. If I didn't know better I'd say that this was a ruse to get me here on time, that there was no "incident" involving Phoebe and a child in her class, and an accusation of pinching.

But I do know better.

"It's just that we are seeing a few of these incidents, now, and I think we need a plan."

I nod my agreement.

A short while later a tearful Phoebe is brought in to the headteacher's office, where I have been given a coffee, a digestive biscuit, and the usual sympathetic platitudes.

It must be so difficult.

We can't imagine what you have been through.

You are all dealing with it remarkably.

Only we're not. We're falling apart at work, and we're pinching our classmates. Allegedly.

"What happened, sweetheart?" I ask, pulling Phoebe onto my lap.

She doesn't answer, and instead buries her head in my chest.

I look at Mrs Chandry expectantly, and what she tells me all but breaks my heart.

Apparently Phoebe told Jacob, a little boy in her class who I've frankly never heard nice things about, that her mummy was going to come back from heaven next week and pick her up.

You can't come back from heaven, he told her. It was a one-way street, he said – or words to that effect.

So she pinched him.

On the arm.

As hard as she could.

I want to tell Mrs Chandry that however much it hurt that

child, it can't have hurt anywhere near as much as Phoebe is hurting right now.

I don't, of course.

Because she already knows that.

Instead I tell her I'll speak to Phoebe.

On our way out, when she is confident that Phoebe is out of earshot, Mrs Chandry asks if I think it might be better if we looked at a school closer to home.

I don't think she's talking about the pinching episode – or how the school would be better off without such a delinquent child. I don't even think she's talking about the fact that I am never here on time to pick Phoebe up.

I think she's talking about all of it – and the fact that maybe we all just need a fresh start.

When all I can do is shrug, she touches my arm sympathetically, suggests we chat about this another time, and then says goodbye.

When I get back in the car, I make sure Phoebe has her head in her Peppa Pig magazine, and then I allow myself to cry.

Chapter Twenty-Eight

We could use some help, clearly.

So I call Amy – Jamie's wife, the child therapist.

I'll be honest, it feels more than a little odd, calling my childhood sweetheart's wife – and the mother of his children – and asking for help. But I need it. And she is the best person to give it.

For almost twenty minutes she just listens. While I tell her how much I miss my friend. How scared I am about the future. How I don't know how I am going to get through it. How I don't know what to do to get Phoebe through it. How I have no idea what is going on inside her little head. How one minute she seems to understand that her mummy and daddy have gone, but the next will be telling her dollies how she thinks they might come and see her at the weekend if she's a really good girl. Or telling her friend she's going to have a dog at her daddy's house. And how one minute she can seem happy – immersed in a television programme, or playing with one of her favourite toys – but the next she can seem sad and withdrawn.

Amy says nothing. She just listens. And it feels so good to talk to someone who doesn't tell me it will get better, that I will get through this, that we all will.

Instead she tells me that what I'm feeling is perfectly normal. And what Phoebe is doing and saying is perfectly normal too – including the bedwetting, and the conversations with her toys, and even the pinching.

And then she just listens again, while I allow myself to cry. For the friend I have lost. For the little girl who is now mine. For the little boy who has no idea how much his life has changed. And for my own children who have accepted the monumental change to their lives with grace and unbounded compassion.

"This is all just part of the grieving process for a small child," Amy tells me eventually.

And then, "Zoe, have you ever heard of the expression Puddle Jumping?"

"I'm guessing you don't mean the kind where we all put on our wellies and make a big old mess?" I say, somehow finding the ability to laugh.

"Correct," she says, and I can hear in her voice that she is smiling. "Children can sometimes appear to move in and out of their grief very quickly," she explains. "A bit like they are jumping in and out of puddles. This is what we mean by Puddle Jumping.

"Imagine a puddle full of sad feelings. A child – like Phoebe – might jump into the puddle when someone close to them has died. But they can't cope with feeling sad for very long. So eventually they will jump back out. They will play with their toys, or chat about their day, or watch something on the television. And they'll seem quite happy – like you have seen with Phoebe.

"Adults tend to stay sad for a longer period of time than children. Ours is more like a river of grief in comparison. Because of that we tend to assume that children are not affected by the death because they seem able to jump out of their sad puddles without any difficulty. But this is just Phoebe's way of dealing with her grief.

"I will send you a link to a video which explains it a little bit better," Amy tells me. "But in the meantime let me look at setting up some counselling for her, as I think that would help. I know someone based in Ferringham who is very good. I think you said you work there?"

"That's right," I tell her. "That would be great, honestly, I can't thank you enough."

"Allow her to talk about Lou and Rich," she adds. "It's important. It might feel instinctive to stop her from doing that. But it's important she has that opportunity."

Promising to call me as soon as she has any kind of update, she says goodbye, and I come off the call feeling like a huge weight has been lifted. I was so convinced I was making a complete hash-up of everything, that just to hear I'm really not was all I needed right now.

I poke my head into the makeshift playroom and find Phoebe sitting on Isla's lap watching something on her phone. She's laughing. It's a real belly laugh, and I realise this is one of those moments she's enjoying out of the puddle.

It warms my heart and yet takes my breath away, how much I love this little girl. This little girl who was never supposed to be mine.

"Who wants to take Stanley to the beach?" I say.

"Me!" she shouts, jumping off Isla's lap.

"Right then, get your coat and shoes on while I go and get Zack up from his nap."

We spend the rest of the afternoon at the beach. We fly kites, and build sandcastles, and dig trenches out to the water. We throw sticks into the sea for Stanley to fetch, shrieking each time he comes back out with them in his mouth and splashes us all as he shakes himself dry.

We get hot chocolates and donuts from the Beachcomber Café, and I tell Phoebe how I've been coming here ever since her mum and I were young girls. She asks me to tell her all about it. So I do. I tell her how her mum once stripped down to her underwear and swam in the sea on a cold winter's day – just because a friend told her she wouldn't. When she came out she was blue, and she had to warm up under the hand-drier in the toilets. I tell her how she worked in the café one summer and was told off for giving all her friends free ice-creams. And I tell her how it was in this very place almost eighteen months ago that she told me that Phoebe was going to be a big sister after all.

When we get home we order pizzas and snuggle up in front of the fire together, with popcorn and sweets. And everything feels like it might just be okay.

Chapter Twenty-Nine

Lou didn't always want children.

When we were younger she said she wasn't sure if she saw herself as a mum.

I think she thought she was too selfish to have children.

She liked her social life – her nights out, her weekends away, her holidays.

And she loved her job. She was ambitious. She wanted to be the best, and if she couldn't be the best then she wasn't interested.

She didn't think she'd be a very good mum.

But she was.

She was a brilliant mum. When it finally happened.

When Phoebe came along she was the centre of Lou's universe. Maybe because she'd waited so long to have her.

Yes, she wanted a career, yes, she was still ambitious, but when she wasn't winning court cases she gave her children everything she had and everything she was. Almost without exception.

She might not have always been there at the gates when Phoebe came out of school, and she might have missed bedtime more often than she didn't, but when the weekends came, she was just a mum. She went swimming, to soft play, to the park, to the zoo.

The girl who once queued for hours for Take That tickets now thought nothing of queuing for hours for tickets to Mister Maker Live just so she could see her little girl's face when she told her where they were going at the weekend.

She taught Phoebe how to write her name, how to bake, how to grow a sunflower. She taught her not to be afraid to try things, to stand up for herself, to love music…

One day I will tell Phoebe all of this.

But for now she just wants to hear about the day her mummy and I met and about all the things we got up to together.

So I tell her more stories.

I tell her how we used to cover our school books in posters of our favourite popstars.

I tell her how we used to go into town together and have lunch at McDonald's, and how Lou would always pick the gherkin out of her burger.

I tell her how we both went together to get our ears pierced, and Lou was so scared she made me go first.

I don't tell her about the jester earrings in the pretty giraffe-covered box in my bedside drawer. The ones that Lou left me when she died. When she asked me to look after her children like they were my own.

I will tell her one day. But not yet.

From time to time she asks to look through all the photos I have of Lou and I from all the years we were in each other's lives. So I indulge her. I am indulging myself too. Because I need to remember my friend. I need to remember how much I loved her, and how I didn't always have this unsettling doubt sitting in the pit of my stomach.

So I let her choose an album from the bookshelf.

There are photos of us in each other's bedrooms, sitting on our bikes, playing netball for the school team…

There are photos of us in front of the Eiffel Tower during a French exchange trip when we were fourteen. We are both wearing berets and laughing uncontrollably at something. I wish I could remember what it was that we found so funny.

And there are photos on the day we got our A Level results. Both of us ecstatic about our success, but at the same time anxious about the next step we'd be taking – without each other by our side.

The photos run out eventually. When digital cameras came along and no one printed half as many anymore.

The more recent pictures of the two of us are on my phone.

I scroll through them, looking for some to show her.

I stop at one of Lou and Rich with Oliver at his eighteenth birthday, when they gave him a cheque for £5,000. They had been saving for him since the day they became his godparents.

He used that money to buy his first car.

I stop at another of Lou and I out running and I giggle.

It had been raining and the fields by Lou's house were waterlogged, but we went anyway, both of us getting stuck in the mud, and barely able to move for laughing so much.

And then there's Lou and Phoebe, just a few hours after she was born.

I look at Phoebe. I look for signs that this is too much. That I need to stop.

But she just smiles and asks me to tell her about the day she was born. Again.

"I was at work," I tell her.

"At work where you look after animals?" she asks, and I nod.

"I was getting ready to leave when your daddy phoned me," I say. "He said you were here, that you were beautiful and that he already loved you more than he could ever have imagined."

She beams at this and looks down at the photo.

"I met you for the first time that night," I tell her. "And Daddy was right. You were beautiful. I looked at your mummy and she cried."

"Was she sad?" she asks, her hands clasped around my phone, an anxious look on her face.

"No," I tell her with a smile. "She was happier than she'd ever been."

And Phoebe laughs. And she tells me that that's silly. Why would someone cry because they were happy?

And I put my arms around her and hold her tight.

———

Lou was wrong. When she said she didn't think she'd be a good mum.

She was a great mum.

Phoebe and Zack are proof of that.

And one day I will tell them how great she was, how they were the best thing that ever happened to her, and how she made sure that even if she was gone, they would be okay.

Chapter Thirty

Some days I wonder why I bothered phoning Amy. Phoebe seems fine. No tears. No tantrums. No pinching. Just laughter, some average playing up at bedtime and a little bit of frustration at having to do reading and learn spellings.

And other days it's like no time has passed at all, like she has only just embarked on her grieving journey, and the road ahead feels insurmountably long.

On Friday I leave work early and I am there at the gates when Phoebe comes out.

She looks sad. Which makes me sad.

But I know that there will always be days like this. And that it won't always be because someone told her that her mummy can't come back from heaven, or because someone told her that their daddy took them to the park at the weekend.

The house is quiet when we get home. Sophie is at Josh's and Isla has a dance class. It's Mike's weekend with the girls and he picks Isla up from dance, so I won't see them until Sunday.

I barely got a word out of Phoebe all the way home, despite a visit to the bakery.

Slipping her shoes off, she goes straight into the living room and switches on the television.

Putting Zack straight into his highchair, I open the back door for Stanley, who obediently trots outside to water the plants.

"Hey, Phoebs," I shout. "Want to help me feed Stanley?"

That question is normally met with an enthusiastic shriek, and a bigger-than-normal portion for the dog when Phoebe insists on holding the almost-bigger-than-her bag of food all by herself.

Not today.

Today it's met with silence.

I walk into the living room where I find her cuddling one of her teddies, her thumb firmly in her mouth.

"You okay, sweetheart?" I ask.

She manages a little nod, but nothing more, so I tell her I'll be in the kitchen with Zack, making her dinner, if she needs me.

I pour pasta into a pan of boiling water and wine into a glass.

"Don't judge me," I say to my little charge in the highchair, who is currently pushing his finger into an elephant cupcake whilst chewing on a piece of orange. No judgement here.

And then Mike calls.

He's running late.

Can I pick Isla up from dance and he'll pick her up from the house?

"I'm sorry," he says, an hour later, after I have abandoned my glass of wine, turned off the oven, got Zack back out of his highchair – orange still tightly gripped in his hand – persuaded Phoebe back into her shoes and coat, piled them both into the car, and driven the eight miles to Isla's dance class to pick her up.

"Zoe?" he says, when I don't respond.

He wants to hear "It's okay." But it's not.

I call Isla down from her bedroom.

"You said you'd help, Mike," I tell him. "But instead it feels like you're making things harder. If that's even possible."

"I had to work. I'm sorry."

I know.

It's all I've heard for the last twenty years.

I had to work.

I had to work.

I had to work.

Until I no longer expected anything from him. It was easier that way. It meant I wasn't constantly disappointed when he didn't show up. For school events. For family dinners. For school pick-ups that he promised he'd be there for.

"Zoe," he says. Again. This time he puts his hand on my arm.

"Don't, Mike," I tell him, shaking my arm free.

He looks hurt, but I just don't have the energy to be sorry.

"We're spending the day with Simon on Sunday," I tell him. "Please have them home by ten."

"Sure," he says. And then: "Do you want me to take Phoebe?"

It takes me by surprise, and it's like a chink of light in an otherwise dark room.

Not because I don't want her here with me, but because it's like he gets it, it's like he has finally heard that I can't do this on my own.

"I can," he says, confusing my silence for scepticism. "She can have my bed and I'll sleep on the sofa. I would take Zack too, if…" His voice trails off and I know he is mentally working out where he would put two teenagers, a five-year-old and a baby. It's not the pokey flat we had when we were starting out, but it's certainly not big enough for a family of five.

But I love that he has offered, even if he is hoping I'll say no.

"It's fine," I tell him. "He's in bed already anyway."

"But I can take Phoebe?"

"Are you sure? Because I know she'd love to. So you have to be sure before I ask her."

"I'm sure," he says. "We'll have a great time. Me and my three girls."

He steps forward, reaching for me, but I step back.

"You're doing great, Zoe," he says instead. "I'm proud of you."

"Thank you," I say, before turning to go and tell Phoebe the good news.

I was right. She is beyond excited about this spontaneous sleepover at Uncle Mike's and immediately drags me upstairs to pack her things.

While Mike is putting their bags in the car, I give all my girls a goodnight kiss – my two big girls, and my bonus little girl.

"Call me if you need anything," I tell Mike.

"I will," he assures me, shutting the boot and getting into the car.

And then it's just me – and my little boy sleeping soundly in his cot upstairs.

———

I last an hour before I call Mike.

"Is she okay?" I ask, before I've even given him a chance to speak.

"She's fine." I can hear in his voice that he is smiling.

"Is she asleep?"

"No. She's watching a movie with the girls."

"Is it suitable?" I ask.

"Yes, of course. I have done this before, you know, Zoe?"

"I know. Sorry. I'm being silly. It's just … well … I miss her."

"It's only been an hour, Zo."

"I know."

"Do you remember when…"

"Yes," I tell him instinctively.

Oliver was eight months old when we left him for the first time to go out for dinner. He was spending the night with my parents. But we didn't even make it to the end of the road before I called my mum to say I was coming back for him. I missed him too much.

I got better, of course. By the time Isla came along I was happily leaving all three of them for as long as my parents would have them. So that Mike and I could have time to ourselves. So that we could enjoy uninterrupted nights making love until we fell asleep in each other's arms, and lazy days sleeping in and eating breakfast in bed.

When did all that stop? I don't even remember.

"She's fine," Mike tells me again, and for a fleeting moment I wonder if he is recalling the same memories.

The house feels quiet without them all. I don't like it.

It's amazing how quickly I have got used to the noise and the chaos.

Realising tonight is almost a wasted opportunity, I sip my wine and message Simon.

> I have the house to myself. Well, almost. Come over.

He replies with a simple thumbs up.

Half an hour later he is on the doorstep with a takeaway, a bottle of wine, and the look of a man who knows he's about to get lucky.

And of course he's not wrong.

Abandoning the Chinese on the kitchen table, still in its white plastic bag with a handful of foil-wrapped fortune cookies, he leads me upstairs to my bedroom.

———————

Sex with someone new is so different to sex with someone you've known what feels like your whole life.

It's fresh.

It's exciting.

It's not rushed like sex with a long-term partner can be – because you know you haven't done it in a while but have to be up early in the morning, or because you're due at friends for a dinner party in an hour but one of you is feeling horny, or because at any given moment one of the three children you have had together could walk in.

You can take your time. To work out what each other likes. Where you want to be touched. And where you don't.

Sex with Simon is good.

Tonight he takes me to a place where I am not a mother, or a godmother, or someone who can save an animal's life. I'm just me.

He makes me forget everything.

And then, after warmed-up chicken chow mein with spring rolls and prawn crackers, he makes me forget all over again.

Afterwards, I ask him to stay.

"Are you sure?" he asks.

"Yes," I tell him, finding my spot on his chest and wrapping my arms around him.

Later I tell Simon my worries about Lou. About what Heidi told me, and Jamie. And about the fact that she and Rich were preparing to live in separate homes.

"Why would she lie to me?" I say. "Why did she tell me her and Rich were moving together?"

"Is that what she said?" he asks me.

"What do you mean?"

"Did she use those exact words? Did she say, 'We are moving to a new house together'?"

I think about it for a moment.

"Well, no. I mean, I guess she didn't use those exact words – but she never said they weren't."

She told me *they* were thinking of moving.

And she didn't *just* tell me that.

She elaborated.

She talked about a fixer-upper.

She painted a picture of togetherness. Of knocking down walls together. Of spending evenings ripping out kitchen units when the kids were asleep. Of designing walk-in wardrobes and choosing bathroom suites with his and hers sinks and a shower big enough for them both.

Why did she do that if they were splitting up?

Were they ever moving together? Or was it always just a lie? And why?

"Do you think one of them was having an affair?" Simon asks me, cautiously. And I know instinctively that he is thinking of the time he saw Lou in the pub with a man that wasn't Rich, soon after meeting her for the first time. "Do you think maybe one of them was cheating?"

The truth is, I didn't.

The truth is, it hadn't even occurred to me.

But now that he has said it, of course I do.

I do think maybe one of them was cheating.

It makes sense.

And it wouldn't have been the first time.

Chapter Thirty-One

The week after we worked out that Lou and Andrew had an 18 per cent chance of being good together as girlfriend and boyfriend, Lou asked him out.

Never one to miss an opportune moment, she spotted him in the dinner queue one lunchtime on her way to netball practice.

"So do you want to go out with me or what?" she asked him.

The poor lad didn't know what to say.

It was unexpected. He was new. He barely knew how to find his way around the school, let alone whether or not he wanted to go out with one of the most confident girls in the year.

But with a bit of raucous encouragement from his new mates stood in the queue with him, he figured he had nothing to lose, and said yes.

A week later they had their first kiss, and a month after that they both lost their virginity.

Somehow I think it made Lou feel like she was back on a level playing field with me. Like she'd been playing catch-up, somehow. Because I'd been the first to have a boyfriend. And the first to do everything that that involved. Including having sex.

I didn't care about any of that.

I was just happy that she was happy.

And she was.

Lou quickly fell in love with Andrew.

And he was besotted with her.

They were the real deal.

And they seemed to defy those 18 per cent odds.

But she wasn't faithful to him. Not completely.

At the end of our first year of A Levels the four of us went on a barge for a week with four other friends.

We were all free of our parents for a week, and we were determined to do that justice.

I don't think there was a single one of us who didn't throw up over the side of the barge that week, and of course more than one of the lads ended up falling into the canal at one time or another.

On the last day we left the barge to go to a pub for the evening and Lou and Andrew had a fight.

She was drunk and was flirting with the barman.

Nothing happened. She got a free drink, stroked his hand flirtatiously across the bar, and then joined the rest of us in the beer garden, where Andrew told her she was embarrassing herself. And him.

She disagreed, of course, and told Andrew he was an idiot.

At which point he walked out of the pub and back to the barge.

They made up later, of course, when the rest of us got back to the boat.

No one was in any doubt about that fact – the walls of a barge being not in the least bit soundproof.

And back then I didn't think anything of that silly little tiff they had in the beer garden of a pub in the middle of Wales.

But given what happened a year later, maybe it was the first sign that in the end that 18 per cent was just not enough for Lou.

Chapter Thirty-Two

In the morning I am woken by the gentle caress of the man lying next to me.

He kisses me softly and slides his hand up my leg, stopping tantalisingly just before that point of no return. And then there it is. That quiet chatter that has woken me every day for the last two and a half months.

I giggle and kiss him back, before slipping out of the bed and pulling on my dressing gown.

Simon is taking his girls to see their grandparents today, so after breakfast with Zack and I he heads off, promising to be back bright and early on Sunday to spend the day with us all.

It feels strange, just being me and Zack, but we make the most of it.

We go to soft play where I sip coffee while Zack crawls over brightly coloured cushions and sits in a ball pit looking totally bemused.

We go into town where we have lunch and buy George Pig pyjamas and two new story books, and a glittery hair band for Phoebe.

And we do the supermarket shop, where Zack plays happily in the trolley, and fends off all the old ladies who want to squeeze his cheeks and tickle his toes.

"What a beautiful little boy you have," one of them tells me.

And I just smile and say thank you. Because she's right – I do.

And we have a lovely time, but all the while I am wondering whether his mummy was stupid enough to risk everything she had. And if so, why.

I am ready for adult company again by the time Simon arrives back at the house on Sunday morning.

He is sat at my kitchen table drinking coffee, Zack sitting happily on his knee, when my ex-husband walks in with the girls.

For a moment everything feels awkward.

Mike looks at Simon.

Simon looks at Mike.

Sophie and I look at their dad and Simon looking at each other.

And Phoebe looks at Sophie and Isla.

Even Zack looks perplexed – that everyone around him seems to have gone quiet.

And then I do what British people do best – and I put the kettle on, retrieving Simon's cup from the table to refill it.

It's hard to know what Mike is most upset about – the fact that Simon is in his kitchen, that he is holding his godson so comfortably, or that he is drinking out of Mike's coffee cup. A World's Best Dad mug the girls bought him for Fathers' Day a couple of years ago.

"Coffee?" I ask, casually, quietly sliding the mug into the sink and choosing a fresh one for Simon's next drink.

"Not for me," Mike says. "I'm meeting Scott for a run."

"Okay," I say, somewhat relieved.

"How did it go?" I ask him, seeing him out.

"It was fine," he says, and I can tell I'm not going to get much more than that, so I tell him I'll see him soon and then I shut the door, feeling inexplicably uneasy.

"I keep thinking about what you said on Friday night," I tell Simon later.

We have brought the children to the beach for a dog walk and an ice-cream.

He takes my hand as we watch Phoebe chase Stanley across the sand.

"About what?" he asks.

"About Lou. About whether she might have been having an affair."

He doesn't say anything. He just holds my hand a little tighter.

"She cheated before," I tell him quietly. It still makes me sad to say it out loud. "Not on Rich. Before him, I mean."

A few days after our final A Level exam Lou and I went on holiday together to Majorca. We met a group of lads on the plane that were staying at the same hotel.

I was newly single, having just split up with Jamie. But Lou was very much still taken.

Despite being single, I had already decided I was not interested in a one-night stand with some guy I met on holiday. But Lou had decided that that was exactly what she did want.

I made it clear I didn't approve. She was with Andrew. She had a boyfriend. But I couldn't stop her. She took some guy – so irrelevant to our life story that I don't even recall his name – back to our apartment one night, and asked me to give her an hour. When I returned the guy was nowhere to be seen and she was sat on the bed, removing her make-up, like nothing had happened.

"Well?" I asked.

"Well what?" she said, with a self-satisfied grin.

"Please tell me you were careful, at least?"

She nodded. And then, "The sex was incredible."

I didn't want to know.

"And now what?"

"It was a one-off," she told me. "It was just something I needed to do."

And as far as I knew, it *was* just that. A one-off. Something that she had to do, for whatever reason.

But I have never been able to forget that night, and how disappointed I was in my friend.

———————

"If she'd done it before, why didn't it occur to you that she might have done it again?" Simon asks me later.

"Because she never told me," I say. "And we told each other everything."

Chapter Thirty-Three

Phoebe and I are on our way to visit her grandma. Rich's mum.

I feel bad that we have not been before now.

I guess I thought seeing a grandma who may not remember her seemed just that little bit too much for a little girl who has already been through so much.

But Margaret remembered Phoebe at the funeral, and if she *still* has moments where she remembers her, then it's unfair to keep them apart.

I'm just hoping today is a good day.

I prep Phoebe on the way. I tell her that if Grandma asks her any strange questions – what her favourite colour is, for example, or who she is – then not to worry, grandmas can sometimes be a bit forgetful...

The home she is in is lovely. It's set in really pretty grounds, with trees and flowers, and a little fishpond for the residents to sit by.

I point the pond out to Phoebe as we walk up the gravel path to the entrance.

She holds my hand and asks when we can go home.

"Soon," I tell her. "We're just going to say hello to Grandma, and then we'll go and get Zack from Auntie Robyn's."

She nods and holds my hand a little tighter.

I sign in at reception and after receiving a few words of sympathy, which I am more than used to now, we head to the day room where I'm told Margaret is watching television.

I watch her from the doorway and she looks up and smiles.

Maybe today *is* a good day.

She has actually only met me a handful of times. Lou and Rich's wedding. Phoebe's christening. The occasional birthday party. The funeral…

I don't expect her to remember my name.

"Zoe," I tell her, so she doesn't have to ask.

It must be hard getting old. Seeing a different person staring at you in the mirror every day. Different to the person you once were. Losing the people you love. Forgetting things.

When she still looks confused I remind her that I was Lou's friend.

"We met at school," I tell her.

And then she is with me.

Phoebe is still holding my hand. Tightly.

I sit down on a chair and pull her onto my lap.

"You remember Phoebe right, Margaret?" I ask.

I watch her face as she mentally rifles through a lifetime of memories, desperately trying to pull out the right file.

I am willing her to say yes.

"Of course I do," she says eventually, before reaching into her handbag and pulling out her purse.

She hands Phoebe a £2 coin.

"Get Mummy to buy you some sweeties," she says.

She immediately looks confused, like she's realised what she's said is not quite right, but she can't figure out why.

Phoebe looks at me, and I give her a little smile – to remind her – see, grandmas can forget things sometimes. And when she rolls her eyes with a little smile herself, I realise I couldn't love her any more if she was my own.

"And this one is for Zack," Margaret says, handing Phoebe a second coin.

"Zack can't have sweeties," Phoebe tells her. "But I can put it in his money box for when he is older."

She nods her agreement with this plan, and then looks at me with a sadness in her eyes that almost takes my breath away.

"My Rich is gone, isn't he?" she says.

I nod and take her hand in mine.

And then:

"He was too good for that woman."

I look around me. Hopeful, maybe, that she isn't talking to me. That she isn't talking about Lou. But I know she is. She may have Alzheimer's but she knows what she is saying. Today, at least.

"What do you mean, Margaret?" I try, while Phoebe fiddles with the two coins in her little hand.

But I have already lost her. She is already looking at Phoebe like she has no idea who she is.

Chapter Thirty-Four

It is impossible not to think about what Margaret said to me, of course.

Were these the incoherent ramblings of an old lady with Alzheimer's? Or was there something in what she said? *Was* Rich too good for my friend?

I guess it's natural to want to only think about a person in a good light when they have died.

We remember all the things we loved about them, how kind they were, how they made us laugh, how their smile could light up a room.

We think about what we miss about them.

We forget that they were human, that they had flaws. Maybe because they're not there to defend themselves. So it seems fairer to only remember the good stuff.

But what if there was bad stuff too?

What if there was a lot of it?

And what if you didn't know about all of it?

Chapter Thirty-Five

When Lou told me she had cheated on Andrew a second time, I was angry.

We were both in our third year at university. For Lou it was her final year.

Her trips home to visit Andrew had become less and less frequent, and I had just assumed she was devoting more of her time to her studies.

But then she called me.

"I think I've met someone," she told me.

"What do you mean, you *think* you've met someone?" I said, frostily. I knew where this was going. "You've already *got* someone," I reminded her.

"His name is Rich," she said.

She'd met him at the student union on a night out at the beginning of the term. He'd made it clear he was interested but she'd told him she had a boyfriend. A few weeks later they had bumped into each other in the bookshop.

This time they got coffee, and each other's emails.

When they met for a third time – this time in the library where they were both studying for upcoming exams – they decided it was fate.

They had lunch together. And then dinner. And then he kissed her. And she didn't stop him.

"And then what?" I asked her. "Did you go back to his place? Your place? A hotel room?"

That last option was unlikely – they were students – but I couldn't help myself. The story felt sordid, so I was simply making it more so.

"Mine," she said quietly. "But I didn't sleep with him," she added quickly.

Was it pride I could hear in her voice? Did she feel she deserved some element of credit for stopping short of having sex with this guy? A kiss and a bit of a fumble under the sheets back at her place were perfectly acceptable, as long as they didn't have full-blown sex?

"He knew you had a boyfriend," I said. And then, "I'm not lying for you again, Lou."

And I meant it.

I'd lied for her once and I wasn't going to do it again.

Andrew was one of my best friends. He deserved better.

But she said it was different this time. She said Rich might be the one.

So I gave her a choice. End things with Andrew, or end things with this new guy. Because I wasn't prepared to lie for her again.

Lou wasn't stupid. She knew I could be pushed, but she also knew I had my limits, and I had reached them.

She phoned Andrew the next day and broke up with him.

He was devastated. I think he thought they'd be together forever. I think we all did.

Chapter Thirty-Six

At the beginning of April, three months after I became a parent to two extra children, I am late to pick Phoebe up for the very last time.

I am about to leave work for school (scrubs off, bag on shoulder, car keys in hand) when an elderly man rushes into the surgery in a blind panic with his dog Peggy, who has just eaten a grape that had fallen on the kitchen floor.

Grapes are incredibly toxic to dogs. And while it won't be fatal to 99 out of 100 dogs, because Peggy's owner lost his wife six months ago and Peggy's brother three months after that, I really can't risk her being that one in 100. So I chuck my handbag and keys at Robyn in reception, shouting at her to please call the school, and I dash to the staff room to change back into my scrubs.

By the time I arrive in the school grounds, Phoebe and Mrs Chandry have given up on me and gone back inside.

I walk into the school entrance where the receptionist informs me that Phoebe is in her classroom with her teacher and she buzzes me through.

I open the door and my heart breaks.

She stays right where she is, barely even looking up, perched on her little chair at her little table, her teacher by her side and the class teddy – Max the Dog – held tightly in her arms.

"I'm sorry, Phoebs," I say, from the doorway.

She hugs Max a little tighter.

Giving Phoebe's arm a little squeeze, Mrs Chandry gets up and joins me over by the door, a look on her face that is both frustration and sympathy in equal measure.

"I'm sorry," I tell her. Because there is nothing else I can say. And because if I say anything else I'm afraid I might cry.

I have a choice to make. I realise that.

I am either okay with being that parent that is met with the disapproving looks from the teachers and the sad faces of my children when I turn up even just a few minutes later than I am expected, ready to make it up to them in whatever way is necessary afterwards, or I am not.

Because there will always be something that gets in the way. A tractor blocking the road. A traffic light that turns red just at the wrong time. A dog that has swallowed a grape and could die if being on time for the school run is more important to me.

Can I live with myself if I let these children down? If I don't live up to the promise I made to their parents?

The thing is, if they were my own children – or rather, when it *was* my own children – I told them the truth. I told them Mummy had a job. An important one. That people relied on me to keep their animals safe, to keep them from dying. So if that meant they had to stand by their teacher for a couple of extra minutes while I waited to safely overtake a tractor after leaving the surgery just that little bit later than I should have done, while I waited at that red light, while I treated the diabetic dog who was fitting in the surgery reception because his elderly owner had not been giving him his insulin properly, then so be it. But how can I tell Phoebe and Zack that right now? After everything they have already been through?

I watch Phoebe in the rear-view mirror. She is still cuddling Max – who she has been allowed to bring home for the weekend, her thumb in her mouth.

"I'm sorry I was late again, sweetie," I tell her.

Looking up briefly, she pulls Max's hood up and puts her thumb back in her mouth.

I want to tell her that tomorrow I won't be. That tomorrow I will be the first person through the school gates when the bell goes. Waiting for her with a beaming smile, ready to hear all about her day. But I can't, because no matter how hard I try, I know there is a chance I won't be. And I know I shouldn't make promises I can't keep. Especially not to Phoebe. She needs the truth more than anything right now.

So I give her that. I give her the truth.

"I will try my best not to be late tomorrow. Okay?"

She nods.

"But if I am late, it doesn't mean I don't love you, right?"

She nods again.

"It just means that something happened that I just couldn't help."

She pulls her thumb out of her mouth.

"Like Mummy and Daddy?" she says.

"What do you mean, sweetie?"

"Like when they went away," she says, her face etched with sadness. "And then something happened. So they couldn't come back to us. So now we live with you. And Sophie and Isla. And Stanley."

And then – just like that – I get it. I suddenly see everything from the eyes of this beautiful little girl. And I know exactly what I have to do.

Chapter Thirty-Seven

I call Mike from the car.

"Can you come over?" I ask him, before I've even said hello.

"I'm just on my way over to Charlotte's," he says. "Is everything okay?"

"Not really. Can you come over? I wouldn't ask if it wasn't important."

"I'll be there in ten minutes," he says.

He's already at the house by the time Phoebe and I get home, sitting at the kitchen table chatting to Sophie, while Isla is raiding the kitchen cupboards for ingredients for next week's food tech lesson.

"I've brought Max home for the weekend, Uncle Mike," Phoebe says excitedly, pulling his Trunki suitcase into the kitchen behind her.

"How wonderful," Mike tells her, despite having absolutely no idea what she is talking about.

She puts Max on the table and starts pulling off his shoes.

"I need to get him ready for bed," she says.

I ask the girls to keep Phoebe occupied for half an hour and then I pour myself a large glass of wine.

"What's going on?" Mike asks.

I sip the wine, waiting for it to wash away the hellish day I have just had.

"I need you to cash in one of our savings plans," I tell him.

He immediately looks alarmed, his mind no doubt darting between all the possible reasons that would have me needing that kind of money.

"What's happened?" he asks. "Why do you need money? Are you okay?"

"I'm fine," I reassure him. "But I need to take a break from the surgery. A proper break. Not just a few weeks. So I need some money to see us through."

"Why? What's happened?"

"This," I say, holding my arms out wide to illustrate exactly what "this" is. My life. As it is now.

"My best friend died," I say. "And so did her husband. And now I have two small children to look after. Right when I thought my days of changing nappies and chanting times-tables were a distant memory."

Mike says nothing. He just waits for me to finish.

"I can't do it, Mike," I tell him. "I thought I could, but I can't. I can't get them to school and nursery, do a full day's work, and still make it back to school for pick-up. The hours just don't stack up.

"I can't put her in breakfast clubs, and after-school clubs, or send her to friends every day. It's not fair. She's my responsibility. And it's too soon."

"You can't leave the practice," he tells me. "Not after everything you've been through to get where you are…"

"I'm failing, Mike," I tell him.

"What do you mean?"

"I'm trying to do what I promised Lou I would do. And I'm trying to be what I was before. But I'm not giving 100 per cent of myself to either role. I need time off one of them. And that can't be Phoebe. Or Zack. Do you know what she said to me today?"

Mike shakes his head.

"She said when I'm not there to pick her up, it might mean something has happened to me, like it did to Mummy and Daddy. Or words to that effect. How can I do that to her, Mike?

"I need to give up work. Just for a while. Just until she is through the worst of this. I have no choice. But I need some of our money to do it."

When Mike and I split up we made the decision to leave our joint savings where they were. It didn't make sense to split them. They were making us a lot in interest. And neither of us needed the money.

"She's already lost Lou and Rich," I tell Mike. "When she comes out of school every day she needs to see me waiting for her. She deserves that." Saying it out loud makes it more real than it already seemed in my head. And before I know it, I am sobbing.

Saying nothing, Mike drags his chair closer to mine. Then he moves my wine glass to the side and wraps his arms around me.

I stay there for a long time. Too long, perhaps. But those arms have held me through so many happy times – and through so many sad times. They have pulled me in for a first kiss; guided me back down the church aisle after saying "I do"; handed me our baby son for that first precious cuddle. They have held me when, despite my best efforts, I lost my first animal following a car accident almost identical to the one which first inspired my veterinary career; comforted me when our firstborn left home; reassured me the one and only time our eldest daughter told me she hated me. They have been there for every celebration, every worry, every fear.

"Promise me you won't do anything rash," Mike tells me before he leaves. "If it's really what you want then I'll get you the money. But think really carefully before you do this, Zo. Sleep on it. We can talk again next week."

And then he leaves, kissing me on the cheek as he walks out of the door.

Chapter Thirty-Eight

I am on my way to the surgery the following week when Mike phones me.

"Have you told the surgery yet?" he asks me, a sense of urgency in his voice. "Have you spoken to Nathan?"

"Not yet," I say. "Why?"

"Don't," he tells me. "I have an idea. Can I come round tonight?"

"Yes, but what is it?"

"I'll explain everything tonight," he says. "I'll bring a takeaway."

He arrives just after we get home from nursery with Zack.

Sophie is at Josh's and Isla is at a friend's, so it's just me, Zack and Phoebe for the evening – and Mike.

I put the takeaway in the oven to keep warm while we put the kids to bed and then we talk.

"So what's your big idea?" I ask him, tipping chicken tikka masala onto two plates.

"Let me help," he says.

I open the bin and drop the empty foil tray into it.

"You can grab the mango chutney from the fridge," I tell him.

He opens the fridge and I can see him scanning the shelves for the jar.

It's strange to think that just a year ago his hand would have gone straight to it.

"Top shelf, behind the pesto," I tell him.

He hands me the jar.

"I didn't mean let me help with the dinner," he says. "I meant I can *help*. I can pick Phoebe up. If you need to be at work, and she needs to see someone there when she comes out, then I can do it. I can do pick-up for you. A few times a week, maybe?"

"You?" I ask, incredulous. I can't help myself. I can't hide my surprise at this suggestion.

This is the man who left all of the childcare arrangements for our own children to me. All the drop-offs. All the pick-ups. All the clubs, and the playdates, and the trips into town when they got older. They all fell to me. Every one of them.

"Yes, me," he says. If he is offended by my scepticism then he's not showing it.

"But I have asked you for help. And you are always too busy," I say. "Nearly always," I say, trying my hardest to be fair.

"I know. You're right," he says. "I've not been there for you and I should have been.

"Twelve months ago I'd have been legally obliged to help, Zoe. If Lou and Rich hadn't changed their will, I mean."

"Really?" I say. "So what about your legal obligation to your own three, then?"

I shouldn't have said that. He is trying.

"I'm sorry," I tell him. "I didn't mean that." Though he knows I did. Just a little bit.

"So what's changed?" I ask him. "What about your work?"

"I'll cut my hours down. It's about time I did. Before I work myself into an early grave."

He'll be kicking himself for saying that. I know he will. No one can mention death in front of me, in any way, shape or form, without feeling like the worst person in the world.

"I'm sorry," he says.

"Don't be," I tell him.

"I just mean I probably need to start taking things a bit easy. I'm not getting any younger."

"I know."

"The bottom line is, I want to help you," he says.

"Why?" I ask. "Why now?"

"Because I don't want you to have to give up everything. Not again, Zoe. You have worked so hard to get where you are. If you step back again, you might never get back to that place. And I wouldn't forgive myself if that happened."

"Why not?" I say.

"Because you gave it up once before," he says. "For me. For our family. And I charged forward with my career while you raised our children. And now you are prepared to do that all over again. For two children who aren't even your own."

"They are my own," I tell him. Again. "They became my own when I left Patrick Massey's office with those papers in my hand."

"You know what I mean."

He's right. I do.

"You'd really do that for me?" I ask him. "For us?"

"Yes, I would," he says. "I will. If you'll let me."

"What does Charlotte think about this?" I ask Mike after we've finished dinner, and after I've had time to digest what he has offered to do.

"She's fine with it," he says. "She understands."

I'm sceptical but decide not to push it.

There's something he's not telling me, though, and that I do push.

"What is it?" I ask him.

"I didn't like it," he says. "When Simon was here. When I brought the girls home."

I go to explain. To tell him that Simon had never stayed before. That that weekend was the first time. That I have always stayed at his.

And then I realise I don't owe him an explanation. I don't owe him anything. I am truly grateful for what he's offered to do for Phoebe and me. But let's just see if this is a promise that he can actually keep this time.

Chapter Thirty-Nine

The next week we move Phoebe to Hartingley Primary
School.

Mike was right – it does make perfect sense. I just didn't want
to admit it.

Hartingley Primary has had a new head since Isla left four
years ago.

The last one saw three Henry children pass through the school.
He knew us as a family. Knew our background, our morals, our
values.

Catherine Alderley doesn't know anything about us.
Everything needs explaining.

"So you're looking for a school place for Phoebe?" she asks
Mike and I, while one of the class teachers takes Phoebe to the
library so we can talk.

"Yes," I tell her. "She's our goddaughter, actually. As I
explained on the phone, her parents – our best friends – they both
died in a car accident a few months ago."

Will I always feel the need to do that? To justify our place in
her life?

Will I tell her new friends' parents that she isn't really mine? Will I turn to the parent next to me at Prize Giving when she's a teenager and announce, "That's my goddaughter Phoebe – her parents died when she was five."?

"Tell me a little bit about Phoebe, Mrs Henry," Catherine Alderley tells me softly.

An hour later we leave knowing this is the right school for Phoebe, just as we knew it was for Oliver, Sophie and Isla when we moved back to Sussex.

———————

She starts the next day and our lives are transformed.

She settles quickly. She likes her new teacher. She's happy.

We have moved Zack too. To the nursery across the road from Hartingley Primary. It was the obvious choice.

I wonder what my friend would think. If we'd discussed things like this when she asked us to be guardians, would she have asked that we keep the children where they were, or would she have told us to do whatever we needed to do to make it work?

The truth is, I don't know what she would think.

But I have had to accept that I don't have all the answers. I don't know what Lou would have done in every situation. I can only decide what's best based on what feels right for my family, and for her lovely children.

———————

Mike stands by his offer to help.

Yes, of course I'm sceptical.

Monday to Friday, between the hours of 8am and 6pm, Mike has never had to put his children first. Financially, yes. Logistically, no.

He has always had someone else to do that.

There has always been someone else to do the school run, to make sure they were doing their homework, or their reading, or their spellings, to drop them off at their clubs, to deliver them to their friends' houses.

Mike has never had to check in with anyone about his schedule – when he needs to be in London at 7.30am in the morning, or needs to attend an evening meeting, or needs to spend the whole of the weekend working on a report for a new client.

He has just taken it for granted that someone else will pick up the pieces.

For the first few years it was me, and after that it was still me, the only difference being I had a childminder to help me. A childminder that *I* found, that *I* booked, that *I* communicated with on a daily basis to confirm which child needed to be where, at what time and for how long.

When Oliver and Sophie were little – and then when Isla came along – Mike was carving out his career. The deal was, I would put mine on hold, I would raise the children and he would support us.

And he took that job seriously.

He was always the first one to take on the extra work, always the last to leave the office, in the hope that it would get him up the ladder quicker, bring in the money faster.

But along with the money and the reputation for being great at his job came the sacrifices – the missed bedtimes, the missed firsts, the missed time with his family that he would never get back.

He has worked for himself for a long time now, though. And for a long time he has earned the sort of salary that means you don't have to worry about money. The sort of salary that puts three children through private school, that pays for foreign holidays every year, that buys all the latest gadgets, the latest clothes, the latest cars.

Mike is the one holding the ladders for others on their way up now.

It is a long time since he has had to put in the sort of hours it takes to prove yourself. But he still does it. Because old habits die hard.

So do I think he has what it takes to actually make Phoebe his priority? I'm not sure.

But he says he does. And I have to trust him. Because if it means I can avoid the alternative, then it has to be worth a shot.

———————

Four times a week he is going to pick Phoebe up from school and stay with her at our house until I am home.

So that I can do the job I love *and* be a mum.

Today is day one.

I left the house this morning with a spring in my step, and a heart full of hope. The sort of hope you feel on New Year's Day – with a clean slate, all your sins of the previous year wiped clean, all good intentions set out – and written down – for the days and weeks ahead.

My late for pick-up penalty points have been wiped and we are starting a new era. One where Phoebe will be among the children beaming at the doors at the end of the school day when she sees Uncle Mike waiting for her.

Today I have dropped a happy little girl off at school, I have delivered a cheerful little boy to nursery, and I have made it to the surgery in time for the morning briefing.

I have already resuscitated one rabbit, spayed two dogs, and removed four rotten teeth from an elderly cat.

I feel like I am winning for the first time in weeks.

I am even able to take a rare lunchbreak with my friend.

I have not had a chance to tell her about our new childcare arrangement.

"You look happy," she says, peeling the cover off a Costa sandwich.

"I am," I confirm.

She looks at me expectantly.

"I've got some help with the kids," I tell her, stirring my coffee.

"That's great! Who?"

"Mike," I say, putting the stirrer down on a napkin and taking a bite of my cheese toastie.

"Mike?"

"Yes. Mike."

"So how's that going to work?" she asks.

"He's cutting back his hours," I tell her. "Just for a few months. So he can pick Phoebe up from school for me."

"And do what with her? Keep her at the flat until you've finished work?"

"No. He'll take her back to the house. We want to keep her world as normal as we can. Or as normal as it can be right now."

She says all the right things but I can see she looks sceptical. But then, I can't blame her for that when it is exactly how I feel.

"How are things going with Simon?" she asks.

"Really well, actually."

"And what does he think about this arrangement?"

"I haven't even told him," I say. "But it's got nothing to do with him. This is a practical arrangement. Nothing more, nothing less.

"I'm not ready to turn my back on my career, Rob," I continue – conscious that I am giving far more explanation than I need to, but unable to stop myself. "Not if I have any kind of alternative. For now this is the alternative. So we're going to give it a go."

"Then I'm all for it," she says, in a show of solidarity that I have always been able to rely on her for.

"And you know I will help wherever I can," she tells me. "You just have to ask."

"I know. And I will. Believe me. I need all the help I can get right now."

And then we eat our lunch. The first lunch we have enjoyed together in a long time that has not been interrupted by one animal-related drama or another.

Chapter Forty

I call Mike on my way to Zack's nursery.

"Yes, I did," he says, answering the call.

"Yes, you did what?" I laugh.

"Yes, I did remember to pick up my goddaughter from school," he says, laughing.

"Am I that transparent?" I ask.

"Yes. You are. But I get it. This is not my speciality, I know. Would you like to speak to her?" he asks.

"No, that's fine. I'll see you both shortly."

"I think she was a bit disappointed to see me, to tell you the truth," he says, as I am about to hang up.

"What do you mean?"

"She told me she gets cupcakes when you're late. But I was early. By a good ten minutes," he adds, for extra brownie points.

"So what did you do?" I ask.

"I took her for cupcakes, of course!"

"Wow that's dangerous," I laugh. "Cupcakes if we're late. And cupcakes if we're early."

"I know, right? I'm going to have to do a few extra miles on the treadmill. We've saved you one, by the way. A bumble bee."

"Lovely, thank you! We'll see you shortly," I tell him, and hang up.

When Zack and I walk through the door, I honestly wonder if I have come home to the wrong house.

I am not entirely sure what I was expecting. Noise, maybe? School bags and shoes abandoned haphazardly through the hallway? My ex-husband dealing with multiple "urgent" emails while three hungry girls snack on packets of crisps and chocolate bars in front of the television?

Whatever I was expecting, it certainly wasn't the scene I am greeted with. Quiet. Calm. School bags and shoes lined up neatly by the front door. Two out of my three girls sat at the kitchen table together chatting. And – perhaps the biggest shock of all – the smell of dinner cooking.

I close the front door behind me and put Zack down on the floor. He immediately crawls through to the kitchen, drawn by the sound of laughter.

"Wow, you guys have been busy," I say, surveying the table – set for dinner, my ex-husband sporting my red gingham apron and matching oven gloves.

The smell of freshly baked cookies fills the room, quickly joined by the smell of lasagne as Mike pulls open the oven and removes a large dish.

"Me and Isla made the cookies," Phoebe tells me proudly.

"They look yummy, sweetie," I say. "I can't wait to try one. Well done!"

"And I *didn't* make the lasagne," Mike grins. "But I *did* go to M&S."

"Even so," I say. "I'm impressed."

And I am.

"I did make the garlic butter for the bread, though," he says, gesturing to the apron and scooping Zack up off the floor for a cuddle.

"How was nursery, big man?" he says.

Zack grins and blows a raspberry. As expected.

"Right. Dinner is served," Mike says, putting Zack in his highchair.

"Brilliant," I say. "But what's with the M&S lasagne? Lasagne's your best dish."

"I knew I'd run out of time," Mike says. "So Phoebe and I popped to the shops after school. I'll cook it from scratch next time," he smiles.

"I'm only teasing," I say. "I didn't expect to come home to dinner. Though I do love your lasagne," I add, just in case he does actually fancy cooking it for us some time.

"Are you staying?" I ask.

Mike loosens the apron ties behind his back.

"I can't," he says, but offers no explanation.

My reaction catches me off guard.

Disappointment.

I wasn't expecting it.

We're divorced. He's helping me out by picking up his goddaughter.

Family dinners weren't part of the deal.

And yet I wanted him to say yes. And I can't get my head around that.

I go to ask him. To find out if the reason he can't stay is because he is seeing Charlotte.

But before I do I stop myself. Because I'm not sure I want to know the answer.

So instead I thank him for his help and tell him I'll see him tomorrow. And I say goodbye, before he can see the disappointment etched all over my face.

Chapter Forty-One

The tidy house doesn't last. Of course it doesn't. But I can live with that.

The kids are happy.

I'm happy.

Mike is happy.

We have found a new normal.

Sometimes I come home to chaos. To mess. To children who haven't done all their homework. To an ex-husband who is catching up on emails and leaving three children to fend for themselves as I throw the fourth into the mix. But I am okay with that.

Because isn't that how most families with working parents get by?

And because it's a small price to pay for being able to pluck maggots from a rabbit's bottom without clock-watching, right?

It's one of the least glamorous elements of a vet's life, but someone's got to do it, right?

On Friday afternoon it's me.

Poor Mortimer has fly-strike – a condition caused when flies are attracted to damp fur. They land on the rabbit – around their bottom usually – and lay their eggs. Eggs that within a very short time will hatch into maggots.

Mortimer has a bad dose, bless him. A bottom literally riddled with maggots. But we painstakingly pick off every last one and make sure he lives to hop another day.

Handing the mildly traumatised little fella back to his owner with a dose of antibiotics and some pain relief, I catch Robyn watching me.

"What?" I say.

"You seem really happy," she tells me. Suspiciously.

"Well, who wouldn't be after picking twenty-seven maggots off a rabbit's bottom?" I ask her, as soon as Mortimer and his owner have left the building.

Her eyes widen.

"You didn't actually count them?" she says.

"I'm not that sad," I laugh. "It was just a guess!"

"Right, well, yeah – besides the obvious maggot-induced joy, you seem happy."

"I am, Rob," I tell her, honestly. "Three months ago, I couldn't imagine ever feeling this positive again. But I do. We are happy. All of us. I am loving being back at work. And Mike and I are trying really hard to make this work for the kids."

"Just for the kids?" Robyn asks me.

"Yes, just for the kids," I say firmly. "So what time will you be over tomorrow?" I ask Robyn, changing the subject.

It is Zack's first birthday tomorrow, and we're having a small party.

"Around 12pm?" she says.

It was only a few months ago that I was helping Lou with Phoebe's fifth birthday party, and yet so much has changed it feels like a lifetime.

I spent the morning building a balloon arch for my goddaughter – blowing up a hundred balloons by mouth because Rich had forgotten to order the electric pump. By the time her little friends arrived I was ready to keel over.

Lou had hired an Elsa and an Anna to come for the last hour of the party and the children were beside themselves with excitement.

But as I recall the princess-themed bouncy castle and the cupcakes decorated with pink glitter icing, another less pretty memory surfaces. And I wonder why I hadn't let myself remember before now.

When I arrived at the house with the girls to help set up, Lou and Rich were in the middle of a blazing row. Lou had been on a work night out the night before and had ended up staying over with a friend rather than getting a taxi home, as it was so late. She turned up just a few hours before the party was due to start and Rich lost it, shouting at her for putting work before her family "yet again". Not to mention the fact that they had a six-month-old baby who needed her.

"Have a word with your friend," Rich muttered, while I stood blowing up balloons, before he took Phoebe upstairs to get her changed into her party clothes. But Lou just rolled her eyes at me as if to say, "Here we go again", so I never did. Instead I tied up the balloons, handed her some paracetamol and quietly opened a packet of chocolate fingers.

I thought about that day last night when I was wrapping Zack's presents. It didn't seem that significant at the time, but now it does.

I don't think my friend *was* happy.

But was she so unhappy that she would risk everything?

Was she cheating on Rich?

Was she with another man the night before her daughter's fifth birthday party?

Was it the man in the pub? The one she was with when Simon saw her?

I wish I had asked her who he was.

I should have asked her.

But I didn't. And so I will probably never know the truth.

And that is hard to come to terms with.

The fact that I probably never knew my friend as well as I thought.

Chapter Forty-Two

P lanning Zack's birthday has felt like such a responsibility.
What would Lou and Rich have done?

What would they have wanted me to do?

We never discussed things like this, so I am left wondering.

How much fuss would they have made? What presents would they have bought and how many? How big would the party have been? Who would they have invited?

And the most important question... Should we be doing what they would have done?

It made me think again about all the things we just don't know.

What did they do on Christmas Eve to prepare for Santa's big visit? How did they explain the Easter Bunny? How did they celebrate Valentine's Day? And how would they have handled the tooth fairy's first visit?

We don't know enough about all of the traditions – big and small – that they have started over the last five years since Phoebe arrived in their lives – or the ones they were yet to start.

How do we make their lives as normal as possible when

there's so much we don't know about what their parents would have done?

It was Robyn who helped me find my way back out of the confusion.

"You are her parents now," she told me simply. "So you need to create your own traditions for them."

And suddenly it all seemed really easy.

Balloons. A cake. A shed-load of presents. And a party.

Zack was awake at 5am this morning. I like to think that was out of excitement for the impending celebrations, but we all know that no one-year-old actually has the faintest idea that it's their birthday. Zack included.

The blue helium balloon with a big "1" on it, tied to his highchair at breakfast, is met with mediocre interest, particularly when Isla spreads Nutella on a piece of toast and has the absolute audacity to put it in her own mouth and not his, prompting a frustrated tug on the balloon ribbon and a brief cry until the situation is remedied by his big sister.

"Here you are, Zacky, you can have mine," she says, thrusting a half-eaten piece of chocolate-covered toast in the birthday boy's hand – and making me feel ridiculously proud of her.

After breakfast we open his cards and a pile of presents – a wooden ride-on bumble bee and a Brio train track from me, some Peppa Pig toys from Mike and some Duplo from the girls. Predictably, he is more interested in the paper and the cardboard boxes that the gifts came in than the gifts themselves.

And then we all get dressed and take Stanley to the beach to wear him out for the rest of the day.

When we arrive back at the house Simon is there.

He has been great the last few weeks. When I told him Mike

was helping out, I wouldn't say he was thrilled, but he didn't make a fuss.

He offered to help, but he knew it wouldn't solve the problem. Phoebe doesn't know him well enough. Not yet.

And though I appreciated his offer, we both knew it was made for the wrong reasons.

He follows us into the house and pulls me in for a kiss.

"I've missed you," he says.

"Me too," I tell him.

My parents arrive just after lunch, closely followed by my brother and his family.

I haven't seen them since the funeral.

"Uncle Luke," Isla shouts, throwing her arms around my brother.

Phoebe looks shyly on from the kitchen table where she is doing some colouring. I can see her trying to work out where she fits in here.

She looks to me for reassurance.

"Is he my Uncle Luke too now?" she asks quietly.

I look at Luke and he smiles. Sliding into a chair next to Phoebe, he pulls a funny face, making her laugh. "I would really like that," he tells her. "If you can put up with an uncle who pulls funny faces and tells really bad jokes." Phoebe giggles and I silently thank my brother for being so amazing.

And then.

"My mummy and daddy have gone to heaven. So me and Zack are living with Auntie Zoe now. And Stanley."

Somewhere along the way Stanley seems to have usurped Sophie and Isla in Phoebe's affections, but we'll let that go for now.

"Yes, Auntie Zoe did tell me that," my brother says.

I am conscious that I am holding my breath as I wait to see

what my brother is going to say next. He's not always great at saying the right thing. But today he nails it.

"What's it like having two new bossy big sisters?" he asks Phoebe.

She giggles and Isla gives him a playful shove.

Sophie comes in with Zack – just up from his nap – and he holds out his arms to my dad.

"Mum, Dad, this is Simon," I say, conscious that there is so much going on, I've not even introduced them yet.

Shuffling Zack onto his hip, my dad shakes Simon's hand.

"Bill," he says, with a smile. "Welcome to the madhouse."

"Janet," my mum then says, before kissing Simon on the cheek.

And then we all move on. Awkward introductions with boyfriends they never thought they'd have to meet, done. All of us relatively unscathed.

"So, Phoebe," my mum says, taking a seat the other side of her at the table. "I hear you are going to have a new bedroom soon?"

In a gesture typical of my firstborn, Oliver has offered to give up his room for Phoebe. It is bigger than any of the spare rooms.

"I'm never there," he said to me when he phoned a couple of weeks ago. "It's her home now."

"Yes, I am," Phoebe confirms, with a big grin. "Uncle Mike is going to paint it for me."

I look at Simon for a reaction, but he either wasn't listening, or is not bothered.

I hope it's the latter. I should have told him. But in all honesty, it didn't even occur to me.

"Well, that's lucky," my mum tells Phoebe. "Because we've brought you a little something to go in it once it's done."

My mum takes a box out of her bag and hands it to Phoebe.

"It isn't my birthday. It's Zacky's," she says, looking at me.

"It isn't a birthday present," my mum tells her. "It's a non-birthday present."

"Oh," Phoebe says, her face lighting up, all explanations of lost parents in heaven now long forgotten.

My parents always did this with my brother and I when we were growing up and again with my own children when they were younger. They would give lots of birthday presents to the birthday boy or girl – and one small non-birthday present to the others.

And now they are doing the same for Phoebe and Zack.

Mike arrives at 2pm with Oliver who has made a special trip for his new baby brother, closely followed by Robyn, and our nextdoor neighbours and their children.

I notice Mike has not brought Charlotte with him.

And there is a brief moment where I feel like the entire room has their eyes on Mike and Simon. The ex-husband and the new man. Waiting for the tension. Waiting for the resentful glances – each of them uncomfortable with the other's presence in my home.

But maybe it's just me.

Or maybe everyone else can only think about what it is they are here for.

If I thought about it too much I'd probably conclude that I am trying to fill the house with people, that I am trying to compensate for the fact that the two most important people are not here. But I'm not going to think about it. Because I am trying my best. I am doing what I can to make this a happy day for Zack.

And do you know what? It really is.

We spend the afternoon opening the rest of his presents – which include a sand pit for the garden from my parents and a hideously noisy musical mat from Simon. We wear shiny party hats and blow party horns, we eat sandwiches and sausage rolls and chocolate fingers and then we light the number "1" candle on a George Pig cake and sing happy birthday.

Phoebe proudly blows out the candle for her little brother and we all cheer.

Yes, it is sad, because this is Zack's first birthday – and his parents are not here to see it.

But it's still his birthday.

So we have blown-up balloons, and wrapped presents, and eaten cake, and all the other things you are supposed to do when it is your child's birthday. And we have done it with smiles on our faces. Not because we have to, but because he is happy. And so is his big sister. And, because of that, we are too.

By early evening most people have left, happy in the knowledge that we have given Zack the best possible birthday we could have.

My parents offer to drop Oliver back at the station and my brother and his family leave soon after.

Which leaves just Mike and Simon.

Not at all awkward.

Especially when Simon casually slips his arm around my waist. Staking his claim?

If we didn't all feel awkward before, then we certainly do now.

"Coffee?" I say to them both, unintentionally – but conveniently – sliding out of Simon's hold in order to reach for the kettle.

"I should get going," Mike says.

And of course I'm relieved. No one needs this level of awkwardness in their life.

But I'm also something else. Something that I can't quite put my finger on. And it's unsettling.

"No Charlotte?" I ask Mike as I open the door to see him out.

He shakes his head.

"You know she would have been very welcome."

"I know," he says. "She was busy."

And then glancing behind me, he squeezes my hand gently, briefly.

"You did a great job, Zo. Lou would have been proud."

And then he gets in his car and drives away.

And with a heavy heart that I cannot explain, I shut the door and go back into the house.

Chapter Forty-Three

Phoebe has been seeing a therapist for a few weeks now. As promised, Amy put us in touch with someone based in Ferringham. Her name is Poppy and she is just lovely.

On the first day she explained to me what would happen and since then it's just been her and Phoebe. I drop her off each week after school and while she's there I pick Zack up and we go to the bakery for cupcakes.

I am not involved. This is for Phoebe. And already she seems happier. While the bedwetting hasn't stopped altogether, it is definitely better, and she is no longer shouting out in her sleep.

Each week she comes out with a smile on her face, excited about the task Poppy has set her. One week it was to write a letter to Mummy and Daddy. Poppy explained to me after the session that for young children writing is a way of expressing their emotions, particularly when the death is sudden. As soon as we got home Phoebe asked for some paper and a pen, and wrote her letter, in between bites of a zebra cupcake. It seemed the most natural thing in the world. She read it out to me at bedtime. Just three lines.

To Mummy and Daddy. I mis you and I love you. I am loking arfter Zack.

As she put it under her pillow for the fairies to take to heaven, I swallowed back the lump in my throat.

Another week Poppy asked me to help Phoebe with a task. I had to start a sentence that Phoebe could finish in whatever way she wanted. This one was harder. For both of us.

"If I could talk to Mummy..." I said.

Phoebe looked at me, tears flooding her eyes.

"I would ask her to come and get me," she said. And once again I was acutely aware of how hard this all is and was filled with doubt as to whether I can actually pull this off.

Somehow I forced myself to go on.

"When I think of Daddy..." I said.

"He is teaching me to ride my bike. But I couldn't do it," she said, her eyes filling up again.

"I will teach you to ride your bike," I told her, pulling her in for a cuddle.

"Or Uncle Mike?" she asked. And I nodded.

One week she says she doesn't want to go. I don't push it. I just call Poppy and I cancel. Just for this week, I tell her. We take Stanley to the beach instead. We buy ice-lollies and she asks if Mummy and Daddy are still dead. And I tell her yes. And then we go home.

Chapter Forty-Four

Lou had been with Rich for four months by the time I met him.

I was hesitant. He stole my best friend. He knew she had a boyfriend but he took her anyway.

It didn't help that I'd recently seen Andrew on a trip home and seen for myself how heartbroken he was.

But I could see what she saw in Rich. Despite his obvious flaws, he was a good guy. And he clearly cared about my friend.

He was ambitious, funny, kind, attentive. But he wasn't a pushover. He would put her in her place. If she was being whiny he would tell her to stop. If she was being needy, he'd tell her he wasn't her parent.

He was perfect for her.

The day they got married was the happiest day of her life.

At least that's what she said…

They got married in the Maldives, with just their parents and Mike and I there. We had two of our three children by then and were well versed in leaving them behind without tears (theirs or ours), so they went to my parents for the week.

It was beautiful.

She was beautiful.

They exchanged their vows on the beach – where the sea really was as blue as it is in the brochures, and the sand as white.

The four of us went diving, and sipped cocktails in hammocks on the beach.

We talked about our friendship. About the future. About our hopes and dreams.

By the time they were married they'd already built a home together, they both had successful careers.

But it was several years before they were ready to take the next step.

Watching her go through one heartbreak after another broke my own heart too.

She asked me once if I thought she was being punished for her past mistakes.

"You don't not get a baby because you cheated on a high school boyfriend," I told her, holding her hand after the fourth brutal round of treatment had brought only one line on the pregnancy test stick.

But she shook her head, in a way that puzzled me.

Chapter Forty-Five

I need a night out. Or so Robyn tells me.

"Come on, Zo," she said to me at Zack's party. "It's ages since we had a night out together."

She immediately looked guilty, of course. For daring to suggest I should have a good time. My best friend died, remember. I'm not allowed to have a good time. I must live in purgatory for the rest of my life.

I smiled. Because she was right.

It *is* ages since we've had a night out together.

On Friday night I drop Phoebe and Zack off at my mum and dad's. It's the first time I've left them both overnight, and I feel anxious. Much like I did when Mike and I left Oliver with my parents for the first time so that we could enjoy a night to ourselves.

"Their pyjamas are in the bag," I tell my mum. "And their toothbrushes, and a couple of story books. Oh, and their favourite toys for bedtime."

"Zoe, your dad and I have been doing this for forty-odd years," my mum says, laughing. "I think we'll be just fine."

But she pulls me in for a hug, because she knows that this is a big deal for me.

I thought my days of leaving my children to be looked after by their grandparents were over.

It turns out they are starting all over again.

"They'll be fine," she says. "Now go have some fun. You deserve it."

If Phoebe is thinking about what happened the last time she waved someone off for the night, then she isn't saying. So I can only hope her mind is filled with thoughts of baking cookies with Granny Janet, of watering the plants in the garden with Grandad Bill, and of snuggling into the top bunk bed in the bedroom with her name on the door.

I pull her into my arms for a cuddle.

"Be good for Granny and Grandad," I tell her.

"I will," she promises.

And then I turn and leave, because I know this time I have to, and because I know that she will be fine.

I meet Robyn at a bar in town.

She already has a glass of wine waiting for me.

"Before you say anything, I know this is a big deal," she tells me. Which makes me cry.

Not a great start to a night out.

"I also figured you'd probably cry," she says. "So I got you a large one." She smiles and pushes the wine over to me, followed by a packet of tissues.

"Baby steps," she says. "They'll be fine, you know that, right?"

I nod, momentarily unable to speak, and conscious that a couple of people on the next table are looking at us.

"I know I have to leave them," I tell my friend. "I know that I can't always be with them, despite what happened – and because of it. But it's not easy."

"Do you want to talk about it?" Robyn asks me. But she knows the answer.

"No," I tell her. "I want to get drunk. I want to have fun."

"Good. Let's do that then. Starting with another drink. Get that one down you, girl. You're playing catch-up."

I obey my friend and drain my first glass of wine, which is quickly replaced with another, and then another.

We order food, we people-watch, and we chat non-stop.

We reminisce – about all the years that we have been friends, and the memories that we share. We talk fondly about our boys at university who are making us so proud every day, both finding their way in this sometimes-unpredictable world, and about our girls whose kindness seems to know no bounds. And we laugh hysterically when we remember the time that Mike tripped over his shoelace in Robyn's garden one summer when he and Scott were having a race and flew headfirst into the paddling pool.

For the next three hours I allow myself to forget. That I lost my best friend. That I am a mum of five. That I am divorced after more than twenty years of marriage. That I am dating again for the first time since I was a teenager. And that I may not have known my best friend as well as I think I did.

When I arrive home at midnight I am unmistakably drunk.

And when I wake in the morning I am hungover. But I also feel a sense of achievement. That we have all managed to take this next big step in our journey together.

And I cannot wait to pick up my young children and tell them how much I love them.

When I arrive at my mum and dad's, my brother is there.

They are all in the back garden, Phoebe helping Grandad plant seeds, Zack in the baby swing giggling as Luke pushes him higher and higher.

"I'll make us all a drink," my mum says, disappearing into the kitchen.

"Have fun, did you?" Luke says, clocking the hangover I am currently wearing.

I grin.

"Actually I did," I tell him. "It was just what I needed. It was harder leaving the kids than I thought it would be, though," I add.

"I'm really proud of you, Zo," my brother says, putting his arm around me. "For what you're doing, I mean."

"It's only what I promised I would do," I tell him. "And I know if it had been the other way around, Lou would have done the same for me."

"Do you really think so?" Luke asks, in a tone I can't quite make out. Doubt? Sarcasm? A request for confirmation?

"Why?" I say. "Don't you?"

"I don't think she was as selfless as you," my brother says, cleverly avoiding the question.

He wants to say more, I can tell. But I don't push him. Because I'm hungover. And because I'm not sure I want to hear it.

"I worry," I tell him instead.

"About what?"

"About whether I'm getting it right. About whether I'm saying the right things, teaching them the right values, giving them the birthday parties that Lou would have wanted, feeding them the foods she would have chosen…"

My brother offers me a bite of his Snickers bar and we both laugh.

"Just be careful not to put Lou on a pedestal," he says. "You're a great mum, Zo. You've always been a great mum. Even with three you've made it look easy. Christ – Jess and I can barely manage with one sometimes!

"And you'll be a great mum to Phoebe and Zack too. You don't have to live up to some idea of the expectations you think Lou may or may not have had of you. She was your best friend, but she wasn't perfect. Far from it."

I know Lou wasn't perfect. Who is?

But my brother isn't talking about the girl who wore her skirts too short, or who wore make-up when she wasn't supposed to, or who once snuck a bottle of vodka into a school disco. I can tell.

I have never asked him about the argument my mum said he had with Lou when we were younger.

Has it never felt the right moment? Or did I just not want to know?

I want to ask him now, but something is stopping me.

Am I frightened of what I might discover? Frightened that it might in some way upset the fragile balance that we have somehow managed to carve out of the devastation of losing my friend.

Either way, I don't ask.

Instead I just hug my brother, for telling me that he's proud of me. Because I'm proud of me too.

Chapter Forty-Six

Going through Lou and Rich's things was always going to be hard – working out what to keep and what to let go – but I had no idea quite how tough I would find it.

We have agreed to push through with the sale of the house. I'm not sure I'll ever know if it was the right decision, but it was what they wanted when they were alive, which is the only concrete reason I have to go with. If they had died just a few weeks later the sale would have already gone through.

I have agonised over whether I should be keeping the house for Phoebe and Zack. So that when they are older they will have it as a way of remembering their parents. So that they can see the home where they were brought into the world, where they made those first precious memories.

But Mike was right. What was I going to do? Keep everything exactly as it is right now? Ready for them to visit when they are older, and are emotionally prepared?

Would I leave the fairy wallpaper on Phoebe's walls? The bright yellow digger stickers on Zack's nursery wall? The wooden playhouse in the back garden that Rich and Mike spent two days building for Phoebe's third birthday? The step that they screwed to the island when she fell off a kitchen chair one day after standing on it to make cupcakes with Lou…

Where does it stop?

How do you choose what to leave and what to pack away? Do you pack away the books on the shelves, the picture frames filled with photos of the four of them, the ornaments Lou and Rich chose together? What about the paintings haphazardly stuck on the fridge, the Peppa Pig cutlery set in the kitchen drawer, the Paw Patrol sippy cup on the draining board?

Do you just leave it all? Because without all those things it is just a shell. And with them it is … well, it's just some kind of museum. Gathering dust and waiting for its first visitors who won't be ready to visit for a long time to come.

Besides, unless you still live there, who really remembers the home where they spent their first years? I know I don't. Not even the hundreds of faded photographs filling my parents' old albums are enough to make me remember the semi-detached house in Mapleton Croft where I lived until the age of five.

We will make sure Phoebe and Zack remember Louise and Rich. They don't need a house to do that.

And we will help them make new memories with us in their new home.

After weeks of being patient, the buyers threatened to pull out.

So I have given the go-ahead.

And soon the house will no longer be Lou and Rich's – or rather Phoebe and Zack's, as it is now legally deemed to be.

So now we need to work out what we keep for them before everything else is either sold or destroyed. It's painful to think that that's what it comes down to – but it really does. We will take what we know they need now and what we know – or hope – will stir up memories somewhere down the line – and the rest will either be sold at auction, donated, or binned.

With no one else to do the job, it falls to me – and other than retrieving what I need for the children, I know I'm not strong enough to do the rest, so I have a house clearance company lined up for that.

"Ready?" Mike asks me.

He is the only person who can help me with this.

I often wonder whether I have given Mike the same support I've expected of him. It wasn't just me that lost my best friend that day. He lost his best friend too.

They met soon after I met Rich for the first time.

"I like him," Mike had said tentatively when we got back home after spending the weekend with them. He knew I had reservations.

"You can't spend the rest of your life being angry with him for taking Lou from this other guy," he told me.

"Andrew," I had reminded him. It was easy for him to forget the name of a guy he'd never met. It also made it easier for him to like Rich.

I guess they didn't have much choice in whether or not they became friends.

Lou and I were friends. So they were stuck with each other.

And they didn't seem to mind.

While Lou and I reminisced about our childhood stories, they made new stories.

When it came to work they had nothing in common. Mike crunched numbers while Rich was a sales director for a pharmaceutical company.

But it didn't matter. They just did what boys do best. They drank pints of beer. They rode their bikes. They played golf together.

When Rich married Lou and asked Mike to be his best man, Mike described him as the best friend he'd never known he needed.

There are just a few letters waiting for us on the mat this time.

I gather them up and open the door to Lou's office.

The desk is still littered with legal papers, and law books from whatever case she was working on.

She was a fantastic lawyer.

She worked so hard. And she rarely lost a case.

Sometimes I just couldn't equate that with the rebellious girl I knew at school. The one who was caught smoking weed when she should have been in a PE lesson. The one who would turn up late for a lesson and would tell the teacher to chill out when they challenged her about it.

She was already a successful lawyer by the time I embarked on my own career.

I remember meeting her in London for dinner one evening when Sophie was about two.

She regaled me with stories of dramatic court cases and lavish dinners with colleagues in expensive restaurants.

For those few hours I would live vicariously through my friend, my own life being filled only with nappies, and pureed fruits and vegetables, and playdates where I spent the entire time negotiating disputes between stubborn toddlers who both wanted the same toy.

"I'm hoping that animals will be far less complicated in comparison," I would tell her, laughing, though those days still seemed so far away.

"You'll do it," she said, crossing her legs and taking a sip of her Sauvignon Blanc, already exhibiting the sophistication you always see in Netflix series – lawyers in expensive suits drinking overpriced drinks just because they can.

"Before you know it, you'll be sticking your arm up a cow's bum, having a good feel and then enjoying a cup of tea with the farmer," she giggled. And there she was – the less sophisticated friend I remembered. The one who once threw up out of a taxi window on holiday in Ibiza and then proceeded to tell Rich she would quite like to marry him one day (whilst he paid the driver and apologised profusely with a bigger than average tip). The one who once threw a chip wrapper into the back of a police van on the way home from a night out. Not things she is likely to have included on her CV when she applied for her First Year Associate position with Massey & Stewart.

Still clutching the letters, I sit down at my friend's desk.

Mike puts a hand on my shoulder and gives it a gentle squeeze.

I don't know where to start. I am torn between wanting to sit down on the floor, in the middle of all of Lou's stuff, and just breathe it in, and wanting to walk out, shut the door behind me and never have to look at it again.

But I know that I have to do it.

When I read Phoebe a bedtime story, she will spot the tooth-shaped dent in the footboard of her bed and I will tell her the story of how Lou and Rich were on their way out for a party, and were saying goodbye to the babysitter, when they heard a scream. At only two, Phoebe couldn't tell them what had happened, but the dent in the wood told the story. She'd been jumping on her new big-girl bed and had fallen and bashed her mouth on the bed frame. I remember Lou calling me, hysterical, telling me that Phoebe wouldn't stop crying and that her mouth wouldn't stop bleeding. "The mouth always takes longer to stop bleeding," I told her calmly. "Just hold a cold flannel to it for as long as she will let you." An emergency dentist appointment the next day confirmed Phoebe had knocked her tooth loose. It re-set eventually, but Phoebe still talks about the day her mouth bled all over Mummy's pretty dress. She doesn't remember. She just sees the dent and everyone else fills in the gaps. But I don't want her to forget now, because it's a memory of her mum, and there will be no new ones to be made that include her.

When Zack is old enough he will ride the wooden trike with the yellow handles – the same one that his sister rode before she moved to a bike with stabilisers, and the same one his daddy rode when he was a boy.

And one day they will fight over the beautiful desk that their grandad made. And when they do, I will smile, knowing I have done a good job in making them yearn for even the smallest of reminders of their past.

I will watch as they look through the photo books filled with memories that Lou was meticulous about making. Phoebe's first month, Phoebe's first year, yearbooks, Christmas books, holiday books, Zack's first month... The book of Zack's first year is conspicuous in its absence, this lovely boy not yet reaching that significant milestone before he lost his parents. It will be down to me to add that one to the collection.

Mike sits on the edge of the desk and slides one of the photo books out of the bookcase.

I watch him as he turns the pages – carefully – as though they might tear, as though they are fragile, like the lives of the people who chose the pictures they hold inside.

He smiles and holds the book up to me, open at a picture of the four of us on a trip to Wales. I was pregnant with Sophie at the time. Rich had just had a button chewed off his brand-new coat by a horse who had wandered over to the edge of the field to say hello. Rich was furious – not helped by the fact that both Lou and I were laughing so much we were crying.

"Was that when a horse ate one of Rich's buttons?" Mike asks, squinting at the photo.

I allow myself to laugh – just a little – and nod.

"It's okay to laugh," Mike says. "It doesn't mean you don't miss them. It just means you're remembering some of the great times you had with them."

He hands me the book and I hold it to my chest – as if the memories inside will bring Lou back to me in some small way.

"Shall we make a start?" Mike asks me gently.

I nod and swallow back the lump that is catching in my throat.

We start downstairs. If feels easier somehow. Less sentimental.

It's hard to get emotional about dining-room furniture, or kitchen gadgets and a drawer full of takeaway menus.

Although, I do pause briefly when I open the utensil drawer and see a bright red slotted spoon, bought last year after Rich – too busy chatting to Mike whilst cooking us dinner one evening – left its predecessor on the hob and it caught fire. Cue loud smoke alarms, one wide-eyed Phoebe asking what all the noise was, and one woken baby who Lou had only just managed to settle.

The spoon was history – the brief exposure to the gas flame turning the three slats into one giant hole that only a large floret of cauliflower would withstand.

I drop the red spoon in the box by my feet, and glance over at Mike who is clearing out the fridge. From his gentle smile I know he gets it. It's a silly memory. But aren't they often the best ones?

And there are other things I can't bear to leave. A framed photograph of Lou and me, taken just after Isla was born – proof that this friendship between two schoolgirls had stood the test of time. The calendar from the kitchen wall that is covered with Lou's writing. Anniversary dates, birthdays, playdates, house viewings ... the words are irrelevant, but the writing is my friend's, and for that reason alone I can't bear to part with it.

Over the next two and a half hours we work our way through the rest of the house.

We empty furniture.

We take photos off the walls and fill boxes with toys and books.

We fill suitcases with the children's clothes – pretty dresses with flowers on them and babygrows covered in dinosaurs.

We pack Phoebe's princess bedding, her pink heart-shaped rug, the butterfly lampshade she chose with Lou when they decorated her "big-girl bedroom".

The fairy wallpaper can't come, we have explained.

Nor can the pencil marks on the wall behind her bedroom door, a record of her growth since the day she first stood independently.

"We can start a new one," Mike tells me gently, when he catches me looking at it.

We take down Zack's cot, and pack up his toys. We take a half-empty bottle of Calpol, and the baby scissors from the bathroom cabinet, the bathmat with the ducks all over it, the soft towels with the character hoods – Cinderella, Dora the Explorer, George Pig, the Gruffalo...

When we reach Lou and Rich's bedroom, I falter.

Mike knows there is nothing he can say to make this easier, so he doesn't even try. He just squeezes my hand as I open the door.

As quickly as we can, we stuff clothes into bags destined for the charity shop, keeping just a couple of items for the children – a blue check shirt of Rich's, and a Christmas jumper of Lou's with three penguins wearing Santa hats – because I know Phoebe loves it.

On a mirrored dressing table underneath the window sit two framed photographs – one of Phoebe and one of Zack – taken when they were each just a few days old, in between them two half-empty bottles of perfume. I sit down on the stool and open the dressing-table drawer.

Lou's wedding ring.

It would have shocked me a few months ago – seeing the symbol of their marriage casually sitting in the bottom of a drawer. Forgotten. Seemingly not needed.

But now it just feels inevitable.

I know now that they weren't happy.

I just don't know why. I don't know why they couldn't get past whatever it was that was making them unhappy.

They tried so hard to have the family that they dreamed of, and then they were willing to just throw it away.

But why?

I take the ring out of the drawer and turn it over in my hand, as if doing so will give me the answers I am looking for.

I don't show Mike.

I know I need to move on. But he can no longer tell me that they were happy. Because I know that's just not true.

I drop the ring into a shoebox along with some other precious things I cannot bring myself to leave. Then I remove the lid of one of the perfume bottles and put the nozzle to my nose. I am instantly engulfed in a sadness that quite literally takes my breath away. It is crushing. I look up in the mirror long enough to notice

Mike drop the bag he is holding and rush to my side, wrapping his arms around me, my hand still firmly around the bottle.

We sit there like that for what feels like forever, saying nothing, the weight of my ex-husband's body the only thing stopping the flood of tears.

Eventually I pull away, wipe a stray tear from my face and put the bottle into the shoebox to take home. I don't know if I will ever be able to smell that scent again without it taking my breath away, but in case I need to, it will be there, sitting in that box – a random collection of nostalgia that might one day, when I am ready, help brighten up a sad day.

And then we continue.

I open Lou's bedside drawer and I feel like I am intruding in a private world.

Bedside drawers are our sanctuary – the place where we should be able to expect that our most private, and most precious things will be untouched. It feels wrong to be searching through them. But who else is going to do it?

The contents resemble my own. Uninspired. Unexciting. Conspicuously free of sexy lingerie. Or sex toys. Or books on how to have multiple orgasms. Instead the drawers are filled with a random collection of things – the pieces that make up the story of my friend – of the life she was living before it was snatched away without warning. Hairbands and nail files, half-empty packets of paracetamol, an empty ring box and a book of quotes about being a mum.

I move the book and it is right then that the delicate edges of our new life begin to very gradually fray.

Underneath the book – and a letter addressed to Santa – is a card. Torn open. Concealed by the otherwise unremarkable contents of this drawer. It looks insignificant, but I know instinctively that it's not.

It feels out of place.

Like it shouldn't be there. Like its very existence threatens to unbalance the new world we are only just beginning to figure out.

I hold it in my hands, not daring to open it, for fear of the truth it holds inside.

The white envelope is nondescript.

It doesn't scream of betrayal or infidelity.

It doesn't tell me that my best friend broke a vow.

But the writing on the front does not belong to Rich.

I have known Rich for more than twenty years. I know his writing. This is not his writing.

I look over at Mike, quietly sorting through the contents of the drawers on the other side of the bed, and he smiles at me reassuringly, oblivious to the discovery I think I might have made.

Could the card in my hand hold the answers I have been looking for?

Could it tell me something about my friend that I never knew she was hiding from me?

Desperate to know the truth, and yet not quite ready to, I smile back at Mike and quietly slide the card into my handbag.

Seven hours after we arrived at the home Lou and Rich made for their beautiful family, the job Mike and I came here to do is done.

In those few short hours it has changed from being the centre of so many happy memories to being just a container. A holding bay for the memories – categorised, marked up and ready to be moved out and stored until we are ready to unpack them, to unpick them, and to piece them back together for the little people that they will eventually mean so much to.

Locking the door for the very last time, we load the bags of remaining essentials into the car and drive away. Both of us silent. Both of us contemplating in our own way the enormity of what we have just done.

Chapter Forty-Seven

I am relieved to get back to the surgery on Monday morning.

In a world currently dictated by difficult decisions, emotional choices, and the complicated needs of two small people, I am grateful for the mundane. For the cat that won't stop vomiting. For the dog that has gone off his food. For the hamster who is still going strong well past the usual sell-by date for these furry friends that aren't supposed to require a long-term commitment.

I fill in paperwork, I prescribe anti-sickness medicines and take bloods to send off to the lab, I laugh with my staff about the funny story on the breakfast show about pets who look like their owners.

And in between all that I read a message from Phoebe's school reminding me it's Pirate Day on Monday and asking all Year 1 parents to send in a carrier bag next week as they will be bringing home their junk modelling projects. The joy I feel at the thought of her bringing home a robot crafted out of old cereal packets and the remnants of a roll of tin foil makes me realise how far we have come.

The card has been burning a hole in my handbag since the weekend, tucked inside one of the photo books from Lou's office.

I haven't been able to bring myself to open it.

I'm scared of what it might tell me about my friend.

I want to believe that I knew her. That the three decades we shared as friends were real. That this – whatever it was – was the only thing she ever hid from me.

I sit in my car outside the surgery, pulling the book out of my bag on the passenger seat.

I look through the pages and see my teenage self staring back at me. I am instantly taken back to my youth – Lou and I in our school uniforms, her shorter-than-short grey skirt, her top button undone in protest behind the knot of her navy-and-grey striped tie, a look of pure rebellion on both our faces. Both of us so young, so sure of ourselves, but with so much to learn about the world.

There are photographs from the barge trip and of Lou in the car her parents bought her for her eighteenth birthday – the same furry dice she'd bought me hanging from the rear-view mirror. And there's one of Lou and I on a camping weekend in Devon when it rained so much, our tent caved under the weight of the water.

I kiss the tips of my fingers, and gently touch the face of the girl on the pages in front of me. My best friend.

Then I slip the card out from inside the front cover and drop the book back into my bag.

I slide the card out of the envelope and open it, my hands shaking.

A Christmas card.

It's not from Rich. I know that much.

Nor is it from a client or a colleague, or an associate at the Magistrates' Court, or the Crown Court, or any other court.

This card is from someone that matters.

I stare at the words inside, feeling the strength of my lifelong friendship crumbling under their weight.

To my darling Lou. The love of my life. Happy Christmas. With love. X

My mind immediately starts flicking through the filing cabinet of memories for something to reassure me, to tell me that this doesn't mean anything.

But I have nothing and can feel a panic rising in my stomach.

For what I am about to unravel. For a friend who clearly had secrets she couldn't share with me. And for a friendship that may not have been everything I thought it was.

I slide the card back into its envelope, put it on the passenger seat, and put my car back into drive before I am completely consumed by the enormity of what I have just seen.

All the way to nursery my eyes are drawn to the writing on the envelope – the loop of the L in my best friend's name that I have never seen her husband use, the neat bold line underneath that somehow demonstrates the audacity of its scriber.

The writing is not Rich's. I know that much, but it feels familiar somehow. Like I have seen it before.

Have I just stared at it for too long? Is that why it is now a familiar scrawl etched into my brain whilst at the same time strange and disconcerting? Or *have* I seen it before?

I pick Zack up and barely hear his carer talking me through his day. I hear "sleep" and "macaroni" and "puppets", but little more.

I strap him into his car seat and get back into the car, picking up the card for another quick look – checking it is real, checking I haven't imagined this scenario in which my best friend was cheating on her husband.

Chapter Forty-Eight

Rich proposed to Lou on holiday in Antigua. On the beach at sunset.

The ring was barely on her finger before she phoned me.

"It was so romantic," she said. "He got down on one knee and everything."

Though I wouldn't have changed my world for anything, I envied her the romantic proposal on a beach in the Caribbean. A backdrop of white sands and delicate fairy lights, the waves glistening under the sunset.

Mike proposed to me – six months pregnant with Sophie – on a rare night out while my parents babysat Oliver.

My hands were so swollen he couldn't get the ring on my finger, and I had barely said yes before I had to get up to use the toilet, as our unborn daughter was pressing so heavily on my bladder.

"I'm so happy for you Lou," I told her.

And then…

"Do you think I am doing the right thing?"

Her question caught me by surprise.

It had never occurred to me that Lou wouldn't say yes if Rich proposed.

———

I wasn't Rich's biggest fan at first, admittedly.

But once I got to know him I loved him and could see how right he was for my friend.

He made her happy.

Lou asked me once what it felt like to love someone so much that you'd be prepared to give up everything.

She had seen me put my career on hold for Mike – for our family – and she wanted to know what a love like that felt like.

I thought – I believed – that eventually that was how she felt about Rich.

So when she asked me if she should marry him, it never occurred to me to say no.

"Do you think he's right for me, Zo?" she asked. "Do you think he's the one? Do you think I should marry him?"

"Do you love him?" I asked.

"Yes, I love him. Of course I love him."

"Then marry him," I said.

But maybe the very fact that she had even asked me that question was everything I needed to know.

Maybe instead of asking her if she loved him, I should have asked her if she loved him enough?

Did she love him enough to give up everything?

———

She'd cheated on Andrew. Twice. That I knew of, anyway.

But I never imagined she would cheat on Rich.

I feel foolish for that now.

She fooled me. Just like she fooled Rich.

Once a cheater, always a cheater. Isn't that what they say?

Chapter Forty-Nine

When I tell Mike that night, he does not react like a man finding out for the first time that his ex-wife's best friend cheated on her husband. Far from it.

He doesn't tell me not to be ridiculous. Or that I must be mistaken. Or that there will be an innocent explanation. For all of it. For the argument Lou and Rich had the night of the accident. For the spare room that Rich had moved into. For the wedding ring sitting redundant in the bottom of Lou's dressing-table drawer. And for the card hidden away in her bedside table.

He says nothing. He just stares at the card sitting on the kitchen table in front of him – like a neon sign declaring my best friend's infidelity.

He looks guilty.

He looks like this is not news to him.

And suddenly my heart is pounding so hard I can barely breathe.

Nothing is impossible.

Nothing is off the table.

I thought I knew my best friend, and I clearly didn't.

And so it is perfectly plausible that she would not stop at stealing my husband.

She said so herself – she wanted to know what it felt like to love someone enough to give up everything.

Did she love Mike enough to give up Rich? To give up our friendship?

"It was you," I say, eventually, the words barely audible.

He says nothing, just runs his hands through his hair. Exhausted. Looking for the right words to say.

And for a moment I am broken.

And then he shakes his head. And I know immediately that it is not an expression of denial. Or even of admission. It is one of hurt. Of crushing disappointment that I could even think that was a possibility.

"Don't be ridiculous," he says eventually.

Of course it wasn't Mike. He was far too busy working to ever find the time for an affair.

"You can hardly blame me," I shout. "You told me to let it go. You told me they were happy. All along you've been telling me I've been worrying for no reason."

"You *have* been worrying for no reason," he says, exasperated. "What is the point in all of this? They are dead, Zoe. They are gone. What good can come of this?"

I know they're gone. But hearing the man I loved for more than twenty years remind me like this stings, and I can't hold back the tears.

"I'm sorry," he says, pulling me into his arms. "I shouldn't have said that."

"Why?" I say. "It's true, isn't it? They are gone."

"I shouldn't have shouted. I'm sorry. Let's get the kids to bed, and then I'll tell you everything I know," he says.

I look at him, incredulous.

Everything?

Everything suggests there is a lot to tell.

Everything suggests I didn't know my friend at all.

"How did you find out?" I ask Mike, when I have kissed my best friend's children goodnight, told them that I love them, told them that their mummy and daddy loved them too. So much.

"Which one?" he says quietly, and I can only stare at him and will back the tears that are threatening to engulf me.

"There was more than one?" I eventually ask. I feel foolish. Naive. Betrayed.

"There were two," he says quietly. "That I know of," he adds quickly. It is a rather late demonstration of his honesty, I know, but the implication that there may have been more only makes it worse.

"Let's start with the first one," I tell him, now resigned to my friend's infidelity, and perhaps deluded that having the detail will make it easier to accept somehow.

"It was three years ago," he says, hardly daring to look at me, aware his own betrayal is hurting me almost as much as my friend's.

He should have told me.

"I saw her with him in a café outside Waterloo Station. It was obvious they weren't just two colleagues having a coffee together.

"I wouldn't have done anything. Not right there and then, anyway. But she saw me, so I went over. And I watched the blood drain from her face.

"She didn't introduce him. She didn't need to. I knew everything I needed to know."

"What did he look like?" I ask him.

It's irrelevant, but I need to know.

"Was he dark? Blond? Tall? Short?"

Who was this man that my friend was prepared to risk her marriage for?

Was it someone she met at work? Someone she met on her daily commute? Someone from the gym? A neighbour? A parent at Phoebe's school that I unknowingly stood next to in the playground in those early days after her death?

Was it the same man that Simon saw her with in the pub?

Does it make it better or worse if it was the same man?

Is one long affair better or worse than a string of one-night stands?

Is a long affair more of a betrayal? Because it suggests more than just sex. Or is it a greater infidelity to go from one to another like sordid notches on a bedpost?

"It was three years ago, Zo."

"Try," I say. "Please."

"What difference does it make?"

"It makes no difference at all," I admit. "But I need to know. Please."

"He was dark-haired," he says. "Wearing a suit."

"Attractive?" I ask.

He shrugs his shoulders.

"I guess so. He was married too," he adds. Quietly. Like he knows this tiny detail makes the whole story more seedy. More significant. More catastrophic. More damning.

When I look at him questioningly, he holds up his hand, wiggles his wedding-ring finger.

And then, I don't know if it is the enormity of what he has just told me, or the sight of the soft dent in Mike's finger, where his wedding ring once sat – or both – but I put my head in my hands and I sob.

He wraps his arms around me. Again. And tells me it will all be okay.

But I'm not sure how it can be.

I feel like I never really knew my best friend. Like she was a stranger. Someone who could go through something potentially so life-changing and not tell me. The person who had known her the longest. The one with whom she shared so many memories.

"I called her that afternoon," Mikes says. "I told her to end it. Or I would tell Rich. And you."

"And did she?" I ask.

"She said she would. She said it was a mistake. A brief fling that didn't mean anything."

"Did you believe her?"

I am in unfamiliar territory now, when it comes to Lou.

I'm in a place where she is someone not to be trusted, where she is someone you would have reason not to believe.

It's disconcerting. And it's painful.

But I need to know.

I don't want half a story.

"I had to believe her," Mike says. "I couldn't let it consume me. Six months later she and Rich came to Dubai with us, and they seemed happier than ever."

I remember. They *were* happy. And we were busy falling apart.

"So I assumed it was exactly what she'd said. A brief fling. A mistake. I don't think she ever told Rich. I guess she just figured there was no need."

"I wish you'd told *me*," I tell him.

"I know," he says softly. "But what would it have achieved? I could see no point in telling either of you. In hurting Rich. In telling you that your best friend had done something that would crush you. It was over as far as I was concerned."

"And the second?" I ask eventually. "Was it the same man?"

"I don't know. I honestly don't. It was about six months ago. Rich found a message on her phone. It was pretty conclusive, let's put it that way. They'd both been away for the weekend. Rich with his work and Lou with hers.

"Let's just say the 'thanks for a lovely weekend' text he found on her phone was not referring to a two-day conference about the workings of the British judicial system."

"What did he do?"

"He confronted her. And she broke down. Said she was sorry. Said it would never happen again. The usual.

"He phoned me that night. Asked me if he could stay at the flat for a few days while he got his head straight."

"Did you tell him? About the first time?"

"No," he says. "I was going to. And then I realised I didn't want to be the reason they didn't get another shot. It had to be his decision. He already knew what she was capable of. If he was prepared to forgive her for that, then it wouldn't have made any difference knowing it wasn't the first time."

"He couldn't forgive her, could he?" I say quietly.

I already know the answer.

Mike shakes his head.

"He was trying to. They sold the house so they could have a fresh start. But he wasn't sure. He suggested they live separately for a while."

"If they were splitting up, why did they go to Heidi and Stephen's wedding together?" I ask, acutely – painfully – aware that had they not, they might still both be alive.

"I don't know. Because it was all arranged? Because she begged him not to make her go on her own? I don't know."

"And this time? Why didn't you tell me this time? They were splitting up. Did you not think I should know?"

"We're divorced, Zo," he says, and it stings for some reason. "It wasn't my news to tell. It was up to Lou to tell you. Or Rich. Not me."

"So why didn't she?" I ask, though I know he doesn't have the answers.

"Honestly, I don't think she wanted to accept it was happening," he says eventually. "She'd screwed up. Twice. And she was hoping beyond hope that she would get another chance. Another opportunity to get it right."

"Is that everything you know?" I ask him.

"Yes," he says. "I promise." I know he is aware how empty his promises feel right now.

He moves my wine glass to the side and takes hold of my hand.

"You need to move on now, Zoe," he tells me. "You are going to make yourself ill trying to figure all of this out.

"She was still Lou. She was still your friend. And the mother of your godchildren. This doesn't change any of that. She loved those children. And she loved you. And right now that is all that is important.

"I mean, look who she chose to be their mum when she couldn't do it anymore."

I allow myself to smile at this. My ex-husband. The charmer. The one who could always make me smile.

"Mike," I say, opening the door to see him out, emotionally exhausted. "Why didn't you tell me? Now, I mean? They're gone anyway. Why didn't you tell me everything?"

He looks at me, his eyes filled with compassion, with love for the mother of his children and with regret that we couldn't make forever work.

"Because you were already hurting enough," he says. And then he closes the door and goes home.

Chapter Fifty

When Phoebe goes back to school after the Easter holidays it feels like the start of a new chapter for us all.

Everyone is happier.

Phoebe is happier.

I am trying my best to move on. To stop dwelling on questions that I will probably never have the answers to.

It isn't easy. But I have to try. For everyone's sake.

Including mine.

On Friday I spend the night with Simon. We've not seen each other in three weeks. He's been busy. I've been busy.

I haven't missed him like I feel I should have.

I have thought about him. Of course I have. But I haven't yearned for him in the way I did for Mike when we first met.

I try to tell myself it's because I'm older. No longer a love-sick teenager. I have more important things to occupy my day than thinking about a boy, and when I'll next see him.

I'm a vet. I'm a mum. I have school runs to manage, and playdates, and dance clubs.

I have spellings and times-tables to chant, a house to clean, a dog to walk.

It can't all be about candle-lit dinners and romance.

But is it that? Or am I just not ready to share my crazy, chaotic, unplanned life with anyone?

Sophie is out so Robyn is babysitting.

It didn't seem right, somehow, asking my ex-husband to have the children so that I can have sex with my boyfriend.

One of the joys of double standards, I guess you could say.

Mike gets to spend all the time he wants with his girlfriend without giving his children a second thought.

I'm being unfair, though.

Mike has been brilliant these past few weeks.

He has really stepped up.

He's not once been late to collect Phoebe.

He's done her reading with her. He's made her dinner. He's comforted her when she's had a bad day – because she's missing her mummy, or just because she didn't like what Theo said about her painting.

He even took biscuits in for the Friday fundraiser. Yes, he bought them from the supermarket, but he still did it.

He's done everything he said he would. And more.

I guess I just wish he'd done it sooner.

"You look great," Simon tells me, kissing me on the lips when he picks me up.

It's been more than ten months now and we're well past the kiss-on-the-cheek greeting. But this doesn't feel right tonight. And I can't shake that feeling.

I want to feel more. And I feel guilty that I don't right now.

Simon has been with me through the darkest time in my life.

It wasn't planned that way.

It was accidental.

He came into my life just before tragedy struck.

And then he stayed.

Out of a sense of obligation, maybe? Or sympathy? Or because I was worth it?

Or maybe because he had been there and was the right person to help me navigate my way through the darkness.

Simon taught me that children are resilient. That they bounce back. From the saddest of places.

He taught me that they are adaptable. And that as long as they feel safe and loved, then they will love you back and just get on with life.

One day they will shout at me that I'm not their mum. That I can't tell them what to do. That they hate the fact that it's me taking them to their school prom and not their mum.

And I will be ready for that.

They will tell me that their mum and dad would have done things differently.

Phoebe will tell me that her mum and dad would have let her stay over at her boyfriend's house despite only being fifteen.

Zack will tell me that they wouldn't have grounded him for skipping school.

They would have given them more pocket money, they'll tell me, more freedom, more time on their phones.

And I will have to tell them – again – that their mum and dad chose me. That they trusted me. To make the best possible choices I could for the people they loved most in the world.

"How has your week been?" Simon asks me, breaking both my thoughts and the silence hanging between us.

"Good," I say.

A few months ago I'm sure he was afraid to even ask that question.

The worst bit about my week these days is a family pet that I've just not been able to save, which though devastating, pales into insignificance when you have to tell a five-year-old over and over again that her mummy is never coming back.

"Polly was back in," I tell him.

"No!" he chuckles.

I told Simon about Polly on our first date. The parrot that won't stop talking.

The first time I ever met Polly, she told me to sod off. Over and over again. I didn't take it personally.

"She has started talking to Alexa, apparently," I tell Simon.

"That's hilarious. What's she saying?"

"Asking her to play Barry Manilow, by all accounts. There's not much I can do about that, obviously. I mean, if that's the music she's into…"

I laugh, and Simon reaches for my hand.

"It's good to hear you laugh," he says.

He seems nervous, and I wonder if he's feeling the same as me. That maybe we are going through the motions. Both of us wanting more, both of us knowing that it can feel better than this. We go out for dinner. We drink wine and eat spaghetti and talk about our children. He tells me that Jenny wants to get a tattoo – and to get her tongue pierced. And I tell him that my best friend was having an affair before she died.

We offer each other our deepest condolences and then we go back to Simon's and have sex.

It's still fresh and exciting. We still have so much of each other to explore. I'm just not sure it's what either of us really wants.

I wake early, quietly slip back into the clothes I abandoned at the side of Simon's bed last night and let myself out.

———

"Maybe you've just had too much going on to really invest in the relationship," Robyn tells me when I get home and try to explain how I'm feeling.

I don't even know myself how I'm feeling, never mind trying to explain it to someone else.

"Tell me you didn't just leave without saying goodbye," she says, putting a coffee down in front of me, and handing Zack a finger of toast.

He drops it on the floor and immediately holds out his hand for a replacement.

"I didn't," I confirm. "I gave him a kiss, and told him I'd see him next weekend," I clarify.

She looks at me questioningly.

I take a swig of coffee and put the mug back down on the table dramatically.

"It's his sister's fortieth," I say. "Big party. All the family."

I'm well aware I should be feeling far more excited about this particular social engagement than I am.

"You could just use him for the sex," Robyn says eventually, holding her hands over Zack's ears theatrically on the final word. "I mean, you said he was good at it," she laughs.

I don't correct her.

"Why not? You survived with none of it for the best part of a year. You've got some serious catching up to do."

"More," I remind her, in reference to the sexual drought in mine and Mike's relationship in our final months together.

"Well then," she says, taking a bite of Zack's banana, and holding it in her mouth a fraction longer than is strictly necessary.

I open the door to the den just to confirm that yes, both Phoebe and Isla are engrossed in Peppa Pig and YouTube and therefore blissfully unaware of the mildly pornographic conversation going on in the kitchen.

When Robyn has gone home Phoebe and I spend the morning working on the latest task set by her therapist.

When I picked her up last week Poppy explained that when they have lost someone they love, children can sometimes worry that they will forget things about them.

So we are making a memory box.

Something she can fill with things that remind her of Mummy and Daddy.

While Sophie watches Zack we go to Hobbycraft where Phoebe chooses a little wooden box, and some things to decorate it with.

"Mummy liked pink," she tells me, pulling a packet of pink sequins down from a hook and dropping it into our basket.

I clock her use of the past tense, and immediately want to wrap my arms around her for being so brave.

But I don't.

Phoebe doesn't know she's being brave. This is just her new normal. When Mummy was here she liked pink things and giraffes. And now she's not here anymore. Simple.

She holds my hand as we walk up and down the aisles,

picking out pink heart-shaped stickers, bottles of glitter and reels of ribbon.

"I need something green too," she tells me quietly as we're stood at the counter to pay, looking shyly at the shop assistant.

"Daddy liked green."

"We won't be a minute," I tell the girl who, though she cannot possibly know the reason for our visit, smiles kindly at Phoebe and tells us to take all the time we need.

No young child should have to do this – make a box in which to store memories of a parent that they have lost, let alone two.

When we get home we tip the contents of the bag onto the kitchen table and set to work.

This is Phoebe's project. Her design. I am merely here to help open packets of glitter and cut coloured ribbon to the specified length.

She is so proud of it when it is done, and I'm proud of her.

When she's ready I hand her a box of Lou and Rich's things from the house.

A pre-selected assortment of items that will mean something but hopefully not make her too sad. Photos. Lou's jewellery. Some little ornaments. Last year's calendar from the kitchen that I can use to help her remember fun times they all had together.

While she's picking out what she wants, I look through the calendar.

All of our birthdays are on there – each marked with our name and a number in a circle.

There's Zack's vaccination appointments, and Phoebe's playdates, the trip to the zoo when Phoebe fell over and cut her hand and got to stroke the giraffes for being so brave.

There are house viewings, and visits to the dentist and days when either Lou or Rich were away for work.

And the weekend Phoebe and Zack came to me at the end of the summer, when they both had to be away at the same time.

"I'm ready, Auntie Zoe," Phoebe tells me quietly.

"Well done, poppet," I say. "Do you want to show me what you've chosen?"

She nods and climbs onto my knee, sliding the items over in front of us both.

Whenever she needs to, Phoebe will look in her memory box.

She'll take out the pretty giraffe brooch that was her mummy's and put it on her dolly's dress for a few minutes before returning it to the box. She'll hold the photo of her and her daddy showing off the snowman they built last winter, and for a moment she'll look like she's gone to that place in her mind. And she'll take out the handkerchief that we sprayed with Rich's aftershave and breathe it in, not fully realising that one day the smell will fade, and so will her memories.

I try not to dwell on the fact that my memory box – if I made one – would now contain a discarded wedding ring and a card that showed me I didn't know my friend as well as I thought.

I want to know who it was that was so special, my friend was prepared to risk everything.

But I know I probably never will.

I have to move on.

So that we can all move on.

Chapter Fifty-One

Mike is decorating Phoebe's new bedroom today. Oliver's old bedroom. Eventually we will also decorate one of the guest rooms for Zack, but that can wait a while, as things for the youngest tend to do.

She has chosen a bright pink paint and some unicorn wall stickers. A change from the fairies in her old bedroom. A new chapter marked by a new mythical creature.

Painting is not Mike's forte.

When he decorated Isla's bedroom a couple of years after we first moved into Newman Gardens, he managed to cover the skirting boards, the ceiling, and the plug sockets with almost as much paint as he got on the walls.

When I politely suggested he might want to get the decorators in next time – that nobody can be good at everything – he said it made him happy to decorate his children's bedrooms.

So I followed him around the room with a damp cloth and a pot of white ceiling paint instead.

When Oliver offered to give up his bedroom to Phoebe, Mike immediately said he wanted to be the one to decorate it.

He wanted her to feel special. This time I never even mentioned the decorators.

———

I pick Zack up on my way home and just after 6pm I walk into what can only be described as a happy house.

The girls are all in the front room – Isla and Sophie watching some American baking show on the television, and Phoebe playing with her dolls on the carpet next to them.

"Hi, girls," I say.

Not one of them looks up. And I smile to myself.

"Where's your dad?" I ask.

Oblivious to either my presence or my question, Sophie comments disparagingly that she's sure she could do a much better job than the contestant on the show who, as far as I can see, is attempting to make a fondant penguin to put on the top of a cupcake.

Isla laughs. "No you couldn't," she says.

"No you couldn't, Sophie," Phoebe says, though it's unlikely she even knows what it is Sophie couldn't do, as she's not even facing the television.

Sophie reaches over and gives Phoebe a little tickle.

"Oi, cheeky!" she says, and Phoebe giggles.

I put Zack on Sophie's lap, with instructions to keep hold of him until I get back.

"Where are you going?" she asks, finally acknowledging my presence.

"Upstairs," I tell her. "To check on your dad."

"He's painting," she says.

"Yes, he's painting," Phoebe confirms, putting a cowboy boot on one of her Barbie dolls.

"I thought you were helping him, Phoebs," I say.

"I did!" she says, with the same indignant tone of a child who has been asked to tidy their toys and has managed to put one solitary Duplo brick in the toy box before acting like they've done a full day's work.

I smile.

"Oh, okay. Well done then, poppet."

I leave Sophie trying to keep Zack on her lap so she can continue watching bakers make Arctic animals to go on top of their winter-themed cupcakes, and head up to inspect Phoebe's extensive painting efforts.

I am halfway up the stairs when the smell of paint hits my nose.

I gently push open the door and see Mike, up a stepladder, roller in hand. He turns around and grins. He has splatters of pink paint up his arms, on his forehead and in his hair.

"Looking good," I say.

"Well thanks," he grins, holding the roller up and striking a pose. "I think the colour suits me."

"I meant the walls," I say, smiling. "Phoebe says she helped you?"

He grins.

"For all of five minutes," he laughs. "And then she decided her time would be better spent watching television with the girls."

"You look like you're almost done," I say, scanning the walls.

"It'll need another coat, I think. It's hard to tell because of the light, but you can still see the green underneath in some areas."

"Are you staying for dinner?" I ask.

I want him to say yes. And that feels unsettling.

———

I look at the man in front of me, with flecks of pink paint in his hair and bits of masking tape stuck to his jeans. He reminds me of the man I once loved. The man who threw his little boy up in the air and waited for him to squeal before doing it again. The man who wanted to paint a purple bedroom for his little girl – even if it looked like she'd done it herself – just to show her how much he loved her. The man who tried his best to be a fun dad to his children – and only fell short because he was so busy making sure he could give them everything they could ever need. Not realising that all they ever really needed was him.

"I've got some chicken in the fridge," I tell him. "Unless you're seeing Charlotte," I add. It's thrown in as an afterthought, and yet it's disconcertingly all I can think about.

He shakes his head.

"No, I'm not," he says, scratching at a bit of paint on his hand. "That would be great. But I can always grab something when I get home."

"It's no bother," I tell him.

"Then thank you – that would be lovely. I'm just going to paint behind the radiator, and then I'll be down."

"Okay," I say, heading out of the door, confused by what I am feeling right now.

I throw some fish fingers and chips in the oven for the kids.

I did, of course, offer Sophie and Isla the more grown-up honey mustard chicken that I am making for Mike and me, but they both jumped at the chance of this throwback dinner, only half-joking that they would be expecting jelly and ice-cream for dessert.

I can't help but wonder whether their choice might also have something to do with leaving me alone with their dad.

My honey mustard chicken is one of Mike's favourites. It has been ever since the first time I made it for him when we moved into our flat.

I'm not really sure why I'm making his favourite dish.

———————

The fish fingers have been demolished and half a tub of ice-cream has been devoured by the time Mike appears, carrying the roller tray and two paint brushes.

Zack crawls across the floor and holds his arms out to him.

Handing me the brushes, Mike scoops him up.

"You look funny, Uncle Mike," Phoebe tells him.

"Why's that, Phoebs?" he grins.

"Your hair's gone pink!"

"Oh no! Has it?!" he jokes.

"Do you think Mummy will like my new bedroom?" she asks.

I am only very briefly thrown by her use of the present tense.

This is just the latest of questions about Mummy and Daddy.

"Do you think Mummy can see me right now?"

"Do you think Daddy will be happy that Zack can say 'ball' now?"

"Do you think Mummy will be cross that I didn't eat my vegetables?"

We have told her that Mummy and Daddy are watching over all of us every day. Making sure that Phoebe is being kind to Zack. That Auntie Zoe doesn't forget to buy the unicorn bubble bath. That Uncle Mike doesn't eat all the Hawaiian pizza.

So I tell her the truth.

"Yes, I think Mummy will love your new bedroom."

Mike offers to put Phoebe and Zack to bed while I finish preparing our dinner.

After kissing them goodnight, he checks in on his big girls, both of whom are FaceTiming their friends and both of whom blow him a swift kiss before shooing him out of their rooms.

And then it's just us.

———

"This looks great," he says, sitting down next to me, and opening the bottle of beer I have set down for him.

"You didn't need to do this, you know. We could have ordered a takeaway."

"I know. I just thought I'd treat you. After doing such a great job of Phoebe's new room."

He pulls a face.

"Well, I'm not sure about that," he laughs. "But she seems to like it."

He sips his beer and I'm suddenly aware of feeling something I have never felt around Mike before.

Nervous.

Right now – sitting together in the home that we built together but no longer share, I am confused by what I am feeling.

Is it just fear? Of doing all of this alone? And desperately wanting someone – anyone – to share the burden with?

Is it nostalgia? For the love we once shared?

Or is it new love?

———

Sitting across the table from him, sharing a dinner I chose only because it's his favourite, talking about our day over a glass of wine and a bottle of beer – it feels wrong.

It feels like I am cheating on Simon.

But it also feels more right than anything has felt for the last twelve months.

"Why are you doing all of this, Mike?" I ask him.

"I just want to make the room nice for her," he says.

"I don't mean that. I mean all of this. Everything you are doing. Picking Phoebe up. Having her every afternoon. Spending so much time with us."

"I told you," he says. "I didn't want you to have to give up your career again."

"I know. But how come you can suddenly find all this time? I'd been asking you for years. To give us all more of your time. To give *me* more of your time. To put your laptop away and look at me. To remember what it was about me that you fell in love with."

He puts his beer down and goes to hold my hand but stops himself and puts his hands on the table instead.

"I never forgot," he says quietly. "I was a fool. I think I just thought you'd always be there. So I focused on making as much money as I could. For us. For the family we'd made. So that we could have the life we'd always dreamed of."

"But we already had the life we'd always dreamed of," I tell him. Not for the first time. "We had three beautiful children. A lovely house. Great friends. Holidays. All the things we could ever want."

"I think I just always wanted us to have more," he says.

I'm aching to reach out to him. To hold his hand and tell him he was all I ever needed.

But I can't.

Because he broke my heart.

He broke his promise that he would never stop looking at me the way he looked at me the day he first told me that he loved me.

All the school runs in the world can't change that.

He finishes his beer and wraps his hands tightly around the bottle. To stop himself reaching out to touch me?

"When you told me you were giving up your job, I knew I couldn't stand by and watch you abandon your dream for a second time," he says.

"I let you do that once before. I asked you to. I couldn't do that again.

"Losing Lou and Rich like that shocked me to the core. It took me a while to realise just how much."

He looks up at me and I see a pain in his eyes that I've not seen before.

Maybe I've just been too immersed in my own grief.

Mike lost his best friend too.

They didn't have the history Lou and I had, but they had been friends for almost twenty years. That's not insignificant.

"He was just a year younger than me," he says. "One minute we were planning a game of squash, and the next he's gone. They are both gone. In a heartbeat. And their children are left without their parents.

"Thank God they have you," he says, hastily brushing a tear from the corner of his eye.

"Us," I whisper, the word barely audible, so crushed am I that it's an "us" that is now broken.

"I looked at what those children have lost, and I think I finally realised that there is more to life than just earning as much as I can," Mike tells me.

"So I took a step back. Christ, I've worked hard enough for the last twenty years to finally put the brakes on a little. To spend a bit of time on something other than work."

"I wish you'd realised this a long time ago," I tell him.

"So do I," he says, running his hand through his hair, a look of resignation in his eyes.

"Is it too late, do you think?" he asks me quietly.

I clasp my hands together on the table, suddenly conscious of the emptiness where my wedding ring once sat, and I look at my ex-husband. Regretful. Changed. Resigned.

"I don't know," I tell him eventually.

Because right now I don't.

Chapter Fifty-Two

That weekend I end things with Simon.

We go to his sister's birthday party together. An 80s-themed party. Fancy dress compulsory. Simon goes as Boy George and I wear a fabulous Rubik's Cube print dress that Sophie and Isla found on Amazon. It has a matching handbag and everything. It's my favourite fancy dress costume ever.

We dance to 80s tunes all night, we cheer as Simon's brother-in-law shows us his breakdancing moves and we drink far too many pina coladas.

And when we get back to the hotel where we are staying for the night, Simon tells me that he loves me.

He knows immediately that I don't love him back.

I tell him I'm sorry. That our timing was shocking. That from the moment I lost my best friend I was lost.

He asks if I have feelings for Mike, and I tell him the truth. I tell him I don't know.

He tells me it's hard to compete with the history that we share.

I want to tell him that he is not competing with the past. I want to tell him that he is competing only with the man my ex-husband has become. Since we both lost our best friends.

But of course I don't.

Because he is not competing at all.

Mike is not mine.

Chapter Fifty-Three

When Mike first told me he'd met someone, it hurt. A lot. I felt blindsided.

This wasn't supposed to happen. Yes, I'd pushed for the divorce. But neither of us was ever meant to meet someone else. That wasn't part of the plan.

It was Robyn who pointed out how unreasonable I was being.

"He's moving on," she told me bluntly, over a bottle of wine and a Chinese, six months after Mike moved out of our family home. "It's what you wanted. You can't be mad at him for that. That's not fair."

It took me a while but eventually I accepted she was right. I had no right to begrudge Mike this happiness, even if it did hurt to hear about him finding the time to take someone out to dinner that he could never seem to find for me.

It feels different now, though.

I don't think I'm hurt that Mike is giving another woman the time I wished he'd given me.

My feelings are far more complex than that.

I think I might be jealous.

Chapter Fifty-Four

The first time Oliver ever called me Mummy – or Mama, at least – my heart melted. He was eleven months old, and Mike and I had taken him to the beach near my parents' house. We had put him down while we unpacked the picnic and the buckets and spades, but he didn't like the feel of the sand on his toes, so he crawled over to me and held out his arms to be picked up.

"Did you hear that?" I said to Mike excitedly. "He said Mama!"

I remember scooping him up and kissing him, over and over again, telling him what a clever boy he was and how proud I was of him.

A woman walking her dog took a photo of the three of us. For Oliver's baby book. A memory of the day he first said my name.

Slow to talk – content long after her first birthday with just pointing when she wanted something – Sophie kept me hanging on far longer, but it was just as magical. And Isla stubbornly refused to say anything but Dada until I bribed her with a chocolate button at the age of fifteen months.

This morning – four months after my beautiful goddaughter

lost both of her parents and became part of our family – I hear the word Mummy for the first time once again. It is unexpected. It is bittersweet.

And yet, somehow, it is no less magical than all the times that came before.

We are running late for school due to an unfortunate nappy incident, so we're in a hurry. Handing Phoebe her book bag, I kiss her goodbye and usher her through the gates, telling her to have a great day, and that I love her.

She is halfway across the playground when she turns around to look at me.

"Bye, Mummy!" she shouts.

I don't think she has even noticed what she has said as she skips off happily, dragging her bag behind her. And I'm sure it's a slip of the tongue. I'm sure what she meant to say was "Bye, Auntie Zoe!"

But it melts my heart once again, nonetheless.

It is as beautiful as it is accidental. As monumental as it is inconsequential.

And it fills me with a guilt that takes my breath away.

"I feel like I am replacing her," I tell Robyn later, a lump catching in my throat.

"You *are* replacing her, Zoe," my friend tells me gently. "She chose you to replace her. When and if she wasn't here to be her mummy anymore.

"It was inevitable that this would happen," she says, always the voice of wisdom. "Phoebe is only young. She will barely remember Lou, if at all. You're her mummy now."

I try to hold back the tears and Robyn hands me a tissue.

"It's okay to cry," she tells me. "You don't get a quota of tears for the loss of your best friend that you're not allowed to exceed. You have to find your own way through all of this, Zoe. You have to make your own rules."

"The enormity of it all just keeps hitting me," I tell my friend. "Over and over again. Like a tidal wave. The moment I feel like we've turned a corner, that the kids are settled, that I am happy – the loss just washes over me again."

"You *have* turned a corner, Zoe," Robyn says. "Phoebe calling you Mummy – whether it was accidentally or on purpose – is proof of that."

Chapter Fifty-Five

I go to bed that night with the image of Phoebe and Zack waving goodbye to Lou and Rich – the very last day they saw them – playing over and over in my mind.

"Bye-bye, Mummy," Phoebe said happily, her little hands pressed against the window as she watched them drive away.

I wake in the night with a jolt.

I slip out of bed and pull on my dressing gown, my heart racing.

The house is quiet, four children sleeping soundly in their beds, two of them cuddled up to teddies that might one day remind them of their first precious years – the only ones they spent with the parents they lost.

I tiptoe down the stairs and into the study where I put the box of things from Lou and Rich's house – the items that didn't make it into Phoebe's memory box.

I pull the calendar out and turn the pages to September.

'RICH – CONGRESS – BARCELONA' it says across several days in the month – in the chunky block capitals he typically used – a work trip he couldn't miss. Not without upsetting his boss.

And on two overlapping squares, Lou's neat handwriting indicating her own work trip – a Law Society conference in Southampton.

Both crucial to their careers. Both unavoidable.

So I had the children.

Zack was just a few months old.

She dropped them off on the Friday evening before rushing to the train station, and I stood at the window with her children waving her off.

"We'll see Mummy when she's back from her meeting," I told them, reassuring Phoebe that we would phone Mummy at bedtime.

I shut the calendar and return to bed, my head a mix of sadness and what I can only describe as disappointment.

———————

I call Mike on my way to work the next morning.

"The weekend Lou went away…" I say.

With her lover, I want to add, but can't bring myself to.

"Her dirty weekend," I clarify instead.

Mike's impatience is audible.

"Not this again, Zo," he says, but I ignore him, undeterred by his desire for me to let this go.

"Was it in September?" I ask him.

"I don't know," he says, exasperated. "Possibly. Wait – yes, I think it was. Because I remember meeting Rich at the pub when he told me, and we were sat in the beer garden. Two boys were chasing each other and knocked Rich's pint all over his shorts.

And I remember him saying to me that beer-stained shorts were the least of his problems.

"Why?" he asks me. "Why do you want to know?"

"Because I had the children that weekend," I tell him. "I had Phoebe and Zack. All weekend. Because Lou said it was a work trip. She said she wouldn't ask, if it wasn't really really important."

I pull into the surgery car park, silence at the other end of the phone.

There is nothing Mike can say to me to make this better. To take away the web of lies I now see running through the very fabric of my friendship.

"I've got to go," I tell him. "I'll see you tonight."

Chapter Fifty-Six

I call Luke the next day. I ask him to come over. I tell him it's important.

"I need to know what you meant?" I tell him when he arrives. "When you said not to put Lou on a pedestal."

He sighs and loosens his tie.

"And I need to know why you weren't planning to come to her funeral.

"Mum told me," I say, when he looks shocked that I even know this.

"Have you got a beer?" he says, sitting down at the kitchen table.

I put a beer down in front of him and hand him the bottle opener.

"Luke?" I urge. "Tell me. Please."

"I just meant she was no angel when we were younger. But you already knew that, right?"

Yes. I did know that. I knew that she smoked the odd joint. That she once cheated in a Science test. That she cheated on her childhood sweetheart. Twice.

What I didn't know was that she was prepared to throw away the beautiful life she had made with the man she said was the love of her life.

I open the drawer where I put the card – not touched since the day Mike confirmed my worst fears.

I put it on the table in front of my brother.

"What's this?" he asks.

"She was having an affair," I tell him.

He barely reacts.

And then:

"It doesn't surprise me," he says. "And it won't have been the first time, I'm sure."

"Sit down, Zo," he tells me, pulling out the chair next to him.

My heart is racing. I'm scared of what my brother is going to tell me.

"What?" I say. "Just tell me, Luke. Please."

"I'm guessing she never told you about Jamie?" he says.

"My Jamie?" I ask. "My first boyfriend?"

"Yes."

"No," I tell him. "What about Jamie?"

So my brother tells me. He tells me how Lou slept with Jamie. My Jamie. A one-night stand. Though Lou wanted it not to be.

"While we were together?" I ask quietly.

"You had just split up," he says. "But she was still with Andrew at the time."

It was one weekend when she was home from university, apparently. Luke saw them together in a night club.

"And?" I say.

"Well, they weren't making small talk, put it that way," my

brother says hesitantly, conscious that this won't be the easiest thing for me to hear.

"As far as I was aware it was just a drunken snog – worst case, a bit of a fumble in a dark corner of a nightclub. But she inadvertently confessed to it being much more a few weeks later, when I told her I'd seen her.

"She told me it didn't mean anything. That it was a drunken shag. So of course I knew. Jamie's version of events was different."

"You spoke to Jamie?"

"Yes. He was your ex. And he'd just slept with your best friend. I was angry. I wanted to know what the hell he thought he was doing."

I think I'd be touched if I wasn't so bloody angry. With Lou. With Jamie. And with my brother for not telling me.

"And?"

"He said she'd been throwing herself at him ever since you'd split up. He said he told her she was insane. That she was his best friend's girlfriend. And that you might not still be together, but he still cared about you. And if he didn't, then she certainly should.

"But that night he was absolutely hammered. He didn't even really know what he was doing, until it was too late. At least that's what he told me."

"Why didn't you tell me?" I ask.

"What good would have come of it?" he says. "You'd met Mike by then. And it was over. Lou tried to get in touch with him a few times, I think. But he said he wasn't interested. And then a few months later he met Amy."

And suddenly it all makes sense. Why Lou didn't seem to like Amy. Why she said she couldn't understand what Jamie saw in her.

She was jealous.

"I'm sorry, Zo. I know it's not what you wanted to hear. But you need to know the truth. Lou was your best friend, I know that. And in so many ways she was a really good person. But she also lied. And she cheated. And so I never want you to look at those children and wonder whether you are living up to Lou's expectations. Because you are a better person than Lou ever was. And they are so lucky to have you."

Chapter Fifty-Seven

After he has left, I can't stop thinking about what Luke has told me about Lou, and Jamie.

How could she have done this?

Was she jealous of my relationship with Jamie all along?

Did she wish she'd got to him first?

Or did he mean nothing to her?

Was it just a drunken one-night stand, with no thought whatsoever to who it might hurt?

I thought she loved me.

I thought she loved Andrew.

They were so happy.

They were the couple you see in films about high school kids.

Everyone wanted what they had, everyone wanted to be what they were. The good-looking boyfriend, who was captain of the school football team. The gorgeous girlfriend, who did well at everything without even trying.

Yes, she cheated on him. But I know that Lou loved Andrew. And that he loved her.

Before he passed his driving test Andrew would think nothing of cycling the seven miles to Lou's house to see her. And Lou would stand at the side of a football pitch every week, cheering him on – unless it rained, when she'd invariably drag me to the pub down the road from the pitch to wait for him before congratulating him on his winning goal with a kiss and a pint of Coke.

They spent every waking moment together. And most nights too, in fact. *And yet that clearly wasn't ever enough for her. She always wanted more.*

I want to know why my friend did what she did.

I want to know why she slept with my boyfriend. I won't even dignify her actions by calling him my ex. Because that didn't matter. He was always mine. He was never hers to take.

I want to know why she had an affair. And who with.

I want to know who Mike saw her with in that café outside Waterloo, who Simon saw her with in a pub shamefully close to where she lived, where her family lived.

I want to know if I ever really knew my friend.

Mike tells me again that I should leave it. That no good can come from knowing. That Lou is gone now, and I will never be able to ask her why she did what she did.

What would I have done, he asks me, if I'd known six months ago. What difference would it have made?

And I don't know.

I don't know what I would have done if she'd told me she was unhappy. Or that she'd been cheating since we were kids. That she'd never stopped cheating.

Two days after my brother's visit, I stare at the boxes stacked in my garage – the ones delivered from Lou and Rich's house – wondering if one of them holds the answers, wondering if one of them contains something – anything – that will tell me why my friend did this. Why she did any of this.

I grab a knife from the kitchen and rip open the boxes. Furious with my friend. Angry that she left me to pick up the pieces of her children's broken hearts, and didn't even have the decency to stay faithful to their daddy before she did so.

I pull out bank statements and birthday cards, legal books, Lou's work diary and a multitude of scraps of paper that may or may not mean something when we are ready to go through all of this stuff properly. But they tell me nothing. There are no illicit messages, no love notes scribbled on Post-its tucked inside the pages of law journals, no receipts for dirty weekends away without Rich.

I scour her social media accounts for clues. For pictures of other men. Men that weren't her husband. Men that weren't the father of her children – the children sleeping soundly upstairs in bedrooms in their new home with me, since their little lives were shattered.

And I look through her phone – returned to me by the police following the accident when I was established to be the legal guardian of her possessions, and her children.

Four days after the accident I had scrolled through it for names and numbers. For people I had to tell. For people who needed to know their calls and texts to this number would no longer be answered.

And then I switched it off, put it in a Ziplock bag along with a Dire Straits CD, a watch, and a pretty silver necklace that she was wearing at the time of the accident. Because one day Phoebe and Zack will want to know everything. They'll want to know what happened. They'll want to know every detail – the car they were driving, the clothes they were wearing, the music they were listening to.

It had never occurred to me that I might one day need to scan Lou's phone for clues that might tell me who she had been prepared to risk everything for.

But if I am expecting to find anything there, then I didn't know my friend.

She was a lawyer. One of the best.

She wasn't going to keep detailed notes on her secret liaisons with her lover. All the times they met whilst pretending they were working late. All the times they jumped into bed together. All the times they laughed at the stupidity of their unsuspecting partners. Of their families. Of their friends. She was far too smart for that.

There are no messages that tell me anything, no declarations of love, no details of arrangements to meet. There's not a single text, or WhatsApp, or email, or anything else to incriminate her.

The only mistake she ever made was to keep that Christmas card, tucked away at the back of her bedside drawer.

"I thought I had moved on," I tell Robyn one day over a rare lunch break together. "But I can't get it out of my head. It wasn't the first time, you know?" I ask.

Robyn sips her coffee, aware this is not a question she is required to answer. She is a sounding board. She is here because I need an outlet. For my frustration. For my confusion. For the heartbreak I am feeling at never really knowing my friend.

"She cheated on her boyfriend when we were younger," I continue. Now in full flow. Purging the indiscretions of my best friend. The one who died and left me to raise her children.

"Did I tell you that? Three times, it turns out. I told you she slept with my ex-boyfriend too, right?" I ask. "My *first* boyfriend. When she was still with Andrew."

"Yes, you did tell me," she says gently.

The waitress delivers our food order – two cheese toasties and a slice of carrot cake to share.

Robyn thanks her quietly and picks up a knife to cut the cake in half.

"But cheating when you're married. That's a whole new level, right? She had children, for God's sake."

"And you have no idea who it was?" Robyn asks me eventually.

"None whatsoever," I tell her.

"Was she still in touch with your ex?"

"Kind of," I say. "She stayed in touch with most people from school in a way that I never really did. They usually just met up at weddings, but I guess sometimes there were random get-togethers. Why?" I ask.

"Well, you've probably already thought of this, but could it have been him? Your ex-boyfriend?"

"Jamie?" I say.

She nods.

"She did it once," she says. "Maybe she did it again. It's a bit of a reach, I know, but maybe it was him?"

I hadn't thought of it, no. Until now.

Chapter Fifty-Eight

You never forget your first love. No matter how it ends.

Everything was new and exciting with Jamie. He was my first kiss, the first time a boy held my hand, the first time I felt like a woman. You never forget that.

And I loved him. I really did. But I knew it wasn't enough. I knew I could love more. And I was right. I could.

While I have no right to be bothered about who he may or may not have slept with after me, knowing now that he slept with my best friend really stings.

He was my past. Not hers.

And she was supposed to be my best friend.

Would it hurt more if I found out that he was having an affair with her? That twenty years later they rekindled whatever it was they had – however brief – when we were eighteen years old? Or would the hurt only be for Rich to feel? For Phoebe and Zack? For the life she had built with them?

I know it won't change anything. Not really. But I have to know.

We meet in Crakeleigh. In the coffee shop next to our old school.

He is there when I arrive. He stands up to greet me, knocking his coffee so that it spills slightly onto the table.

He looks older than I remember. Inevitable, of course, but I hadn't registered this at the funeral. I guess I had other things on my mind.

"Hey, Zo," he says, wiping the table with a napkin.

He hugs me. And instantly I am eighteen again. Saying goodbye to him, both of us preparing to go off to university and find ourselves.

"How have you been? How are the kids?"

Ordering a coffee, I take my jacket off and sit down.

"They're doing really well," I tell him, slipping my jacket over the back of an empty chair.

"Phoebe has moved schools. She's at Hartingley now, where my own kids went. It wasn't an easy decision, but it was the right thing. She's really settled there though, and at home too. She still gets sad and asks why Mummy and Daddy had to die. But it's getting easier. We've come a long way."

The conversation feels fake – knowing what I'm here to ask him.

But I'm also aware there's every chance I am wrong.

"Amy has been amazing," I say. "The therapist she found for Phoebe is great. Phoebe loves her."

"And their little boy?" he says. "I'm really sorry, I don't remember his name."

"Zack. He's fine. He's so young. I honestly don't think he will ever remember them. It's so sad, but I have kind of found my peace with that."

"So?" he says eventually, reminding us both that I asked him here for a reason.

I wait while the waitress delivers my coffee, taking the damp napkins from our table as she leaves.

"Were you having an affair with Lou?" I ask him, wasting no more time on small talk.

"What?! No!" he says. "Of course not! I barely ever saw her!

"I lost touch with her a long time ago," he continues. "I lost touch with everyone, really. The only reason I was at Heidi's wedding was because I work with Stephen."

"Did you ever sleep with her?" I ask him.

It's a test.

I know the answer.

I want to know if he'll tell me.

He looks down at his hands. Twists his wedding ring on his finger.

"I need you to tell me the truth," I tell him.

I already know the truth, of course. But I need to know if he will tell me it. I need to know if I can trust him.

"Yes," he says eventually. "Once."

And I feel nothing.

Because she's gone and I can't get angry at her? Because it makes no difference now? Or because I never loved him the way that I loved Mike?

"It was a mistake," he says, wanting to fill the silence. "From my side, at least. Lou wanted more. But I didn't. And then I met Amy.

"How did you find out?" he asks.

"My brother told me."

I look at Jamie and I can tell.

I can tell there is more to this story.

"What is it?" I ask him.

And so he tells me.

He tells me that after their drunken rendezvous Lou missed her period.

So she took a pregnancy test.

And it was positive.

She told Jamie. But she didn't tell Andrew. Because there was no way of knowing whose it was.

Not that it would have made any difference.

She was eighteen.

She wasn't ready to be a mum.

So she had an abortion.

"I remember," I say.

"She told you?" Jamie asks, surprised.

"No," I tell him. "But I remember not seeing her. For what felt like months. She'd tell me she was busy. That she had too much work on. That she had exams. And I believed her. I had no reason not to."

Knowing everything I now know, the words sting.

I didn't know she had an affair. I didn't know she left her kids with me so she could have a dirty weekend away with her lover.

And I didn't know she once slept with my first love – and then got rid of a baby that might have been his.

Was this what she meant when she asked if she was being punished for her past mistakes? When she didn't fall pregnant after years of trying?

Did she think she was being punished for sleeping with Jamie? For having an abortion? For cheating on Andrew over and over again?

The lies just keep coming.

But I feel nothing.

It's done now.

Mike was right. None of this will bring her back. Or undo the past.

"I'm sorry, Zoe," Jamie says. "I wish it had never happened."

"It's okay," I say. Because it is. It's done now. We can't go back and change any of it.

So I tell Jamie about what brought us to this point. About the card, about what Phoebe told me about them sleeping in separate beds, about Rich wanting to split up.

"That explains a lot," he says.

They were arguing at the wedding, he tells me. Rich wanted to go, but Lou didn't. He left for a while and Lou just got more and more drunk. When he came back they had words and then left, without saying goodbye to anyone.

"Whatever it was that was going on, I was not involved," Jamie tells me. "I'd love to be indignant that you even thought I might be. But I know I lost that right a long time ago."

"Yes, you did," I confirm.

"I hope you find the answers you're looking for, Zo," he says.

And then he kisses me on the cheek and we say goodbye.

Chapter Fifty-Nine

"You are never going to find the answers you are looking for, Zoe," Mike tells me later when I get home. "You have got to let this go now."

He's right, I know.

"Do you want a coffee?" I ask him, switching the kettle on.

He shakes his head.

I've had a day from hell at the surgery, and I'd much rather be reaching for the wine, but I have to pick Isla up from a friend's later. So coffee it is. Unless Mike is able to pick her up…

"I can't, I'm really sorry," he says.

"No worries," I tell him, reaching in the cupboard for a mug.

"I'm meeting Charlotte," he adds.

He sounds apologetic. But he shouldn't be. He has done what I told him to. He has moved on.

I haven't told him about Simon and I breaking up, though I'm sure the girls probably have.

"I could tell her something has come up," he says, awkwardly, fiddling with his keys.

290

"No, it's fine," I tell him.

And then I turn away. I spoon coffee into the empty mug. I check my phone while I wait for the kettle to boil. I wipe an imaginary spillage from the worktop. Anything to avoid showing him that that is exactly what I want him to do.

Chapter Sixty

Eventually the weeks of our new life begin to slip by unnoticed.

It isn't always perfect.

There are times when grief will engulf me out of nowhere. When I miss my friend so much, I can hardly breathe. When despite all of her lies, I am gripped by an indescribable heartache. When I am enraged by the unfairness of it all.

Out of nowhere I will be struck by a memory. Something simple will make me think of my friend. Something as mundane as crossing the road, or sewing on a button, or stirring a pan of pasta with a slotted spoon.

There are moments when Phoebe will jump back into her puddle of grief for longer than I am used to, and I worry that she will never fully emerge.

And there are times when I can't be everything to everyone and I feel like I am making a complete mess of it all – like when Isla or Sophie need me, and I can't be there – because I am picking up Zack or attending a meeting at Phoebe's school – and I worry about the sacrifices that they have had to make for this to work.

But most of the time we are okay.

And I wonder why I ever thought I had to give up everything I'd ever worked for to make this work.

I look at Mike and I realise that he saved us. He stopped everything from going bad. Just by being there for us. More than he has ever been before.

I wish it hadn't taken this for him to do it.

I wish things could have been different.

Eventually Phoebe starts an after-school club. It's just three days a week, but it means I can pick her up just before I get Zack.

It also means Mike isn't around as much.

It was always going to be this way. This was never going to be forever. But I find myself in uncharted territory. I find myself missing him – the man I decided I no longer wanted to spend the rest of my life with.

And I look forward to the days when I know I am going to see him.

Even though I know he is no longer mine.

Today is one of those days.

Mike is looking after the children so that Robyn and I can go out.

I arrive home to the sound of drilling. I've bought Phoebe a new cabin bed and he is putting it together. Her old bed bears the memory of the day she bashed her mouth, but I need her to feel special. A new bed for a new bedroom. We need to make new memories.

I've ordered some unicorn bedding and matching curtains which should arrive tomorrow, and she is so excited.

She kicks her shoes off in the hallway and runs upstairs.

Following her up with Zack in my arms, we open her bedroom

door to find Mike leaning over the bright pink bed, fastening the last of the slats into the frame.

He looks up at me and smiles. Clearly unimpressed that her bed is not ready to climb into immediately, Phoebe leaves the room in search of the girls.

"I thought you were going to drop the kids off and go straight out?" Mike says.

"I thought I'd come home and change first," I tell him. "You know, make a bit of effort. Ditch the scrubs for an outfit slightly more suited to a night on the town…"

He laughs and fastens another screw.

The truth is, I wanted to see his face. To hear his voice. Even just for a few minutes.

"I'll give Zack his bath before I go."

"I can do that," he says. "I'm almost done here. You go and get ready."

I do what he says. But I don't feel the excitement I should be feeling. Right now I can think of nothing I'd like more than a night in front of the telly with a takeaway. And Mike.

I consider phoning Robyn and cancelling, but I know she would kill me. So I don't.

Instead, I wait for Mike to take Zack from me and then I go and run myself a bath.

I have just climbed in when there is a knock at the door. It's Sophie. With a glass of wine and an offer to drop me in town when I am ready, so that I can have a couple of drinks with Robyn.

She hands me the wine and tells me she loves me.

I tell her I love her more. And before she has had a chance to escape I tell her that I'm proud of her.

"It was Dad's idea," she says, pulling a face. But it doesn't change anything.

An hour later I am scrubbed and polished – my hair blow-dried and straightened, my nails painted, and looking good, apparently, in some new skinny jeans, a bright pink top and some leopard-print boots – picked out for me by my daughters, as heaven forbid I should be allowed to choose my own footwear for a night out.

"What do you think?" I say, doing a quick twirl for the team – all of whom, except Zack, are now sat around the kitchen table eating crisps and dips and playing Uno.

"You look lovely, Mum" Isla tells me.

"Yes, you look lovely, Auntie Zoe," Phoebe confirms.

Sophie nods her approval.

Mike says nothing, but gives me a little smile, before killing his eldest daughter's hopes of a third win with a Draw 4 card.

"Yellow!" he shouts, adding insult to injury for Sophie, who clearly has a hand completely devoid of this colour card.

"I hate you!" she tells him, before reassuring Phoebe that she doesn't really.

"I have to take Mum now," she says. "So shall we just say I won?"

Isla and Mike both laugh.

"Right, Phoebs, shall we get you up to bed while Sophie drops Auntie Zoe off for her night out?" Mike says.

"But I want to stay up with you and Isla," Phoebe protests.

"Well, maybe another twenty minutes then," Mike says. Pushover. "And then straight up to bed. Okay, Phoebs?"

She takes the deal.

"Can we play Uno again, Isla?"

Isla looks at Mike with a face that says she is ready to disown him. But of course, she agrees.

"Night-night, Phoebs," I say.

"Night-night, Auntie Zoe," she says, wrapping her arms around my neck, the deck of Uno cards gripped tightly in her little hand. "Love you."

In the car Sophie checks where she is dropping me off to meet Robyn, before we travel in silence, both of us lost in our own thoughts.

And then she takes me by surprise.

"You're doing a great job," she says. "You know that, right, Mum?"

"Thank you, sweetie," I say.

"I mean it. The way you have dealt with all of this. It's amazing. I'm so proud you're my mum."

Her words take my breath away and I feel an overwhelming rush of pride for my eldest daughter.

"I do worry about you and Isla sometimes," I tell her, eventually.

"Why are you worried about us? We're fine."

"You'd only just got your heads around your dad and I splitting up," I explain. "And now you're having to share me with Phoebe and Zack. They're so young, and they need so much more of my time. I worry that you and Isla are missing out."

"We're not missing out, Mum," she says. "It's Phoebe and Zack who would be missing out if it wasn't for you. Look at what they've lost. I don't know how I would ever get over it if I lost you and Dad."

It's not often my eldest daughter tells me how she's feeling, but when she does, she tugs hard on the heartstrings.

And I'm lost for words.

I'm not going to tell her that it will never happen. That she'll never lose me. I know all too well now that I just can't do that.

"They'll be fine," I tell her instead.

"They'll be fine because of you, Mum. Because of everything you are doing to make up for what they've lost. They're so lucky to have you. We all are."

And in that moment, driving into town to meet my friend who is no doubt going to make me drink copious amounts of alcohol before ordering chips and curry sauce in the early hours of the morning, I feel so incredibly proud of the beautiful, kind, thoughtful daughter I have raised.

Yes, she might roll her eyes at me when I ask her if she's done her homework, or when I question the value of the umpteenth TikTok video she's staring at on her phone whilst sprawled out on the sofa, and she might cringe when I ask her how serious she is about Josh, or tell her that I was young once and am available for advice, should she ever want or need it, but despite all that I – or rather we – do appear to have raised a daughter who really does care. About me. And more importantly, about others.

I am mentally congratulating myself on the great job I have done when we arrive at the bar where I am meeting Robyn.

"Go get drunk," my daughter tells me, as her own parting piece of advice.

And then one more for good measure.

"Mum," she tells me as I open the car door.

"Yes?"

"Dad is still crazy about you. You know that, right?"

"Don't be ridiculous," I tell her, my heart racing inexplicably. "We're divorced. And your dad is with Charlotte now."

"No, he isn't," she tells me. "They split up weeks ago."

And then she pulls the door closed behind me and drives away.

Chapter Sixty-One

I meet Robyn at the trendy new wine bar that has just opened in Ferringham.

Even its name is trendy. *Wine.*

I'm not sure if they just ran out of money for the signwriter, or if it's meant to be a play on words, the clientele supposedly coming here to whine after a hard day at work? Or maybe I am just too old to be frequenting such trendy bars and I simply don't get it.

Robyn is already here when I arrive. Already halfway through her first glass of Malbec.

The bar is still quiet – most of the Friday night drinkers aren't generally out until us oldies are getting ready to head home to our beds – so we have somewhere to sit, at least.

Until about three weeks ago it was a musty old pub – still boasting the same carpet that was put down more than twenty years ago, still displaying the same tatty beer towels and shredded beer mats.

New owners took it over and within forty-eight hours of the

cheque clearing, they had ripped out the insides like Nick Knowles in an episode of *DIY SOS*.

Wood panelling was swapped for bare brick walls; identical old pine tables that wobbled and spilt precious sips of beer at the slightest knock were swapped for purpose-built cast-iron structures in the shape of wine glasses; and ready-salted and prawn-cocktail flavoured crisps were swapped for roasted parsnip chips, olives and *caprese* bites.

"They've done a great job," I say, looking around.

Lou would have loved this place. Before she had Phoebe, she probably spent every other night in a place like this. And then after, as many as she could get away with. She loved a night out. She loved all the wining and dining that was part and parcel of her job.

Did she take her lovers to places like this?

I feel so incredibly sad now that every thought of my best friend is interjected with what "bad Lou" would have done. I can't just wonder whether she would have loved a place like this, whether she would have sat with colleagues and shared bowls of antipasti while discussing how she nailed her cross-examination. I have to wonder, too, if she ever left with the tall, dark, handsome stranger whose hand skimmed hers provocatively as they both ordered double gin and tonics at the end of a tough day in the city.

I feel cheated. Of the good memories with Lou. Of when we were just two girls with the world at our feet. Of the girl who asked if she could sit next to me and became my best friend.

"Another one?" Robyn says, drinking the last of her wine, breaking my thoughts of what Lou might or might not have done in a place like this.

"Why not," I say.

While Robyn goes to the bar, I look around me, at the couples clearly talking to each other for the first time – brought together by alcohol and a mutual attraction – or maybe by arrangement following a swipe on Tinder or some other dating app. The thought of it horrifies me. It was so easy when I met Mike. Dating these days feels too much like hard work.

"I think it's time to find you a new man," Robyn tells me, putting the drinks on the table. "You need to get laid. Again," she clarifies when I point out I already have.

"I have no idea why you didn't just stay with Simon for the sex, if it was that good," she giggles, taking a large swig of wine and scanning the bar for options.

"Because I have morals," I point out, laughing despite myself.

"Morals are not going to satisfy your needs, young lady."

She looks over the top her glasses, continuing to scan for potential suitors.

I know she is joking. I know she doesn't actually think I am going to walk up to the nearest good-looking man in this bar and proposition him.

But the fact that we are even having this conversation is confirming to me something I think I already knew.

"I think I might be falling in love with Mike," I tell Robyn, because I can't keep it inside any longer.

She tells me that she already knew, of course. That she's known for weeks. That she was just waiting for me to work it out.

And then she smiles a little smile, knocks back the rest of her Malbec and announces that we are going to need another one. And let's make it a large one.

Over more wine, and something to help soak it up, Robyn tells me that she saw this coming. That as soon as Mike offered to help with Phoebe and Zack, we might as well have ripped up the divorce papers. That the day he left work early for the first time to be there for me and these children, he might as well have just moved back in.

I tell her it's too late. That Mike doesn't feel the same way.

"I pushed him away," I tell her. "I gave up on our marriage. And now he has moved on. You said so yourself when he met Charlotte – it's what I wanted him to do."

It was me that wanted the divorce. To be free to start again with someone else one day. To be free to love someone the way I once loved him. To fall in love with someone the way I once fell in love with him.

I just never imagined that someone would be him.

———

My friend – slightly drunk and slightly giddy in the knowledge that she was right – just smiles at me.

"Zoe Henry," she says. "Your ex-husband is madly in love with you. Anyone can see that. Why do you think he split up with Charlotte?

"Because she's not you," she says before I have a chance to even try and answer the question.

"Because he loves you. I have never been surer of anything in my life.

"Go home," she tells me. "Go home and tell him how you feel."

"I can't," I tell her. "What if you're wrong? Or what if you're right, and I tell him, and it all goes wrong again?"

"It won't," she tells me, pushing her hand through a collection of empty glasses to hold mine. "You won't let it."

I wish I had her faith.

But all I can think about is how much I loved Mike – almost

from the day we met. We made a family by accident and it turned out to be the best thing that ever happened to us. We built a life together. A home. We made memories. And it still went wrong.

I want to stay here. In this wine bar with my friend. Eating olives and *caprese* bites and drinking copious amounts of red wine. Where I can pretend none of this is happening. Where I don't have to think about telling Mike that I'm in love with him, about risking everything we have worked so hard to achieve these past few months.

When the taxi pulls up outside my house I take a deep breath and put my key in the door.

I'm suddenly unsure.

Could I just be feeling overwhelmed at what I have taken on? Grateful for the support Mike has been to me over the last few weeks? And confusing that with something else entirely. Or could I be falling in love with him all over again?

I put my bag in the kitchen then go through to the lounge where Mike is asleep on the sofa – the sofa where he spent so many nights in the year leading up to our divorce. Working late. Watching rubbish on the television until the early hours of the morning. Not wanting to come to bed. Not wanting to admit our marriage was over.

Now he's here because he's trying to fix things. To be there for his family. To be a dad to two children who have lost everything.

Is it too late? Or *can* we fix this?

I put my hand on his and he stirs. And then smiles up at me.

"I'm sorry I'm so late," I tell him.

"Don't be," he says, sleepily. "Did you have a good time?"

"We did. How were the kids?"

"Good as gold," he says, sitting up and rubbing his eyes.

And then, "I better get going."

Stay, I want to say.

Stay for a drink.

Stay for the night.

Stay forever.

I play the scene over and over in my mind where I tell him how I feel.

I imagine a scenario where he tells me he feels the same. And I feel so happy. And then I imagine one where he tells me he has moved on, that he will always be a dad to our now five children, but nothing more. And I feel so crushed I can barely breathe.

I am terrified of breaking the life we have built over the last six months – the new life we have given Phoebe and Zack.

"Thanks so much for tonight," I say instead.

"You don't have to thank me," Mike tells me, picking up his keys. "I love spending time with the kids. See you next week?"

"See you next week," I confirm, opening the front door.

And then he steps outside, and I shut the door behind him.

Chapter Sixty-Two

It's Friday before I see him again.

I've missed him.

Phoebe's after-school dance class is cancelled, so he's picking her up for me.

I'm glad of a busy day.

When you have what feels like the entire animal population needing emergency care, it is hard to find time to think about how you are almost certainly in love with your ex-husband. At lunchtime I decline an invitation to join Robyn for a quick bite at the new café around the corner. Because I know she will quiz me. I opt instead for a solo trip to Pret A Manger where I eat two bites of a tuna baguette and a handful of salt and cider vinegar crisps.

And I message my eldest daughter.

> Soph please can you make sure you're home when I get back this evening. Thanks, Mum x

She texts back immediately.

> Why? I told Josh I'd go round to his to study.

To study? Honestly, she must think I was born yesterday.

> I'll explain later. Please Soph. It's important. Thanks honey x

K.

Though a little calmer, the afternoon flies by and before I know it, I am throwing my scrubs into the laundry bin and swapping them for my jeans (new) and Crew shirt (also new). I am pulling a brush through my hair when Robyn appears in the doorway.

She studies me for a fraction longer than is strictly necessary.

"You look nice," she says. Curious. Suspicious. I say nothing.

"New top?" she says.

"What? This old thing? Had it ages," I say, avoiding eye contact.

"Hmm."

I look at her, still pulling the brush through my hair, which by now is exhibiting a super glossy shine.

"What?" I ask, smiling.

"Nothing," she says, with a quick smile and a barely visible twitch of the eyebrows, before turning her attention to the coffee mugs in the sink.

"Phone me later," she says without looking up, as I take my car keys out of my handbag and shut my locker door.

"Of course," I tell her.

And then I am on my way home to my family.

They are all in the lounge when I walk through the door with Zack.

Mike is lying face down on the carpet. Sophie is lying on top of him. Isla is lying on top of her. And Phoebe is balanced on top of all of them. It's like a scene from *The Enormous Turnip* – though the challenge here is squashing Mike, not pulling up an overgrown root vegetable.

I say hi and hear a muffled response from Mike.

I drop my handbag on the floor beside me and gently hold Zack on top of Phoebe to help them finish the job. Excited to be joining in with whatever game this is, he stamps his feet on her bottom, which makes her laugh.

"Right you lot, off your dad now so he can breathe!" I say.

He may biologically only be Sophie and Isla's dad, but it feels significant somehow when they all tumble off Mike obediently, no one feeling the need to point out this minor detail.

"So why am I here?" Sophie asks, getting straight to the point.

I beckon her into kitchen, where I explain to her that I need some time to chat to her dad and ask her to take the rest of them out.

She wants to know what we're going to talk about, obviously.

Teenagers are nosy and Sophie is no exception.

"Just stuff," I tell her, thrusting a £20 note into her hand.

They have all had tea apparently, except Zack – because my ex-husband has become so bloody good at looking after his children – so I ask her to take them to McDonald's for a milkshake and an apple pie.

I tell her she can keep the change, which seems to swing it in my favour.

She pushes the note in her pocket and shouts to her sister.

"Come on Isla, we're going to McDonald's."

"Can I come too?" Phoebe shouts, running through to the kitchen holding her Cinderella handbag.

"We're all going," Sophie tells her. "Go put your shoes on."

"Thank you," I mouth.

By now Zack is on his way to find out what all the fuss is. He stops in the doorway and sits on his bottom to assess the situation, an oversized jigsaw puzzle piece in his hand.

He is not impressed when Sophie picks him up and starts putting his coat back on and he realises he has had all of five minutes with his favourite man before being whisked back out again.

Isla is in the hallway helping Phoebe put her shoes on. In the minute and a half since being told she is going to McDonald's she has managed to change into a Snow White dress, swap her handbag for one that matches her outfit, and accessorise appropriately with four bracelets and six hair clips.

"You look beautiful, Phoebs," Isla tells her, fastening her buckle.

"You know you could have just called Dad and talked to him on the phone," Sophie mutters as she pulls on her own coat and picks up the car keys.

She's right. I could.

But this is not a conversation I want to have with four children listening in.

I'm scared. But I need to tell Mike how I feel.

How can I be mad at my best friend for not telling me what was going on in her life – for not telling me how she was feeling – if I am not prepared to share my own feelings with Mike?

Was she scared? Was she afraid to admit that she was

unhappy? Was she afraid to tell me about the mistakes she had made when we were young? That she had had no choice but to have an abortion, and then spent years trying for a baby and wondering if she was being punished.

I don't want to spend my life wondering what might have happened if I'd only told Mike I still love him.

I want to give him the chance to tell me he feels the same. Even if it turns out he doesn't.

———

Making sure Zack is securely fastened in his car seat, I wave as they drive away, and then I go back into the house.

When I walk into the lounge Mike is asleep on the sofa, his hands in his lap, his head resting on one of the bumblebee cushions we picked out together when we redecorated.

It's a scene I've seen a million times. My husband, exhausted from a long day, working hard to make sure his family had everything they could dream of.

I sit next to him, and he stirs slightly.

I look down at his hands – the same hands I held for the first time over two decades ago, now just a little older, with a few more stories to tell of numbers crunched, babies held, flat-pack furniture assembled.

Those hands have held me so many times. Made me feel loved, kept me safe, comforted me. I have not missed them in the year we have been divorced. But today I miss them more than I could even put into words. It's as if a dam has been broken, and an immense love, held back by the years of not having enough time to be us, has been suddenly released, in full flow, crashing over and wiping out all the time spent apart, all the missed opportunities, all the weary silences. And rendering them completely insignificant – these things that once ultimately drove us apart.

I put my hand on his – startling him, and he pulls away.

He opens his eyes and – seeing me there – slips his hand back where it was, under mine. Then he looks at me. Confused? Hopeful? He is trying to work this out, trying to put together the pieces of this strange jigsaw. One minute he is at the bottom of a pile-on, at the mercy of his children, and the next they are gone, and his ex-wife is waking him from a gentle slumber, holding his hand.

And then he kisses me.

And suddenly I am eighteen again. In the arms of the cute, hot guy who deemed me worthy of an extra Murray Mint.

Still cute. Still hot. Just older. Better.

We kiss for eternity, neither of us wanting to pull away, both of us getting our fix of a drug we've been deprived of for too long.

Eventually he pulls away, holds my face in his hands, looks at me.

He says nothing. And nor do I.

I simply wrap my arms around his neck – the need to hold him overwhelming me.

But he is going nowhere, he is right where he wants to be, and so am I.

He tells me that he has never stopped loving me.

He tells me that he hoped I might come back to him one day. But never dared dream that I actually would.

We stay like that, in each other's arms, until the children arrive home, both of us sure that this is the start of something good.

And when he leaves he holds my hand and kisses me softly.

And I am as intoxicated as I was the first time around.

Maybe even more.

Chapter Sixty-Three

It's a week before I see him again, and it feels like forever.

I have not been able to stop thinking about him.

I am like a teenager again – only just stopping short of scribbling his name on my metaphorical pencil case.

He has phoned me every night and I have lived for those phone calls – as much as I did the first time around when he'd call the phone box at my university accommodation. Maybe more.

From that first phone call back when we were just kids – when my sweaty neighbour thumped his fist on my bedroom door and announced a guy called Mike was on the blower – I was relaxed – a cocky teenager who was confident that this "guy" really liked her.

But this time around I'm less self-assured. Maybe it's because I've got more to lose. My heart is more fragile now. Because I lost him once before, and then I lost my best friend too. And then I learned she wasn't the person I thought she was.

I need to see him. I need to look in his eyes again and know for sure that he feels the same.

We're going out for dinner.

I guess you could call it a date.

A first date.

A far cry from our first first date when we were both carefree and had our whole lives in front of us.

Sophie is at Josh's so Robyn is babysitting, but I don't want the children to know anything about this – not yet – so I am meeting Mike at the end of the road.

Robyn picked the kids up for me, as I had a late appointment at the surgery and by the time I get home they are in the kitchen tucking into macaroni cheese with home-made garlic bread.

Mike is meeting me at 7pm.

I look at my watch before sneaking a piece of bread from Phoebe's plate.

She scrunches her nose up at my dreadful behaviour.

Biting into it, I mentally rifle through my wardrobe for a date-night outfit and come up with nothing.

"Dark jeans, white vest top with the sequins around the neck, blue jacket," Robyn says casually, getting up from the table, taking a bottle of wine from my wine rack and pouring me a glass.

I put a spoon of macaroni in Zack's mouth and nod my approval.

Robyn takes the spoon out of my hand.

"You are not needed here," she says, swapping it for the glass of wine.

"Take this and go and get ready."

"Yes, miss," I say, which makes Phoebe giggle.

"Shout if you need me," I add, on my way up the stairs.

"We won't," she shouts, rolling her eyes for Phoebe's benefit, which makes her giggle again.

An hour later I am ready.

"You look pretty, Auntie Zoe," Phoebe tells me, tearing her eyes away from the television screen for just long enough to look me up and down.

"Thanks, sweetheart," I tell her.

"Are you going out for dinner?" she asks.

"Yes, that's right, Phoebs."

"Where are you going? Are you going to McDonald's?"

Robyn giggles. And so do I.

The truth is, I don't care where we're going. I only care that it's Mike I'm going with. Though I am probably a little overdressed for a Big Mac and a milkshake.

I kiss the children goodnight and thank Robyn for being amazing and then I walk up to the end of our street.

And there he is. Waiting by his car.

My first love. My only love.

And just like that, my nerves disappear.

"You look lovely," he says with a smile.

I'm sure I could be wearing my scruffiest leggings with the hole in the bum, and a jumper that's older than our firstborn, and he would have said the same. In fact, if I remember rightly, he did say something very similar when I turned up for our second date on the running track wearing a pair of Adidas cycling shorts and a mismatched running top. But I thank him and take comfort in the knowledge that he has not lost any of his charm in the last twenty-five years.

"I've booked us a table at Romano's," he tells me.

"Not McDonald's, then?" I say.

"We can go to McDonald's if you like," he laughs.

"Romano's is perfect," I tell him.

Romano's is my favourite restaurant. When we first moved back to Sussex, we'd go there as often as we could. Date Night. Time for him and I to be together, just us, to make sure we didn't forget why we were together. My mum and dad would have the kids overnight and after indulging in our favourite Italian foods and far too much red wine, we'd take a taxi home and make love until we were both exhausted, and then we'd fall asleep in each other's arms. I miss those days. I want them back.

The restaurant is still quiet – and we are shown to a table for two, tucked away in the corner.

"I bought you something," Mike tells me, taking a small gift bag out of his jacket pocket and placing it on the table in front of me.

I put my hand in the bag and pull out a packet of Murray Mints.

And I laugh – a little louder than I intended, attracting the attention of the only other couple in the restaurant.

They look young. I want to tell them not to make the same mistakes we made. I want to tell them to make time for each other, no matter how busy life gets. I want to tell them to never stop telling each other how they feel.

"I didn't have time to go to Tesco's and the corner shop only had the small packs," he says, apologetically.

"I love you," I tell him, before I can stop myself.

"Steady on," he says. "It's only a packet of mints." And we both laugh.

But then…

"I love you too. I always have."

"I'm sorry I divorced you," I tell him.

"That's okay," he says. "I would have divorced me too."

"Would you?" I ask. "Because I need to know that if we do

313

this – if we get back together – that we'll get it right – that we won't be back here again, in another twenty years' time."

"I'm hoping I'll be retired by then, so it's unlikely," he says, smiling.

"Seriously though, Zo. I'm done with the ridiculous hours. With devoting my whole life to my job. I'm exactly where I want to be right now. I want to be part of the kids' lives. And yours. I want to be there for all of you.

"Does that answer your question?" he asks.

"Yes, it does," I say, holding his hand.

We eat our food in virtual silence.

It's a comfortable silence. One that neither of us feels the need to fill. Both of us aware that each of us is processing the enormity of this in their own way. Both of us feeling the same rush of something indescribable that we first felt almost twenty-five years ago when I slipped my hand into his for the very first time.

"I don't want to rush things," I tell him later. "Things are still so strange for Phoebe and Zack. They are just starting to adjust to their new life. They are happy. They know what's what. Phoebe knows you pick her up from school sometimes. And then you go home. I don't want to confuse her."

"I understand," Mike says.

Just like the first time around, we both know that we will take the next step when we are both ready.

As we leave the restaurant and walk to Mike's car, I slip my hand in his.

"Lou and Rich would be happy," I tell him quietly.

He squeezes my hand and we both quietly acknowledge that this may be the one good thing to have come out of this tragedy.

We pull up outside the house and I look at Mike.

"I want to kiss you," I tell him honestly. "But I'm worried that I won't be able to stop. That I won't be able to tell you to leave."

He says nothing for a moment. He just runs his hand gently across my cheek, his touch like electricity running through my body.

"Would you rather kiss me and never be able to stop, or never kiss me again?" he asks me eventually, with a cheeky glint in his eye.

And I smile.

"Do you want to come back to the flat?" he asks.

"Yes," I say, without hesitation, reaching for my phone to let Robyn know.

"Good," he says, taking the handbrake off and pulling back out onto the road.

Chapter Sixty-Four

W e park up outside Mike's flat – a first-floor two-bed in a small purpose-built block only a couple of miles from the house. The flat we'd bought as a buy-to-let shortly before we split up, so it just made sense for Mike to move in there.

He leans over and kisses me softly on the lips, before grabbing his keys and getting out of the car.

He runs around to my side and opens the door for me, then holds both my hands in his, both of us right now needing to feel the touch of the other.

We take the stairs to the first floor and he unlocks the door. I can feel my heart racing.

"Do you want coffee?" he says.

I shake my head.

"I'm guessing you don't want tea either, then?" he says, and I smile.

And then the desperation that we are both feeling is finally too much and we cannot get each other's clothes off quickly enough.

He pushes my jacket off my shoulders and drops it on the floor, immediately reaching for my top and lifting it over my head in one swift move, stopping only briefly to look at me before he holds my face gently and kisses me.

And then it's my turn as I reach for his belt, unbutton his jeans, slip my arms around his waist, desperate to pull him close to me, to feel him against me, to remember what it feels like to have him inside me.

Mike has always been great in bed. Right from that first time in my university bedroom, when I abandoned my Animal Health Management assignment with four paragraphs to go, knowing I couldn't wait another moment to sleep with this man I had fallen head over heels in love with.

He knew intuitively where to touch me, how to hold me, when to kiss me – and I went to places I had never gone with Jamie – places I hadn't even realised existed.

And as the years went by – and he got to know every inch of my body – he only got better.

He has forgotten nothing since we were last in each other's arms like this.

And when we are done – both of us exhausted from the urgency of it, both of us glistening with sweat – we lie facing each other, covered loosely by the white sheets he bought the day he moved out of our home and into the flat.

Mike runs his hand slowly down my back, stopping at my waist before pulling me closer and holding me tight.

"I love you," he whispers.

And then, just like our first first time, we do it all over again.

Chapter Sixty-Five

The weeks that follow go by in a blur.

I feel like a teenager all over again.

I wake in the morning thinking about Mike, and I go to bed in the evening still thinking about him.

It catches me by surprise that I can feel the same excitement twice over for the same man I have slept next to for the last two and a half decades.

I feel the same rush I felt all those years ago. In some ways it's better. Because this time we know what to do to change the ending.

———

We need to make time to be together, for the dinner dates, for the early nights, for the walks along the beach when it's just the two of us.

We need to give the spontaneous kiss, the touch of a hand or the cheeky glance that suggests a promise of something more at the end of the day.

We need to keep making each other a priority.

We are taking things slowly.

Mike is not packing his bags and moving back in.

Not before we are sure we have got it right this time.

Sometimes he stays over.

And when I go to bed, he is not working, or loading the dishwasher, or catching up on emails – no matter how important – he is right there next to me, holding me close.

I was worried about Phoebe. I was worried that seeing us together again would confuse her. We prepared a speech. An explanation for why we were apart, but now we are not.

But no speech was needed. She didn't care in the slightest. The first time Mike stayed over, she simply climbed into bed with us in the morning, stuck her thumb in her mouth and switched on Peppa Pig.

This time around, no introductions are needed. Mike knows my friends, my family, my colleagues. And they know him.

My parents are thrilled that we are back together.

They were devastated when we called time on our marriage. They have always loved Mike. Ever since I brought him home for the weekend, when I already knew this was the real thing.

When he had put us on the train back to Bristol at the end of that weekend, my dad had pulled me in for a hug and whispered in my ear.

"He's a keeper," he had said. But I already knew that.

When I take Mike to visit my parents for the first time – the second time around – my dad shakes his hand – the way he has always done, while Mum just hugs him, tells him she likes his shirt and makes him a cup of tea.

We have dinner with friends, we enjoy days out, we walk

along the beach holding each other's hands, and the hands of our children.

We cheer together as Zack masters walking, we sit side by side at Phoebe's parents' evening, both listening with immense pride as her teacher tells us how well she has adjusted to her new school and how happy she is, and we laugh together with our daughters over a takeaway and the latest must-see Netflix comedy series.

We spend time with our new expanded family.

Our children have got what they always wanted – their mum and dad, back together.

And Phoebe and Zack have a new family.

———————————

But six months after I left Patrick Massey's office with a pair of jester earrings and two extra children, our new-found happiness is threatened in a way we never could have imagined.

Chapter Sixty-Six

It's our first night alone at the house since we got back together.

The girls are both at friends and my parents have offered to have Phoebe and Zack for a sleepover.

Mike phones me on my way home from work, both of us almost high on the anticipation.

"Are you almost home?" he asks.

"About twenty minutes away," I say, stopping at a red light and silently cursing it for holding me up.

"Hurry," he says. "I want you."

And I hang up, laughing at the two of us, behaving like the teenagers that we once were.

But when I get home all thoughts of him ravishing me on the doorstep are forgotten.

Dropping my keys on the hall table, I call his name.

"In here," he says.

"I was expecting to find you naked," I joke. "Would have saved us a bit of time."

But he doesn't laugh.

"Look at this, Zo," he says instead.

I hang my bag on the kitchen door and squint at the book in his hand.

"That's one of Lou's photo books," I say. "Where did you find it?"

"In the kitchen drawer. I was looking for the number for the Chinese."

"It's the one I took from the house when we packed up their things," I tell him. "I put the card inside the pages."

I take the book from him and open the cover.

"See?" I say.

He takes the book back and puts the card on the table.

"I think he's in here, Zo," he tells me, pointing at the book.

"Who is?" I say, confused.

"The man from the café. The one I saw Lou with."

"What are you talking about? Those pictures are from years ago."

"I know," he says. "And I'm not sure. But think it's him, Zoe."

"Show me," I tell him.

He opens the book and flicks through a few pages, stopping at a photograph of Lou and I with two boys, in the same school uniform, the same navy-and-grey striped ties, tied around their heads like bandannas.

He points his finger at one of the boys.

"Him," he says.

"I could be wrong. But I think it was him."

Andrew Robson.

Lou's first love.

The one she told me she liked as she swung on a swing when we were seventeen. The boy she dated for four years. Until Rich came along and swept her off her feet.

"Are you sure?" I ask Mike.

"I'm not sure, no. I mean, this picture is from twenty-five years ago. But it looks a lot like the guy I saw her with."

"Wait," I say.

I run upstairs and take Lou's phone out of my bedside table.

It's flat, so I plug it in.

Her passcode wasn't difficult to crack that day the police handed it over to me. Phoebe's date of birth.

Waiting for the phone to come on, I stare at the picture of the four of us – Lou, Andrew, Jamie and me. So happy. So confident. Our whole lives ahead of us. That picture was taken just after we'd all sat our last A Level. We went straight to the pub and got blind drunk – Lou and I on Pernod and blackcurrant, and Jamie and Andrew on Jack Daniels and Coke.

"Wasn't he from around here?" Mike says, breaking my thoughts.

"Yes," I say. "He was."

I am distracted, though. I am remembering a time when Lou told me that she loved Andrew. That the boy on holiday was a mistake. That she couldn't imagine ever loving anyone more. That she thought she would marry him one day. Probably. And then she met Rich. So I told her to pick one of them, and fast. And she picked Rich.

"Maybe he never left the area," Mike says. "How come I never met him?"

"He went to university in Edinburgh," I say. "He never really came home in the holidays."

"Maybe they just never lost touch? Or maybe they just met by chance in London? Or maybe they worked together?"

So many maybes.

Maybe she never did pick one of them. Not really.

It's a bit of a stretch – but my mind is in a spin.

I have gone from believing my best friend was happily

married, to discovering she had an affair, to finding out that that affair might have been with her first love.

"Wait," I tell Mike, recalling how when I first saw the card, the writing felt oddly familiar. It was not Rich's writing. I knew that. But there was something strangely recognisable about it.

Dropping Lou's phone on the table, I run back up to my study, reach up to the top shelf of my bookcase and pull out my school yearbook. Faded, and worn at the edges, but still as precious as the day they were handed out to us on our last day of Crakeleigh High School.

I flick through the pages to find my own, and scan the messages that fill the white space. And there it is:

I'll miss you Zo-Lo. X

Zo-Lo was a nickname I acquired almost as soon as I started at Crakeleigh. Starting at the school after everyone else, Andrew never really knew me by any other name.

Back downstairs, I lay the book out on the kitchen table, open at the incriminating page. I pull the card out of the envelope and hold it next to the book.

To my darling Lou. The love of my life. Happy Christmas. With love. X

Our writing changes over the years. I know that. But the *Lo* in my name and the same letters in Lou's are unmistakably – devastatingly – similar.

Were they still in touch all that time?

When I moved back to Sussex and Lou suggested we meet up with the boys – and I said no – did she do it anyway? Without me?

Was that where it all started?

Did Lou love him back?

Was he the love of her life too?

Were they still together the night she and Rich died?

Jamie said Andrew was at the wedding. Was that why Lou and Rich were fighting? Did Rich know?

"I'm sorry, Zo," Mike says. "I should have told you. Years ago. I can see that now. I thought I was doing the right thing. You know that, right?"

I nod, but I am already far away.

I am at the house party where Lou lost her virginity to Andrew, afterwards declaring that she loved him, and that she couldn't imagine ever not loving him. I am in Ibiza where we all went on holiday together in our last year of school. Where Lou got food poisoning and Andrew sat by her bedside for three days straight. I am on the phone hearing her tell me that she'd done what I asked. That's she'd picked Rich. And that she hoped she'd made the right decision.

"I need to know," I tell Mike.

"Need to know what?" he says.

"I need to know if she ever really ended it. I need to know if she never stopped loving Andrew."

"What difference will that make?"

"I don't know," I tell him.

And I don't.

But I don't think I am going to like the answer.

Chapter Sixty-Seven

There is a reason they say some things are best left well alone.

And that's because they are.

I have tried to resist the temptation to be drawn into Facebook.

I have an account, but rarely access it. I don't post photos, or like things, or share funny videos. And I have friend requests that have been sitting there for months.

But I am quickly immersed in Lou's Facebook account.

I click on the app on her phone and there's my friend. Dressed in the blue Ted Baker dress I helped her pick. Next to her husband in a dark suit and co-ordinating blue tie. Both of them smiling. At the wedding they attended just before we lost them both.

I feel a lump catch in my throat.

It will have been one of the last photographs ever taken of them.

And there are others from that same wedding.

The bridesmaids, the hen party crew, the bride and groom cutting the cake, Lou and Heidi, Lou with Jamie and his wife…

And then there it is. A picture of Lou with Andrew. Her first love. At their friend's wedding. He is not tagged in the picture, but I know it's him.

And of course it's probably only because I know what I do, but her smile seems bigger, the glint in her eye brighter, her arm just a little bit tighter around his waist than it really needs to be.

I show Mike.

"Him?" I say.

He nods. He doesn't say anything. Instead he wraps his arms around me, aware that I am wondering once again if I ever really knew my friend, and feeling like I am losing her all over again.

Why couldn't she tell me?

And what else was she hiding?

I click Lou's contacts and am taken to a list of 472 friends. All in alphabetical order. And there he is, underneath Abigail Browning, a mutual friend from school, and Adam Cotterill, a colleague at Massey & Stewart.

Andrew Robson.

I can see why Mike was pretty sure. He really hasn't changed at all. A few grey hairs, a few lines around the eyes, but otherwise the same good-looking boy I remember. Popular with everyone. The boy who once pushed me, fully clothed, into the hotel pool in Ibiza; the boy who got drunk on Hooch in Ecstasy and told me how much he loved my friend.

I click on his name and the images in front of me immediately fill in the gaps of the last twenty years.

A wife. Three children.

Holidays abroad. On beaches, and ski slopes, and sightseeing in capital cities.

A dog who is clearly idolised by the entire family.

A job where he wears a hard hat.

And a first love that he clearly couldn't forget.

"What are you going to do?" Mike asks me, getting a Marks & Spencer ready meal out of the fridge, our night of passion clearly off the table for now.

"I'm going to message him," I say.

"And say what?

"Ask him to meet me."

"And then what?"

"I haven't got that far yet," I snap. I know Mike would rather I just left this. But I can't.

"I'm sorry," I say. "He might not even respond."

"But if he does? And he agrees to meet you? What is the end game here, Zo?"

"What do you mean?"

He opens the oven and pushes the lasagne in. Tapping the door shut with his foot, he puts the oven glove down on the island and looks at me.

"What are you hoping to achieve?"

"I want to know why she did it?" I tell him quietly. "I want to know if it meant anything.

"I want to know why she married Rich, if it was Andrew she really loved. I want to know why she cheated on him. Why she had a one-night stand in Majorca. Why she slept with Jamie. Why she did all those things, if it was him she really loved."

"And then?"

I get a bag of salad leaves out of the fridge and tip them into a bowl.

"And then?"

Was it the brief fling she had Mike believe it was?

Or was it something more?

Did she keep going back? Was she unable to tear herself away from the first man she ever loved?

Was he the one that broke her marriage? The one she left her children with me for, when she said she was working? The one Simon saw her with in the pub?

Or was that someone else? Another lover she was prepared to risk everything for? How many were there? And was Andrew even the first?

I think about what Rich's mum told me. That Rich was too good for Lou.

Did she know?

Did she know that Lou had cheated on her son?

Were there more men?

Were there more affairs?

What else did she do to deserve this scorn?

I can't ask Margaret.

She won't remember even saying it.

"What a smashing woman Lou was," she'd probably say.

But I know now that she wasn't.

"And then what?" Mike asks me again.

"Zo?

"When you've met this guy and he tells you that he loved Lou. Or that he didn't. And that it was just the fling she told me it was. Or that it wasn't. Then what?"

"I want to know why she didn't tell me," I say quietly.

He takes the empty packet from me and holds my hands in his.

"Maybe she just didn't want you to know," he says. "Maybe she was racked with guilt. Maybe she was just worried you'd tell Rich. Maybe it *was* just a stupid mistake that she wanted to forget as quickly as it happened.

"I know you want to know, but I'm not sure you're ever going to find the answers you're looking for.

"And none of this is going to bring her back, Zoe. She's gone. She did what she did and nothing is going to change that. So you need to move on now."

I know he's right. I know she's not coming back.

But I was friends with Lou for more than thirty years, and right now I feel like I never really knew her.

If she could keep something like this from me, then what else did she not tell me?

What else do I not know about my friend?

Andrew feels like a missing piece of a puzzle. A piece I need to find.

And once I find it – *if* I find it – then maybe I *can* finally let this all go and move on.

That night Mike and I do make love.

But it's not the urgent, desperate sex we were both expecting when he called me on my way home from work this evening.

It's not the barely make it to the bedroom, tear each other's clothes off kind of sex we've had at any opportunity now since we realised what we'd both foolishly given up.

It's slow and it's tender. Mike holds me close – like he's afraid to let me go, and when we are done I cling to him like he can save me – from the devastation that I can feel in my heart is about to unfold. Because I am getting to know the friend I thought I already knew. And I am beginning to understand what she may have been capable of.

Chapter Sixty-Eight

We meet the next day.

In London.

He offers to travel to Sussex, but I don't want him here. I don't want him anywhere near where my friend was meant to have a life without him.

So I travel to London where we meet at a coffee shop just outside Waterloo Station.

I stare at the door, unable to go in.

Now I'm here, I don't know what I am expecting.

Will I look at him and understand why she did what she did? Will it be that simple?

Or will I never get the answers I am hoping for?

When I eventually enter the coffee shop it's empty, but for the young barista, who is diligently wiping down the counter in front of her.

"Morning," she says, enthusiastically. Her voice full of hope for the day ahead.

"Morning," I say, my own voice doing little to hide the anxious feeling in the pit of my stomach.

"What can I get you?"

I order a coffee and a pastry that I know I won't touch.

"Take a seat," she tells me. "I'll bring it over."

I have the entire coffee shop to choose from and am working out where best to sit to interrogate my dead friend's first love about their illicit affair when he walks in the door.

And I am back at school. In the sixth form block. Fiddling with the cuffs of my jumper. Giggling with Lou and Andrew in the corridor between lessons because Mrs Sanford, the English teacher, has just told Jamie he is an imbecile. I don't even remember why.

"Hi, Zo-Lo," he says quietly.

I haven't been called that since I left school.

"Hi, Andrew," I say.

And then, without warning, he envelops me in a hug that literally takes my breath away.

Eventually I pull away. To look at my friend. The boy I have not seen in twenty-five years.

"You haven't changed a bit," he says, a gentle smile on his face.

"Nor you," I say.

He has the odd wrinkle here and there. The odd grey hair. But then we're a few years older than we once were.

He looks empty. Broken. Like he has lost someone dear to him?

He orders a coffee and we sit together at a table in the far corner of the coffee shop.

We sit in silence while we wait for his coffee to arrive, neither of us ready to show our cards.

"I know you and Lou had an affair," I tell him eventually, his coffee delivered, sugar added, spoon stirred gently.

He nods.

I'm not telling him anything he hasn't already assumed. It's no great coincidence that I have contacted him after all these years.

"How?" he says.

"It's a long story," I tell him, suddenly conscious of the journey that has brought me here. "I was clearing her house and I found a card," I say. It's enough detail for now.

How did you know it was me? he wants to ask, but doesn't. He knows it doesn't matter.

"You said she was the love of your life," I tell him.

"She was. I never stopped loving her."

"She was married," I tell him. "And so were you."

"I know. We both knew that. But we couldn't help ourselves."

"How did it happen, Andrew?" I ask him.

He sips his coffee, contemplating reliving something that is clearly already so painful.

He starts to tell me the story. *Their* story. The one only they will ever truly understand.

He had been living in London for years. But his parents were still in Sussex. On a trip home one weekend, he bumped into Lou. In the supermarket, of all places.

"Seeing her brought back feelings in me that I had kept buried for so long. She broke my heart all those years ago. It took me a long time to get over it."

"But you did get over it, right?" I ask him. "You got married. You made a vow. You had children. And a dog."

"Yes," he says softly. "I did."

"So what happened?" I ask. "One minute you're bumping into each other in the vegetable aisle at the supermarket where you both grew up, and the next you're both risking your marriages for a quick shag?"

I can't help myself, and he flinches.

"It wasn't like that," he tells me.

"What was it like then, Andrew? Enlighten me? She had a family, for God's sake. And so did you."

"I loved her."

"I know. You said. But it was years ago, Andrew. We were just kids."

"You don't understand," he says. "I mean I *loved* her. I loved her back then. And when I saw her again I *still* loved her."

"And then what?" I ask him. "What did you do?"

"For a long time, nothing," he says. "We met for coffee. Once. But other than that, nothing. And then we bumped into each other again. This time in London. And it felt like fate.

"We met for a drink," he says. "And I kissed her. I couldn't not. And she didn't push me away."

"And then you just happened to end up in bed together?"

"Yes," he says quietly. "Pretty much. We spent the night together. At a hotel. And it was like our first time all over again.

"After that it was like we were back at school. Falling in love. Sneaking every opportunity we could to be together. To see each other. To hold each other. She worked in London, so it was easy enough."

"But you were both married," I remind him.

"I know. And we both felt terrible. But the pull was too strong."

I want to tell him about Jamie. I want to tell him how his first girlfriend loved him so much that she cheated on him with his best friend. And with a complete stranger while she was on holiday with me. And then again when she met Rich. But I don't. What good would that do? It won't change anything.

The coffee shop is filling up now. Young couples sit opposite each other messing about on their phones, practically ignoring each other while they drink coffee and share millionaire's shortbread and chocolate croissants. An elderly man orders a pot of tea and hooks his walking stick on the back of his chair while he waits for it to be delivered to his table. A mum tries to negotiate with a toddler who is furiously rejecting all offers of help as he attempts to push the little cardboard straw into his carton of apple juice.

"When?" I ask him. "When did it all start?"

He says nothing for a while. He just looks down, twisting his wedding ring – the one that says he made a vow, the one that confirms he belongs to someone else and should never have done this.

Eventually he looks up at me, and I can tell in his eyes that he knows it's going to hurt me.

"Three and a half years ago," he says, so quietly that I can barely hear.

But I do.

I do hear him telling me that his affair with Lou spanned not just a few months but several years.

And I know then that this was so much bigger than I could ever have imagined.

And all I can feel is sadness. Because I think I came here looking for reassurance that I did know my friend. That whatever this was, was not important, and that she was happy with the life she'd made. But I know now without a doubt that I didn't know her, that this *was* important, and that despite the beautiful children she fought so hard to have, she just wasn't happy.

"If you loved her that much, why were you not at her funeral?" I ask him, suddenly remembering that he wasn't there.

He says nothing at first. But he looks anguished. Apologetic.

"I wanted to be there," he says.

"But you had something else on?" I ask. It's flippant, I know, but I can't help myself.

He looks hurt, but also like he knows he has no right to be.

"I told Nicky about the affair," he says.

"Your wife, I assume?"

He nods.

"I was devastated when I heard the news from Heidi, and I couldn't hide it from her."

"So I'm guessing she's no longer your wife?"

"No. She is," he tells me, and I can't hide my surprise.

"Did you tell her how long it was going on?" I ask, with more than a little cynicism.

He looks uncomfortable, which answers my question.

"Of course you didn't," I say. "There's no way she'd still be with you if you did."

"She said she was prepared to give me another chance."

"That was very big of her. I'm not sure I could have done that."

"But she said if I went to the funeral she would walk away."

"Do you actually still want to be with her?" I ask him. "You said you loved Lou. Do you love your wife too?"

"I don't think I even know how I feel anymore," he says. "But I've been married a long time, and if Nicky is prepared to give me another chance, then I need to take it. For my girls' sake, if nothing else."

"You may have been married a long time, but that was not a brief fling you had there, Andrew. It was a full-blown affair. One that lasted more than three years."

"We did stop for a while," he says, as if he is suddenly recalling a brief moment when they both questioned what on earth they were doing, when they remembered they had families at home – children who were waiting for them to tuck them in, a husband and a wife who loved them and deserved better.

"Oh, well done, you," I say, and he winces, his face betraying a guilt that he has clearly struggled with.

Well, I'm struggling now.

I want to leave. I want to go home and tell Mike that I love him. I want to hold my children tight and tell them I'll never do anything to hurt them.

But I am compelled to stay.

"So why *did* you stop?" I ask Andrew. "If you loved each other so much, why didn't she just leave Rich? Why didn't you leave your wife?"

"I said I would. But Lou kept saying she wasn't ready. That it was a big step.

"And then, out of nowhere, she just ended it. I was devastated."

"Did she say why?" I ask him.

He shakes his head.

"Not at the time. But a few months later she called, and we met. She was pregnant.

"For a moment I thought it was mine, of course. But it couldn't have been."

Why not? I want to ask. *Why couldn't it have been yours?*

But I don't. I stay silent, convinced that Andrew can surely hear the pounding in my chest.

"I knew Phoebe was conceived through IVF after years of trying for a baby. But I thought they'd stopped trying. If I'd known they were having IVF again, I would have ended it. There and then. Honestly, Zo-Lo, I would have.

"I felt like such a fool. I honestly believed that she loved me, that we were going to be together one day, when the whole time they were going through IVF, trying for another baby."

And it is in that very moment – when Andrew tells me how my friend broke his heart when she made a baby with another man – that I realise I may have started something that I might just not be able to undo.

———————

I put my hands under the table so that Andrew can't see them shaking.

And I am sure the pounding in my chest is now as visible as it is deafening to me.

Andrew is still talking.

But I hear nothing after "IVF".

I am filling in the gaps. I am counting all the lies my friend has told. The people she has betrayed. The friends she has involved.

It's all right there in front of me.

She had an affair with her first love. Then she found out she was pregnant. So she broke his heart and convinced her husband that after years of trying for another baby, they had suddenly got lucky.

So Andrew never had any way of knowing that the baby could be his.

And then what?

I don't need to ask. And Andrew can't tell me anyway. He doesn't know the truth.

So I fill in the blanks myself.

Zack was born. And he completed their family. And Lou was happy. For a while, at least.

But leopards don't change their spots. Eventually she was back in touch. And Andrew couldn't say no. Because she was like a drug that he couldn't get enough of. So while they once again pretended to be working late and had sex in hotel rooms, Rich was left at home with his daughter, and the newborn son *who may or may not have been his.*

"Zoe?" Andrew says, putting his hand on my arm, pulling me back from a place in my mind where I am doing my best friend's job, where I am weighing up the evidence, where I am building a case against her. And it is clear she is guilty as charged.

"What?" I say.

"Do you want another coffee?"

I am suddenly aware of the barista stood over our table, clearing our plates, asking if we'd like anything else.

I look in my cup where there is still a little left.

"No. Thank you," I say.

I need to go. I need to work out what the hell I do now.

"She called me," Andrew says, answering the question I haven't yet asked. "When Zack was a few months old. She said she missed me.

"I asked her again. To leave Rich," he says. "I told her I would look after her. And the children. But she couldn't do it."

"But you carried on anyway?" I ask him. "Even after they'd had another baby? Even after she'd said she wouldn't leave Rich?"

"I'm not proud of myself," he says quietly.

I need to get out of here.

I need to get away from Andrew.

I don't want him to look at me and see that Lou lied to him too.

I drain my coffee and tell him I have to go.

"Thank you for meeting me," I tell him, looping my bag over my arm and onto my shoulder.

"It's been a long time," he says. "It was good to see you. I just wish it had been under better circumstances."

I nod my agreement.

And then I say goodbye, before he can see the look on my face. The look that says there was no IVF, that Lou was lying to him, and that there is every chance that Zack may be his.

"I loved her, Zo-Lo," he tells me, as I turn to leave.

"I know," I tell him. "Me too."

Chapter Sixty-Nine

When I get home the house is empty.

Mike has taken the kids out.

I think he knew I might be a mess, and he didn't want the kids to see that.

But I don't think either of us could have ever imagined just how messy this might be about to get.

I pull off my shoes and drop my handbag on the hall table before heading straight up to my study.

I drag the box in the corner over to my desk and open it. I pull out two baby books. A record of the first year of Phoebe and Zack's little lives. A pink book for Phoebe. A blue one for Zack. Stereotypical. But absolutely the right choice for each of them.

I slide Phoebe's into the bookcase alongside my own children's. I can look at hers another day.

I hold Zack's in my lap, the spine stretched a little with the volume of photos glued inside, despite him not even being a full year old when the last picture was lovingly added.

Lou fared better than me at filling these books.

Oliver's was bulging with information. On his first words, his first tooth, his first steps.

Sophie's was completed with slightly less enthusiasm, with a toddler tugging at my hands, tickling his baby sister, demanding my time.

And honestly, Isla's was barely even opened. When life calms down, I'll fill it in. That's what I've always told myself. I am still waiting for that time to come, of course. The last few months have guaranteed that it is still a long way away.

I look at the pictures of Zack, turning the pages one by one.

In hospital, the day he was born. In his pram a few days after they brought him home, with Phoebe pushing him, reaching her little arms up to the handles, a big smile on her face. In the bath. In his cot. In his highchair.

I always thought he looked like Rich. But is that just something we say? An instinctive reaction when you see a baby for the first time? "Oh, doesn't he look like you?", "He's got your nose, that's for sure.", "I can really see you in him when he smiles."

I look for signs of Rich in the pages in front of me. And I look for signs of Andrew. Both with equal determination. But the truth is, I just see Zack. The little boy who has become mine. And who I can't bear the thought of losing.

Chapter Seventy

Mike was right. When he said I should leave well alone.

Before I started digging, I could justify Lou's affair as a moment of weakness, a moment of stupidity – a few brief moments of stupidity, at worst.

Now I know it was more than that. Far more.

Now I know that Zack might not be Rich's son. That he probably isn't.

In the days that follow I say nothing. Not to Mike, not to Robyn, and definitely not to the girls.

I am scared to say it out loud.

I am scared that if I say it out loud it will make it real, it will become something I have to face. And I don't want to face this.

So I tell Mike he was right. I tell him that it was a brief fling that ended shortly after that day in Waterloo. That they did what he had asked.

I don't want to lie to him.

But I can't tell him the truth.

Because I don't want it to be the truth.

I want all of this to go away. I want Lou to have been happy. I want her never to have bumped into Andrew, or had coffee with him, or started an affair with him. I want her never to have loved him.

I want Zack to be Rich's. Because that makes him mine now. And I don't want to lose him.

When I am not in surgery – where my concentration can literally be the difference between life and death – I am consumed by my best friend's affair – and the far-reaching consequences it could be about to have for me and my family.

I find myself staring at Zack. As he plays. As he eats. As he sleeps soundly in his cot, in the new bedroom we have just finished decorating for him, with the dinosaur stickers on the walls and the dinosaur curtains hanging at the window.

I try to see Rich in his features. When I can't, I try to see Andrew instead. And sometimes I convince myself I can see his eyes, his smile, the shape of his chin. Other times I can't. And that's when my mind spirals into a place where my best friend was having affairs left, right and centre. With the postman, with the milkman, with the colleague in the office next door to hers.

And then momentarily I convince myself that neither of these men are Zack's father. That his father is another man altogether. Someone else she bumped into in the supermarket, maybe. In the frozen aisle, swapping recommendations for tasty pizzas and to-die-for desserts.

And I know it's crazy. Because she was a good person. I know she was. I knew her for more than thirty years. A few mistakes – even big ones like this – don't wipe all of that out. Surely.

But what else didn't I know about my best friend? What else

did she lie about? *Was* Andrew the first man she ever had an affair with? The only one? One of many? Or was he the last in a long line?

Or was she just very unhappy and not able to tell me?

When I am not obsessing over the lies Lou told in the months leading up to her death, I am obsessing over what I do next.

Can I do nothing?

Do I have to tell Andrew? That Lou lied to him. That he may have another child? That his three daughters may have a baby brother?

I should do the right thing. I know that. I should tell him the truth. Whatever he did or didn't do, he deserves to know that Zack might be his. Doesn't he? And if it turns out Zack's dad didn't die in a car accident six months ago, then doesn't he deserve a chance to know his real dad?

But I can't bear it. I literally can't bear the thought that we might lose Zack. Or that his little world – and that of his sister – could be blown apart yet again. After everything they have already been through this year. He deserves better. They both do.

What if I just said nothing?

Would that be so terrible?

What if I had never seen that card?

We were happy.

We were beginning to make a life together.

Can we just pretend this never happened?

No one knows.

Andrew suspects nothing. As far as he is concerned, Zack is Rich's. He is not knocking at my door to claim a child he thinks might be his.

Chapter Seventy-One

"Let's have a day at the beach," Mike announces on Sunday morning a week later.

I have been trying to forget.

I have dropped Phoebe and Zack off every morning and kissed them goodbye. I have put on scrubs and performed intricate surgeries on family pets and ploughed through piles of paperwork. I have taken my children to dance classes and therapy sessions. And I have cuddled up to my ex-husband at night and told him how much I love him.

I have been trying to forget how my world changed the moment I found out about Lou's affair.

And I have been trying to pretend that I still live in a world where I am the guardian to two children who lost everything.

Even though I know one of them might not have.

"A day at the beach sounds perfect," I say, hopeful it will give me some respite from the moral dilemma that is raging in my mind.

The sun is shining and the beach is already busy by the time we arrive.

By the expert way Mike is dragging Zack's pushchair backwards through the sand, you can tell he has done this before.

"This will do," he announces, dropping the picnic bag on the sand.

This would normally be where he parks himself on a deckchair and starts scrolling through a thousand emails on his phone, telling me that no, it really can't wait, and yes, he'll play with the kids in just a few minutes.

Instead he kicks off his shoes, pulls out a bucket and spade and starts digging.

"Are you going to help me, Phoebs?" he asks.

"Yes please," she says, looking suitably excited.

I help her take off her shoes and socks and then, on Mike's instructions, she obediently begins digging a big mound of sand with her little pink spade.

"What are we making, Uncle Mike?" she asks him.

"Anything you want," he says. "How about a mermaid?"

Her face lights up.

"Daddy can make sand mermaids," she says excitedly, and Mike immediately looks at me.

It is a while now since she has mentioned Lou or Rich in this way. Like they're just "away", due back any day now…

So we wait, like we always do when she's sharing a memory with us, and then she giggles.

"We put my bikini top on her," she says, a big smile on her face.

Pushing a strand of hair out of her eyes and leaving a trail of sand in its place, she goes quiet for a moment, her little mind lost in this beautiful memory. And then she asks us if we think they have sand in heaven.

"I think they probably do, don't you?" Mike says.

She thinks about it and then nods and carries on digging.

"So, a mermaid then, Phoebs?" Mike checks, glancing over at me with a smile.

These moments used to be followed by a period of sadness, where she'd look at photos of Lou and Rich and ask us to tell her again why they had to die.

But now – more often than not – she is just sharing a memory. She is just telling us about something that made her happy. Like when Mummy put her hair in bunches for Lilly's birthday party. Or when Daddy took her on the big slide at the park. Or when they went to the beach and made a mermaid in the sand.

I want to bottle these memories for her so that she never forgets.

But I know I can't do that, and that makes me sad.

———

"I know!" Phoebe announces excitedly. "Let's build a unicorn!"

"A unicorn?" Mike asks, clearly concerned that her expectations may be a little grander than his sand-sculpting abilities.

"Yes. A standing-up unicorn," she clarifies, in case he thought he was going to get away with a unicorn having a snooze on the beach.

"You got it, Phoebs," he says.

And I have no idea quite how he will pull this off or if he even knows himself, but right now I don't think I could love him any more if I tried.

An hour and a half, one ice-cream and one paddle in the freezing-cold water later, Ursula the Unicorn is born – complete with shell-encrusted horn.

The name was Mike's idea – Ursula being the only name he could think of that began with a U.

Even Isla is impressed at her dad's artistic efforts.

"It's pretty good, to be fair, Dad," she says, pouring the contents of a miniature packet of Skittles into her mouth, and Mike smiles proudly.

We have just enough time to take a few photographs before Zack – who has been watching with quiet disinterest from an inflatable dinghy – throws himself out of the boat and grabs Ursula's horn, crushing it in his little hands.

Isla and I immediately burst out laughing – and fortunately so does Phoebe – whilst Mike, clearly mourning the lost hour it took him to make a sand sculpture that defied gravity, takes a few seconds longer than the rest of us to see the funny side.

As we walk off the beach at the end of the day, Mike lifts Phoebe onto a wall and starts dusting the sand from her feet with a towel. She is tired and is making a fuss, complaining that it's hurting her toes.

"Okay, Phoebs," he says, still rubbing her foot with the towel, her shoe under his arm. "Would you rather keep going to the beach, and have to have the sand dusted off your toes every now and then? Or never go to the beach again?"

"Never?" she says. "So we would never be able to build another Ursula?"

"Exactly that," he says.

"I like the beach," she says with a smile, and holds out her other foot to prove it.

It's been a good day.

We have made memories.

We have eaten ice-creams, and made sand unicorns, and smiled as Zack put handfuls of sand in his mouth like all of our other children once did.

But as we arrive home I realise that all the happy memories in the world will not make me forget what I now know.

As I take Zack out of his pushchair, he holds his arms out to Mike.

"Dada," he says.

And my heart all but breaks.

———————

I *can* say nothing.

I *can* pretend that this never happened.

I can pretend that Lou was happy and that she and Rich had two beautiful children together.

Because no one knows.

Not even Mike.

No one suspects a thing.

But *I* know.

And if Zack is Andrew's son, then I don't think I could live with myself if I said nothing. How could I deprive him of hearing his son call *him* Dada one day?

Chapter Seventy-Two

I wake up every morning and I remember that my best friend had an affair. And that that affair may or may not have produced a little boy. And I feel sick, and sad, and disappointed, and scared – all at the same time.

I drive to work and wonder how many times Andrew met Lou off the train in London, snatching time together before they went to work.

I cook dinner for my new extended family and wonder how many times Lou and Andrew shared romantic dinners in London's finest restaurants, all the while winning Nicky and Rich's sympathy for having to work late yet again.

And I kiss Phoebe and Zack goodnight and wonder how many times Lou missed those precious moments so that she could have sex with her first love instead.

I find myself staring at Andrew's number on my phone, my thumb intermittently hovering over the dial button, changing my mind each time I am about to make contact with the glass screen.

If I call him, if I tell him, then I know I can't un-tell him. I can't take it back. It will be out there, and I will have set in motion something that I won't be able to stop. Something that I know in my heart is more likely than not to end badly. For me, for Mike and the kids, for Phoebe. And for Zack.

Chapter Seventy-Three

Nine days after I drank coffee with Andrew and learned how he and Lou had spent the last three years of her life betraying everyone they loved – where they held hands in London restaurants, had sex in boutique hotels in their lunch hour and reminisced about their teenage years – I crack.

I realise I can't do this alone. I can't carry this monumental secret to my grave. I need to share it – so that it doesn't weigh so heavily on my own heart. So I tell Mike everything.

I leave out only the fact that I momentarily considered saying nothing at all. To anyone. Ever. I don't want Mike to know this. I don't want him to be disappointed in me. To doubt that I'm a good person. Because really I am just scared.

I know he won't be able to make it go away.

I know that him knowing won't make it any less likely that Zack is Andrew's. But if it turns out he is – and I lose him – then I will need Mike to pick up the pieces. I will need him to hold my hand like he has every other time I have needed him to. More than ever.

When I walk through the door he is loading the dishwasher.

I put Zack in his highchair and peel him a banana before pulling out a chair and sitting down.

"You okay?" he asks, dropping a handful of spoons into the cutlery holder.

I shake my head and can already feel the lump rising in my throat.

"I lied to you," I tell him.

"About what?" he says. "How much you love me? How much you love my lasagne?"

"I'm serious, Mike."

He looks up and can see as much in my face.

"Sorry," he says, shutting the dishwasher door.

"Sit down," I tell him.

So he does.

But before I can tell him, Phoebe comes running through from the playroom, clutching a handful of Lego.

"Hey, Phoebs," I say. "Good day at school?"

"Yes," she says, dropping the Lego on the table in front of me.

"Can you pull Stephanie's hair off for me?" she asks.

"Sure," I say with a smile.

I pull the peculiarly styled plastic hair off the Lego head and hand the pieces back to her.

"So what did you do at school today?" I ask her.

"Stuff," she says, with a cheeky grin, now familiar with the stories of how Oliver, Sophie and Isla always used to give this response to the same question.

"What kind of stuff?" I try.

"Felix bit Jasper on the knee because he wouldn't let him play with the building blocks, so they both got told off in Mrs Alderley's office," she says.

"Oh, right," I say. "That doesn't sound very good. Anything else?"

"Not really," she says.

"What did you have for lunch?" I ask.

"I can't remember. Can I go now?" she asks.

"Of course you can," I tell her, handing her the rest of the Lego pieces from the table and planting a kiss on her forehead.

"I just need a quick word with Uncle Mike and then I will run you a bath."

"Okay," she says, skipping out of the kitchen, Stanley following close behind.

I look at Mike and my eyes fill with tears.

"What is it, Zoe?" he says.

"I lied to you," I tell him again. "About Andrew. When I met him in London."

"What do you mean?"

"It wasn't over, Mike. It was never over. When you saw them in London they were in the middle of a full-blown affair."

He is as shocked as I was.

"She had no intention of ending it."

"What, ever?" he asks, incredulous. "So they were having an affair this whole time?"

"They broke up briefly," I tell him.

"When?" he asks.

I go to tell him and the words won't come out.

"When?" he asks me again.

"When Zack was born," I say.

And then I crumble.

Zack looks at me, puzzled, and Mike swiftly pulls him out of his highchair, delivering him to his eldest daughter in the living room before returning and shutting the kitchen door.

He wraps his arms around me and holds me.

If he has worked it out, then he isn't saying.

I want to push him away. I want to punish him for believing my friend. For not telling me. For not giving me the chance to stop this before it became too big for any of us to ever get over.

But I can't. Because I need him.

"Zo," he implores me as I sob in his arms.

"Tell me. Please. What is it?"

I look up at my ex-husband, my first love – my only love – the man who helped me find happiness again in the face of the worst kind of grief.

And I realise that he can't help me. That he can't stop this from happening. No one can.

Chapter Seventy-Four

Leaving Mike to process the enormity of what I have just told him, I put the children to bed.

I bathe them. I clean their teeth. I read them stories and hand them their favourite toys. I do all the things that, just six months ago, I didn't need to do, but that now are as much my need as theirs.

When I tuck Phoebe in, in the cabin bed I bought for her, and the unicorn duvet that we picked out together, she wraps her arms around me and cuddles me.

"Night-night, Mummy," she says.

In that moment it is the very best and the very worst thing she could have said to me.

I don't correct her.

I don't need to.

Instead I hold her tight and tell her that I love her too. Because I do.

I love her. And I love Zack.

And my heart aches at the thought of losing him.

I kiss her and tell her I will see her in the morning. And then I kiss her baby brother, and I wonder if my days of doing this might be numbered.

"Do I have to tell him?" I ask Mike later.

But I know the answer.

He squeezes my hand.

"Would you rather tell the truth or risk living a lie?" he says.

"Neither," I tell him.

Whenever Mike has asked me these questions, I have never cheated. I have never chosen "neither". I have chosen the baby over the career, I have chosen the hypothetical life without pizza, I have chosen the never-ending kiss. But this choice is just too hard.

"I don't want to stop Zack knowing the truth," I say. "If it is the truth. But I don't want to tell Andrew he could be his. Because if I tell him, then I might lose him."

"If you don't tell the truth, then it might come out anyway. One day. In a few months, or in a few years. And then it will be too late to do the right thing. And you will risk losing him anyway."

I know he is right.

"What then?" I say. "What happens when I tell him?"

"Let's just take this one step at a time, Zo," he tells me. "We don't know anything for sure yet. We only know that there's a chance Zack might not have been Rich's son."

I brush a tear from my face, and wipe my hand on my jeans, desperately trying to hold it together.

"But if he wasn't, what then?" I say, barely able to get the words out. They are too painful to even contemplate, let alone say out loud.

SARAH LEFEBVE

"Then we will get through it," he says. "Like we have everything else that life has thrown at us. Together. But we are a long way away from that scenario right now."

Chapter Seventy-Five

I t is clear that we need some help.

We are intelligent people. Between us we can save animals and we can crunch huge numbers. But how do we even begin to fathom out what to do with this? With the knowledge that my godson, who was orphaned when both of his parents died, might not actually be an orphan after all.

Zack might have a dad. A dad that, given half a chance, I know, would love him like I do.

Where do we even start?

I am not ashamed to admit that, yes, I have asked Google.

And judging by the multitude of results it generates, *How do you find out who your child's father is?* is a far more commonly asked question than you'd think.

Along with *What if my husband is not the father of my child?* and *How do I tell my husband he is not the father?*

What is not so common, though, is *How do you find out who your godson's father is? The one you are now guardian for, because both his parents have died, including the father who might not be the father after all...*

According to the links I do find, paternity can be determined by blood tests and DNA. And whilst a lot of the sites talk about samples from the mother, the potential father and the child, paternity can also be determined without samples from the mother.

Which is handy, of course.

You can even do it without the father's knowledge.

Which is a dangerous thing for me to be reading right now.

Before I know it, I will be going undercover, following Andrew on his way to some coffee shop, lurking in the corner, ready to pounce when he gets up to leave, scouring his empty seat for a single strand of hair, then placing it in an envelope alongside one of Zack's hairs and sending it off to some dodgy backstreet lab that will tell us with 99.999 per cent certainty whether our world is about to be shattered.

Schools have broken up for the summer holidays. I have booked Phoebe into a summer camp for the first two weeks. I drop her off each morning before I drop Zack at nursery and pick her up on my way back to get him. For the next two weeks my parents are having her, which she is equally excited about. And for the last two weeks we are going on holiday. I have even managed to convince Oliver and Sophie to join us. Our first holiday as a family of seven.

Mike is making the most of Phoebe's packed summer schedule to put in a few extra hours at work.

And in my spare time – of which there is, of course, always very little – I am brushing up on the law.

I need to know where I stand.

I am Zack's legal guardian.

But I became his legal guardian when he lost both of his parents.

If it turns out he didn't lose both of his parents, do I automatically lose that status?

My head tells me that that is obvious. It makes sense.

But my heart is aching for nothing to make sense. My heart wants me to be his legal guardian, no matter what. My heart wants me to be able to tell Andrew that Zack is mine. That he can't have him. That I won't let him take him away.

———

Wanting answers, despite not being sure if I am ready to hear them, I call Patrick Massey.

It seems ironic, somehow, that the law firm where my friend was such a success professionally, could now be advising me on the absolutely monumental mess she made in her personal life.

"Massey," he says, the epitome of formality.

"Hello, Patrick," I say. "This is Zoe Henry. Lou's friend…"

He says nothing, and I picture him taking a sip from his crystal tumbler, squinting at the sunlight beaming through his window, trying to place me.

"Lou Smithson," I offer.

"Yes, of course. I'm so sorry, Mrs Henry. It's been one of those days."

One of what days? I want to ask. Because right now I'd gladly take one of any kind of days over my own.

"Please call me Zoe," I tell him. Again.

"Zoe. Sorry. How are you?"

"I'm well," I tell him, knowing that I wouldn't even begin to know how to answer this question truthfully. "But I do need your help with something, if that's okay?"

"Of course," he says. "What can I do?"

"Would I be able to come and see you?" I ask him. "It's kind of complicated. I'm sorry. I know you are very busy. But I really would appreciate it. I wouldn't ask if it wasn't really important."

"Of course," he tells me.

"How does next Tuesday work?"

We confirm a time and then I hang up.

Patrick Massey was the right person to call.

But I am scared.

Seven months ago he told me I had to care for a little boy called Zack, but soon he might be telling me that I have to give him up.

———

I hope I have done the right thing.

I have watched enough legal dramas to know that whatever I tell Patrick Massey will be kept confidential. I think...

Despite this, of course, I know my imagination will run wild. I will not be able to stop myself from imagining scenarios where Patrick tells everyone I know that his protégé was having a sordid affair right up until her death. That I have no legal right to keep the child she left me in her will. And that he belongs to a man he has never met.

———

"Do you not think we need to speak to Andrew about this first?" Mike asks me when I tell him about my meeting with Patrick.

His use of the word "we" is not lost on me.

This is our problem now. Not mine.

And I am so glad I have him by my side.

Yes, I probably should tell Andrew first. He might tell me he doesn't want to know if Zack is his.

He might tell me that he's not interested in finding out he has another child.

But I know Andrew.

He wouldn't tell me anything of the sort.

He would tell me that if Zack was his, he would love him immediately.

He would tell me that if Zack was his, he would spend every day making up for the fact that he missed the first year of his life.

So the truth is, I need to know whether we should be doing everything in our power *not* to speak to Andrew about this.

If Patrick Massey tells me that Andrew could just walk into my house and take Zack, I honestly don't know what I would do. What would it do to Zack? What would it do to Phoebe? Haven't they been through enough?

"I need to know if he can take him," I tell Mike. "I need to know where we stand."

He wants to tell me that no one can take Zack away from me. I know he does. He wants to fix this.

But he knows he can't fix it.

He knows he can't tell me that no one can take Zack away from me.

Not if Andrew is his dad.

Not even Patrick Massey can tell me that.

I am not stupid.

I am just desperate.

Desperate to stop Phoebe and Zack's lives from falling apart around them all over again.

Desperate to stop my own life from falling apart.

"He might not be his, Zoe," he says instead, holding me, trying his best to stop my heart from breaking all over again.

Chapter Seventy-Six

In the days before I meet Patrick I try to keep things normal.

I get the children up. I feed them. I take them to nursery and summer camp and I pick them up at the end of the day.

I play with them, make them dinner and run them a bath, and I tuck them in at night.

I try not to hold Zack too tight, not to cuddle him more than I normally would, not to wonder whether these might be my last days or weeks with him.

On Monday Phoebe sees Poppy. She's doing really well right now, but Poppy has prepared us for the fact that these times will come and go. She won't always seem like she is doing well.

"Just keep encouraging her to share how she is feeling," she told me. "In whatever way she wants to do that."

When I pick her up she tells me she wants to draw a picture of her family.

Draw a picture of us, I want to say.

We're your family now.

We love you.

But of course I don't.

Instead I put the paper and colouring pencils on the table and give her a little cuddle.

"That's a lovely idea," I say.

But half an hour later my heart breaks when I realise that is exactly what she has done.

We're all there – Mike, me, Isla, Sophie, Oliver and Zack. All of us standing in a line, neatly labelled underneath our feet in her tiny writing. Even Stanley makes it onto the picture. And I want to cry. Because it is the first picture she has drawn of us as a family. But it may be the last while we still are one.

She puts down her pencil and looks up at me hesitantly, as if she is looking for approval somehow, as if she is wondering whether she has got it right. We *are* her family, aren't we?

I put a beaker of milk and a biscuit on the table next to her and kiss the top of her head.

"I love it," I tell her.

"Shall we put it on the fridge?"

She nods, slides another piece of paper in front of her, and tells me she's going to do another one.

"What are you going to do now?" I ask her.

"A picture of my other mummy," she says, kneeling up on her chair. "The one that is in heaven."

She looks in the pencil box, her little face full of concentration, carefully choosing the perfect pencil for this very important project.

I look away, hiding a sadness I don't want her to see.

To Phoebe it's simple. She has two mummies now. No more, no less.

I am here, by her side. The other one is not. The other one never will be again.

I leave her drawing while I bathe Zack, and by the time we come back downstairs she is colouring in Lou's dress. A pink dress with purple flowers on it.

"Do you think Mummy would like it?" she asks me, hesitantly.

I tell her I do, of course.

I tell her I think Mummy would think it was the best drawing she'd ever seen. And Phoebe beams with pride.

But inside I am angry.

The woman in the drawing is happy. She has a pretty dress with purple flowers, and a smile that would light up a room.

But the woman in the picture is also a liar and a cheat.

I am angry that my friend is putting me through this. That she is putting us all through this.

Isn't it enough that she went and died, and left us to pick up the pieces?

Now we have to figure out how to clear up a mess that none of us could ever have imagined she could make.

———

On Tuesday I drop Zack and Phoebe off and then leave my car in the station car park before taking the train into London.

Mike offered to come with me.

"I should be there," he said. "I *want* to be there. We're a team now."

But I told him I need to do this alone.

It's me Lou picked. It's me that walked out of Patrick Massey's office in February having been named as sole guardian of her children. If I am going to be told that that no longer stands, then I want to be the first to hear that. Alone.

I buy myself a coffee at the station before boarding the train.

In different circumstances it would feel like a treat. A whole morning to myself. No children to sort out. No animals to stitch up, or vaccinate, or de-magot. Just me, a cappuccino and my phone.

But I can't feel excited today.

I sip my coffee and stare out of the window.

I watch a couple and their young son get off the train at Clapham Junction. Getting off ahead of the little boy, they each hold one of his hands as he tentatively steps onto the platform, all of them excited for the day ahead. For me, though, every mile closer to Waterloo feels like a mile closer to my new world falling apart.

I take the underground to the City, my mind suddenly back in the day I last made this journey. The day I arrived empty-handed and left with a pair of jester earrings and two more children.

I exit the station and make the short walk back to the offices of Massey & Stewart, wondering if this time I will leave having been told I may be down to just one.

I hope I don't. I love them both so much. More than I already did. More than I ever thought was possible.

I sit down on the leather sofa outside Patrick's office and pick up one of the magazines from the table in front of me. I open it but the words all merge into one, my mind unable to think of anything but how much my life has changed in the last seven months, and how I don't want it to change again.

The door opens and Patrick emerges from his office.

"Mrs Henry," he says, giving me a warm smile. "Zoe."

"Hi, Patrick."

He opens the door to his office. "Come in. Please."

I have come so far since I last sat in this office. I have gone through so much and come out the other side. Happy. Still me. Just with two extra, amazing, wonderful children. And a new start with the love of my life.

"So how can I help you, Zoe?" Patrick asks me. The same

crystal tumbler on his desk. The same pen. A different pile of papers to shuffle.

"I need some advice," I say, hesitantly. "But it's difficult to explain."

"Well then, why don't you just have a go? And we'll take it from there?"

I nod.

And then I tell him my story.

I tell him about the card. And the photo book. And my best friend's first love.

I tell him about the affair she had with him. And the fact that she lied to him about Zack. About having IVF.

He listens attentively. Lifting his pen to write down the odd note.

"So now I just don't know," I tell him. "I don't know if he's Zack's real dad or not.

"And I don't know if I should tell him that I think he might be. And – if I do tell him … well, then could he take Zack away from me? Could he take him away from all of us? Because I don't think I could bear that. I don't think any of us could."

Patrick hands me a tissue and waits patiently while I dab the corners of my eyes. He writes a few more notes on the paper in front of him and then puts down his pen. And he looks at me earnestly. Which I know is not a good sign.

"If you believe this man – Mr Robson – to be Zack's father, then you have both a legal and a moral obligation to tell him, Zoe. But I think you already know that, right?"

I nod, allowing a stray tear to run down my cheek.

"And what happens once I do that?" I ask him quietly.

I know it's already a foregone conclusion that I will. How can I not?

"Well, that is up to Mr Robson initially. If he agrees that he may be Zack's father, then he can make an application for what's called a Declaration of Parentage."

"What is that?" I ask. "What does it mean?"

"A Declaration of Parentage declares whether a named individual is the legal parent of another person under English law," he says. "If Mr Robson makes an application to the courts, and the courts believe he has grounds for the application, then they can order a paternity test to be carried out."

Mr Robson.

It sounds so formal.

No longer my childhood friend, but the opposition in a potential custody battle. For a child who seven months ago didn't need either of us, but who we both now want to love, or will want to in Andrew's case.

"If that paternity test then proves he is the father, then he will be named as such on the Declaration."

Giving me a moment to process the enormity of what he has just told me, Patrick reaches across his desk and puts his hand on mine.

It is a gesture that threatens to push me over the edge into a place I might not get back from.

"A Declaration of Parentage is not the same as parental responsibility, though, Zoe," he tells me gently.

"Right now that parental responsibility – for both children – lies with you. And you alone. Based on the stipulations in Louise and Richard's wills.

"If it was proved beyond any reasonable doubt that Mr Robson was Zack's biological parent, then he would have to make a separate application for parental responsibility. If he wanted to pursue that role."

Would Andrew do that?

Would he want to be Zack's dad?

I don't know him. Not really. I haven't known him since we

were teenagers. But I can't believe that the man I sat with in the coffee shop – the one who told me how much he still loved Lou – wouldn't want to be part of his son's life.

He has given his three girls a great life.

Just a handful of photographs on Facebook are enough to know that.

I think he would want to make sure he gave his son the same love, the same life.

"Does that help, Zoe?" Patrick asks, breaking my thoughts.

"Yes," I tell him. "Thank you, Patrick."

"I know it's probably not what you wanted to hear," he says. "But it's important to know you have options. Right now you are Zack's only parent, Zoe. Any other parent seeking any kind of involvement in his life would have to convince the courts that that involvement was in Zack's best interests."

"I understand," I tell him. "I really do appreciate your help, Patrick. You have my address, of course. For your invoice."

He shakes his head.

"I wouldn't dream of it," he tells me. "Please just keep me posted. Will you do that?"

"Of course."

"And if you need any further help, please just pick up the phone. Okay?"

"I will," I confirm.

He goes to shake my hand and instead clasps it gently between his own. A lump catches in my throat and I hurriedly say my goodbyes.

I walk to the station. I get on the train back to Ferringham. I watch the people around me go about their daily lives. Some of them no doubt leading lives even more complex than my own. Some of them blissfully unaware of just how complicated life can be.

And I contemplate what I do next.

Chapter Seventy-Seven

I call Mike as soon as I am on the train, but I am unable to speak. If I speak I will cry. And if I cry I will not be able to stop. But I need to hear his voice. I need him to tell me everything will be okay, even though I know it won't.

In my head I have already lost Zack. He is Andrew's, and Andrew wants him.

In my head I am packing his clothes, and his toys – all the things I have already packed once before.

In my head I am telling Phoebe that she lost two parents but Zack only lost one. What a lucky boy.

———

I haven't stopped crying since I arrived home. I picked Zack up from nursery early. Brought him home. Cuddled him. Breathed him in. Mourned his mum all over again. And then I told Mike we might lose him.

"It might not come to that," he says, as I sob in his arms. "Let's just take it one day at a time."

"I won't make it easy for him," I tell Mike later, haphazardly tipping pasta into two bowls and pouring sauce on top, while he researches *Declaration of Parentage* on his laptop.

It was not supposed to be like this.

We have just found each other again.

We were supposed to be ripping each other's clothes off at every opportunity.

We were supposed to be thinking about how lucky we were that we got another chance.

Instead we are spending every waking moment researching family law, and trying to calculate the likelihood that any court would not give custody of a little boy to a living parent over a family friend.

Mike pushes his laptop to the side as I put our dinner on the table.

But I can't eat. Instead I just push my fork around the bowl, feeling lost.

"You need to eat something," Mike tells me gently.

"I won't make it easy for him," I say again. "I will tell him there is a chance that Zack is his. But I won't share with him what Patrick told me. He can find it all out by himself."

And he will, of course.

I know that.

It is only a matter of time before he knows everything I know.

"I'm sorry," I tell Mike, putting my fork down.

"What are you sorry for?" he says.

"For doing what you told me I shouldn't. For going looking for answers to questions I should never have asked."

"There is no point in regretting something you had to do," he says gently. "She was your friend. She lied to you. And you wanted to understand why."

"Do you think she knew?" I ask Mike, brushing away a solitary tear. "Do you think she knew Zack might not be Rich's? Do you think she just thought she could get away with it? That no one would ever find out?"

Mike simply nods. Yes. Yes to it all.

Yes, he thinks she knew.

Yes, he thinks she thought she could get away with it.

And she would have done, wouldn't she? If she hadn't died.

I can no longer hold back the tears and so I leave them to fall silently instead, while the man who has never stopped loving me watches me helplessly, knowing there is nothing he can do to stop them.

All he can do is hold my hand.

"She chose me," I whisper, eventually, even though I know it means nothing.

I call Andrew the next day.

Chapter Seventy-Eight

I know now what Lou meant.

When Zack was born and she said to me, "You would never split them up, would you, Zo?"

She knew.

She knew back then that Zack might be Andrew's.

But she couldn't tell me. She didn't want to tell me.

Instead she asked me to keep a promise that she knew I might never be able to keep. Not when the truth came out. And the truth always comes out.

It's not up to me now – what happens to Zack.

I will fight for him. In the same way I would fight for Oliver. Or Sophie. Or Isla. Because I love him.

But loving him might not be enough.

Chapter Seventy-Nine

Andrew doesn't question why I need to see him again. He just asks me where and when.

Robyn arrives first. She is taking the children to hers. I don't want them here. And this is bigger than a trip to McDonald's with their big sister.

I open the door and she says nothing. She just pulls me into her arms and holds me.

Mike ushers the girls through the hallway, Phoebe chattering excitedly about how she is going to plant a sunflower with Auntie Robyn, Isla and Sophie both conspicuously quiet, both acutely aware something serious is happening. Then he hands Zack to Robyn, along with two £20 notes.

"Use this to get a takeaway," he says.

But she tells him not to be so ridiculous and drops the money on the hall table. She tells him that she'll keep them all for as long as we need.

And then all that's left to do is wait for Andrew to arrive.

He is prompt. He knocks on the door at 5.30pm exactly.

This time Mike is with me. This time I agreed we were a team.

"Ready?" he asks, giving my hand a reassuring squeeze.

"No," I tell him. And then I open the door, to set this metaphorical, potentially heartbreaking ball in motion.

Now that he is here, I need to just tell him.

So I do.

Introductions done, and coffee made, I rip off the band aid in one swift tug.

"Zack might be yours," I say.

He looks as you would imagine. Stunned. Confused. Floored.

"She lied to you, Andrew," I tell him, when it's clear he doesn't even know what to say. It's brutal, but it's needed.

"There was no IVF. They had given up. They had accepted that Phoebe would be their only child. They couldn't bear to go through it all again. The heartbreak when it failed. The crushing disappointment."

He still says nothing. He is processing what I have told him in the same way I was when he told me he couldn't be the father.

And he is probably wondering why Lou lied to him if she really loved him the way she said she did.

But that piece of the jigsaw we will never know.

"Phoebe was a shot in the dark," I tell him.

"They had tried for years. And then they had IVF. Five times. Phoebe was their last go.

"They wanted more children. They never wanted just one. But it wasn't to be. So they had grieved for the children they wouldn't have and moved on...

"And then Zack came along. After she'd slept with you," I add, just in case it's not already clear.

"There is a chance he is Rich's, of course. But based on everything I have just told you, there's a far greater chance he's yours."

"Is he here?" he asks me eventually, his words barely audible.

"No. He's with my friend," I tell him. "They all are."

"Can I see him?"

"Not yet."

"So what happens now?"

"That's up to you," I tell him.

He leaves our house a different man to the one who walked in here an hour ago. Bewildered. A little broken. The possibility of another child. A son. And the same question I had just a few days ago – what the hell to do now?

"I think she did love you, Andrew," I tell him as he gets into his car. "And I think she did want to be with you. I just think she wanted a family more."

He attempts a smile and tells me he will be in touch.

But when I do hear from him, it is not a phone call, or a text message asking if we can meet. It is a letter from Dennell & Clifton – family law solicitors.

It was inevitable, I know. I was foolish to even hope that we could keep this informal. That we could work it out ourselves. That he would tell me he wasn't too worried that he might have another child out there. Why rock the boat, hey? Everyone was settled.

But it still hurts when the letter from Claudia Dermott LLB

lands on the doorstep informing me that they are contacting me on behalf of their client Mr Andrew Robson.

Chapter Eighty

I call him on my way to the surgery.

"You couldn't just pick up the phone?" I shout when he answers. No "Hi, Andrew" pleasantries.

"I'm sorry, Zo-Lo," he says. "I wanted to. Believe me. But the solicitor said I should keep it formal."

"Don't call me Zo-Lo," I say. "Don't you dare call me that when you are about to rip my heart out."

He says nothing. Doesn't confirm or deny the accusation.

"That's what you're going to do, right?" I say, my heart pounding in my chest, willing him to say no.

I pull over, not convinced I am safe to drive.

"Are you still there?" he says, eventually.

"Yes."

"Can I see you?"

"What for? To dig the knife in a bit deeper?"

"To talk. To explain."

"What's to explain? You want to know if he's yours. So you can take him away from me. I get it."

"It's not like that, Zoe. Please. Meet me."

I agree to meet him after work. We arrange to meet at the pub in the village and then I hang up.

———————

I am grateful for a packed ops list when I arrive at the surgery. I'm glad of a long-overdue dental treatment, and an operation to remove a suspicious mass from the lung of a four-year-old cat. I'm even happy to deliver a few booster vaccinations if they will make the day go that little bit quicker.

I collect Phoebe from her summer camp where she has been on a scavenger hunt, and made birdfeeders out of empty water bottles, and generally had the time of her life. And I collect Zack from nursery and wonder what nursery he will go to if he turns out to be Andrew's.

And I drop them both home to Mike and the girls and tell him about my meeting with Andrew.

"Do you want me to come with you?" he asks me. "I can ask Sophie to watch the little ones."

"No. I want to do this by myself," I tell him. "I want to know what he is planning."

"Okay. Just try and keep calm, okay?"

"I will."

———————

He is already at the pub when I arrive. Halfway through a pint.

He stands up when he sees me.

"Can I get you a drink?"

"I'll get my own," I tell him. It's petulant, but I can't help it.

I order an orange juice and bring it to the table.

"I'm sorry, Zoe," he says. "I wanted to call you. To tell you

382

what I was doing. But the solicitor told me to keep it formal. That things can get difficult if they get too personal."

"Why did you?"

"Why did I what?"

"Why did you want to call me?"

"Because I care. I did a bad thing, Zo-Lo. We both did. Me and Lou. But I'm not a bad person. I loved her.

"What did the letter say?" he asks.

"It said you have made an application for a Declaration of Parentage."

"That just means…"

"I know exactly what it means," I tell him.

"As his legal guardian it's up to you whether he has the paternity test."

"I know that too. And if I don't agree then the courts can make me," I say, saving him the job.

"Yes," he says, quietly. Embarrassed. Uncomfortable. Ashamed.

"You know she cheated on you, right?" I tell him.

He looks confused.

"When we were teenagers?" I say. "She cheated on you. Three times, at least. You know that, right?"

He didn't. That much is clear.

I wasn't going to tell him. It wasn't planned.

I have gained nothing by telling him. I have only made him hurt more.

But I am hurting because of what she did, so I want him to too.

He looks crushed, and I am suddenly crushed for him.

"I'm sorry," I tell him. "I shouldn't have told you. That was a low blow. It was a long time ago. We were just kids."

"I don't blame you," he says.

I stop short of telling him that she cheated on him with his best friend, and that she aborted a baby that might have been his.

I am angry, yes, but that feels like a step too far.

Nor do I tell him that Rich was leaving Lou. If that's what he was doing. The details are irrelevant. I figure that knowing Lou was finally going to be free before fate cruelly stepped in and took her from all of us is probably more than he can bear right now.

For a while we just sit there, both of us staring into our drinks, neither of us knowing what to say next, what to say to make this feel any less impossible than it does.

"I don't want to take him away from you, Zoe," Andrew tells me eventually. "She chose Rich. And then she chose you. I just need to know if he is mine."

"For now?" I say. "And then what? When you find out he's yours? What happens then?"

"I don't know," he tells me, honestly. "But what I do know is that he has been through enough in his little life. And I am in no position to look after a baby."

"Nicky's not up for raising your lover's child then?" I say. "A step too far for her, is it?"

"She wants a divorce."

"So I was right?"

"I had to tell her," he says. "This is too big. Even for me to hide," he adds, because he knows it is what I am thinking.

"She could forgive the affair. But not a child."

"Remember, he might not be yours," I tell him. More for my own benefit than his. I need to hold onto that bit of hope, no matter how small it is.

"I know. But she's already convinced he is," he says.

Despite myself I can't help feeling sorry for him.

He has lost Lou. He has lost the love of his life.

And he has lost his family, whether Zack is his or not.

Either way.

"Look, Zoe," he says. "My point is, I'm about to become a single man for the first time in more than twenty years. I am going to have a hard enough job seeing the three kids I already have, without trying to be a full-time dad to a child I've never met.

"But I do want to know if he's mine, Zoe.

"Right now that little boy is happy," he says. "With you. And your family. But he just might have another family that want to love him too."

And I can't argue with that.

"Can I meet him?" he asks, both hands wrapped tightly around his beer glass, trying to hide the hope in his heart.

"Not yet," I tell him. "He's not yours yet."

Chapter Eighty-One

The next day I contact Andrew's solicitors. I ask them to clarify the next steps. And I remind them that I am not Zack's real mum. That she isn't here to interrogate about all this. So go easy with me.

Claudia Dermott is not what I expected.

I expected her to tell me to prepare to say goodbye to Zack. I expected her to tell me that there isn't a hope in hell that I will get to keep him. That she is going to prove he is Andrew's. And then he is going to take him from me.

Instead she is kind. She is gentle. She is understanding.

She talks me through the process, pausing frequently to check I have understood.

We have to provide a DNA sample from Zack for testing. A swab – from the inside of his cheek.

Andrew will need to do the same.

Both samples will be analysed. And the results will tell us with almost 100 per cent certainty if they are related.

And then I will know if Zack belongs to us. To Mike and me. To Phoebe, and to Isla, and Sophie and Oliver.

How incredibly simple it would appear to be to turn our lives irretrievably upside down.

"Is this where you came for the will reading?" Mike asks me, as we sit outside Patrick Massey's office the next day, waiting to speak to him.

Patrick won't tell me anything I don't already know.

He will tell me that I have to agree to the test, I know that.

But I can't do this without him.

I am a vet. I have no legal knowledge other than what I have found through Google. I know even with Patrick Massey's help, I have only a slim chance of this going my way. Without him that chance diminishes significantly. Painfully. Catastrophically, maybe.

"Yes," I tell Mike. "It feels like such a long time ago."

I think about how I felt that day. How devastated I was. How badly I already missed my friend. How scared I was to tell her little girl that she wasn't coming back.

"I'm sorry I wasn't here for you," Mike says softly, holding my hand.

"You *were* here for me," I tell him. "You were the one at home, remember? Playing Junior Monopoly and dishing out copious amounts of Maltesers."

He smiles at this.

"I mean I'm sorry I wasn't here *with* you," he says. "You should never have had to do that on your own. I'm sorry you had to deal with *all of this* on your own."

"You're here now," I tell him. And then he just holds me, wishing he could make all of this go away.

"Zoe," Patrick says, smiling in the doorway.

"And you must be Mike? Come in, please, both of you."

As expected, Patrick does tell me I need to agree to the test.

He tells me – us – that we all need to know who Zack's father is so that we can move on, so that we can start to make some sense out of all of this.

But he says if it comes to it, then he will give us his best solicitor.

And then he tells us what we already know but don't want to hear.

"It would not be an easy fight, Zoe," he says. "You need to prepare yourself for that."

I hold Mike's hand just a little bit tighter and I nod. It's the best I can do.

The following day Claudia sends me a list of court-approved testing laboratories.

Andrew has said I can choose. So I pick one at random. If there is bad news to deliver, it makes no difference who it is that delivers it.

I pick a company called CellSure. I register online. Numb. Wondering what Lou would say if she could see me now. Would she expect me to say no? Would she expect me to fight this? I don't know. I thought I knew her. But I can't have.

She made me promise I would never split the children up, but she knew it was a promise I might never be able to keep.

As part of the registration I am asked to nominate a GP surgery for each "test subject" where the tests will be sent for administering.

I call Andrew to check where he wants to have his test. He suggests we go together, but I tell him no. I need to keep him away from Zack for as long as I can. When he meets him, it will be because I can no longer stop it from happening.

So I enter the details for Andrew's own surgery.

When the tests are received at the nominated locations, we have to take two passport-sized photos. To prove who we are. To prove I am not trying to get away with testing the wrong child, I am assuming. I don't mind this, or being charged £353 plus VAT for the privilege. I just want to know the truth.

I get the call from the GP surgery the following week, not long after my parents have left to take Isla and Phoebe back to their house for a few days.

If we have to do this, then the timing couldn't be better, at least.

I make an appointment to take Zack in the following morning on my way to work.

Andrew texts me to ask me if I've heard anything, to tell me he is having his test the next day.

I reply with a simple yes. It's all I can manage.

The nurse is the same one who gave Zack his MMR immunisation just a few weeks ago. So she knows us. She knows what we have been through as a family. And now she is here with us, carrying out the test that will help decide whether he is still a part of that family.

Her name is Maggie.

I show her the passport photos I had taken of Zack last month so that we could take him on a family holiday – the ones I had to get the doctor in the next room to sign to confirm they were of Zack Smithson, the little boy for whom I have parental responsibility.

Is he really Zack Robson?

And if he is not – if he is Rich's son, and he belongs with us – will he one day be Zack Henry? Would we do that? Would we change their name so they can really be part of our family?

She takes them from me and puts them on the desk in front of her while she completes the paperwork that came in the pack from CellSure.

And then she asks if I am ready.

I tip my head back, to stop the tears that are threatening to come, and I take a deep breath and nod.

"It will only take a second," she tells me kindly, holding up the agreed chocolate button to entice Zack to open his mouth.

Before he is even aware of what is going on, she has inserted the swab inside his mouth, scraped it gently but firmly across his cheek and removed it again.

She pops the swab into its plastic tube container and the chocolate button into Zack's mouth. He is nonplussed at the procedure, but apparently happy with the reward, scrunching his nose up in delight.

"All done," she says.

"Have you had to do many of these?" I ask her, genuinely interested in her answer.

"A couple," she says. "You'd be surprised."

And then she rubs my arm sympathetically.

"This can't be easy for you," she says.

"It's not," I confirm. "But then, what can I do?"

I put Zack down on the floor and hold his hand. He is walking well now. A little stumbly when he is tired, but otherwise a pro.

"Wave bye-bye to Maggie," I tell him, and he holds his free hand up in the air and wiggles his little fingers.

"I'll be keeping everything crossed for you, Zoe," Maggie tells me. "I really will."

I thank her, of course. But I know in my heart that that might just not be enough.

Chapter Eighty-Two

We have had to tell the girls.

There were only so many times I could explain away my tears with stories of injured animals that I just couldn't save, or watching a particularly moving film, or just missing my friend.

The maturity with which they both reacted made me so proud.

Their first thought was for me.

How was I?

And their second thought was for Phoebe.

What would this do to her? How could she lose her little brother after everything else she had already lost?

Only then did they tell me how much *they* would miss him if we couldn't keep him.

Chapter Eighty-Three

They say it's often the waiting that's the hardest. Don't they? For exam results? Or pregnancy test results? Or waiting to hear if you got that dream job over all the other applicants?

But that's not really true, is it? Not if the outcome is not the one you want?

If you don't get the results you were hoping for, if you want to be pregnant and you're not – or if you don't want to be and you are, or you didn't get that job because there was someone who was just that little bit better than you, then the waiting – the *not* knowing – is a far better option, isn't it? Because it gives you a little bit of hope, at least.

So if the not knowing is easier to bear, then it begs the question – why did I set all this in motion?

I could have thrown that card in the bin – not even opened it, maybe, put the book with all the others in the bookcase, and just moved on.

We were happy. We had come through the worst, and we were out the other side. Enjoying life. Remembering Lou and Rich, but not letting their deaths define us. Not letting them stop us from laughing at a joke, from smiling at a sunset, from shrieking with joy when Zack took more than three steps by himself, or when Phoebe learned to tie her shoelaces.

I have threatened all of that now.

But I know in my heart that given the choice, I would do the same again.

I would open the card. I would want to know who it was from. I would want to know what secret my friend had been hiding. And when I discovered the man whose writing was inside – the one who was telling my friend how much he loved her – I would want to see him. To ask him why he did it, why he took something that wasn't his to take. And yes, when I pieced it all together, I would tell him he might have a son.

Because that's the right thing to do. Because I couldn't live with myself if I knew something that big – that potentially life-changing – and didn't say something. Even though it might crush me. Even though it might mean I lose my friend all over again.

Chapter Eighty-Four

The next six days are the longest of my life.

I drop Zack off at nursery. I go to work. I pick him up. All the time wondering how long I have left with him in my life.

I watch him – playing, eating, sleeping – willing myself to see Rich in him. In his smile, in the colour of his hair, in the shape of his ears.

I stare at photos of him with the same aim. I want him to be Rich's so badly.

I take new ones, deleting them in frustration if they don't serve my purpose.

If you could actually will something to be true, then it should be.

I sit with him in the evenings, I let him fall asleep in my arms, so I can feel close to him, so I can breathe in his sweet scent.

I leave work early, just so I can pick him up early, so I can spend a few extra precious moments with him. While he is still mine.

"It's not a fait accompli," Mike tells me on day five.

It is, of course. It *is* "something that has been done and cannot be changed"…

Whichever man is Zack's father has been his father since the day he was born. Since the day he was conceived. We just might not have known it.

But I know what he means. He means it could go either way. Until we open that piece of paper, it's anyone's game.

It's a game Lou set in motion when she chose to sleep with another man.

And then she died. Leaving me to pick up the pieces.

I am angry at my friend.

I am angry that she betrayed her husband. That she lied to me. That she died and left two children without her.

And I feel guilty for being angry. Because she was my best friend. And I should be able to forgive her. Because a few mistakes shouldn't wipe out more than thirty years of memories. Even if one of those was a monumental mistake.

Chapter Eighty-Five

It is on the kitchen table when I arrive home from work on Monday evening. Along with a Matalan sales brochure and a Pizza Hut flier. Looking equally inconsequential. And yet capable of turning our lives upside down.

They have been the longest six days.

And yet, I am not ready.

I am not ready to know that I might have to give up this little boy. This little boy that I never expected to be mine, but who I love as if he were my own flesh and blood.

I stare at the envelope that contains our fate. Zack's. And mine. And Phoebe's. And Isla's and Sophie's. And Oliver's. And Mike's.

How is it that one piece of paper can have such far-reaching consequences?

———

I put a slice of Soreen on Zack's highchair table, cut up into small pieces, and he kicks his legs excitedly, immediately picking one up and squeezing it in his little fist.

Andrew doesn't know that he likes Soreen. He doesn't know that he sleeps with a little blue elephant. Or that he loves bath time. Or that he has the most ticklish feet in the world. He doesn't know anything about him.

Sophie sits on the chair next to me and wraps her arms around me.

I love her so much.

"Are you okay, Mum?" she asks. She knows I am not.

I bathe Zack, refusing both Mike and Sophie's offers to do it for me.

I need this time. I hold his little hand as he plays with the bubbles and kicks his feet in the water.

Then I wrap him up in his hooded towel with frogs on it and take him through to his bedroom. The one we decorated to make it feel like home.

I get him into his pyjamas and cuddle him. He has no idea. No comprehension of how his little life might be about to change. Again.

Mike puts his head around the door.

"You okay, Zo?"

I nod, and he comes into the room. Gently plants a kiss on Zack's cheek. And then another on mine.

I am so glad I have him by my side.

I don't know if I could do this without him.

He leaves me to read Zack a bedtime story. To tuck him in with his blue elephant by his side. To tell him that I love him and that I will always love him. No matter what.

And then I am ready.

Chapter Eighty-Six

He is Andrew's son.

I knew already, in my heart.

This piece of paper just proves it.

It's not dissimilar to a list of exam results. A list of codes. A list of numbers next to them. Only there are two names instead of one.

Child: Zack David Smithson
Alleged Father: Andrew James Robson

The "interpretation" is detailed clearly at the bottom.

Probability of Paternity: 99.9996%

The alleged father is not excluded as the biological father of the tested child. Based on testing results obtained from analyses of the DNA loci listed, the probability of paternity is 99.9996%. The probability of paternity is calculated by comparing to an untested, unrelated, random individual of the Caucasian population (assumes prior probability equals 0.50).

It leaves no room for doubt. Unless I want to hang onto that 0.0004 per cent, of course.

Chapter Eighty-Seven

The next day I call Robyn and ask her to find cover for me, and I spend the day crying.

I cry until I have no tears left.

I cry for me. For Phoebe. For Isla and Sophie and Oliver. For Mike. And for Zack, who didn't ask for any of this.

A respectable – and no doubt painful – twenty-four hours after we both receive the results, Andrew phones.

"Can I see you?" is all he says when I answer the call.

———

Isla and Phoebe are at my parents'. Sophie is out. And Zack is in bed asleep.

Mike lets him in and brings him through to the kitchen, where I am sat staring at the DNA test results, willing the numbers to change.

"Can I get you a drink?" he asks Andrew.

"A coffee would be good," he says hesitantly.

"What do you want, Andrew?" I say, getting straight to the

point. It's why he's here, after all. "Are you going to take him away from me? From us? From his sister?"

I wasn't sure I had any more tears left, but there they are, and judging by the look on Andrew's face, he has cried his fair share in the last twenty-four hours too.

Mike stands behind me and wraps his arms around me while I sob.

I know it is hurting him more than anything that he can't save me from this.

He gestures to Andrew to sit down. He looks at him, gives him the briefest of smiles.

Without saying anything, I know he is asking him to be patient. To give me time to come to terms with what I knew in my head was true, but hoped in my heart wasn't.

So Andrew pulls out a chair next to me and sits down, puts his hand on mine. Gentle. Reassuring.

"No," he says. "I'm not."

And I look at him, my eyes stinging from all the tears they have cried.

I don't even dare hope that he is telling me the truth. I can't.

"I know you have no reason to believe me, Zoe. But I am not here to take Zack away from you. I just want to be part of his life.

"I did a bad thing. I know that. But I am not a bad man, Zoe. I loved Lou. I have loved her most of my life. And I really believe she loved me too.

"I'm a good dad," he says. "It's the one thing in my life that I can be really proud of.

"And I want to know my son. I want him to know me.

"Zack has three sisters," he says.

"He has three sisters here," I tell him.

"So he has three more. He's a lucky boy.

"I want to see him," he says.

I shake my head instinctively. I know I can't stop this. But I can't bear the thought of it.

"I can request it through the courts," he says. "But I wanted to come to you first."

Mike brings the drinks over, sits down next to me and holds my hand.

"Listen to him, Zo," he tells me. "Let's try and keep this good. For Zack's sake."

"Please, Zo-Lo. I just want to see him. For him to know me. To grow up knowing that I'm his dad."

"I'll think about it," I say eventually.

"Thank you.

"And I want to help," he says. "Financially, I mean."

"I don't need your money," I snap.

"I'm sorry. Maybe that came out wrong."

"Zack and Phoebe won't ever want for anything. Lou and Rich made sure of that."

"Then I'll set up an account for him. He can have it when he's older."

"That's up to you," I say.

And then, "Do you really not want to take him away from me?"

I sound desperate, I know that.

But I *am* desperate.

I need him to tell me he's not going to take Zack away from me. Again. I want him to tell me over and over and over again, until I can start to believe it.

"No," he says. "He has been through enough. And he is in the best place here. With you. And Phoebe. And the girls."

He looks at Mike.

"And Mike."

I am compassionate enough to know that that can't be easy to admit. He has already missed out on the first year of his son's life. And now he's willing to hand him over to another man to raise.

"You can all give him everything he needs. I couldn't even contemplate taking him away from all of that," he says.

"Especially now. I have no idea what my future holds.

"I mucked up, Zo-Lo. Big time. And right now I need to make sure my girls are okay.

"But I have to be part of his life. I couldn't bear it if I weren't."

I look at him. I look for signs that he's lying to me. That he will take this little boy away from me. That he will break my heart. And I see none. So I have to trust him. Because without that trust I have nothing.

"He's upstairs," I say. "He's sleeping."

I can see in his eyes that he hardly dare believe what I might be saying.

Mike squeezes my hand gently. Proud. Tender. Supportive. My rock.

Andrew follows me up the stairs. I stop briefly in the hallway. Take a breath. Check for a moment that I am doing the right thing.

And then I quietly open the door to Zack's room.

To show Andrew his son.

Chapter Eighty-Eight

It takes his breath away, of course. The image of his little boy – his son – sleeping peacefully, his blue elephant clutched in his little hand.

It triggers something in his heart. Like the first sight of our children always does. When you see that little person that is part of you – your flesh and blood – for the very first time. And you know that you will do anything and everything to protect them. To make them happy. To ensure they have everything they dream of.

That first sight just came a little later for Andrew.

He looks at me and smiles. Absolute wonder in his eyes. Along with tears of indescribable joy.

"Thank you," he whispers.

Zack stirs in his cot, so we quickly turn and leave the room.

"He's a light sleeper," I say.

"I know nothing about him," he says, genuine sadness in his voice.

And I know it will be down to me to change that. To teach him everything I know about his little boy. His favourite foods. His favourite toys. His favourite television programme. What makes him giggle. What makes him cry. How he loves to be thrown in the air, and cuddled, and to ride on his Uncle Mike's shoulders. And how he loves his big sisters more than anything in the world.

"You'll learn," I tell him.

Chapter Eighty-Nine

Two days later we head to Spain. The love of my life and I, and our five children.

Oliver has joined us. He wants to get to know his new little brother and sister. And they are excited to spend time with him too.

We needed this time. All of us. We needed to forget what brought us all together – and just *be* together.

There is still a lot to be decided, but for now that can wait.

I am ready for a break. Mike and I both are.

We have become parents again. It's different this time, but it's also the same. We get them up. We feed and clothe them. We take them where they need to be and collect them at the end of the day. We teach them. We love them. More than life itself.

We spend the days wrapped in happiness. We lie in the sun. We build sandcastles in the shape of unicorns and dinosaurs. We eat ice-cream for breakfast, and dinner at ten o'clock at night. Just because we can. We enjoy the time with each other and don't ever feel guilty for being happy. Because we deserve it. Phoebe and Zack deserve it.

Mike and I watch our children laughing and having fun and we think about how we almost threw it all away.

We make love at every opportunity. We walk along the beach holding hands. We kiss – whenever the children aren't watching – and whenever they are. And we vow to never again forget how much we love each other – and the beautiful family that we made, together, in one way or another.

And when we get home – and there are piles of washing to be done, and kids to be taxied around, and work to be caught up on – we do all of that. But we don't forget the stuff that's really important. The kiss when we walk out the door, the cuddle at the end of the day – even if there is no energy left for anything more, the cheeky look that says there just might be, and the *I love yous* – even though we already know it, because you can never hear those words too many times.

Chapter Ninety

I haven't spoken to Andrew since that day at our house, when he saw his son for the first time.

I asked him to give me time. To give me the space I needed to think about how we can make this work.

There are so many questions.

What will Zack call him?

Will he be Daddy? Or will he be happy just being Andrew?

What will we tell Phoebe? And eventually – when he is old enough to understand – Zack?

How often does he want to see him?

And where will he see Zack? Here, with all of us, or in his own home – with all of Zack's other relatives – relatives that just a few short weeks ago we had no idea even existed.

I wanted to draw up paperwork. I wanted him to sign a contract, a piece of paper, the back of a receipt from my last supermarket shop – anything to hold him to his promise that he won't take Zack away from me.

But it wouldn't serve any purpose, Patrick told me. It wouldn't be worth the paper it was written on.

"He is Zack's biological father, so he will always have the right to apply for parental responsibility," he told me.

"That doesn't mean he would automatically get it. But he can always apply, no matter what he has promised you – even if it is written down."

So for now I have to trust him.

And he has done what he promised. He has given me time. And now I am ready.

A week after we get home from Spain, I send him a photograph. His little boy. On the beach. An ice-cream in his hand, and the biggest smile on his face.

Our boy, I write on the bottom of the picture before clicking send.

And then:

> Come for Dinner? Tomorrow?

Zack is still up when he arrives, in his highchair, busy squishing a piece of banana in his little fist.

He looks over at the stranger in his kitchen and holds his hands up to Mike, seeking reassurance.

"Dada," he says, and my heart melts. But it also breaks a little. For Rich, who thought this little boy was his. And for Andrew, who knows he is his.

Mike wipes his hands and lifts him out of his highchair.

"Can you say hi to Andrew," he says, and Zack buries his head into Mike's chest.

We wait a second or two and he looks up. Smiles. Scrunches his little nose.

"I bought him something," Andrew says, handing me a gift bag.

"Why don't you give it to him yourself," I suggest, giving it back to him.

He takes out a little brown bear with a blue ribbon around its neck, and hands it to Zack.

He takes it from him and rewards him with another smile.

"There's something in there for Phoebe too," Andrew says. And my heart melts all over again. Because they are a pair. They lost everything together, and because of that they will go through life with each other by their side. Each other's greatest ally. And he has recognised that.

I call her through and introduce her.

For now he is just Andrew. Auntie Zoe's friend. Nothing more. Nothing less.

Polite, but interested in nothing but what is in the bag, she pulls it out to reveal a fluffy pink unicorn, and I smile.

"You couldn't have got it more right if you'd tried," I tell him.

She skips off excitedly to join the girls in the den, Stanley hot on her heels, intrigued about this new fluffy kid on his patch.

"How have you been?" I ask Andrew a little later, as Mike pours us both a glass of wine.

It has been over three weeks since we last met, so he has had plenty of time to think, to work out what he wants, to change his mind. And that scares me a little. A lot.

"Okay," he says. "I took the girls to visit my parents for a few days."

I remember his parents. Of all the parents they were the most relaxed, never thinking anything of allowing twenty or thirty teenagers to drink themselves stupid in their home – their argument being that they'd rather we did it there, where they knew we were safe, than somewhere else where they didn't.

"They live in Cornwall now," he tells me, smiling at the same memory he can see in the glint in my eyes. "They retired down there a couple of years ago."

"And Nicky?" I ask – afraid to, but at the same time afraid not to.

He tells us he's moved out.

He tells us he went home after he'd seen his son for the first time, and his bags had been packed for him.

"Do you think she'll ever forgive you?" I ask.

"Probably not," he says. "I didn't really try very hard, if I'm honest. It was always Lou that I loved. I was living a lie."

I wondered once what would be worse – knowing that Lou had one affair that meant something – or a whole string of one-night stands that meant nothing.

Hearing again how much Andrew loved her, I know now that that was better. She might not have been happy in her marriage, but I think she was happy with him. And if Zack has to be another man's child, then I would rather it was someone she loved. I would rather it was someone who made her happy, no matter the circumstances.

"Nicky and I will never get back together, Zoe," Andrew says. "We're not going to join forces and take him away from you. I told you I wouldn't do that, and I meant it.

"I promise you, Zoe. I just want to know my son. It is going to be hard enough being a part-time dad to my girls. My job is not your typical nine to five. It demands far too much of my time."

I look at Mike when he says this and I smile.

"Where are you living?" I ask him.

It matters. Is there room for Zack? Space for Andrew to be a dad to him?

"I've been staying with some friends," he says. "But I'll be moving into a flat in a few days. It's only small. A two-bed. But it'll do for now. Until I can sort something more permanent."

Stay in the two-bed, I want to tell him.

Where there is room for all your children to visit, but none of them to live.

And he knows it's what I am thinking.

"I have three children, Zoe. Three *other* children," he says, still adjusting to his father-of-four status.

"I've been sleeping on my mate's sofa. And my upgrade on that is going to be a rented two-bedroom flat. I can't be a full-time dad to Zack. But I do want to get to know him. Will you let me do that?"

I look at the man in front of me. The man who stole my best friend's heart when she was just a girl. And then again, years later, when she was someone else's. And I know in my own heart that he is a good man, that he is a good dad, and that he deserves a chance to know his son.

"I will," I say.

Chapter Ninety-One

When I first walked out of Patrick Massey's office as guardian to two young children who had lost everything, I wondered why I'd never asked Lou what she wanted me to do. Why I'd never asked her what she wanted for them.

I never asked whether I should sell the house, whether she'd be happy if Phoebe moved schools, or whether she'd be happy for her children to call me Mummy one day.

I never asked who their friends were, or their favourite songs, or what they were afraid of.

I never asked about Santa, or the tooth fairy, or the Easter Bunny.

But in the end that didn't matter. We are finding our own way. We sold the house. We moved Phoebe to a new school. She calls me Mummy and I don't correct her.

Phoebe has made new friends. Her favourite song changes

every day. And we bought a princess night light because she's afraid of the dark.

Santa will leave his presents under the tree, just like he has at our house since Oliver was born. The tooth fairy will rummage down the side of the sofa for a coin to leave under their pillows, just like she has virtually every time a Henry child has lost a tooth over the years. And the Easter Bunny will do her thing when the times comes too.

We're happy.

I didn't really need to ask those questions. I knew I would do the right thing. And so did Lou. It's why she picked me.

What I didn't know was that there were bigger questions that I needed to ask.

Did Lou ever stop loving Andrew? Was he always the love of her life?

If she hadn't died that night, would she have ever told Rich the truth? About how she really felt? About the little boy who wasn't his? Or did he already know but simply couldn't forgive her?

Would she have ever told *me* the truth?

About any of it?

About Jamie.

About Andrew.

About Zack.

I will never know why she did what she did.

And I am okay with that.

Because she was my friend. My best friend. For more than thirty years. From the moment I threw my school bag on the floor and declared the seat next to me hers. And I loved her. And that's really all that matters. And so for as long as I live, I will love the children she trusted me enough to raise as my own.

Chapter Ninety-Two

When Mike and I married the first time round, we did it quietly. Just us, a posy of tulips, and my parents as witnesses. We just wanted to be married. We didn't care about the fuss and the frills. I walked into that registry office as Zoe Louis, and I walked out as Zoe Henry. That was all that mattered.

Today we have all the fuss, and all the frills.

I have the white dress, and the glittery shoes, and the new sparkly diamond ring.

We have our friends and family with us – to witness the best day of our lives, to see us promise to never again forget how much we mean to each other and to never stop making time for us.

Among them is Robyn. The one who stood by me through the toughest time in my life. And the one who always knew that this day was inevitable. That one day Mike and I would realise how much we meant to each other. And that our family would be together again. Only bigger. Better. Stronger. With more love than anyone could ever need.

I have my three beautiful girls with me. The best bridesmaids any bride could ask for. And Mike has our son by his side. His best man. The boy who came along sooner than we'd have planned but started something truly wonderful. Our family.

As for our youngest – well, he is with his daddy. In the front row.

He will be two in a few short months. He is walking confidently now. Making mischief with his big sisters. Getting into everything he shouldn't be. Smothering Stanley with his over-exuberant cuddles. Giving me the runaround. Me. No longer his Auntie Zoe, but his mummy.

He will never remember a time when we were not his family. And I am okay with that. Because one day I will tell him all about the mummy and daddy that loved him when he was born. And how they had to go to heaven, so we got to be his family. We were the lucky ones that got to love him when they couldn't anymore.

And one day we will explain that he got lucky. That he might have lost one daddy, but he gained two more, who both love him beyond measure.

Phoebe loves school. She'd rather be at after-school clubs with her friends every day now than come home with boring old Mummy and Daddy. So Mike is back to work as normal. But he has found a balance. He works hard, but he plays hard too. And we come first. Always. Me, Oliver, Sophie, Isla, Phoebe and Zack.

I touch my hands to my ears. Checking that the jester earrings are still there. The ones I put in my ears this morning for the first time since the day I opened that pretty little box with the giraffes on it. A gift from my best friend.

I don't have her by my side. But I do have her children. *My* children. And I am thankful for that.

At the instruction of the vicar, Mike leans in for his kiss and Phoebe giggles.

"I love you, Mrs Henry," he tells me.

"And I love you," I say.

Outside the church Andrew brings Zack over to us.

Clutching the little brown bear with the blue ribbon around its neck, our little boy is happy in his arms.

Andrew has lived up to his promise. He has taken the time to get to know his son. He has visited him. Played with him. Cuddled him when he has been ready. And he has asked for nothing more.

Zack loves his new big sisters. And his new grandparents. And his new aunties and uncles.

They have all opened their hearts to him. And to Phoebe too. Because they come as a package. They lost everything together that night almost one year ago. So anything they have now is for them both. Soft toys. Treats. Days out. Extra parents, and aunts and uncles.

Andrew has moved. He has bought a house in Ferringham, not far from the surgery. He has the girls to stay every other weekend. And once a month he has Zack to stay too – and Phoebe.

She loves Uncle Andrew. Mummy Lou's friend. He makes pancakes and lets her lick the Nutella spoon. And the trampoline in his garden is even bigger than ours. So what's not to love?

I can't be sure that one day in the future he won't change his mind, that he won't want Zack to be with him, that he won't fight me for custody. But I can't live in fear of what might or might not happen.

Right now he is being the best dad he can to a little boy who has already lost more than anyone deserves to in their life.

And I can't ask any more than that.

There are all kinds of families in life. There are single-parent families, families with two mums, or two dads, step-families and adopted families. And then there is our family. Three big kids, two little ones. And a mum and two dads – none of whom were there when their youngest was born. But all of them just trying to be the very best they can for two children who lost everything and yet gained so much.

And after all, wouldn't anyone rather have too much love than not enough?

Acknowledgments

Thanks first and foremost to the wonderful team at HarperCollins who have waited patiently whilst I procrastinated endlessly over writing book number two – who knew it would take a pandemic to inspire me to write again.

Thank you to the now Publisher Charlotte Ledger who made me believe I could do it, to Nicola Docherty who diligently worked with me on several rounds of structural edits and to Simon Fox for his eagle-eyed line edit. But most of all, thank you to my editor Jennie Rothwell, whose unwavering patience meant more to me that I can ever say, as I worked to churn out almost 100,000 words whilst navigating a busy full-time job and an even busier family life.

It took what often felt like forever, but I did it.

Thank you to Liz Jones, my bestie, whose faith in my friendship inspired the initial premise of this story – of the lengths you would go to for a friend.

It will likely be the first time in 25 years that she has thought of this story, but thanks to my friend Katie Hannah (or Katie Hemingway as she was back then), who once came to school wearing a pair of jester earrings that I loved and have never forgotten and who, having bought me the closest alternative she could find, really did promise – albeit jokingly – to leave them to me in her will.

A big thanks to Clare Lissmann, a friend who more than anyone understands the pressures I put on myself – to have a successful career; to be a good mum; to be a supportive wife and, despite having less than no spare time, to still volunteer for countless school fundraising events. Clare gave up her own minimal spare time to share with me the workings of a veterinary practice and the training she has undergone over the last 25 years to become a Clinical Director – the role I chose for Zoe Henry.

Thank you to Brian Keegan – my good friend of more than 30 years – and his family, who guided me on some of the complexities of family law.

Thank you to all my friends who unknowingly gave me the inspiration for a scene, or a line of text, or a little piece of backstory, or who simply kept me motivated to finish this story just by asking how it was going.

I could not have done any of this without my family – without their belief in me, their support, and their understanding when I was locked away in my office (listening to music that they hate but knew inspired me) while I was writing what was often an emotional story.

Thanks to Sean who indulged me as I read out excerpts with no context and no background, expecting him to comment constructively. And thanks to my children Freya and Max, who are ready and eager to read what I have written when I determine them old enough!

And last but most certainly not least, I owe a debt of gratitude to my mum who stepped in more times than I can remember to look after her grandchildren while I was writing, editing, or staring at a blank screen waiting for inspiration. She helped me to achieve a dream: to be the author of another story that I could share beyond the safety of my own family.

Thank you, Mum. I love you.

ONE MORE CHAPTER

YOUR NUMBER ONE STOP

FOR PAGETURNING BOOKS

The author and One More Chapter would like to thank everyone
who contributed to the publication of this story...

Analytics
Imogen Wolstencroft

Audio
Fionnuala Barrett
Ciara Briggs

Contracts
Laura Amos
Inigo Vyvyan

Design
Lucy Bennett
Fiona Greenway
Liane Payne
Dean Russell

Digital Sales
Laura Daley
Lydia Grainge
Hannah Lismore

eCommerce
Laura Carpenter
Madeline ODonovan
Charlotte Stevens
Christina Storey
Jo Surman
Rachel Ward

Editorial
Janet Marie Adkins
Rosie Best
Kara Daniel
Simon Fox
Charlotte Ledger
Jennie Rothwell
Sofia Salazar Studer
Helen Williams

Harper360
Emily Gerbner
Ariana Juarez
Jean Marie Kelly
emma sullivan
Sophia Wilhelm

International Sales
Peter Borcsok
Ruth Burrow
Bethan Moore
Colleen Simpson

Inventory
Sarah Callaghan
Kirsty Norman

Marketing & Publicity
Chloe Cummings
Grace Edwards
Katie Sadler

Operations
Melissa Okusanya
Hannah Stamp

Production
Denis Manson
Simon Moore
Francesca Tuzzeo

Rights
Ashton Mucha
Alisah Saghir
Zoe Shine
Aisling Smyth
Lucy Vanderbilt

Trade Marketing
Ben Hurd
Eleanor Slater

**The HarperCollins
Distribution Team**

**The HarperCollins
Finance & Royalties
Team**

**The HarperCollins
Legal Team**

**The HarperCollins
Technology Team**

UK Sales
Isabel Coburn
Jay Cochrane
Sabina Lewis
Holly Martin
Harriet Williams
Leah Woods

**And every other
essential link in the
chain from delivery
drivers to booksellers
to librarians and
beyond!**